THE
STATE SCHOOL

a novel by Jack Dempsey

RPSS Publishing - Buffalo, New York

Book design by Mark D. Donnelly, Ph.D.

www.rpsspublishing.com

publisher@rockpapersafetyscissors.com

ISBN:978-1-956688-28-3
Printed in the United States of America
First Edition

10 9 8 7 6 5 4 3 2 1

This book is dedicated to my wife Kristin,

who has enriched my life beyond its wildest

dreams, and blessed me with four

amazing children, Kyle, Ian, Jude, and Eamon.

I would also like to extend a special thanks to

Mr. Mike Donnelly, – who has been my closest

lifelong friend, and is the inspiration behind the

character Murphy Doherty in this story.

CONTENTS

INTRODUCTION

Well, look who's back, it's Jack O'Leary! And he hopes to capture the hearts and minds of his readers with his new book entitled, "The State School," which is the sequel and follow-up story to his first book, "Sharing the WEALTH."

O'Leary, who after working a year as a vocational counselor at an agency that employs the handicapped called WEALTH Industries, has now decided to leave the agency and accept a counselor position at a state-operated residential facility for mentally challenged individuals.

Jack O'Leary is very excited about the prospects of beginning the next chapter in his life, and hopes that this new adventure that he is embarking on will equal or maybe even surpass the incredible experience that he enjoyed at WEALTH Industries.

As the story unfolds, O'Leary realizes that in order for him to survive at the State School, then he may need to alter his thinking, and learn to utilize some very unconventional counseling techniques, so that he can not only be effective in his job, but try to maintain his sanity as well.

O'Leary's client caseload poses him with some very interesting and unusual challenges, and often times the clients that he works with can be funnier than a barrel full of monkeys.

There are times when O'Leary feels more like a parole officer than he does a vocational counselor. And on occasion, O'Leary has had to rely more on his wits and Irish luck than on any of the tried-and-true counseling techniques that he learned back in graduate school.

The reader will catch a glimpse of what it is like to be a client who is trapped in the State system, and to also get the chance to peek behind the mysterious dark door of institutional living. So sit back and enjoy a story that is filled with a unique blend of humor and poignant moments, and experience life at the State School, which is like no other story that you've ever read before.

CHAPTER ONE

"Well, that's the last of it Jackie boy, I don't think we forgot anything." Dad said, as he latched the back door of the trailer, and then slipped the padlock through the hasp.

Just then Mom frantically rushed out of the house and handed me a picnic basket full of food, and a small cooler filled with some ice cold drinks.

With tears streaming down her face, Mom bravely said, "Here ya go Jackie, just in case you get hungry or thirsty along the way."

Dad then jokingly remarked, "Geez Winnie, he's not exactly going cross-country. It's only a two hour trip, ya know!"

As Mom wiped the tears from her eyes, she snarled at Dad by saying, "Listen Jack Sr., you deal with his leaving in your way, and I'll deal with it in mine."

"Well, on that note, I guess I better be shoving off." I said, softly.

Dad then piped up and asked, "So Jackie boy, do you want me to go over the directions with you one more time, 'cause it's really no trouble?"

"Nah, that's okay Dad, I've got it all resigned to memory. After all, I'm a chip off the old block, right Mom?"

"That's right, dear." Mom replied, as she struggled to muster a smile.

I gave Mom and Dad one last hug and then jumped into the car. As I turned the ignition, I told Mom and Dad that I'd give them a call just as soon as I arrived at the developmental center.

As I slowly pulled away from the curb, I fondly gazed back at my parents in the rearview mirror. Although Mom was heartbroken to see me go, she and Dad both knew that I was making the right decision in taking the State job at the developmental center.

Once on the interstate, I could feel my stomach beginning to growl, so I reached into the picnic basket and grabbed one of the maw decker sandwiches that Mom had made for my trip.

As I nibbled on my sandwich, I was thinking how excited I was to be starting the next chapter in my life. I then had thoughts of Bob Watson swimming through my head, and I knew in my heart that I was trained by the very best.

I then shifted my attentions over to Ms. Alice Albright, who would now be my new boss and mentor at the developmental center. I was hoping that I could foster the same relationship with her as I had achieved with Bob Watson.

As I continued to push down the highway, I began to think back to the day of my job interview, and how Ms. Albright kept referring to the developmental center as the State School.

At first, her recurrent State School references didn't seem to faze me in the least. But now that I've had some time to think about it, I found her constant usage of the term to be quite odd. Especially since the State abolished the term State School years ago, because the reference was considered to be politically incorrect, and had too many negative connotations attached to it.

Apparently, the State decided to rethink its position on how they viewed institutionalized clients, so the State Legislature enacted a law which mandated that all of its state-run institutions be referred to as developmental centers instead of State Schools.

The State's decision to rename all of its state-run institutions was the first step in letting the general public know that people living in these types of facilities had just as much value in life as anyone else. And that going forward, these individuals should not be looked upon as a blemish on society.

Furthermore, the Governor decided to put his money where his mouth was. So the Governor recommended that hundreds of millions of dollars be allocated into the state budget every year, so that individuals residing in these state-run institutions could be taught some basic skills, and skills that would enable them to become more independent and self-reliant. And with any luck, maybe these poor and unfortunate souls could somehow achieve a better quality of life.

So after exiting the interstate, it then spilt me onto a very quaint and scenic country road, which I travelled for about ten miles, and then I spotted the sign for the developmental center.

As I slowly drove up the hill that led to the main campus of the facility, I was keeping an eye peeled for Building 31, which was the building designated for temporary staff housing.

So after parking my car in front of Building 31, I then spotted a flowerpot that was sitting next to the front door, where I was told that a key to the on-grounds apartment would be stashed.

As I entered the apartment, I was thinking how fortunate I was that the facility was providing me with a place to live until I could secure my own accommodations in town.

So after a brief inspection of the apartment, I decided to give Mom and Dad a quick call and let them know that I had arrived safely. Mom was ecstatic to hear my voice, whereas Dad was more interested in knowing how heavy the traffic was on the interstate.

I then gave my fiancée Christine a call and told her all about the new apartment, and that I would talk with her later tonight and fill her in on all of the particulars of my day.

So after settling my belongings, I then decided to stretch my legs a bit and take a leisurely walk around the grounds, so that I could become more familiar with my new surroundings.

As I strolled along the cobblestone sidewalks, I was in absolute awe of the sprawling landscapes that embedded the entire property. Courtyard after courtyard was draped in a canopy of exquisite and meandering flower beds, which were rich in color and impeccably maintained.

The lawns were a brilliant shade of green, and there wasn't a single weed to be found. It was truly a botanical paradise. And if you didn't know any better, you'd almost think that you were vacationing at an exclusive five-star resort, instead of working at a state-operated facility that was home to mentally and physically challenged individuals.

The following day, I reported to the Human Resources Office at 8am, where I met with Ms. Rita Spinelli, who was the Personnel Administrator that hired me. Apparently, there was some paperwork that needed to be satisfied before I could officially start in my new position.

Rita was her usual bubbly self, as she offered me coffee and pastry, and then took me through the tedious paperwork process step-by-step.

We spent roughly two hours completing all of the forms. And when we were finally done, Rita humorously remarked, "Well, you're probably ready for a day off now, right Jack?"

So after completing all of the required paperwork, Rita and I took a leisurely stroll over to the Rehab Building so that we could meet up with my new boss, Ms. Albright.

As we entered the Rehab building, we made our way down a long and poorly lit hallway. When we approached Ms. Albright's office, her door was slightly ajar. Rita lightly tapped on the door, and we heard a voice from inside the room say, "C'mon in!"

When Ms. Albright saw us standing in the doorway, she got up from her desk and walked straight over to us with her hand extended, and then greeted me in a rather ho-hum sort of way by saying, "Hello, Mr. O'Leary."

"Good morning, Ms. Albright!" I eagerly replied, as I shook her hand with zeal.

"So Mr. O'Leary, I take it that Rita has done her part with you?" Ms. Albright asked, in a rather stoic and businesslike tone of voice.

I replied, "Yes, she has. So I guess you can say that I'm all yours now, Ms. Albright."

Rita lightly chuckled at my quipping reply. However, Ms. Albright wasn't the least bit amused by my rather funny and witty remark, and just stood there looking at me like a statue.

As Rita was preparing to exit the room, she pleasantly said, "Well Jack, if there's nothing else, then I'll leave you in the very capable hands of Ms. Albright. Oh, and please don't hesitate to call me if you have anymore additional questions or concerns along the way."

"Thanks Rita, I'll certainly keep that in mind." I answered appreciatively.

Once Rita left the room, Ms. Albright turned toward me and straightforwardly asked, "So would you care to see your new office now, Mr. O'Leary?"

"Uh, yes ma'am, I would. Oh, by the way Ms. Albright, I was wondering if you wouldn't mind calling me Jack."

"Certainly, Jack it is." She replied, in a rather dull sort of way.

As we left Ms. Albright's office, I was a bit taken aback by her standoffish disposition, as if she had just woke up on the wrong side of the bed. And what's more, but I was also wondering why she didn't ask me to be on a first name basis with her as well.

Then again, perhaps Ms. Albright makes it a policy not to get too chummy with any of her subordinates, and prefers to maintain a certain level of professional distance with them.

Anyway, as we proceeded to make our way down the dimly lit hallway in complete and utter silence, it struck me as odd that Ms. Albright didn't try to engage me in any type of small talk, or even inquire as to how I was adjusting to town or my new living situation.

We then stopped at the last door on the left, where Ms. Albright removed a tarnished brass key from the side pocket of her beige cardigan sweater. She slid the key into the cylinder, turned the lock, and then handed me the key, while saying in a rather matter-of-fact sort of way, "Well, welcome to your new office, Mr. O'Leary."

As we entered the room, I noticed that it was much larger space than the one that I had at WEALTH Industries. Although the walls were chipped and cracked, I was happy to see that my new office had windows. This was certainly a substantial upgrade from the previous office that I had at WEALTH Industries, which looked more like a broom closet than a professional office.

Ms. Albright then grunted, "So why don't you stow your belongings in your office, and then I'll give you a quick tour of the building Mr. O'Leary."

As I slung my backpack off of my shoulder, I was thinking that there was something dramatically different about Ms. Albright today than the last time we met. She seemed rather distant this morning, and lacked the spark that she had exhibited on the day of my interview.

She actually reminded me of a grumpy old schoolmarm, or maybe even a spurned spinster.

Quite frankly, but I thought that Ms. Albright and I had actually hit it off quite well on the day of my job interview, and maybe even established some sort of a connection.

So I wonder what changed?

Then again, maybe she's not a morning person, or perhaps she hasn't had her first cup of coffee yet.

In any event, this wasn't the time or the place to be chartering those waters, so I just decided to let the matter go and see how the rest of the day unfolded.

As we entered the south corridor of the Rehab Building, Ms. Albright pointed out all of the various clinical departments that were housed there. She then rifled off a brief description of each department, and as she knocked them off one by one she never broke stride.

I found it a bit odd that Ms. Albright never gave me the chance to ask her any questions, nor did she even bother to introduce me to any of the people that we passed along the way.

And to make matters worse, she made some rather disparaging remarks about several of the clinical departments, along with some mean-spirited comments toward its department heads.

Frankly, I didn't think that her off color comments or bold characterizations regarding the departments or its department heads were appropriate, - at least not on my first day anyway.

Despite my feelings on the matter, I certainly wasn't going to challenge Ms. Albright's authority or views on the subject. After all, she was my boss, and it was my first day on the job.

As we continued to walk along, Ms. Albright kept spewing venom at every turn. I really thought that Ms. Albright would be more diplomatic than this. I guess I was expecting her to take a more positive approach by telling me that the dark ages of institutional living were finally over, and that we were now entering the dawn of a new era.

Well, perhaps my views on the matter were nothing more than wishful thinking. But that's exactly how I would've presented the situation, if I had been in her shoes anyway.

When the tour was over, Ms. Albright and I walked back toward our offices in complete and utter silence. Which once again struck me as odd, and made me feel a little uncomfortable.

As I was unlocking the door to my office, Ms. Albright informed me that her staff was allotted thirty minutes for lunch, and made it a point to say that the policy was strictly enforced.

It would seem that Ms. Albright likes to run a very tight ship.

So as Ms. Albright turned to walk away, she then informed me that she would check back with me after lunch. And if the truth be told, I was actually quite happy to be rid of Ms. Albright for the next thirty minutes. Her extremely starchy disposition was beginning to wear thin on me.

As I sat at my desk, I began to wonder if Ms. Albright was this surly all the time, or was she simply having a bad day. As I pondered the question, it then occurred to me that the noon hour was approaching, and that the clock was ticking on my allotted thirty minute lunch hour.

Well, since I didn't pack a lunch today, I thought I would head over to the commissary and see what the "blue plate" special was for today.

When I entered the commissary, it was absolutely bustling with activity. I grabbed a lunch tray and some utensils off of the rack, and then quickly found my place in line.

A sign behind the counter read, "Today's Blue Plate Special, - Hot Roast Beef Sandwich with Mashed Potatoes and Gravy."

"Mmm…, that sounds pretty good," I thought to myself.

As I observed the young girl behind the counter, she struck me as a very energetic person. She was quite engaging to all of the customers, and she had a smile that could light up a room.

When it was my turn to order, I promptly asked her for the "blue plate" special.

As the young girl handed me my plate of food, she pleasantly said, "Here ya go, sir. Excuse me, but are you a new employee, because I haven't seen you in here before?"

I quickly responded, "Why yes, as a matter of fact, today is my first day."

The young girl replied, "Well, I think you're really gonna like it here, sir."

I quietly chuckled at her enthusiastic comment, and then humorously quipped, "Well, if you keep feeding me like this, then I'm sure I will."

The young girl softly giggled at my amusing reply, and then pleasantly said, "My name is Becky, what's yours?"

"Hi Becky, my name is Jack O'Leary. It's very nice to make your acquaintance."

Becky smiled, and then spiritedly replied, "Likewise! Well, it's been nice chatting with you, and I hope you enjoy your lunch." She then shifted her attentions to the next person in line.

I poured myself a cup of coffee, and then headed over to the cashier to pay for my lunch.

The young girl behind the cash register scanned my lunch tray, and then affably said, "That'll be two dollars and twenty-five cents, please."

With a look of surprise, I then replied, "Really, are you sure you added it up correctly?"

The young girl seemed a bit flustered that I questioned her. So she glanced back down at my lunch tray again, and then scanned the items one more time. She then confidently said, "Yep, one special and one cup of coffee, so that will be two dollars and twenty-five cents, please."

As I reached into my pocket to pay for my lunch, I then whimsically replied, "Why that's gotta be the best deal in town."

The young girl chuckled, and then bashfully said, "Well, I guess that's why we get so much foot traffic in here for lunch every day, sir."

I quickly replied, "Hey, at these prices, I think you'll be seeing me in here again, and often. May I ask what your name is?"

She quietly answered, "Kelly."

"Well, it's a pleasure to meet you Kelly, my name is Jack O'Leary."

"It's nice to meet you too, Mr. O'Leary. I hope you enjoy your lunch."

As I left the cash register, I scouted out a place to sit down. I then spotted an empty table across the way, so I headed straight for it. As I placed my lunch tray down on the table, I heard a throaty voice say, "So, I see you ordered the "blue plate" special."

The voice was that of Ms. Albright, who was sitting all by her lonesome eating lunch.

I paused a moment, and then awkwardly said, "Oh, hello Ms. Albright, I didn't see you sitting there. May I join you for lunch?"

Ms. Albright then half-heartedly grunted, "Sure, pull up a chair."

Seeing Ms. Albright in the cafeteria took me completely off guard.

For some reason, I wasn't expecting to see her in amongst the living. I guess I just assumed that she would be all curled up in a musty old coffin somewhere for the next thirty minutes, nibbling on a piece of tartare au jus.

As I was getting ready to take a mouthful of food, I was praying that I wouldn't dribble any beef gravy down the front of my shirt, because that wasn't exactly the impression that I was hoping to make on Ms. Albright today.

Suddenly, I began to have some second thoughts about joining Ms. Albright for lunch.

In retrospect, maybe I should've simply said, "hello Ms. Albright," and just kept walking towards the other side of the cafeteria. But that would have been extremely rude, and completely out of character for me to do.

Ms. Albright then said, "So I saw you talking with Becky and Kelly. Those two kids are quite friendly, wouldn't you agree?"

"Uh, yes…, very pleasant indeed. In fact, all of the employees that I've met here so far are very nice."

But then quickly thinking, - "Well, that is, everyone but you Ms. Albright."

Ms. Albright sarcastically snarled, "Becky and Kelly aren't employees, those two kids live right here at the State School. Boy, they sure had you fooled."

She then began snickering at me, in a very cynical and condescending manner.

Although I felt somewhat embarrassed by my faux pas, I just smiled and simply replied, "Yeah, well, I guess you're right Ms. Albright, they did have me fooled."

Ms. Albright continued by saying, "Well, I suppose it's an honest mistake, especially since they are two of the brightest kids that we have living here at the State School. Those two girls have been living here since they were infants. Both of them were conceived out of wedlock. And back in the old days, it was considered taboo for single mothers to raise a "love child" all on their own. So many of the out of wedlock newborns became custodial wards of the State."

"That's very interesting," I said.

Ms. Albright wiped her mouth with her napkin, and then flippantly replied, "Well, so much for the history lesson."

She then tapped the crystal on her wristwatch with her forefinger, while snidely saying, "Well, you better get crackin' on that lunch of yours, Mr. O'Leary. By my calculations, you have about ten minutes left until your back on the clock again."

At that point, Ms. Albright got up from the table, discarded her trash, and then walked out of the cafeteria without even the slightest hint of a good-bye.

As I began plowing through my mashed potatoes and gravy, I was thinking that Ms. Albright should've given me at least five more minutes to finish my lunch, especially since she wound up bending my ear for the last fifteen minutes.

Well, be that as it may, but I was able to polish off my lunch in record time. And I even managed to make it back to the Rehab Building with an extra two minutes to spare.

When I walked by Ms. Albright's office, I noticed that she was on the telephone. I then started to wonder if she was calling the commissary to see if I was still over there eating lunch.

I'm sure that Ms. Albright will be knocking on my office door any minute now. So that being said, I started to rack my brains as to what I could do to look busy until she shows up.

As I looked around my office, I noticed that there were two dusty old filing cabinets that were both sitting in the far corner of the room, so I thought I would take a peek inside of them.

When I opened up all of the drawers of the first filing cabinet, I saw that all of the drawers were empty, except for a few yellowed and outdated folders in the bottom drawer.

As I was about to open up the top drawer of the second filing cabinet, I heard an ominous voice from behind me say, "So did you find anything interesting in there yet, Mr. O'Leary?"

When I turned around, I saw Ms. Albright standing in the doorway.

Ms. Albright seemed to have a rather disgusted look on her face. And at that moment, I felt like a child, who's mother just caught him red-handed in the cookie jar right before dinner.

So not knowing what to say at that point, I simply replied, "Um, well, the only thing I found so far were a few yellowed and outdated files."

Ms. Albright then grunted, "Uh-huh, well, why don't you try opening up the top drawer of the filing cabinet that you're standing next to Mr. O'Leary."

When I opened up the top drawer, I saw that it was completely crammed with files. Ms. Albright then said, in a rather blasé tone of voice, "Welcome to the people on your caseload."

Ms. Albright then walked over to where I was standing. And as she ran her hand across the top of the files she said, "These files represent all of the clients in Buildings 12 and 13 who are currently receiving vocational services. I'd like you to start reviewing the files immediately, so that you can familiarize yourself with the types of programs that we provide. Any questions?"

"Uh, no ma'am," I promptly replied.

"Splendid, well, I think two weeks should be enough time for you to organize the files. And upon completion of your assignment, we will then discuss a strategy. That will be all."

Ms. Albright then did an about-face and exited the room. She left without even the slightest hint of a "good-bye," or even the feeblest of attempts in wishing me "good luck."

I then thought to myself, "Well, so much for orientation!"

Obviously, I wasn't expecting Ms. Albright to hold my hand. But I was hoping that she would've at least taken the time to sit down with me, and perhaps she and I could've reviewed some of the case files together.

Well, apparently that's not gonna happen!

From the looks of it, there must be at least two hundred files sitting in this filing cabinet. This assignment was going to be a lot of work in a very short amount of time, but I was fairly confident that I could get the job done within the allotted time frame that Ms. Albright requested.

Based on what I've seen thus far, Ms. Albright didn't strike me as the type of supervisor who tolerates frivolous excuses, or is willing to entertain extensions on overdue assignments.   As I began cracking the case files, it was becoming quite apparent to me that the clients on my caseload were extremely challenged individuals.

When I worked at WEALTH Industries, I had some clients on my caseload that were considered intellectually challenged. However, the clients at WEALTH Industries were a helluva lot more capable than the clients that I would be working with here at the developmental center.

I guess the old adage, "One man's ceiling is another man's floor," may aptly apply here.

In reviewing the case files, I found that the vocational services that the clients were receiving here at the developmental center were extremely rudimentary in scope, with a major emphasis being placed on teaching them to discriminate color and shape.

At first, I wasn't quite sure why these specific concepts were being targeted. But as I delved deeper into the case files, I was acquiring a better understanding as to the reasons why.

Apparently, color and shape discrimination was part of an overall strategy in having the clients sort laundry here at the developmental center. The program involved having colorful geometric shapes, such as, circles, squares, and triangles, sewn onto the inside tags of clothing, and these shapes and colors represented specific buildings and or living units here at the facility.

So after identifying the specific color and shape, the client would then toss that article of clothing into the corresponding laundry bin, and the clothes were then folded and delivered to the various living units throughout the facility.

It should also be noted that the clients were actually paid a nominal amount of money for their efforts, which they could then use to purchase items at the commissary or community store.

I thought that teaching the clients to sort laundry by shape and color was a pretty clever idea. And although it might seem a bit primitive, I actually found it to be a creative form of job engineering.

So after spending a tedious week of organizing the case files, it was nice to receive a visit from my fiancée Christine over the weekend. Christine not only helped clean the apartment from stem to stern, but she also rustled me up a couple of delicious homemade meals as well.

Although I had a wonderful time with Christine this weekend, at one point she wound up reading me the riot act, because she discovered all the empty pizza boxes and fast food wrappers that were piled up in the trashcan in the back alley. Christine also made it a point to say that she doesn't want to see a fast food graveyard the next time that she comes back to visit me.

So in an effort to appease her, I said that I would try to eat healthier during the week. But in the back of my mind, I was thinking that I'll have to remember to dump the trashcan in the back alley before she comes back to visit me again next week.

As week two rolled around, I was beginning to discover that this assignment of mine was actually going a lot slower than I had originally anticipated. I thought that I would be knocking these case files off quicker than this, but these files were in pretty rough shape.

Fortunately, Ms. Albright has not been hounding me for any updates or progress reports on my assignment. But nevertheless, I'm still quite confident that I can get it all done on time.

And if it means that I have to bring some work home with me every night so that I can finish up this assignment, then that's what I intend to do. Because I really want to make a good impression on Ms. Albright. And with any luck, maybe even try to creep into her good graces.

Well..., assuming that she has any, that is.

By Thursday afternoon, I wrapped up the last of the case files. Although it was a daunting assignment, it proved to be not only educational for me, but very enlightening as well.

As I sat at my desk, I was still quite hesitant to tell Ms. Albright that I was finished with my assignment. I guess all of my apprehensions on telling her were all based on fear.

Thus far, Ms. Albright doesn't seem to be too impressed with me. And maybe she's even having some second thoughts about hiring me in the first place. So I thought that if I could really wow her with this assignment, then maybe she'd look at me in a more favorable light.

Although Ms. Albright wasn't requiring me to submit a written report to her, I thought it might be a good idea to draft some sort of synopsis or summary anyway, because it would be a more effective way to describe all of the meat and potatoes that were contained in the case files.

In addition to providing Ms. Albright with a written report, I thought that some type of visual aid might also be helpful in giving her a better understanding for what was stored in the case files as well.

So keeping all of that in mind, I decided to take a drive into town and purchase some poster-board and colorful pastel markers from the art supply store, so that I could design some sort of presentation that might really impress Ms. Albright.

Now by most creative standards, my artistic talents may be considered primitive at best. But for my purposes, it should suffice.

After all, how hard can it be to screw up a pie chart or even a simple bar graph.

Actually, I think if Dr. Stevens were here right now he would be applauding my efforts, and simply overjoyed that I was utilizing some of the practical knowledge and applications that I had acquired in my statistics class back in graduate school.

The way I see it, I need to knock this assignment right out of the park so that I can impress the hell out of Ms. Albright. And if going the extra mile means that I have a shot at making her happy, then that's what I intend to do.

Because up until now, - my cheery disposition and extremely dull looks haven't gotten me anywhere.

So after working into the wee hours of the morning, I finally finished up my art project. As I looked over my schematics, I thought that it wasn't half bad.

It wasn't exactly Picasso, but I thought it was still good enough to do the trick.

The next day, I knocked on Ms. Albright's door and informed her that I was finished reviewing the case files. I then asked her if we could set up a time to meet, to which she replied, in her usual stodgy tone of voice, "Well, I guess there's no time like the present, Mr. O'Leary."

So after excusing myself for a moment, I then beat it down to my office and gathered up all of the materials that I needed for my presentation. Ms. Albright looked a bit stunned when she saw me come waltzing back into her office with my written report and schematics in hand.

As the presentation unfolded, Ms. Albright and I engaged in a very lively discussion, and she seemed quite taken by my efforts. She said that the information I provided her should prove to be very useful in developing future vocational programming and development at the facility.

In fact, Ms. Albright almost bowled me over when she emphatically said, "This is very impressive work Jack, and I must say that you've certainly exceeded all of my expectations!"

At the risk of sounding dramatic, but Ms. Albright's unbridled enthusiasm this morning was certainly a far cry from her usual starchy disposition. And for the first time since coming on board, I was beginning to think that I may have turned the corner with Ms. Albright, and that today may be the start of a whole new relationship for us.

When the meeting concluded, Ms. Albright wanted to know if she could hold onto all of the presentation materials for a few days, so that she could share my findings with Mr. Kramer, who was the department head, and held the title of Director of Rehabilitation Services.

The following Monday, Ms. Albright came by my office and informed me that she and I would be visiting Buildings 12 and 13 this morning, which just so happen to be the two buildings that all of the clients on my caseload currently reside in.

As we took the short walk over to Building 13, Ms. Albright gave me a brief overview of the building, and pointed out some of the key people that I would be meeting over there as well.

Before entering the building, Ms. Albright made it a point to say that she expected me to display the utmost professionalism at all times, and to be sure that I made myself "accessible."

In addition to that, she also said that she didn't want to hear any negative reports about me in the Unit, and to watch my P's and Q's, - because I was representing the Rehab department.

Once in the building, we headed over to the Main Office so that we could meet with Ms. Fields, who is the Team Leader for Building 13. Ms. Albright was hoping that Ms. Fields would not only give us a brief overview of the building, but give us a quick tour of the building as well.

When we went by the Main Office, Ms. Albright asked the receptionist if Ms. Fields was available. But apparently, Ms. Fields was already up on the living units making her daily rounds.

Ms. Albright told the receptionist that we would take a quiet stroll around the building, and chances are that we would probably bump into Ms. Fields somewhere along the way.

As we headed towards the living units, I must admit that I was feeling a little bit jittery. I then told myself, in a calm and reassuring way, "Hey, if Ms. Albright can do it, then so can I."

The plan this morning was to visit as many living units in Building 13 as we possibly could, because we were also slated to visit Building 12 right after we were done in Building 13.

As we traipsed from one living unit to the next, I saw that each of the living units were all designed the same way. When you first entered the unit, there was a large open seating area. And in the back of each living unit were the sleeping quarters, which were all laid out dormitory style.

When we walked into the open seating area, which was called the dayroom, I saw some pretty bizarre and unusual behaviors. The living units were all noisy and chaotic, and there didn't seem to be any semblance of law and order whatsoever. None of the clients that I saw were very interested in socializing with one another. Unless of course, they decided to get up out of the seat and run around the room, and then haul off and slap someone across the face for no good reason.

If anything, the clients were more interested in spending their time engaging in all sorts of self-stimulating or ritualistic type behaviors than they were at interacting with one another.

Many of the clients were running around willy-nilly with no clothes on. And the ones that were dressed were all wearing some type of one-piece jump suit, which looked to be made out of some sort of heavy canvass material, so that the clients wouldn't try to rip it or tear it to shreds.

Despite all of the strange things that I saw, what really stood out in my mind the most was how sterile the environment was, and the fact that the clients had no privacy whatsoever.

Now back in the old days, institutions like the State School had only one objective in mind, which was to squeeze as many clients onto a living unit as humanly possible. And any thought of creature comforts or personal space or privacy was not even a consideration.

Yet, as we walk out of the shadows of the dark ages, and head directly into the light of the 21st Century, we still continue to warehouse the mentally challenged as if they were nothing more than wooden crates.

As Ms. Albright and I continued to visit one living unit after the other, I found it very disconcerting that the clients were being subjected to live such a spartan existence. There wasn't a single picture, throw rug, or knick-knack to be found, nor were there any decorative blinds or curtains hung on any of the windows. And the one question that I kept asking myself was, - why?

Then again, perhaps this sterile existence was simply a health and safety issue.

For instance, if privacy screens were to exist in-between each of the beds, then this might obstruct the staff's line of sight, and prevent them from adequately supervising the clients.

Or what if one of the clients decided to take a picture off of the wall, or grab a knick-knack from the coffee table, and then use it as a weapon to try to hurt someone on the living unit.

After all, many of the clients who live here at the State School are profoundly retarded. And at the end of the day, client safety trumps a warm and cozy environment every day of the week, and twice on Sunday.

Although I wanted to share my philosophical ideas with Ms. Albright, I kept my thoughts and comments strictly to myself, because I wasn't quite sure what her views were on the subject.

Up until now, it's been nothing but an uphill battle with Ms. Albright, and the last thing that I needed right now was to say something that might jeopardize my recent good standing.

So when we finally caught up with Ms. Fields, she was just finishing up her rounds in the building. As Ms. Fields and I shook hands, she struck me as a very warm and pleasant woman, and someone who could probably teach Ms. Albright a thing or two about social etiquette.

Ms. Fields stated that there were lots of things to do in the building, and she was looking forward to sitting down with me at some point and hearing my ideas on vocational programming.

Ms. Albright then pointed out to Ms. Fields that I would also be responsible for providing vocational programming in Building 12 as well, and that we were planning on heading over to Building 12 right after we were finished up in

Building 13.

As we walked along, Ms. Fields gave us a brief overview of the types of programs that were being offered in the building. And then she wanted to know if we would like to take a quick peek at one of the areas that was designated for client programming.

We then followed Ms. Fields down a poorly lit staircase that led to the basement of the building. As we proceeded down the stairs, I was a bit taken aback that formalized programming was being conducted in a dark and dank space like this. The air quality was despicable. And not only was it drenched in mildew, but it was so pungent that it was almost impossible to breathe.

And to make matters worse, but the program area that we were touring was situated right next to the boiler room. The compressors were so loud and rickety that it sounded like I was standing right next to a jet engine. And as Ms. Fields attempted to explain the nuts and bolts of the operation, I could barely hear a word she said due to the constant cranking of the machinery.

In addition to that, the lighting was so poor that I could barely see ten feet in front of me. And if that still wasn't enough cause for alarm, there were exposed hot water pipes and electrical conduit that ran the entire length of the ceiling rafters.

Needless to say, but the aesthetics of this designated program area left a lot to be desired, and it didn't strike me as being the ideal space that was conducive for formalized instruction.

It then prompted me to wonder, "When was the last time that OSHA was out here for a routine field inspection?"

When the tour was over, we thanked Ms. Fields for her time, and then Ms. Albright and I made the short walk over to Building 12.

As we walked across the courtyard towards Building 12, I was praying that Ms. Albright wouldn't ask me what my impressions were of Building 13. Because based on what I just saw, I wasn't all that impressed. And fortunately for me, Ms. Albright opted not to say a word about it.

Upon entering Building 12, we ascended a large oak staircase that led up to the second floor where all of the administrative and professional offices were located. We walked into the Main Office, and then Ms. Albright asked the secretary if Ms. Neff was available, who is the Team Leader for Building 12, and the person who would be giving us a tour of the building.

When Ms. Neff appeared in the outer office, she and Ms. Albright engaged in a few light pleasantries. Apparently, Ms. Albright and Ms. Neff have known each other for almost thirty-five years. And from what I understand, they both came up through the ranks together.

So after chatting for a few more minutes, Ms. Albright introduced me to Ms. Neff, and then proceeded to tell her that I would be assigned to oversee all of the vocational programs in Building 12 and Building 13 effective immediately.

When Ms. Neff shook my hand, she never smiled or made me feel the least bit welcome, and she actually took a page right out of Ms. Albright's handbook on social etiquette by merely grunting, "hello."

I then thought to myself, "No wonder why these two starchy old birds are such good friends, they probably graduated from the same finishing school."

As we walked along, Ms. Neff struck me as a no nonsense administrator, and someone who likes to run a pretty tight ship.

When passing by the living unit staff, they all seem to snap to attention and almost cower in her presence. Ms. Neff came across as being a wily old veteran, who knew every trick in the book, and the chances of pulling the wool over her eyes was somewhere between slim and none.

The living units in Building 12 were all the same architectural design and layout as that of Building 13. The décor in Building 12 was just as stark as it was in Building 13. And what's more, the clients that resided on these living units were just as wild and crazy as Building 13 too.

It was like something right out of Ripley's believe it or not!

I noticed that all of the clients in the building were bone thin and extremely hyperactive, and many of them were running around the living unit like chickens with their heads cut off.

And without any clothes on too!

I saw all sorts of bizarre behaviors going on, which frankly were beyond explanation, and mere words can't even begin to describe.

Although the building was clean, there was still a noticeable stench of urine and feces in the air, yet I could also detect a subtle hint of bleach that filtered throughout the building as well.

When the tour was over, Ms. Neff introduced me to some of the clinical staff, most notably, the building psychologist and the building social worker.

For some reason, these two guys seemed more like "CIA operatives" than they did clinicians. And it wouldn't surprise me one bit, if they spent the majority of their day doing damage control missions for Ms. Neff. My instincts were telling me that something wasn't quite right with either of these two shady characters, so I better watch my back.

So after finishing up with Ms. Neff's Praetorian Guard, she turned to Ms. Albright and asked, "Alice, do you have enough time in your schedule to meet with

Mr. Wohlers right now?"

Mr. Wohlers was in charge of Buildings 12 and 13. He was not only a very influential man here at the State School, but someone that you didn't want to lock horns with either.

As we headed over to Mr. Wohler's office, Ms. Neff turned to me and candidly said, "Listen Jack, if you have any issues or concerns regarding Building 12, then I would appreciate you coming directly to me, and not pestering Mr. Wohlers about it. Are we clear about that?"

"Um…, yes, ma'am." I said, attentively.

Ms. Albright then decided to throw her two-cents worth in by saying, "In other words, you need to follow protocol and proper chain of command, - no lone wolf antics, got it, Jack."

I just nodded my head, and quietly replied, "Yes, I understand, Ms. Albright."

Ms. Neff then proceeded to knock on Mr. Wohlers' office door, and I heard a voice from inside the room say, "C'mon in!"

When Mr. Wohlers saw us enter his office, he stood up and flashed us his million dollar smile. He then came from around his desk and gave Ms. Albright a gentle hug, while cordially saying, "Hello Alice, it's so good to see you again, my dear."

Ms. Albright, who suddenly became as giddy as a young school girl, then light-heartedly replied, "Likewise Henry, it's been a while since I've been in your neck of the woods."

Mr. Wohlers nodded his head agreeably and lightly chuckled.

Ms. Albright then said, "So Henry, I would like to introduce Mr. Jack O'Leary, who is our newest counselor on staff, and the person that will be assigned to your Unit."

Wohlers then turned in my direction and smiled, and as he extended his hand to me, he gregariously stated, "Well, it's a pleasure to meet ya young man!"

Mr. Wohlers and I then exchanged a firm handshake. And at the same time, we were both quietly sizing each other up as well.

I then cordially said, "It's a pleasure to meet you too, Mr. Wohlers."

Wohlers then asked, "So tell me Jack, what are your impressions of the Unit thus far?"

Before responding to Mr. Wohlers, I quickly thought to myself, "Uh, you gotta be kidding me, right?"

Despite having a million thoughts and ideas floating through my head, I decided that the only prudent thing to do right now was to just lie through my teeth, so I simply said, "Well, I'm very impressed with what I've seen thus far Mr. Wohlers, and I'm quite eager to get started in your Unit."

Mr. Wohlers smiled, and as he patted me on the back, he replied, "Excellent! Well, I look forward to having you aboard. And if you should have any questions or concerns, then Ms. Neff and Ms. Fields are both at your disposal. Just make sure that you don't let me down, okay boy!"

As we were leaving Building 12, Ms. Neff asked me if I would furnish her with a copy of my work schedule as soon as possible.

Just as I was about to respond to Ms. Neff's request, Ms. Albright beat me to the punch and said, "We'll make sure we get that schedule to you by close of business this week, Betty."

Ms. Albright and I then walked over to the commissary to get a bite to eat. And after ordering our food, we found a nice quiet table next to the window to sit down at.

As Ms. Albright was unfurling her napkin, she nonchalantly asked me what my impressions were of the two buildings that we visited this morning.

After thinking a moment, I decided to choose my words very carefully, and then replied, "Well, everyone over there seems very nice, and I think that I can do a good job in their Unit."

As Ms. Albright reached for her beverage, she adamantly said, "Well, I'm quite sure that you will. But a word to the wise, just make sure that you watch your back over there."

I was somewhat perplexed by her rather ominous remark, and then cautiously replied, "Uh, I'm sorry Ms. Albright, but I'm not quite sure what you mean by that."

Ms. Albright then explained, "Well, sometimes people like to take advantage of others, and I'd hate to see a nice young man like you get caught in the switches."

"Okay, well, thanks for the head's up Ms. Albright, I'll certainly keep that in mind."

And for the next twenty minutes, we just sat there eating our lunch in complete and utter silence.

CHAPTER TWO

Well, I've been working here at the State School for close to three months now, and I wish I could say that my relationship with Ms. Albright has gotten better. But sad to say, it really hasn't, and my relationship with Ms. Albright continues to be lukewarm at best.

I keep telling myself over and over again that I need to accept the fact that Ms. Albright is an emotionally challenged individual. And despite all of my efforts in trying to win her over, she continues to be a total enigma to me.

Although Ms. Albright is clearly not my cup of tea, she is nevertheless my supervisor. And I need to come to terms with the fact that I don't have to be her best friend, I just need to do my job to her satisfaction.

Thus far, the work schedule that I've adopted for Building 12 and Building 13 seems to be working out quite well. And to quote Ms. Albright, I have been making myself "accessible."

The other day, as I was getting ready to make my way over to Building 13, the telephone rang. And to my surprise, it was Dr. Stevens on the other end of the line, as he enthusiastically said, "Jack, my dear boy! So where have you been hiding yourself? I thought I would've heard from you by now. I trust that everything is going well."

"Dr. Stevens, what a pleasant surprise! How are you?"

"Ah, I'm doing quite well. And even better, now that I'm speaking with you, my boy! So tell me all about your new position with the State."

"Well, it's certainly a much different role than the one that I had at WEALTH Industries, and I'm in charge of the vocational programming and development of over two hundred clients."

"Impressive," Dr. Stevens replied.

"Well, daunting might be a better description, Dr. Stevens. My superiors are all expecting me to come up with some fresh new ideas, but I don't have a clue as to where I should start."

"Yes, well, you'll figure it out, my boy." Dr. Stevens encouragingly remarked.

"So tell me Dr. Stevens, was Bob Watson able to fill my position at WEALTH Industries with one of your eager young minds from the university?"

Dr. Stevens quietly chuckled, and then said with his usual vigor, "As a matter of fact, he did. One of my prize students accepted the position shortly after you left WEALTH Industries."

"I see, well, so much for my office chair getting cold, eh Dr. Stevens. I hope Bob Watson didn't take advantage of the poor fellow." I humorously quipped.

Dr. Stevens chuckled, and then stated, "Well, you needn't worry yourself about that, my dear boy. Because Lenore coached the young man in much the same way that you coached her."

"Really now…," I replied.

"That's right, - and if that still wasn't enough leverage on poor old Mr. Watson, Lenore wound up spilling the beans by telling the young man that Mr. Watson was in dire need of filling the counselor position, ASAP."

"Ah yes, ASAP, Bob's patented little expression." I said, reminiscently.

"Indeed! So tell me Jack, are you finding the work rewarding?" Dr. Stevens inquired.

"Yes, but it's much different than what I thought it would be, Dr. Stevens."

"I see. And is your supervisor a trained professional?" Dr. Stevens asked, in a somewhat serious tone of voice.

"Oh yes, Ms. Albright has a master's degree in the field. And when I applied for the position, she made it quite clear to her superiors that the facility only canvass applicants who were extremely qualified, and possessed a master's degree from a fully accredited program."

"So tell me Jack, you wouldn't be referring to Ms. Alice Albright, now would you?"

"Why yes, do you know her?"

"Indeed, I do. However, I had no idea that Alice worked at a state-operated facility. She's a tough old bird, but extremely thorough." Dr. Stevens said, astutely.

"Yeah, well, I would say that's a pretty accurate assessment, Dr. Stevens. I wish I could say that we had a good working relationship, but I just can't seem to get on her good side."

"Well, if memory serves me correctly, I don't recall Alice having a good side. Oh, forgive me Jack, I shouldn't be taking potshots at former colleagues. She's actually a very good clinician, but her people skills, well, they certainly leave a lot to be desired."

"Well, I'm glad you feel my pain, Dr. Stevens." I said, as we both chuckled in unison.

"Yes, well, just give it some more time, my boy. When Alice and I first started working together, we often locked horns. But as time went by, we grew to become very good friends."

"Well, I'm not ready to throw in the towel just yet, Dr. Stevens." I said, humorously.

Dr. Stevens exuberantly shouted, "That's the spirit, my boy! Just stay the course, and things will work out just fine between you and Ms. Albright, you'll see."

"Yeah, thanks, I hope so Dr. Stevens. Well, I probably should get back to work, I'm not sure if Ms. Albright has my phone line tapped," which prompted Dr. Stevens to quietly chuckle.

"Oh, before I let you go Dr. Stevens, I just wanted to know how Lenore was doing."

"Ah, she's doing splendidly, my boy. Mr. Watson relies on her in much the same way that he relied on you. She misses you dearly. However, she's making the necessary adjustments, and seems to be totally immersed in her work." Dr. Stevens said, proudly.

"Good, that's exactly what I was hoping you'd say, Dr. Stevens. I'll try to give her a call one of these days."

"Yes, please do, she'd love to hear from you, my boy." Dr. Stevens spiritedly said.

"Well, thanks again for the call, Dr. Stevens."

"No thanks needed, my boy. Ta-ta! And don't forget to stay in touch."

So after speaking with Dr. Stevens, I felt so inspired that I thought I would swing by Ms. Albright's office and touch base with her before heading over to Building 13.

Since taking over my new assignment, I haven't had much interaction with Ms. Albright. Although one might think that's a good thing, but in a strange sort of way, I miss not seeing her on a daily basis. I can't really explain it. Perhaps I liken it to my childhood experience with the Nuns, who always fascinated me on how they spent their free time all cooped up in the convent, and wondering what types of clothes they wore, or things they did to occupy themselves.

I lightly knocked on Ms. Albright's door, and I heard her quickly say, "C'mon in."

"Good morning, Ms. Albright. I haven't spoken with you in a couple of days, and I just thought that I would stop by and touch base with you before heading over to Building 13."

Ms. Albright put down her pen, and with a slight burst of enthusiasm she remarked, "Well, talk about timing, I was just writing you a quick note. Apparently, Ms. Fields and Ms. Neff are extremely happy with your work performance thus far in their Unit. And not only are you making yourself accessible, but you're always where you say you'll be. Nice work, Jack!"

"Well, thank you, Ms. Albright. I'm happy to hear that the Team Leaders are pleased."

"Just keep up the good work, and let me know if I can be of any assistance over there."

"Okay, I'll keep that in mind. Thanks again, Ms. Albright."

When I left Ms. Albright's office, I felt like I was standing on top of the world. I could feel an added bounce in my step, as I cut across the courtyard towards Building 13. Not only was it nice speaking with Dr. Stevens this morning, but Ms. Albright actually threw me a compliment as well. And instead of her usual dull and starchy disposition, she actually radiated with some appreciable optimism.

So given the fact that I was in such good spirits this morning, I thought I would break my normal routine, and check out some living units in Building 13 that I don't normally frequent.

The living units that I was intending to visit this morning were comprised of individuals that function in the profound range of mental retardation, which means that they have an IQ score of less than 20. And as a result, these clients rarely get the chance to leave their living unit.

And trust me, - based on what I saw this morning, I can certainly understand why!

As I visited one living unit after the other, I introduced myself to the staff and explained to them who I was and what my duties were here in the Unit. I told the staff that I simply came by to make some observations, and to assess what types of abilities the clients on their unit had.

Although the staff appeared to be friendly, I could sense that their radar was up a bit, and that they really didn't appreciate the fact that an outsider was snooping around their living unit.

As a rule, the living unit staff are not overly fond of strangers who just so happen to walk onto their unit completely unannounced, and their initial reaction is to become highly suspicious.

Now despite the fact that every living unit that I've encountered thus far here at the State School has been nothing short of science fiction, this one particular living unit that I visited this morning in Building 13 was unlike anything else that I've ever experienced before in my life.

As soon as I walked onto the unit, I was immediately broadsided by a group of unruly clients, who meant me no harm, and were merely running around the dayroom haphazardly. And the staff that was chasing after them looked like they were trying to corral a bunch of chickens.

It was like watching a Road Runner episode on Saturday morning cartoons.

As I stood there watching all of the mayhem that surrounded me, one of the living unit staff sprinted passed me, and then humorously shouted, "Hey, you, new guy, don't just stand there, help us round 'em up!"

Apparently, I picked the wrong time to visit this particular living unit, because this was usually the time of day when the living unit staff was scheduled to bathe and shower the clients.

Despite all of the bedlam that was happening around me, the staff actually had a pretty good handle on things. And under the circumstances, I would have to categorize what I was witnessing this morning as organized chaos.

As I watched the staff showering the clients, it kinda reminded me of an assembly line operation. The staff would march three clients into the shower stalls all at the same time, - and then soap 'em up real good, and then spray 'em all down.

Once the clients were all squeaky clean, they were released back out into the dayroom to just run around naked, until the staff was able to get some fresh clean clothes on them to wear.

When I walked back into the dayroom, I saw a client that caught my eye whose name was Sebastian. From the moment I arrived, to the moment that I finally left, Sebastian did nothing but stomp his feet and clap his hands, while humming some sort of catchy and bewitching melody.

And as God is my witness, but the melody was so haunting and mesmerizing that I found myself humming that same exact melody over and over again for the rest of the day as well.

As I continued to be totally captivated by Sebastian, one of the living unit staff came up to me and sarcastically said, "Hey pal, why the hell are you wasting your time with any of the clients on this living unit for? Half of 'em are deaf and dumb, and the rest are just plain dumb!"

Needless to say, but I was absolutely appalled by what this staff person just said to me.

Now granted, I'm sure that working on these living units day after day isn't easy. But that doesn't give anyone the right to ridicule people that simply can't defend themselves, and are literally at the mercy of others every minute of their lives because of their cognitive deficiencies.

But I think what really infuriated me the most today was that I didn't have the courage to stand up to that lousy son-of-a-bitch and say something to him. And even though I've only been working here for a few short months, I still should've opened my mouth and said something.

As I was walking back to my apartment at the end of the day, I kept thinking about the living units that I visited today, and how affected I was by some of the cruel and dehumanizing comments that some of the living unit staff directed toward these utterly defenseless clients.

Although I found most of the staff today to be quite genuine, there were still some that were a bit gruff and a little mean. And in my view, they had no business working in the human services field whatsoever. And these are the types of staff that can give a facility a bad name.

When it was time for bed that night, I was so mentally exhausted that it didn't take long for me to fall asleep, and I can vividly remember having a series of strange and bizarre dreams.

One of the dreams that I remember having was a dream about me dying. Now I'm not exactly sure how I died, but I dreamed that I was floating through a long dark tunnel. And as I traveled through this dark tunnel, I can only describe it as watching a video of my entire life.

After passing through this dark tunnel, I saw a multitude of people standing in line out in the middle of a beautiful green meadow. When I asked the person ahead of me why we were all standing in line, she said that we were all waiting to speak with Saint Peter at the Pearly Gates.

While I waited in line for my private audience with God's right hand man, I glanced over my shoulder at the multitude of people standing behind me, and I seemed to recognize someone in the crowd who looked vaguely familiar to me.

At first, I couldn't place who he was. But then it suddenly dawned on me that the person standing in line behind me was Sebastian, who was the client that caught my eye this morning on one of the living units that I visited in Building 13.

In a bit of a quandary, I then asked him, "Hey Sebastian, what are you doing here?"

Sebastian smiled, and in a calm and gentle voice he answered, "Well, I think the answer to your question is fairly obvious, wouldn't you agree?"

So after hearing his rather witty reply, I paused a moment and then incredulously said, "Sebastian, you can talk? The staff on the living unit told me that you were unable to speak."

Sebastian then quietly said, "Well, now that I'm no longer trapped in my earthly body, I can express myself in ways that I couldn't before. Because in Heaven,

- all things are possible!"

The following day, before heading over to Building 12, I decided to swing by Ms. Albright's office so that I could bounce a few ideas off of her regarding vocational planning.

Up until now, I really haven't shared any of my thoughts or ideas with Ms. Albright. But based on some of the eye-opening experiences that I had yesterday, I thought that this might be an ideal time for me to pick her brain a bit, and perhaps get pointed in the right direction.

When I tapped on Ms. Albright's door, she was at her desk trying to unjam a stapler. And based on some of the gnarly obscenities that she was mumbling, I think the stapler was winning.

So when Ms. Albright saw me standing there in the doorway, she glared at me for a split moment, and with daggers in her eyes, she then snarled, "So whatta you want, Mr. O'Leary?"

Well, at that point, it didn't take a rocket scientist to figure out that this wasn't the ideal time for me to have an in-depth conversation with Ms. Albright regarding vocational planning. So in an effort to keep it friendly, I told Ms. Albright what an outstanding job that she and Mr. Kramer were doing here at the developmental center with regards to vocational programming.

Suddenly, Ms. Albright slammed her stapler down on the desk, and then vehemently shouted, "What do you mean, what Mr. Kramer has done! I'll have you know that I built this program from the ground up! Mr. Kramer hasn't done a goddamn thing since coming on board! And quite frankly, I'm getting a little sick and tired of everyone giving him all of the credit!"

I quickly thought to myself, "Whoa! Where was all of this anger coming from?"

Here I thought I was doing something nice by giving Ms. Albright a compliment. But in the process, she winds up blowing her stack, and then letting me have it with both barrels.

Well, so much for extending the olive branch!

I then shifted into damage control mode, as I apologetically said, "Gee, I'm sorry, Ms. Albright. I didn't mean anything by it. I just assumed that you and Mr. Kramer collaborated with each other in developing all of the vocational programs here at the developmental center."

Despite my efforts to rectify the situation, Ms. Albright became even more enraged, as she snidely remarked, "Well, you know what they say about assumptions, right Mr. O'Leary! I'll have you know that Mr. Kramer is nothing but a charlatan, who seems to rub elbows with all the right people, seeing how his "rabbi" out at the State Capital found him such a nice cushy job!"

"A rabbi? What does she mean a rabbi?" I wondered to myself.

Ms. Albright then spiraled completely out of control, as she shouted, "I'll have you know that I was in line to be the Director of Rehabilitation Services here at the State School, but then Kramer comes waltzing through the door, and snatches the promotion right out from under me!"

"Again, I'm really sorry, Ms. Albright. I had no idea of the situation here."

"Yeah, well, isn't there someplace that you need to be right now, Mr. O'Leary?" Ms. Albright sarcastically uttered.

"Uh, yes ma'am." I said, as I slinked out of the room.

As I headed over to Building 12, it suddenly dawned on me for the first time that I may have just uncovered the source of what's been eating away at Ms. Albright, and why she has been harboring so much anger and hostility towards me.

Obviously, I struck a nerve with Ms. Albright this afternoon. And for the first time since coming on board, I can honestly say that I really felt sorry for her.

Ms. Albright has been suppressing so much anger and resentment toward Mr. Kramer that even the mere mention of his name was enough to send her completely into orbit.

Well, I'm sure there's a lot more to the story than meets the eye. But for now I think it's in my best interest to maintain a very low profile with Ms. Albright, and to avoid her at all costs.

I wound up hanging out in Building 12 longer than usual this afternoon. I didn't want to head back to my office any earlier than I had to and run the risk of bumping into Ms. Albright.

When I finally made it back to my office, it was close to five o'clock and everyone had cleared out for the day. All of the lights in the building were completely shut off, and the only sounds that you could hear were the sounds of old and worn out creaky pipes.

As I slung my backpack over my shoulder and then turned for the door, I was shocked to see Ms. Albright standing in the doorway of my office.

Suddenly, my autonomic nervous system kicked into high gear, and my entire body was on full alert. Although my heart was racing, I tried very hard to play it cool, as I nonchalantly said, "Oh, hi Ms. Albright, how's it going?"

Ms. Albright softly replied, "Hello, Jack. Um, I waited around for you this afternoon because I wanted to apologize for my extremely unprofessional behavior earlier. Um, I really shouldn't have spoken to you that way, and I hope you can find it in your heart to forgive me."

Although I was a bit stunned by her genuinely sincere and contrite tone, I simply said, "Of course, Ms. Albright. Let's just put the whole incident behind us, shall we?"

Ms. Albright replied, "Well, that's very big of you Jack, thank you very much."

There was a brief moment of silence, and then Ms. Albright continued by saying, "Um, I actually had something else that I wanted to say to you. I know that I've been riding you pretty hard since you've been here, and I'm very sorry for the way that I've been treating you."

"Well…," I quietly uttered.

Ms. Albright continued, "What's really ironic is that I like you very much, yet for some reason, I've been displacing a lot hostility towards you. In fact, I liked you the minute I met ya."

I gently replied, "Well, thank you Ms. Albright, the feeling is mutual."

Ms. Albright continued, "To tell you the truth, there were a number of people here at the State School who were interested in your position, and they would've given their eye teeth for a promotion. But I chose you instead, because you struck me as someone who was very special."

"Well, thank you, ma'am." I quietly replied.

Ms. Albright chuckled a bit, and then humorously said, "Gee, all of this apologizing is giving me quite an appetite. Are you hungry?"

"Um, yeah, a little…," I cautiously said.

"Well, good, because I'd like to treat you to dinner. It's the least that I can do. In fact, there's a great little diner in town, nothing fancy, but I think you'll enjoy their cuisine."

"Um, yeah, sure, that sounds nice, Ms. Albright." I said, agreeably.

When we walked into the diner, we managed to nab the last table in the joint.

As I glanced around the premises, I found it to be nothing more than your typical greasy spoon. But as soon as I tasted the food, then I realized why every table in the house was taken.

So after scanning the menu, I wound up ordering a tuna on rye with a side order of fries. And Ms. Albright opted for a BLT on whole wheat, and a hearty bowl of chicken noodle soup.

We then topped off our scrumptious meal with a nice hot cup of coffee, and a big wedge of apple pie-a-la-mode. So not only did we have an appetizing meal, but for the first time since coming on board, Ms. Albright and I actually got to know each other on a more personal basis.

When we finished our meal, Ms. Albright picked up the tab and I laid down the tip.

As I drove away from the diner, I was thinking how glad I was that Ms. Albright and I went out to dinner. It seemed to clear the air between us, and provide us with a whole new start.

Although I'm not a psychiatrist, but I think Ms. Albright's little hissy-fit this afternoon was very cathartic for her, and it seemed to be just the ticket in revitalizing our stale relationship.

Anyway, I need to keep telling myself that Ms. Albright is still my supervisor, and I'm sure that we'll continue to bump heads with each other along the way. But it's different now, because she finally seems to be in my corner, and trying to work with me and not against me.

Over the course of the next three months, I began to delve deeper and deeper into my assignment. The split schedule between the two buildings has been working out quite well, and the staff that was assigned to me in the program areas were generally reliable and trustworthy.

Once again, I seem to be having less and less interaction with Ms. Albright. And even though she is still my immediate supervisor, and I'm required to keep her in the loop, she has been relegated to the role of a figure head.

For all intents and purposes, I seem to be answering exclusively to the two Team Leaders now. And thus far, everything seems to be working out quite well with both of them.

As I've gotten to know the two Team Leaders better, it was my definite impression that neither one of them particularly liked each other.

Although they were quite cordial to each other in public, I could sense there was some bad blood between them, and that they merely tolerated each other for appearances sake only.

These underlying passive-aggressive tendencies of theirs were fueled by an incessant desire to please Mr. Wohlers, who seemed to thoroughly enjoy the acrimony that existed between them.

Frankly, one would think that Mr. Wohlers would want to resolve this toxic relationship that existed between them, yet Wohlers did everything in his power to encourage the rift.

Every week, Mr. Wohlers would hold individual close-door sessions with each of the Team Leaders, so that he could essentially browbeat them into believing that one Team Leader was out performing the other. And what's more, he would also threaten them by saying that if he didn't see a stronger effort from either one of them, then this sub-par performance of theirs would be reflected in their job evaluation, and then promptly placed in their employment file.

I'm not really sure why Mr. Wohlers subscribed to this line of thinking. Not only were his methods considered cruel and unusual, but Wohlers was also an ordained minister by trade, and actually shepherded a small church for five years before taking employment with the State.

As far as I was concerned, Mr. Wohlers tactics bordered on psychological abuse. But what's really most disturbing was that Mr. Wohlers didn't seem troubled by his underhanded methods, and felt that the competition that existed between his two Lieutenants was actually a very healthy way of cultivating a better delivery of service throughout the Unit.

So just to give you some perspective on things, Wohlers was one of five Unit Chief's that worked here at the State School, and all five Unit Chief's answered exclusively to the Director.

If the truth be known, but the Unit Chiefs only told the Director what they absolutely had to. And most of the time they operated in a vacuum, and kept their cards very close to the vest.

From what I understand, these five Units were like worlds unto themselves. Wohlers was by far the most powerful and influential of the five Unit Chiefs, and he was probably the most ruthless and vindictive of the bunch as well.

Yeah, that's right, - a man of the cloth, an ordained minister.

As time went by, I found myself referring to the developmental center more and more as the State School. It's funny how foreign that term was to me when I first heard Ms. Albright reference it, but now it seems to roll off of my tongue without any hesitation whatsoever.

Well, except of course, when the top brass is around.

The Director, the Unit Chiefs, and even the Team Leaders for that matter, don't like hearing the staff use the term State School while in their company, or else the person saying it might take a hit to their wallet, or maybe find themselves standing on the unemployment line.

Although the top brass can say or do whatever the hell they want, they seem to hold the rank and file to a much higher standard, and expect us to follow the rules precisely to the letter.

Quite honestly, but the fact that a double standard even exists is completely wrong.

But then it shouldn't come as any big surprise to hear, especially since the top brass controls the game.

So just remember, if you wanna continue to stay in the game and remain at the table, then you better learn to play by the house rules, or else you'll be standing on the outside looking in.

Lately, there seems to be some dissention in the ranks between Mr. Kramer and the five Unit Chiefs. Apparently, Kramer and the five Unit Chiefs were embroiled in some sort of turf war, because the Director has been toying with the idea of restructuring the facility's work force.

Naturally, the Unit Chiefs would like the Director to side with them by instituting a unitized model, which would then provide the Unit Chiefs with more staff and a lot more power.

Whereas Kramer is hoping that the Director will continue with the current model, which is the centralized model, so that Kramer and all of his department head cronies can continue to wield their power and remain a constant thorn in the side of the Unit Chiefs.

Well, after months of deliberation, the Director has finally made a decision, and he has decided to throw the centralized model out the window and go with the unitized model instead.

So that being said, the Director has instructed Kramer to devise some sort of restructuring plan, which means that Kramer will be forced to relinquish all of his staff, and divvy them up to the various Unit Chiefs throughout the facility.

When the Unit Chiefs were informed of the Director's decision, they all celebrated by going out to dinner and enjoying a nice juicy steak. Meanwhile, Kramer and his department head flunkies were so devastated that they decided to drown their sorrows at the local tavern in town.

To tell you the truth, but I don't think that any of the clinical staff here at the State School really cared one way or the other as to what model the Director chose. Because in all likelihood, they would continue to function in their current work assignment anyway.

Then again, the fact that the clinical staff was no longer under the watchful eye and constant scrutiny of Mr. Kramer anymore was certainly a plus, and a major cause for celebration.

So now the question that seems to be on everyone's mind is, "What will become of Mr. Kramer?"

But for me the more pressing question was, - "What will become of Ms. Albright?"

Mr. Kramer will undoubtedly land on his feet. And although he may have sustained a few blows to his incredibly large ego, I don't think Kramer is too worried about what his fate will be.

As Ms. Albright pointed out to me several months ago, "Kramer has a "rabbi" at the State Capital." So come hell or high water, they'll find something for Kramer to do, - that's for sure.

On our last official day under Mr. Kramer's regime, he decided to have one last meeting with us. As we all sat around waiting for the meeting to get underway, we all wondered what Mr. Kramer would say to us.

Would Kramer take a moment to thank us for all of our efforts? Or would he simply cry in his beer, and sling mud at the five Unit Chiefs, especially Mr. Wohlers.

It shouldn't come as any big surprise, but Kramer and Wohlers had a very acrimonious relationship, and they have been butting heads with each other ever since Kramer came on board.

In public, Mr. Kramer and Mr. Wohlers acted like they were the best of friends. But the minute you got those two clowns behind closed doors, they fought like cats and dogs.

So once the meeting got underway, Mr. Kramer started right in on how incompetent the five Unit Chiefs were, and that they had absolutely no idea on how to provide adequate clinical services to individuals that were developmentally disabled.

And what's more, Kramer stated that without his guidance and expertise in overseeing all of the day-to-day operations of all of the clinical programs here at the developmental center, then not only would these programs suffer, but they would be severely compromised as well.

Obviously, the accusations that Kramer was making was nothing but complete bullshit, especially since Kramer hasn't stepped foot onto a program area since the day of his interview.

Well, it's hard to believe, but I've been working here at the State School for exactly one year now, and much has transpired in my life.

For starters, I finally convinced Christine to marry me. My wedding day was simply amazing, and Christine looked absolutely beautiful.

Mom made all of the arrangements for the church, and Dad was able to swing a deal with Mr. Flaherty in renting out his swanky Irish restaurant for the reception.

And of course, it goes without saying, but Mr. Migliori performed his magic in making us the most exquisite and delicious wedding cake imaginable.

So among the many guests that were in attendance, I was pleased to see Bob and Anna Watson, Dr. Stevens, C.D., and also Lenore Richards, who was accompanied by her fiancé.

I hadn't seen Lenore since the day that I left WEALTH Industries, so needless to say it was great seeing her again, and we certainly had a lot of catching up to do.

At the reception, Dr. Stevens peppered me with all sorts of questions regarding the types of vocational services that we offered at the State School, and he even marveled at our ingenuity in utilizing simple geometric shapes and colors as part of our overall work program strategy.

Dr. Stevens then remarked that he couldn't wait to get back to his classroom, so that he could tell his students just how utterly innovative these job engineering ideas of ours really were.

When the reception was over, Bob and Anna Watson, Lenore, and Dr. Stevens were some of the last few remaining stragglers that stayed to the bitter end.

Dr. Stevens, who by his own admission had one too many apple martinis, then decided to catch a ride home with Bob and Anna Watson, because he wasn't in any condition to drive.

As Lenore was getting into her car, she thanked Christine for giving her some great ideas for her upcoming wedding. And then told us to be on the lookout for our invitation in the mail.

Bob Watson then pulled his beautiful Lincoln Town Car up in front of the restaurant, so that he could pick up his wife Anna and Dr. Stevens.

As Anna Watson and Dr. Stevens climbed aboard, Bob rolled down his car window and said to me, "Listen Irish, if you have any problems up there at that facility of yours, then don't be afraid to give me a call. Just remember, I know the top guy up there personally, okay."

"Thanks Bob, I won't forget." I said, with an appreciative smile.

As I glanced into the back seat, I noticed that Dr. Stevens was having difficulty fastening his seatbelt. He kept fumbling to clasp the buckle, and he wasn't having any luck. So I opened up the back door of Bob's car, and literally climbed into the backseat to secure his seatbelt for him.

Once Dr. Stevens' seatbelt was secured and snapped into place, he gave me a big thumbs-up, and then he tapped Bob Watson on the shoulder and amusingly quipped, "Home, James!"

The following day, Christine and I got up at the crack of dawn and headed to the airport, so that we could catch a flight to the Bahamas for our honeymoon. We were absolutely thrilled about spending the next ten days in paradise, and just getting away from civilization for a while.

When I finally came back to work after my honeymoon, I couldn't believe the amount of paperwork that I needed to catch up on. As I was sifting through my mail, I was surprised to see a message from Mr. Kramer that read, "Jack, please give me a call at your earliest convenience."

After reading the message, I thought it was rather peculiar that Mr. Kramer would want to speak with me. Especially since I don't work for him anymore, I work in Mr. Wohlers' Unit.

As a matter of fact, even when I worked for Mr. Kramer I never spoke or met with me in private, because Kramer would usually delegate all of the day-to-day matters to Ms. Albright.

Well, seeing how my curiosity was piqued, I picked up the phone and quickly dialed Mr. Kramer's number.

The call rang through and then Mr. Kramer's secretary patched me through to his office.

When Mr. Kramer came on the line, he seemed rather chipper, as he boisterously replied, "Hi Jack, welcome back from your honeymoon!"

"Thanks, Mr. Kramer. So what can I do for you?"

"Well-Jack, I was wondering if you could stop by my office this morning and chat with me for a couple of minutes. It shouldn't take too long."

"Um, yeah, sure, I can do that Mr. Kramer."

Kramer then casually said, "Actually, I have a hole in my schedule right now if you wanna pop over to my office."

"Yeah, okay, I'll be right over Mr. Kramer."

When I reached Kramer's office, his secretary congratulated me on my recent wedding, and then she told me to go straight into Mr. Kramer's office because he was expecting me.

I tapped on the door. When Mr. Kramer saw me walk into his office, he stood up and extended his hand, and then said in a rather cheery tone, "Hi Jack, thanks for coming by, why don't you take a seat. So the reason I wanted to meet with you today was because…."

Just then Mr. Kramer's secretary buzzed his office and promptly said, "Sorry to interrupt you Mr. Kramer, but the Director is on the line and he'd like to speak with you right away."

Kramer placed his hand over the speaker of the phone, and then said in a rather smug and cavalier tone of voice, "Sorry Jack, but can you wait in the outer office while I take this call from the Director. Oh, and uh…, shut the door, please."

"Certainly, Mr. Kramer." I quietly answered.

So I sat in the outer office twiddling my thumbs for about five minutes, and then Mr. Kramer popped his head out from behind his office door and said, "Okay Jack, c'mon in."

Kramer ushered me back into his office and then shut the door behind me. As Kramer made himself comfortable in his big cushiony leather chair, he then casually asked, "Okay, so where were we? Ah yes, so the reason I called you in here this morning was to discuss....."

Mr. Kramer's secretary buzzed his office again, and then hastily said, "I'm sorry to interrupt your meeting with Jack again Mr. Kramer, but Dave Philcox is on the line for you. Would you like to speak to him, or should I take a message for you?"

Kramer quickly replied, "Um, no, I'll take the call Karen. Sorry Jack, but can you wait in the outer office for me again? And, uh…, shut the door, please."

So once again, I got up from my chair and headed back into the outer office, so that the "Prince of Darkness" could take his precious phone call from Dave Philcox.

As I exited the room, I quietly thought to myself, "Kramer must think that the entire universe revolves around him."

Quite honestly, I can understand Kramer needing to take the Director's call. But kicking me out of his office a second time, so that he can talk to Dave Philcox was just downright rude.

Anyway, the phone call that Kramer just received was from a guy named Dave Philcox, who just so happens to be Mr. Kramer's right hand man. Not only is Dave Philcox a "yes" man and a brown noser, but he's also a no good dirty scoundrel whose completely rotten to the core.

The only reason why Dave Philcox puts up with Mr. Kramer and all of his constant petty bullshit is because Dave Philcox is hoping to get a nice big promotion out of it someday.

But if I were in Dave Philcox's shoes, then I wouldn't get my hopes up, because Mr. Kramer is known for making promises that he can't keep.

From what I understand, Mr. Kramer promised to give Dave Philcox my job a year ago. But at the eleventh hour, Ms. Albright was able to convince Mr. Kramer to only consider outside candidates, and to not waste time on interviewing any of the applicants here at the State School.

Ms. Albright was heard telling Kramer, "Why should we scrape the bottom of the barrel here at the State School, when we can skim the cream of the crop with an outside candidate."

Well, by my calculations, Kramer has been on the telephone for a good ten minutes now. And if you ask me, it's extremely inconsiderate of him to keep me waiting like this.

As I glanced at my watch, I could hear Kramer laughing his ass off on the telephone. And the conversation that he was having with Dave Philcox didn't sound business related to me at all.

Dave Philcox is not only a snake, but he's an absolute idiot as well. And he is certainly someone who can't be trusted, which is exactly why Mr. Kramer values him so much.

When Mr. Kramer finally finished up his conversation with Dave Philcox, he opened up his office door, and then casually waved me back into his office while saying, "C'mon in, Jack."

Mr. Kramer then turned to his secretary, and in a smug tone of voice he said, "Karen, I'd like you to hold all of my calls, I think Jack has been inconvenienced enough this morning."

Kramer then quietly chuckled to himself, as he closed his office door behind me.

As Kramer plopped himself down in his big leather chair, he nonchalantly asked, "So how are things in Mr. Wohlers' Unit? Are there any problems that I should know about?"

"Um, no, no problems at all, Mr. Kramer. Everything is going quite well over there."

"Good, well, I figured as much, or else I would've heard something." Kramer replied.

There was a brief pause, and then Mr. Kramer said, "Well, you're probably wondering why I wanted to meet with you this morning, eh Jack."

"Um, well, yeah…," I quietly said.

"Well, as you know, our reconfiguration plan is up and running, and it's my job to make sure that we have a smooth transition throughout the facility with regards to all of our programs."

Kramer then reached across his desk and handed me a sheet of paper.

As I perused the paper that Kramer just handed me, he pompously said, "This schematic represents all of the Units here at the facility that are currently receiving vocational services. And as you can see, you're listed as providing vocational services to Buildings 12 and 13."

"Um, yes, I see that." I said, as I continued to study the handout.

I quietly thought to myself, "Why is Kramer wasting my time by discussing the obvious? He must be on some sort of fishing expedition, but I'm not quite sure what he's fishing for."

Kramer then continued, "Now technically, you're under the auspices of the Unit Chiefs. However, the Director has instructed me to oversee all of the vocational programs here at the developmental center, especially since I was the main architect in developing these programs."

"I see," I quietly answered.

Kramer continued by saying, "Ya know, I've been hearing a lot of good things about you from Mr. Wohlers. And take it from me, but Mr. Wohlers is not one to go out of his way to say something nice about someone unless he's really impressed with them."

I simply replied, "Well, I'm happy to hear that Mr. Wohlers is pleased with my work. But to be honest with you, the only time I ever see Mr. Wohlers is at client case reviews, which are meetings that are designed to focus on treatment plans and client progress."

Mr. Kramer gave me a real sarcastic look, and then viciously snarled, "Uh Jack, I think I know what a case review is, okay."

"Oh, right, of course you do. Sorry, Mr. Kramer."

"So, uh…, there's nothing out of the ordinary happening in Mr. Wohlers' Unit that you'd like to discuss with me, huh?" Mr. Kramer asked, as he twirled his pen through his fingers.

"Um, no, not really…," I said confidently.

"Excellent! So how long have you been working here Jack, about eight months?"

"Um, actually, it's been a little over a year now. I can't believe how fast the time has gone."

"So, uh…, how's married life treating ya?" Kramer casually asked.

I quickly thought to myself, "If Kramer thinks that I'm going to divulge any aspects of my personal life to him, then he's crazier than some of the clients that I work with."

So I just simply replied, "Ah, it's great, thanks for asking Mr. Kramer," which of course was the absolute truth.

"Okay, well, thanks for coming in Jack. I'll continue to monitor the situation in your Unit, and I'll be in touch with you if I have any further questions."

"Yeah, okay, thank you, Mr. Kramer."

As I left Mr. Kramer's office, I was wondering what the real reason was for being summoned into his office this morning. He seemed to be asking me a lot of questions about Mr. Wohlers, and whether or not there were any problems to report in his Unit.

Although Kramer may have telegraphed his punches a bit with regards to Mr. Wohlers, he was careful not to tip his hand. My radar was telling me that he was definitely up to no good. And in all likelihood, he was probably laying the groundwork for his next strategic career move.

As it turns out, my meeting with Mr. Kramer lasted a lot longer than I had expected. And by the time I made it over to Building 13, the morning work program had already ended.

When I headed back upstairs, I saw Mr. Wohlers exiting the building. As Mr. Wohlers reached for the door handle, he spotted me out of the corner of his eye, and then energetically said, "Hello there, young man! Say, I've been hearing a lot of good things about you from my two trusty Lieutenants, Ms. Neff and Ms. Fields. Hey, just keep up the good work, okay boy!"

Wohlers then flashed me his million dollar smile, and as I proceeded through the door, he enthusiastically patted me on the back.

Mr. Wohlers then sauntered across the courtyard whistling a happy tune, as if he didn't have a care in the world.

CHAPTER THREE

So let me ask you something? Have you ever experienced a moment in time in which you suddenly realized that life as you know it may never be the same again?

Well, this was certainly the case for me, the day that Ms. Neff asked me to review the case file of a client named Bobby Diggs.

Little did I know, but crossing paths with Bobby Diggs would be a defining moment in my life, and completely transform my way of thinking in how I viewed the State School.

Bobby Diggs, with all of his crazy schemes and hair-brain ideas, would enable me to look at institutional living through a more panoramic lens. And not only provide me with a much broader understanding of the State School, but help me to discover things about myself that I never knew even existed.

When I first met Bobby Diggs, he was living on the behavioral unit in Building 12, which was a highly secure and restrictive living unit, and arguably the worst unit at the State School.

Over the years, Bobby has resided on multiple living units here at the State School. But for the past five years, he has been living exclusively on the behavioral unit in Building 12.

By the time I met Bobby Diggs, I had already been working here at the State School for about a year and a half, but I wasn't all that familiar with the inner-workings of the behavioral unit. So Ms. Neff thought that it might be a good idea for me to visit the behavioral unit and meet some of the brighter clients that resided on that particular unit, - most notably, Bobby Diggs.

From what I understand, the clients on the behavioral unit were nothing but a bunch of troublemakers, who were constantly getting into mischief, and didn't like following the rules.

And what's more, - they felt that the rules didn't apply to them anyway.

As a result of committing these various misdeeds and wrongdoings, they were banished to the behavioral unit for a indeterminable amount of time as a way of teaching them a lesson.

Now this may go without saying, but the clients who were stuck on the behavioral unit lived a very spartan existence, which meant no TV, no grounds privileges, no nothin'!

So the last thing that any of these hooligans wanted to hear was, "pack your bags, 'cause you're going on a little vacation," which is how the living unit staff would reference it when the clients were told that they were being shipped to the behavioral unit as punishment for their sins.

The clients hated the behavioral unit with a passion, and they would commonly refer to the behavioral unit as the "lock up" ward. And over time, I actually found myself referring to the behavioral unit as the "lock up" ward as well.

So you can only imagine how surprised I was the day that Ms. Neff asked me to review the case file of someone residing on this particular living unit, especially when it was common knowledge throughout the facility that the behavioral unit was comparable to living in Siberia.

When I stepped onto the behavioral unit that day, the first sound I heard was a blood curdling scream, which seemed to be coming directly from the back hallway of the living unit.

The screams were so scary that it sent an icy chill right down my spine. And to be quite honest, but I wanted to run for the door and get the hell out of there as fast as I possibly could.

Apparently, the client who was doing all the screaming was caught red-handed stealing a cup of coffee out of the staff lounge. And as a result of getting caught, he became quite violent, so he needed to be escorted to a safe and secluded area, which is called the time-out room.

Or as it's commonly referred to behind closed doors as, the "box."

So as I headed in the direction of all the yelling and screaming, I passed by a handful of clients who were all huddled together in the far corner of the dayroom. They were all quietly snickering amongst themselves, and I'm sure that all of their so-called amusement had something to do with the guy that was making all the racket in the back hallway of the living unit.

When I reached the back hallway, I saw a group of staff standing outside the time-out room. As I approached them, I asked if I could be of any assistance. The unit charge said that everything was under control, but if I wanted to stick around and watch all of the fireworks unfold, then I was certainly welcome to stay. As the staff quietly chatted amongst themselves, I decided to sneak a peek at the client who was making all of the fuss inside the time-out room.

At first glance, he reminded me of some sort of wounded animal that was just captured in the wild. He was screaming a healthy string of profanities at the top of his lungs. And at the same time, he was banging his head repeatedly against the thick steel door of the time-out room.

Then, without even the slightest hint or warning, this wild animal stopped banging his head, and then pressed his face up against the plexiglass window of the time-out room door.

With blood streaming down his forehead, and a look of venomous distain on his face, he shouted, "Hey, I don't care what you fuckin' people say, I have my rights! And if you don't get me the hell out of here right now, then I'm gonna have the Director fire all of your good-for-nothing-asses, including that fat little bald guy who's hiding directly behind you!"

At that point, all of the staff that was standing outside the time-out room began to laugh out loud. And in one synchronized motion, they all turned their heads and glanced directly at me.

As my eyes nervously darted back and forth from one staff person's face to the other, the living unit charge then humorously quipped, "Hey Jack, it looks like you better start dusting off your resume, because Bobby Diggs is gonna have you fired right along with the rest of us!"

I hastily replied, "You mean that guy in the time-out room is Bobby Diggs?"

The living unit charge answered, "Yep, welcome to Bobby's world!"

Since starting here at the State School, I would have to say that I've met some pretty unusual characters, but no one tops the list like Bobby Diggs.

Bobby Diggs has resided here at the State School for over forty years. And according to his records, Bobby Diggs was born to parents who were both mentally challenged themselves, and actually lived right here at the State School for a number of years just like Bobby.

So it would seem that Sir Isaac Newton's theory was correct after all, - "the apples don't fall far from the tree."

Bobby was the youngest of seven children. And although all of his siblings were no smarter than him, it was decided by Child Protective Services that Bobby be institutionalized at the tender age of four years old. And from that point on, Bobby became a ward of the State.

Despite the fact that Bobby has a list of psychiatric problems a mile long, he can also be quite friendly and extremely thoughtful as well. And at times, he seems to have more insight and compassion than some of the staff that are being paid to supervise him on the living unit.

Bobby is a very complex individual, - one minute he'll bend over backwards to help you out of a really tight spot, and then moments later he'll throw you completely under the bus, so that he can save his own neck.

Over the course of his forty years here at the State School, Bobby has developed some rather sophisticated survival skills, ranging from lying, stealing, conniving, and his most precious skill of all which is playing the role of the victim.

These less than admirable traits of Bobby's have sent him packing to the behavioral unit a number of times, and you would think by now that Bobby could learn from his past mistakes.

But unfortunately, Bobby continues to be a very slow study. And for the past forty years, Bobby has been stepping on the same behavioral landmines over and over and over again.

Although Bobby is clinically diagnosed as having a multitude of psychological disorders, the one diagnosis that seems to describe Bobby to a tee is his borderline personality disorder.

In short, Bobby has difficulty getting along with the world around him. And although many brave and courageous souls have tried to slay the demons that haunt Bobby from sun up to sun down, no one has had any luck in turning Bobby's totally snakebit life around.

At Bobby's last case review, Mr. Snead, the building psychologist, threw his hands up in the air when describing the laundry list of indiscretions that Bobby has exhibited over the past year, as he simply said, "Bobby just doesn't know how to get along with anyone in the sandbox."

Although Mr. Snead's colorful metaphor wasn't exactly scripted in the most clinical of terms, I think his depiction of Bobby was pretty darn accurate and right on the money.

For all intents and purposes, Bobby has an insatiable desire for attention, which probably stems from the fact that he was abandoned by his parents at such an early age.

These feelings of abandonment are quite prevalent here at the State School. And despite the staff's best efforts, they will never be able to remedy what's really ailing clients like Bobby.

From what I understand, Bobby's parents were actually quite relieved when Child Protective Services forced them to relinquish Bobby into the care of the State School. Because that meant that Bobby's parents had one less mouth to feed, and one less kid to worry about.

Sad to say, but Bobby's parents viewed him as nothing more than a financial obligation.

Unfortunately, Bobby has deluded himself into thinking that the only reason his family left him behind here at the State School was for them to get situated in a new place to live.

But once his family finally gets settled, then they intend to file a petition with the State, so that Bobby can be reunited with them, and they can all live together again happily ever after.

The day that Bobby's family finally said "good-bye" to him, they packed up all of their worldly belongings and then retreated as far away from the shadow of the State School as they possibly could, and hoping never to be heard from again.

To put it bluntly, Bobby doesn't want to live at the State School anymore, and he wants to be left to his own devices.

Bobby has stated over and over again that he wants to be discharged immediately, so that he can track down his family, and then start living the life that he has always dreamed about.

Yeah, I guess it would be safe to say that Bobby is in a little bit of denial. Bobby seems to think that his family still loves him, and that someday they will all be reunited again.

But unfortunately, - that's never gonna happen.

Life for Bobby Diggs is one big endless cycle. Bobby is good, and then he's bad, and then he's good again, and then he's bad again. And this merry-go-round of erratic behavior spins round, and round, and round.

Although Bobby is a relatively bright guy, - every day for him is like groundhog's day.

As I've mentioned before, Bobby is a very complex individual, and the list of personality flaws that describes him ranges from soup to nuts. Bobby believes that all of his transgressions are not only justified, but warranted as well. And he simply can't understand why no one at the State School likes him, or why they can't look at life through the same fractured lens as he does.

Essentially, Bobby feels that the world is totally against him. And that everyone here at the State School is not only out to get him, but holding him back from realizing his true potential.

When Bobby gets really frustrated, and he starts to feel like he is at the end of his rope, then he'll usually play the suicide card. And when Bobby utters those five magic words, "I'm going to kill myself," then he essentially turns the living unit upside down and topsy-turvy.

Now depending on the severity of the situation, Mr. Wohlers will either show up and make a cameo appearance, or else he'll have Ms. Neff handle the matter entirely.

But if Wohlers does show up, then you can bet your bottom dollar that there'll be hell to pay for Bobby, especially since Wohlers doesn't like to leave the friendly confines of his office.

Oh, and God help you if Wohlers is notified at home, and he has to be pried out of bed or get up out of his easy chair. Because if that's the case, then it's usually game over for Bobby.

Now on a more humorous note, the one personality flaw that Bobby has which always seems to tickle my funny bone is Bobby's delusions of grandeur.

According to Bobby, he feels very stymied in life. And often times, Bobby can be heard saying, "If my goddamn social worker would get up off of his big fat ass, then maybe I could make something of myself. Like go to college, so that I could learn to be a doctor or a lawyer."

Meanwhile, Bobby has never spent a minute of his life in any type of formalized school or classroom setting, nor does he possess any type of scholastic or remedial skills whatsoever.

And when asked how Bobby would remedy this glaring blemish on his academic record, Bobby would simply say, "Well, I know some doctors and lawyers that ain't so smart either."

Now on a more positive note, Bobby does possess some fairly developed life skills. And there are times when Bobby seems to have more mechanical aptitude and ability than some of the staff that are being paid to supervise him around the clock.

Unfortunately, Bobby just isn't smart enough in the areas that really matter.

Over the years, Bobby has seen many of his contemporaries leave the State School, yet Bobby can't seem to understand why he hasn't had the same opportunities to leave as they have.

What Bobby fails to realize however is that all of the clients who have been permitted to walk through the Pearly Gates of the State School have all agreed to play by the rules.

Yet, Bobby seems to think that the rules don't apply to him, and that he can do whatever the hell he wants. In Bobby's mind, he truly believes that there is some sort of conspiracy theory going on, and that everyone here at the State School is plotting against him.

Year after year, Bobby proudly marches into the conference room to attend his annual case review. Annual case reviews are a big deal for Bobby, so he always makes sure that he looks his Sunday best for his meeting.

Bobby's hair is all slicked back, and he's usually decked out in a shirt and tie. And in Bobby's mind, he thinks he looks like a million bucks.

But in reality, Bobby looks more like Moe Howard of the "Three Stooges."

Before the meeting gets underway, Bobby will strategically go around the room shaking hands with everyone and smiling like a crooked politician. As Bobby shakes your hand, he'll usually toss you a compliment, and then casually ask how the family is doing.

Years of living here at the State School has taught Bobby how to be a real smooth talker. Bobby knew just how to work the room. And if you didn't know any better, you'd almost think that Bobby had a pretty good year. But as we all know by now, trouble seems to follow Bobby wherever he goes, and that's exactly why he's been stuck at the State School for over forty years.

So after buttering up the staff, Bobby would find his seat right next to Mr. Wohlers. And with bated breath, he would listen to the staff give their reports on his "progress" for the year.

Despite the fact that the deck is always stacked against him, Bobby remains the eternal optimist. And he hopes that this will be the day that he gets his ticket punched by Mr. Wohlers, so that he can leave the State School and start living the life that he has always dreamed about.

Yeah, Bobby yearns for the day that Mr. Wohlers will shake his hand and then wish him well in all of his future endeavors.

But alas, Bobby's dream of leaving the State School is only a figment of his imagination, as he listens to Mr. Wohlers invariably say year after year, "Well Bobby, based on all of the reports that I've heard today, your request to leave the facility is hereby denied."

So after finally hearing his fate, Bobby would then throw caution to the wind and scream, "You people have no right to keep me here against my will! You're all nothing but a bunch of baloney shitters, and I'm gonna make damn sure that the parole board hears all about this!"

Every time I heard Bobby threaten to contact the parole board, I would quietly chuckle to myself, especially since our agency had nothing to do with the Department of Corrections.

Just for the record, - we were a developmental center, and not a correctional facility. But as far as Bobby was concerned, living at the State School was comparable to being in Alcatraz.

As I got to know Bobby a little bit better, he struck me as someone who should be doing more with his life. To my way of thinking, Bobby had too much time on his hands. And as the Nuns would often say back in parochial school, "Idle hands are the devil's workshop."

Well, call me crazy, but I decided to make Bobby Diggs my "project." I wanted to make a real difference in Bobby's life, so I asked Ms. Neff if we could meet to discuss a few ideas.

When I met with Ms. Neff, she agreed that Bobby should be doing more with his life. But given the fact that Bobby lived on the behavioral unit, then he wasn't allowed to enjoy any of the social amenities that the facility had to offer, nor could he participate in any off unit activities.

Be that as it may, Ms. Neff said that she would take the matter under advisement. And if she thought that my idea had any merit, then she would pass it by Mr. Wohlers for his approval.

A few days later, I received an unexpected phone call from Mr. Wohlers.

Now under normal circumstances, Mr. Wohlers was not in the habit of making phone calls to subordinates, especially subordinates who were as far down on the food chain as I was.

As a rule, Mr. Wohlers delegated all day-to-day matters to his two Team Leaders, who would then do all of the leg work, and then report back to Mr. Wohlers with their findings. So when I heard Mr. Wohlers' voice on the other end of the line, I was shocked to say the least.

Mr. Wohlers was not one for formality, so he simply cut to the chase, and asked me why I've taken such a strong interest in someone as cunning and as mischievous as Bobby Diggs.

I then decided to lay all of my cards on the table, so I told Mr. Wohlers that Bobby had too much time on his hands, and he seemed to lack any real direction in his life as well.

So after hearing what I had to say, Mr. Wohlers said that he would be willing to make an exception in Bobby's case, and give him the chance to earn some money. But if Bobby should happen to make a mistake, then don't be looking for anymore additional favors in the future.

I thanked Mr. Wohlers for getting back to me, and then reassured him that I wouldn't take any unauthorized liberties without going through the proper chain of command first.

To which Wohlers replied, "Good, see that you don't, because I don't like surprises!"

When I told Bobby the news, he was absolutely ecstatic, and he thanked me over and over again for taking such an interest in him. To Bobby's credit, he was actually a very hard worker, and he had a reputation for being one of the better "working boys" at the State School.

The term "working boy" is a slang expression, and it basically means that clients perform a variety of chores around the living unit. And in return for their efforts, the staff would reward them with various items, such as, coffee, cigarettes, or a handful of goodies from the cupboard.

Bobby was a bonafide workhorse, so motivating him really wasn't going to be a problem, especially since Bobby has been known to work steadily from sun up to sun down.

Now even though I promised Bobby a job, I really had nothing lined up for him yet. I knew that I had to come up with something, but the only job listed on the job board was a truck driver's helper position on one of the laundry trucks. But in order for me to make this happen, then I might need to schmooze Mr. Kramer a bit, so that he would consider Bobby for the job.

Initially, Kramer balked at the idea of giving Bobby a job, especially since Bobby resided in Mr. Wohlers' Unit. And Kramer wasn't interested in doing any favors at all for Mr. Wohlers.

Quite honestly, but Mr. Kramer seemed to get more pleasure out of saying "no" to Mr. Wohlers than he did at saying "yes" to a client who was only trying to better themselves in life.

When you think about it, Mr. Kramer's juvenile behavior was no better than some of the hooligans that resided on the behavioral unit. And Wohlers, well, he was no choirboy either.

Frankly, I had no allegiance to either Mr. Kramer or Mr. Wohlers. And when it came right down to it, my only real concern was helping out Bobby Diggs, who I actually liked a helluva lot more than Mr. Kramer and Mr. Wohlers put together.

Well, after weeks of negotiating, and perhaps one or two empty promises that I made to Mr. Kramer, he finally decided to approve the work placement for Bobby Diggs.

If the truth be known, but the only reason that Kramer even approved the work placement for Bobby was because Kramer was banking on Bobby to screw up. Which would then give Mr. Wohlers' Unit a black eye, and put a great big smile on Mr. Kramer's face.

So the only thing left for me to do now was to convince the Transportation Supervisor that Bobby Diggs was the right man for the job, which was not going to be easy.

After all, Bobby has been wreaking havoc here at the State School for over forty years, and during that time he's built up quite a reputation, as well as burned a lot of bridges too.

On the day that I met with the Transportation Supervisor, I decided that my best course of action in selling Bobby to him was to accent the positives, so I tried to point out all of Bobby's capabilities, to which he bluntly said, "Uh, I'm already aware of Bobby's capabilities. He's capable of setting off a five-alarm fire, and burning the entire place right down to the ground."

Oh yeah, did I happen to mention that Bobby has a history of arson too.

As a boy, Bobby enjoyed setting fires in dumpsters. And although he has not exhibited this type of behavior in many years, these past flagrant acts of his are still counted against him, and continues to be the first thing that pops into people's minds when hearing Bobby's name.

So after much discussion, I was finally able to convince the Transportation Supervisor to take a chance on Bobby. But in order for me to seal the deal, I had to promise the Transportation Supervisor in writing that I would take full responsibility for Bobby Diggs and all of his actions.

I guess you could say that I was putting my fate squarely in Bobby Diggs' hands. To say that I was nervous would be an understatement. Even on a good day, Bobby was a loose cannon.

Yet, here I am, sliding all of my chips into the center of the table, so that I can bet it all on Bobby Diggs, and his devil-may-care attitude.

It's sheer madness I tell you! Especially when the only cards that I'm holding in my hand right now are nothing but a lousy pair of deuces, and Bobby's solemn word that he'll be good.

Well, over the course of the next three months, Bobby put his nose to the grindstone and worked extremely hard in improving all facets of his life.

As part of our deal, Bobby was required to sit down with the building psychologist and draw up a behavioral contract. The contract even stipulated that if Bobby didn't get into any mischief for the next three months, then he would earn the right to be transferred over to the open unit, which was certainly a nice incentive for him to stay on the straight and narrow.

Actually, I heard through the grapevine that the living unit staff was laying 20/1 odds that Bobby would violate the terms of his behavioral contract even before the ink had a chance to dry.

Well, in hindsight, maybe I should've taken that bet. Because three months later, Bobby wound up meeting all of the terms of his behavioral contract, and he was finally getting the chance to be transferred from the behavioral unit and be placed onto the open unit.

When the building psychologist met with Bobby that day and told him that he was being transferred over to the open unit, Bobby couldn't believe his ears.

So now that Bobby was being transferred over to the open unit, this will undoubtedly mean that the quality of his life will be elevated to a whole new level, especially since clients that reside on the open unit had all sorts of privileges, most notably, grounds privileges, which meant that Bobby was allowed to roam the entire grounds of the State School unsupervised.

Oh, my God! Talk about a recipe for disaster!

Now even though Bobby met all of the stipulations of the behavioral contract, he was still encountering some problems, and the living unit staff was starting to question his placement on the open unit. The word on the street was that Bobby was getting away with murder, especially since he wasn't being as closely supervised on the open unit as he had been on the locked unit.

When Mr. Snead heard that Bobby was taking some unauthorized liberties, he decided to draw up another behavioral contract for Bobby. When Bobby sat down with Mr. Snead that day, Bobby didn't think that a new behavioral contract was warranted.

Despite Bobby's objections, Mr. Snead pointed out to him that behavioral contracts were designed to be progressive in nature. And in order for Bobby to remain on the open unit, then he needed to abide by all of the modifications that were built into the new behavioral contract.

So seeing how Bobby really didn't have a leg to stand on, he reluctantly agreed to the new terms of the behavioral contract, and then sealed the deal by signing his John Hancock to it.

Well, it goes without saying, but Bobby violated the terms of his new behavioral contract even before the ink had a chance to dry. And when the staff on the open unit told Bobby to pack his bags because he was being shipped back to the lock up ward, Bobby was absolutely livid.

At that point, Bobby felt that a move back to the lock up ward was a violation of his civil rights, so he demanded to speak to Mr. Snead. Bobby thought that Mr. Snead would give him a second chance, or at the very least, give him a slap on the wrist and tell him never to do it again.

But like always, Bobby misread the situation entirely.

When Snead sat down with Bobby, he reviewed the contract with him clause by clause, and then told Bobby what he needed to do in order to gain access back onto the open unit again.

Well, this little Greek tragedy with Bobby happened time and time again. It's absolutely staggering the number of times that Bobby Diggs flip-flopped between the open unit and the locked unit, and so the living unit staff started referring to Bobby as a "frequent flyer."

So after a while, Snead began to realize that the behavioral contract that he drew up for Bobby simply wasn't working. Snead then decided to up the ante, so he drew up a new contract which stipulated that if Bobby was in breach of the terms, then he would lose his truck driver's helper job until he earned the right to be transferred back to the open unit again.

This new addendum to the behavioral contract was a very tough pill for Bobby to swallow, especially since Bobby loved the status of working on the trucks and earning money.

Naturally, you would think that Bobby would try to make more of a concerted effort at toeing the line, so that he could maintain his job and his living situation. But Bobby just couldn't control himself, as he continued to wreak havoc, and be a constant thorn in the staff's side.

When I first started working with Bobby, I thought that he was nothing but a victim of circumstance, and that all he really needed was for someone to help him deal with whatever adversity life had to offer. But as time went by, I came to realize that Bobby is his own worst enemy, and that the only adversity that Bobby really needs shielding from is from himself.

Bobby is like a mouse on a wheel, who is forever running, but he never seems to get anywhere.

One day, as I was entering Building 12, I saw Bobby scampering out of the building. As I held the door open for him, I inquisitively asked, "Hey Bobby, where are you off to in such a big hurry? You better be heading over to work, because it's almost nine o'clock."

As Bobby glanced over his shoulder, he hastily replied, "I know, but first I gotta go buy a newspaper out of the vending machine for Mr. Askew. But don't worry, I'll be back in a jiffy!"

Bobby sprinted across the courtyard towards the vending machine. He slid the money into the coin slot, pulled the lever, and then plucked a newspaper out of the rack. He then rolled the newspaper up in his hand, and high-tailed it back to where I was standing at Building 12.

As Bobby ran towards me, I quickly asked him, "Hey Bobby, do you want me to bring the newspaper upstairs to Mr. Askew, so that you won't be late for work?"

Bobby was completely out of breath, and then replied, "Nah, that's okay Jack, 'cause Mr. Askew promised to give me a cup of coffee if I got him the newspaper, oh boy, oh boy, oh boy!"

I then said, "Alright, well, I'll call the transportation garage and cover for you this time. But let's not make a habit of it, okay Bobby?"

"Thanks, Jack! I promise that this is the last time, oh boy, oh boy, oh boy!"

So after giving the transportation garage a call, I glanced out the window and saw Bobby running like a jackrabbit across the courtyard in the direction towards the transportation garage.

As I watched Bobby scurry away, I was trying to imagine what it must be like to be in his shoes. Not only is Bobby retarded, but he suffers from a multitude of psychiatric disorders too.

Bobby is under so much scrutiny all day long that it's a wonder that he can even function. All it takes is for Bobby to piss off one staff person throughout the course of his day to make his life miserable, especially when most of the staff around here didn't like Bobby in the first place.

Quite honestly, but most of the living unit staff here at the State School thought that Bobby had the Life of Riley, - "three hots and a cot," and not a single care in the world.

Meanwhile, the living unit staff was struggling to rob Peter to pay Paul, so that they could meet all of their financial obligations, and try to keep their heads above water.

Well, I've been working in Mr. Wohlers' Unit for almost two years now, and the client caseload that I'm assigned to continues to present me with some very interesting challenges.

The two buildings continue to be polar opposites of each other, with Ms. Fields instilling a more gentle approach in Building 13, whereas Building 12 tends to be a bit more hard-nosed.

For some reason, Mr. Wohlers seems to favor Building 12 more than he does Building 13. And if you ask me, he seems to treat Building 13 as if it were his "red-headed stepchild."

Which is quite ironic, - seeing how it bears the dubious number 13 attached to it as well.

Lately, Bobby Diggs has been hitting on all cylinders with regards to his work placement and his living situation. That being said, Bobby continues to have his critics, who truly believe that he's still the same old Bobby, but he's learned to do a much better job at covering his tracks.

Although Bobby can certainly be quite challenging at times, it's still very disconcerting to me when I see some of the living unit staff exerting more time and energy in trying to catch Bobby in a lie or a malicious act, then actually teaching him right from wrong.

In fact, some of the staff has even stooped so low as to try to entrap Bobby in various wrongdoings, so that he will violate the terms of his behavioral contract, and then be shipped back to the lock up ward. That way Bobby can become someone else's problem and not theirs.

Apparently, Mr. Kramer is quite surprised by Bobby's success as well, especially when he was banking on Bobby to screw up, so that Bobby would give Mr. Wohlers' Unit a black eye.

Based on Bobby's recent success, the powers to be were wondering if I might be able to work my magic on several other difficult clients living here at the State School. And there's been some talk that maybe one or two of these hooligans may be transferred into Mr. Wohlers' Unit.

Although Mr. Kramer is thoroughly disappointed that Bobby is doing well in his current work placement, it doesn't seem to prevent him from taking all of the credit for Bobby's success.

Occasionally, Mr. Kramer will toss me a bone, and mention my name to people in high places by saying, "Jack O'Leary is doing a fine job at following my directives to the letter."

So on the coattails of Bobby Diggs' recent success, the Director has ordered the transfer of a client named Tommy Gerard into Mr. Wohlers' Unit.

For the past year and a half, Tommy has been raising hell in one of the other Units here at the State School, so the Director has decided to have Tommy transferred immediately into Mr. Wohlers' Unit, or as Mr. Wohlers commonly refers to his Unit as, "The Shores of Tripoli."

When Bobby Diggs heard that Tommy Gerard was being transferred onto the same living unit as him, he was fit to be tied. Bobby and Tommy have known each other for well over thirty years, and they have "enjoyed" a bit of a sibling rivalry with each other since they were kids.

Despite Tommy's recent reign of terror, I actually find him to be a pretty likeable guy. Tommy functions in the borderline range of intelligence. And between you and me, but I think he's even a little smarter than one or two of the living unit staff that are being paid to watch him.

Bobby was extremely jealous of Tommy, and viewed Tommy as an imminent threat. Not only was Tommy brighter than Bobby, but Tommy had a "gift."

Well..., that's what Tommy's family called it anyway.

Tommy was clinically diagnosed as being a savant.

And when it came to numbers, Tommy was a regular Einstein!

Tommy also had a penchant for remembering people's birthday's too. And not only could he tell you what day of the week that your birthday fell on in this calendar year, but he could also tell you what day of the week that your birthday has fallen on in past calendar years as well.

So you can only imagine the entertainment value that Tommy presented to the living unit staff. It was like having a front row seat at the local comedy club every single night of the week.

Yeah, I'll admit it, even I gave the wheel a few spins with Tommy, and found the experience to be utterly fascinating.

One morning, Tommy approached me on the living unit, and then proceeded to tell me when my birthday was and how old I was going to be that year.

At first, it didn't strike me as being all that unusual, because Tommy always remembers everybody's birthday, and then enjoys spitting it out to them every time he sees them.

But what really struck me as being remarkable was that in a matter of seconds, Tommy was able to tell me what day of the week my birthday fell on for the past ten years in a row.

To tell you the truth, I was so impressed by Tommy's uncanny abilities that I found myself rummaging through an old supply locker later that afternoon in hopes of finding some outdated calendars, so that I could see if Tommy was right.

And come to find out, Tommy was correct on all "counts," - pardon the pun.

In private, the living unit staff enjoyed referring to Tommy as "Rain Man," because of his incredible savant abilities, and the fact that he could spit out numbers with the greatest of ease.

Not only was Tommy a real whiz when it came to remembering people's birthdays, but he also enjoyed computing complex mathematical problems in his head as well, such as three, four, and even five digit multiplication problems.

Tommy was always badgering the staff to quiz him, so that he could calculate difficult math problems in his head, and then spit out the answer faster than you can say Jack Robinson.

Sometimes the living unit staff would tease Tommy by asking him what 1+1 or 2x2 was, which of course would drive Tommy totally out of his mind, and then cause him to shout at the top of his lungs, "Aw c'mon, that's way too easy! I want you to give me a real hard one, okay?"

It got to the point where Tommy wouldn't stop hounding us unless we gave him a real difficult problem to figure out in his head. So in order for us to keep our sanity, we all decided to carry little pocket calculators with us at all times, just in case we got ambushed by Tommy.

As time went by, Bobby could see that the staff was totally infatuated with Tommy. And as a result, Bobby was starting to revert back to some of his old mischievous ways again.

Bobby was so jealous of Tommy that he decided to hatch a plan, so that Tommy would be accused of doing something wrong and totally against the rules. That way Tommy would be sent to the lock up ward, and Bobby could resume his role as kingpin on the open unit again.

Well, like everything else in Bobby's life his plan simply backfired on him. Bobby was now caught in a lie, which resulted in him being banished to the lock up ward instead of Tommy.

So now that Bobby was back on the lock up ward, he was forced to toe the line, so that he could meet the terms of his behavioral contract, and earn his way back to the open unit again.

Upon meeting the terms of his behavioral contract, Bobby was then permitted to go back to the open unit. But the minute that Bobby cast his eyes on Tommy, he would get so riled up that he would wind up doing something foolish, which would then cause Bobby to violate the terms of his behavioral contract, and Bobby would be back on the lock up ward within the hour.

Unfortunately, this little scenario of Bobby's would happen time and time again, and became one big endless cycle for Bobby.

By now, it was getting to the point where Bobby was spending more time on the lock up ward than he was on the open unit. Bobby just couldn't control himself around Tommy Gerard.

Meanwhile, Tommy was living the Life of Riley, as he entertained the troops with his incredible savant talents, and enjoyed all of the social amenities that the open unit had to offer.

Well, it took roughly a year and a half before Bobby finally figured out that he was only hurting himself by targeting Tommy. So Bobby decided to mend some fences with Tommy, and just learn to accept him for whom he was.

Now although Bobby and Tommy seemed quite chummy on the surface, this new found friendship of theirs didn't seem real genuine to me. But be that as it may, Bobby decided to hop on the Tommy bandwagon and see where the ride would take him.

In Bobby's mind, "If you can't beat 'em, then you might as well join 'em!"

Well, today is Bobby's annual case review, and it's hard to believe that another year has flown by. When I saw Bobby on the open unit this morning, he appeared to be very excited. He was joking around and being overly friendly, even to clients that he considers his sworn enemies.

As I've said before, Bobby always gets charged up on case review day. And in Bobby's mind, case review day was bigger than Christmas and his birthday put together.

It's certainly no secret that Bobby has had a pretty rough year.

But to Bobby's way of thinking, it was nothing more than a few bumps in the road, or some minor misunderstandings that he may have had with some people.

Bobby seems to think that if he's good for a couple of months, then he's got a legitimate shot at leaving the State School. But being good doesn't necessarily mean that you'll be allowed to pack your bags and stroll through the Pearly Gates that lead you directly into paradise.

So anyway, as I was chatting with a few of the clients in the dayroom, Bobby approached me and then light-heartedly asked, "Hey Jack, are ya coming to my case review this morning?"

I quietly replied, "Of course, Bobby. I wouldn't miss your case review for the world."

Bobby excitedly blurted out, "Really…, oh boy, oh boy, oh boy!"

He then continued by saying, "Hey, I got a real good feeling about today, and I think Mr. Wohlers is gonna let me leave the State School when he hears how good I've been this year."

As I searched for the right words to say, I couldn't help notice the look of anticipation on Bobby's face. I'm sure that Bobby was expecting me to agree with him, and to tell him that the odds were certainly in his favor that he'd be leaving the State School by close of business today.

Despite the fact that Bobby didn't have a snowball's chance in hell of being discharged anytime soon, I just couldn't lie to him. So I decided to serve him up a big scoop of vanilla by saying, "Well Bobby, I guess we'll just have to wait and see how it all plays out today, okay."

Bobby was so excited about the prospects of leaving the State School that he began to scratch the back of his head with both of his hands, as he exclaimed, "Oh boy, oh boy, oh boy!"

I guess you could say that I chickened out on Bobby this morning. But there's no talking to Bobby on case review day, because Bobby only wants to hear what Bobby wants to hear.

But then, isn't that true for all of us too?

The way I see it, in roughly two hours from now, Mr. Wohlers will be dropping the axe on Bobby, and citing chapter and verse as to why Bobby should remain here at the State School.

So in the meantime, what's the harm in prolonging Bobby's fantasy just a little bit longer.

Before leaving the living unit, I had a curious thought pop into my head, so I decided to ask Bobby a question, "Hey Bobby, if you were to be discharged from the State School someday, then what would you do with all of your free time?"

Without any hesitation whatsoever, Bobby blurted out, "Well, probably sit around and drink beer all day, and then have sex all night, just like the staff does here."

I simply couldn't believe my ears, as I shockingly replied, "What! Is that what you really think the staff does when they're not on duty?"

Bobby straightforwardly said, "Yep, 'cause that's what they told us on the ward."

It never seems to fail, but whenever I have a conversation with Bobby Diggs, he always manages to add at least one more piece to the puzzle as to why he's living right here at the State School, and probably will be for the rest of his life.

Bobby hasn't the vaguest idea of what it's like to function in the real world, especially if he thinks that the staff is enjoying nothing but a hedonistic lifestyle when they're off the clock.

No wonder why Bobby wants out of the State School so badly.

From Bobby's perspective, it's nothing but fun and games outside the four walls of the State School. I wouldn't want to be in Bobby Diggs's shoes for all the tea in China. Bobby has some serious misconceptions about life, and all of the responsibilities that seem to come with it.

As much as it pains me to say it, but Bobby is better off staying right here at the State School than he is at trying to survive out in the real world. At least we know that Bobby is safe here, and that he won't wind up being the lead story on the six o'clock news some night.

When I walked into the Building 12 conference room for Bobby's case review, he was already seated at the table. As usual, Bobby had his hair all slicked back and he was wearing his patented shirt and tie. And once again, I had thoughts of Moe Howard dancing through my head.

Bobby then leaned over and asked me how he looked for his "court hearing." Although I was tempted to laugh, I just smiled and told Bobby that he looked really sharp for his meeting.

Now a typical case review has Mr. Wohlers sitting at the head of the table, with the Team Leader seated at his immediate right, and the client being reviewed seated at Mr. Wohlers left.

As far as I was concerned, Wohlers never seemed prepared for these meetings, and relied solely on the information that was being spoon-fed to him by the staff sitting around the table.

So as Wohlers listened to the reports, he would turn towards the client sitting next to him and do his "inspection." Such as, checking their fingernails, looking behind their ears, examining the inside of their mouth, and even pulling up their shirt to check for any marks or bruises.

Mr. Wohlers' motto was, "Let's keep 'em clean, and let's keep 'em healthy!"

I always found Mr. Wohlers' examination of the clients to be quite comical, and it always reminded me of someone who was buying livestock at a cattle auction.

As a rule, Wohlers never liked to hear any negative reports about the clients. And when he did, he had a look of total distain on his face. In a strange sort of way, I think that Wohlers viewed the clients as his children. And as such, he expected his children to behave at all times.

So when Mr. Wohlers heard some less than stellar reports about Bobby this morning, he was quite dismayed to say the least, and he felt as though Bobby had somehow let him down.

The look on Mr. Wohlers' face reminded me of a disappointed father, who just watched his kid strikeout in the bottom of the ninth with the bases loaded to lose the championship game.

Mr. Wohlers looked Bobby straight in the eye, and then sternly said, "Bobby, what do you have to say for yourself with regards to all of these bad reports that I'm hearing about you?"

Now ordinarily, Bobby will usually blame everybody and his brother for all of his misfortunes in life. But seeing how Bobby was totally outnumbered in the room, he just decided to play opossum and say, "Well, I'm sorry that I let you down Mr. Wohlers, and I promise that it'll never happen again!"

Wohlers would then firmly say, "Well, see that it doesn't!"

When the meeting was over, Bobby would always breathe a huge sigh of relief. And even though he didn't hear what he wanted to hear, in Bobby's mind, - a tie is still better than a loss.

A few weeks later, the transportation garage notified me that they finally had enough of Bobby's shenanigans, so they've decided to pull the plug on Bobby's truck driver's helper job.

When Bobby heard that he was fired, he was absolutely shocked. As far as Bobby was concerned, he thought he was doing a good job over there, and that he even deserved a raise.

So now that Bobby lost his job, the only other work option available to him was sorting laundry down in the Work Activity Center. Which Bobby hates with a passion, because the pay was lousy, and there was no social status attached to the

Work Activity Center whatsoever.

For the next several months, every time I saw Bobby he would hound me to death for a better paying job. So to keep him at bay, I would usually tell him that I was working on it. I'm not really sure if Bobby knew that I was stringing him along, but I didn't know what else to do.

Despite the fact that Bobby was a real hard worker, none of the work supervisors here at the State School wanted anything to do with him. Bobby was a legend in his own mind. And not only was Bobby mischievous, but he talked non-stop and he was also a chronic complainer too.

So who in their right mind would want to put up with that all day, right?

Over the years, Bobby has worked at every job imaginable here at the State School. And suffices to say, but he's built up quite a reputation, and burned an awful lot of bridges as well.

Every time I approached a worksite supervisor to see if I could place a client in there department, the first thing out of their mouth was, "Sure, as long as it's not Bobby Diggs!"

By now, Bobby was really beginning to wear me down. And he was becoming such a nuisance for me that it seemed like every time I turned the corner Bobby would be right there.

In fact, I was beginning to wonder if Bobby had slipped a GPS tracking device inside the heel of my shoe.

So that being said, I was a bit surprised one day when I bumped into Bobby over at the commissary, and he never even tried to pester me about getting him a better paying job.

And what's more, he barely said hello, which made me wonder even more.

One morning, as I was cutting across the courtyard toward Building 12, I saw a man who was loading newspapers into the vending machine. The man was obviously a courier for the local newspaper, and the State School was one of the stops on his delivery route.

At first, his movements weren't all that unusual. But for some reason, my eye continued to be drawn to the man as I watched him loading the stack of newspapers into the machine.

As I got closer to the man, I thought I heard him mumbling a few choice words under his breath. Although I couldn't make out what he was saying, he seemed to be rather agitated.

I then paused a moment, so that I could listen more intently to what the man was saying, and it sounded like he said, "Shit! Where the hell is all of the money?"

When I approached the man, I asked him, "Excuse me, sir. But is there a problem here?"

As the man ran his fingers through his bushy brown hair, he replied, "Well, I think that someone is ripping me off. For the past week or so, every time I come by to load the machine, I find that all of the newspapers are gone, but there's only fifty cents in the coin box."

"Huh, that's odd...," I quietly mumbled.

The man then said, "Well, if this keeps up, then I'll be forced to pull the machine."

I then asked him, "Is this your usual time of day to load the machine with newspapers?"

"Yep, same time every day." The man said, as he scratched his head.

"Okay, well, if you can just hang in there for a little while longer, I'll see what I can do for you. I think I have a pretty good hunch who the culprit might be." I said, with a coy smile.

"Gee thanks, I really appreciate it! To tell you the truth, this is actually the first time that I've ever had a problem here at the State School, and I'd hate to pull the vending machine out of here, because it's been a real good moneymaker for me." The young man said.

I quietly chuckled to myself, when I heard the newspaper courier refer to us as the State School.

It's funny, but it really doesn't matter if you work here or not, because everybody you talk to refers to this place as the State School.

In fact, I'd even bet my whole paycheck that the Director refers to this place as the State School too.

Well..., behind closed doors anyway!

So after the newspaper courier finished loading up the machine, he thanked me once again for looking into the matter for him, and then he was off to the next stop on his route.

As I headed over to Building 12, I was thinking to myself, "Well, the trap is set, so now let's see who comes sniffing after the bait."

It just so happens that the Building 12 staff lounge overlooks the courtyard where the vending machine is located, so it was the ideal vantage point for me to stakeout the crime scene.

The fact that there was only fifty cents in the coin box indicated to me that someone was crafty enough to buy one newspaper, and then help themselves to the rest of the stack of papers.

Although I didn't say a word to anyone, I had a very short list of suspects as to whom the culprit might be, and it was only a matter of time before someone surfaced and then took the bait.

So as I continued to keep a pretty steady eye on the courtyard, who of all people should come strolling by, - but none other than good ole' Bobby Diggs.

As I watched Bobby make his way toward the vending machine, he looked like he was up to no good. And the closer that Bobby got to the machine, the more suspicious he was becoming.

Bobby kept glancing over his shoulder to see if anyone was watching him. So seeing that the coast was clear, Bobby rummaged through his pants pockets and took out a couple of coins, and then slid the money into the coin slot. Bobby then pulled the handle on the vending machine door, and quickly snatched the whole stack of newspapers that were lined up inside the machine. Bobby then took off like a jackrabbit in the direction of the community store.

Although it pains me to say it, but Bobby Diggs did exactly what I thought he would do.

The vending machine held about forty newspapers. And at fifty cents a clip, - that amounted to roughly twenty bucks, which wasn't a bad day's profit for Bobby.

As I watched Bobby scamper away, I was extremely disappointed in him. I just couldn't believe that Bobby would stoop so low as to steal from someone like that. He probably thought that he had a pretty good racket going for himself, and that he wouldn't get caught.

Once again, Bobby was only thinking of himself, and it simply never occurred to him that he was putting someone else's livelihood in jeopardy.

Later that day, I went up on the living unit so that I could speak to Bobby. It was almost time for supper, so I knew that Bobby would be there because Bobby never misses a meal.

Sure enough, as I walked onto the living unit, I saw Bobby sitting on the couch watching some television. I still hadn't said a word to anyone yet about the missing newspapers, because I wanted to talk to Bobby first, and see whether he'd lie about it, or if he'd actually come clean.

I strolled over to where Bobby was sitting, and then nonchalantly asked him, "Hi Bobby, so how was your day?"

"Oh, hi Jack. My day was pretty good." Bobby replied, with a big smile on his face.

I sat down next to Bobby, and then casually asked, "So tell me about your day,

Bobby?"

"Well, um…, I worked in the laundry workshop this morning, and then in the afternoon, I went over to the community store and bought some candy for myself." Bobby said, proudly.

"Oh really, because you don't get paid until Friday, and today is only Wednesday, right?" I asked, very matter-of-factly.

"Well, uh…, I got some money out of my account." Bobby shrewdly said.

"I see, well, I guess I can talk to Mr. Askew about that, right. Isn't he the one who's in charge of handling your account?" I casually asked.

"Well, uh…, maybe you shouldn't ask him." Bobby replied, as he began sweating bullets.

"C'mon Bobby, so where did you get the money to buy the candy today?"

"Um, tips from selling newspapers." Bobby said, in an extremely evasive way.

"You mean snitching newspapers, right?"

"Hey, whatta ya mean by that Jack?" Bobby replied, in a very defensive manner.

I just stared at Bobby for a moment, and then disappointedly said, "Listen Bobby, I know all about you stealing newspapers out of the vending machine."

Bobby was absolutely shocked that I knew anything about the stolen newspapers. And at that point, he realized that the jig was up. With tears streaming down his face, he quietly sobbed, "I'm sorry, Jack. I promise that I'll never do it again, okay?"

"So is this the first time that you've stolen newspapers, Bobby?"

"No…," Bobby sadly murmured.

"So how long have you been snitching newspapers out of the vending machine?"

"Um, about a week or so." Bobby said, dejectedly.

"That's right, and do you know how I know that Bobby?"

"How…?" Bobby impetuously asked, as his eyes bugged straight out of his head.

"Because I talked to the newspaper man today and he told me, that's how."

"Oh, so I guess I'll have to pack my bags and go to the lock up ward now, right?"

"Listen Bobby, as it stands right now, no one else knows about this little caper of yours except you, me, and the newspaperman."

"Really...!" Bobby said, excitedly.

"Yeah, that's right. However, tomorrow morning you have some explaining to do to the newspaperman. Because not only do you owe him an apology, but you owe him a lot of money too. Don't think you're gonna wiggle your way out of this one so easily."

"You're right, and I promise to pay him back every penny. But whatever you do, please don't tell my sickologist, because he'll send me straight to the lock up ward if he finds out."

I then corrected Bobby by saying, "The term is psychologist Bobby, not sickologist."

Bobby thought a moment, and then replied, "Oh, I thought it was sickologist, 'cause they only work with sick people like me."

I then continued, "Listen Bobby, I'm willing to work with you on this. But what you did was wrong, and I'm leaving it up to the newspaperman as to what the consequences will be."

"Yeah, alright, I understand, thanks Jack." Bobby sheepishly said.

"Okay Bobby, now this is what we're gonna do, I want you to meet me at my office tomorrow morning at eleven-thirty. The newspaperman is gonna be there too, and he wants to talk to you about this, okay?"

"Yeah, okay, but this whole thing would've never happened if you could've gotten me a better paying job, ya know!" Bobby viciously snarled.

"Now just wait a minute Bobby, don't try to pin this on me. Stealing those newspapers was wrong, and you better start owning up to it." I staunchly replied.

"Okay, you're right, I'm sorry, I'm sorry," Bobby said, backpedaling.

The next day, I called the newspaper company and spoke with Mr. Schaffer, who was the courier that I met yesterday in the courtyard. I told Mr. Schaffer that I found out who the culprit was in stealing the newspapers, and then asked him if he could meet me around eleven o'clock at my office so that we could try to straighten everything out.

When Mr. Schaffer came by my office, I told him what Bobby had done and how he had tried to outfox us.

To my surprise, Mr. Schaffer was actually quite impressed by Bobby's ingenuity. And instead of wanting to reprimand Bobby, he actually wanted to know if he could hire Bobby as a newspaper delivery boy in lieu of the vending machine that was positioned out in the courtyard.

Although Mr. Schaffer took me completely off guard by his suggestion, I told him that I would be willing to supervise Bobby and serve as his newspaper manager.

But that being said, I also told Mr. Schaffer that we still needed to teach Bobby a good lesson regarding the error of his ways in stealing the newspapers.

Around eleven-thirty, there was a knock on my office door and it was Bobby Diggs. And when Bobby walked into my office, he looked as white as a ghost.

As I went to introduce Bobby to Mr. Schaffer, Bobby perked right up and said, "I already know Mr. Schaffer, because I've seen him loading the newspapers into the vending machine."

Mr. Schaffer quietly nodded his head, and then simply replied, "Hello, Bobby."

I then took charge of the meeting by saying, "Well Bobby, I've explained the whole situation to Mr. Schaffer. And as you can probably guess, he's not very happy with you."

As I read Bobby the riot act, I could hear Mr. Schaffer snickering in the background. Schaffer knew that I was only putting on an act, but Bobby was too rattled to even notice.

"Well, um…, I'm really sorry for what I did, Mr. Schaffer." Bobby said, as he bowed his head for forgiveness.

"Listen Bobby, Mr. Schaffer said that he's willing to give you a second chance for what you did, but only under two conditions. First, that you pay him back all of the money that you owe him. And secondly, that you promise never to do something like this again." I sternly said.

"I promise…, I promise…," Bobby shrieked with excitement, as he feverishly scratched the back of his head with both of his hands.

"Settle down, Bobby!" I said, as Mr. Schaffer cracked a smile, and then lightly chuckled.

"Hey Bobby, just out of curiosity, but how long did it take you to sell all forty of those newspapers that were in the vending machine?" Mr. Shaffer asked, with considerable interest.

"Um, not long, maybe an hour. I probably could've sold a lot more too." Bobby replied.

Mr. Schaffer then asked, "Hey Bobby, let me ask you something else. How would you like to work for me selling newspapers here at the State School?"

"Really…! Wow! That would be great, oh boy, oh boy, oh boy!" Bobby exclaimed, as he excitedly scratched the back of his head with both of his hands again.

Mr. Schaffer smiled, and then casually said, "Well, it sounds like you're a natural born salesman Bobby. What if we start you off with fifty papers a day? And if you think you can sell more than that, then I'll bump it up some more, okay?"

"Yeah, okay, oh boy, oh boy, oh boy!" Bobby excitedly replied.

So after sealing the deal with a handshake, Bobby agreed to sign on as Mr. Schaffer's newspaper delivery boy here at the State School, and I would be Bobby's newspaper manager.

Every afternoon, Bobby would come by my office and pick up his bag of newspapers, and then circle the grounds of the State School.

When Bobby was done selling his newspapers for the day, he would then come back to my office and drop off his newspaper bag and money satchel, where he and I would count the money together, and then secure the funds under lock and key.

It was rare for Bobby not to sell all of his newspapers. Bobby enjoyed standing outside the front entrance of the community store hawking his papers. And if by chance he should have any newspapers left over, then he would head over to Building 12 and sell them to passersby.

Bobby took a lot of pride in working for the newspaper company, and he told everyone he knew that he was working for them in an official capacity. Especially since the name and the insignia of the newspaper company was stamped in bold lettering on his canvass delivery bag.

As far as Bobby was concerned, working as a newspaper delivery boy was the greatest thing that ever happened to him in his entire life.

Selling those newspapers had much more prestige for Bobby than working as a truck driver's helper in the transportation garage. Because Bobby was working for a company that was located right in the heart of town, and not situated on or anywhere near the State School grounds.

As far as Bobby was concerned, he was in a class all by himself, and it gave him absolute bragging rights over all of the other clients that were working here at the State School.

In Bobby's mind, he considered himself to be the top dog here at the State School, and he certainly let all of the other clients know about it as often as he possibly could.

As I look back on it now, stealing those newspapers was a terrible thing for Bobby to do.

Yet, in a strange sort of way, I really admire Bobby's resourcefulness. Bobby was able to find a way to rectify his financial woes, when all other conventional methods had failed him.

Once again, Bobby had to rely on his trusty survival skills. And who's to say that I wouldn't have done the same exact thing if I were in Bobby's situation too.

Well, at the end of the day, Bobby wound up working nine months for the newspaper company. And through no fault of his own, Bobby was forced to eventually relinquish his job.

Apparently after conducting a routine audit, the Department of Labor cited the newspaper company for being out of compliance with their Fair Labor Laws regarding the disabled. And in order for the newspaper company to avoid being subjected to a pretty hefty fine, and a possible shut down to the company, then they needed to cease all ties with Bobby Diggs immediately.

When Bobby heard that he had to give up his newspaper delivery job, he was absolutely devastated.

With tears in his eyes, Bobby pleaded, "Please Jack, can't you just call up the Department of Labor and tell 'em that it's okay with me, and that I promise to keep my mouth shut."

Geez Bobby, if only it were that easy!

When it was all said and done, Bobby was selling about seventy-five newspapers a day. I know that Mr. Schaffer was very disappointed the day that he had to say "good-bye" to Bobby. And when they shook hands for the last time, Bobby was heartbroken and completely devastated.

As a token of appreciation, Mr. Schaffer gave Bobby a bright yellow windbreaker, with the name of the newspaper company embossed in fancy black lettering on the back of the jacket.

When Bobby slipped on the jacket, his tears of sadness were instantly transformed into tears of joy. And as Bobby vigorously scratched the back of his head with both of his hands, he excitedly mumbled, in typical Bobby style, "Oh boy, oh boy, oh boy…!"

Chapter Four

Well, Bobby continues to be down in the dumps since losing his newspaper delivery job, and all he wants to do all day is just mope around the living unit and feel sorry for himself.

The staff has been scratching their heads and wondering why some obscure government regulation would result in the newspaper company handing Bobby his pink slip, especially since the regulation that the Department of Labor cited had nothing to do with Bobby in the first place.

And the one question that keeps circulating around the Unit is, "Why is the Department of Labor interested in what any of our kids here at the State School are doing anyway?"

Just for the record, but the old-timers that work here at the State School frequently refer to the clients as kids, mainly because the clients are developmentally stunted, and much of the behavior that they exhibit mirrors that of children.

Anyway, to satisfy my curiosity, I decided to contact the Department of Labor so that I could get some clarification regarding their Fair Labor Laws, specifically, - the subsection of the law that pertains to Bobby and the newspaper company.

When I finally got someone to explain the subsection of the law to me, they wound up citing some cockamamie regulation that had nothing to do with Bobby's situation whatsoever.

Which I knew would be the case. But when it comes to making sense out of any of the government regulations that on the books, it's like fighting a five alarm fire with a water pistol.

Now granted, federal agencies like the Department of Labor are solely in existence to serve as government watchdogs, so that they can insure that people's rights are being upheld.

But at the end of the day, I think the actions taken by the Department of Labor did Bobby Diggs a terrible injustice. Because delivering those newspapers meant the world to Bobby, and it gave him a great sense of joy and purpose in his life and something to look forward to every day.

To be honest, but I'm actually quite surprised that the Department of Labor would waste all of its valuable time and precious resources on such an insignificant case like Bobby Diggs.

Now if these government watchdogs would really like to sink their teeth into something, then why not go after Corporate America, who has been committing environmental atrocities and unfair labor practices for years, and costing the American taxpayers millions of dollars.

Anyway, despite the fact that Bobby has had a pretty rough couple of months, Bobby was all smiles the day that Mr. Schaffer called and invited him to attend the annual Christmas party at the newspaper plant.

During their brief time together, Mr. Schaffer grew to be quite fond of Bobby. And even though Bobby wasn't associated with the newspaper company anymore, Mr. Schaffer felt that Bobby deserved the right to attend the annual Christmas party anyway.

Mr. Schaffer even invited me to come along too, probably because he needed someone to keep a steady eye on Bobby, so that Bobby wouldn't wind up stealing the place blind.

Lately, there have been some rumblings circulating throughout the facility that state and federal officials have been meeting behind closed doors to discuss some upcoming changes.

Apparently, the federal government is on the verge of appropriating hundreds of millions of dollars, so that state agencies such as ours can design and implement specific programs to teach clients to be more independent in their lives, and these programs are being referred to as habilitation services.

However, it's still not clear as to what these types of services really are, or what any of these proposed programs may even entail.

The rumor mill is usually pretty accurate, so it's only a matter of time before we hear an official announcement that there will be some major shake-ups in store here at the State School.

So in the wake of all of these impending rumors, I received a phone call one late Friday afternoon from Mr. Wohlers' secretary, who wanted to know if I was available to meet with Mr. Wohlers and the two Team Leaders to discuss a few programming ideas pertaining to the Unit.

As I entered the Building 12 conference room, Mr. Wohlers and the two Team Leaders were already seated at the table, and they were quietly chatting amongst themselves. Wohlers had me take a seat, and then he began the meeting by telling us that the federal government was in the process of allocating hundreds of millions of dollars to individuals with developmental disabilities, and that our facility is hoping to qualify for some of these proposed federal funds.

Mr. Wohlers then humorously quipped, "Apparently, the Commissioner wants us to start teaching these kids some new tricks," which prompted the two Team Leaders to quietly snicker.

Wohlers then continued by saying, "Approximately three quarters of the clients living here at the State School, oh, pardon me, I, uh…, meant to say the developmental center…,"

Upon hearing Mr. Wohlers' amusing slip of the tongue, the two Team Leaders began laughing in the background, which then prompted Mr. Wohlers to join in on the laughter as well.

Wohlers took a minute to collect his thoughts, and then said, "So, as I was saying, three-quarters of the clients that reside here at the developmental center are functioning between the severe to profound range of mental retardation, and the rest are either in the moderate or mild range, well, with a few exceptions of course. The Director has instructed all of the Unit Chiefs to come up with a comprehensive plan, so that we can start delivering habilitation services to all of our clients by the next fiscal quarter, and thus be eligible for federal funding."

Ms. Neff then spoke right up and staunchly replied, "Well, I think it's about time that we started working with the lower functioning kids that live here, instead of just the smart ones."

Mr. Wohlers nodded his head, and quietly said, "Yes, I wholeheartedly agree, Betty."

Wohlers continued by saying, "So, I'd like to meet back with all of you in one weeks' time. And at our next meeting, I expect to have a written proposal in my hand, and a clear cut strategy on how we intend to provide habilitation services to everyone in the Unit. I will then review the proposal, and submit it to the Director for his approval. Just remember, the days of clients existing on the back wards are finally over!"

So the following Monday, the two Team Leaders and I assembled in Ms. Neff's office so that we could devise a plan for Mr. Wohlers.

It didn't take long for us to realize that this assignment was going to be a monumental task. And in order for us to design it to Mr. Wohlers' specifications, then we would be burning the midnight oil. We all knew that Mr. Wohlers expected results, and not any flimsy excuses.

By Thursday, I was mentally exhausted, and I think the intensity of this assignment was finally catching up to me.

Of course, my mental state of mind worsened every time I walked by Askew's office, only to see him and Snead drinking coffee and reading the morning newspaper. Meanwhile, the Team Leaders and I were slaving over this grueling assignment that Wohlers directed us to do.

I kept asking myself over and over again, "Why are Snead and Askew so privileged, and why aren't they helping us out on this proposal?"

By Friday morning, we finally put the finishing touches on the proposal, so that we could present it to Mr. Wohlers that afternoon for his approval.

When we walked into Mr. Wohler's office, he was all shits and giggles, as he excitedly rubbed his hands together and stated, "Well, I'm very eager to see what you all came up with."

As the meeting got underway, Ms. Fields volunteered to be the spokesperson for the group. And as always, she was poised and articulate, and made very good use of the charts and schematics that we had designed to help illustrate and explain the basic framework of our proposal.

We not only defined what our mission statement was, but we also provided a tentative program schedule too. And an in-depth analysis on how we were planning to utilize the staff.

Throughout the meeting, Wohlers would nod his head periodically, yet I had the distinct impression that he was not overly impressed with what he was hearing.

Upon conclusion of the presentation, the first thing out of Wohlers' mouth was, "Well, it's a start, but what I've heard thus far sounds more "cookie cutter" than cutting edge. And I'm sure I don't need to remind you, but I expect this Unit to be the flagship program of the facility."

I quickly thought to myself, "Hey Wohlers, are you kidding me? Do you have any idea how hard we worked on this proposal? Maybe you should've had your two golden boys Snead and Askew work on the proposal instead."

When I glanced at the two Team Leaders, I could tell that they were just as disappointed as I was. For crissakes! We poured our heart and soul into this project, only to have the boss say that it's still not good enough.

As we sat there licking our wounds, Wohlers began to rifle off some key points of interest that he wanted us to incorporate into the proposal for our next follow-up meeting.

I then thought to myself, "Hey Wohlers, are you completely off your rocker?"

Just to be clear, but Mr. Wohlers' Unit had a census of over two hundred clients, and he wanted us to design and implement a state of the art program for each and every one of them.

Mr. Wohlers actually thinks that we will be able to transport nearly two hundred severe to profoundly retarded individuals off of their living units every day, and onto a totally foreign and unfamiliar program site, so that our facility can qualify for millions of dollars in federal funding.

Oh, my God! Has Wohlers completely lost all of his faculties?

This proposal was beginning to sound more like an episode of "The Walking

Dead" than it was a way of teaching the clients to be more independent and self-reliant in their life.

Wohlers then turned towards me, and straightforwardly asked, "Jack, will any of these new changes have any impact on our clients that attend the Central Rehab program? You know what a bastard that Kramer can be, especially since he was passed over for promotion again."

In the background, I could hear the two Team Leaders quietly chuckling to themselves, and seemingly quite amused by Mr. Wohlers' colorful language in how he referenced Kramer.

I then interjected, "Well, as it stands right now Mr. Wohlers, we have roughly thirty-five clients who are currently involved in the Central Rehab program, and I really don't anticipate losing any of those work slots. In my opinion, it wouldn't be in Mr. Kramer's best interest to start chopping clients out of his program, especially now."

Wohlers then remarked, "Well, yes, I see your point. But I wouldn't put anything past that son-of-a-bitch, because Kramer is completely rotten to the core. In fact, why the hell do we even need Kramer in the first place? I mean, as far as I'm concerned, they aren't doing anything different over there than we could be doing over here, right?"

As I listened to Mr. Wohlers rake Kramer over the coals, he seemed to be making a pretty valid point. And if I were in Mr. Wohlers' shoes, I probably would've reacted the same way.

Despite the acrimonious feelings that Wohlers has for Kramer, they're both two birds of a feather, and one is just as unscrupulous as the other. Both Wohlers and Kramer are accustomed to getting their own way. And when they don't, then there's usually hell to pay.

What Wohlers fails to realize is that in order for us to operate any type of work program here at the State School, then we need to be in strict compliance with the Department of Labor.

As it stands right now, Mr. Kramer has the final say as to what types of work programs are operated here at the State School. And in order for anyone to get Mr. Kramer's stamp of approval, then he is going to make damn sure that we are in strict compliance with all of the Department of Labor laws and regulations that are on the books.

The Department of Labor is a pretty tough bunch. And from what I hear, the margin for error between compliancy and delinquency is pretty slim.

Now if the Department of Labor happens to do a random inspection, and finds even the slightest hint of impropriety with regards to any of the laws or regulations that are on the books, then the DOL has the authority to revoke your operating certificate and shut your program down.

Obviously getting caught with your pants down by the Department of Labor would be Mr. Kramer's worst nightmare, especially when these operating certificates are the only thing that's keeping him in a job around here. Mr. Kramer is so paranoid about losing his precious operating certificates that he probably tucks them under his pillow at night for safe keeping.

From what I understand, the application process for obtaining a Department of Labor operating certificate is an extremely comprehensive and time consuming procedure, and Kramer was damn lucky that those DOL certificates were already in place when he came on board.

The fact that Ms. Albright did all of the leg work in securing all of those DOL certificates is just one more reason why she harbors so much anger towards Mr. Kramer. And to add insult to injury, but Ms. Albright was then overlooked for promotion because Kramer has a "rabbi" at the State Capital, who managed to use his power and his influence so that Kramer could land the job.

So before wrapping up our little soiree, Wohlers mentioned that Snead would be joining us the next time we meet. Apparently, Snead has some rather interesting thoughts and ideas that he'd like to share with us regarding habilitation services, especially in the area of documentation.

Well, let's just hope that Wohlers isn't counting on Snead to be the linchpin for success. Unless of course, we're trying to decide on which blend of coffee is best suited when reading the morning newspaper every day.

The following week, the two Team Leaders and I met back with Mr. Wohlers. And as promised, Snead was in attendance as well. So after dispensing with a few pleasantries, Wohlers then lateraled the ball over to Snead and asked him to conduct the meeting.

Although it pains me to admit it, but Snead actually impressed me today on how thorough his presentation was. Up until now, I thought that Snead's sole area of expertise was limited to scouring the newspaper and being an aficionado on coffee. But apparently, I was quite mistaken.

As Snead presented his information, he provided us with a number of handouts, such as, a comprehensive list of client IQ levels, as well as a breakdown of each client's ability in the areas of bathing, toileting, dressing, eating, and what types of behavioral deficiencies they had as well.

Snead pointed out that in order for us to qualify for federal funding, then we would need to come up with a standardized way of documenting the services that we were hoping to provide. Snead also made it quite clear that the federal government was not about to hand over millions of dollars to the State. And in exchange, the feds would simply smile and take our word for it.

So that being said, Snead proceeded to pass out a variety of data sheets for us to peruse, so that we could decide on which one of them would be best suited in documenting the services that we were hoping to provide to the clients.

Some of the data sheets that we were considering actually had step-by-step instructions that were built right into the form. And since all of these psychometric inventories already had a proven track record, and were recognized as being measurable yardsticks in the field, then Snead recommended that we choose one of them as the foundation for our documentation system.

Snead then decided to take the conversation in a whole new direction by citing some rather obscure and irrelevant case studies that had nothing to do with the subject at hand.

When Snead finally concluded his convoluted spiel, he quietly leaned back in his chair and looked quite pleased with himself, and then patiently waited for Mr. Wohlers to pat him on the back and give him his long-awaited "that-a-boy" Snead.

To Snead's chagrin, Mr. Wohlers looked more confused than impressed.

Mr. Wohlers then shouted, in a rather irritated tone, "For crissakes, Snead! This is your area of expertise! So just pick out the data sheet that you think we need, and then tell us how to fill out the goddamn form! This meeting is adjourned!"

So after weeks of tweaking the proposal, we finally got it right. The only thing left to do now was for Mr. Wohlers to bring the proposal over to the Director's Office for his approval.

As we all waited on pins and needles to hear back from the Director, Mr. Wohlers was sitting up in his ivory tower firing off one spicy memo after the other. And all of these less than friendly communiques were beginning to incite the fury of the living unit staff.

I'm not sure if Wohlers was trying to keep the staff in the loop, or simply annoy the hell out of them. But either way, tensions were beginning to mount and tempers were starting to flare.

As I've mentioned before, Mr. Wohlers possessed a very unorthodox supervisory style. And as far as I was concerned, he didn't have the slightest idea on how to manage people at all.

Despite the fact that Mr. Wohlers is an ordained minister, and professes to be a man of God, he has a real mean streak in him. It's almost sadistic, - and he doesn't seem to know where to draw the line between constructive criticism and mental abuse.

Every day when the living unit staff reported to work, they would automatically check their mailboxes, so that they could catch up on reading the latest nasty memo from Mr. Wohlers.

The one memo that was definitely raising some eyebrows amongst all of the living unit staff was the one that talked about all of the dramatic changes that were looming on the horizon, specifically, in the way that we do business here at the State School.

Quite honestly, but the last thing in the world that the living unit staff wanted to hear was that there was going to be some dramatic shake-ups here at the State School, especially when the rank and file is so resistive to change.

And trust me, but even the slightest change in the living unit staff's routine was enough to knock them completely off kilter.

So after weeks of anticipation, Mr. Wohlers finally fired off the memo that had everyone in the Unit chirping, which was…, - "The Director has approved the proposal!"

This lengthy three page memo, which read like the Monroe Doctrine, outlined every aspect of the proposal. And in the body of the memo, Wohlers had the audacity to say that the Director intends to use "his" proposal as the blueprint for the rest of the facility to follow.

Once again, Mr. Wohlers was taking all of the credit.

After reading Wohlers' three page memo, the staff felt so nauseous that we all wanted to take a swig of some bicarbonate of soda, so that we could all try and settle our stomachs a bit.

So now that we got the green light from the Director, Wohlers summoned his two trusty Lieutenants into his office, so that he could give them their marching orders on how to proceed next with "his" proposal. Because Wohlers only had sixty days to get the plan up and running.

Of course, getting the proposal approved by the Director was the easy part. But now the hard part was getting the plan put into motion by the sixty day deadline.

Up until now, the living unit supervisors have been kept virtually in the dark with regards to providing any input with the new proposal. Which for the life of me, I really don't understand.

As far as I was concerned, the living unit supervisors were the linchpin in getting this monstrosity up off of the ground.

So that being said, I wish that somebody would explain to me why Wohlers and the two Team Leaders haven't consulted with any of the living unit supervisors sooner than this.

When Ms. Fields and Ms. Neff finally unveiled their plan to the living unit supervisors, their jaws dropped straight to the floor, as they replied, "Uh, you gotta be kidding us, right?"

I'm sure that Wohlers didn't want to say too much to the living unit supervisors, because he was afraid that they might spill the beans to the living unit staff. It's certainly no secret that the living unit supervisors frequently socialize with their subordinates outside of work, and the living unit staff seem to view their supervisors more in the context as friends than they do bosses.

Wohlers has always lived by the motto, "Loose lips, sink ships!"

So that being said, Wohlers decided that the proposal was only on a need to know basis, and that the living unit supervisors didn't need to know.

I wish I had a nickel for every time the living unit staff cornered me on the Unit, and then asked me on the Q.T., "C'mon Jack, you go to all the meetings, so what's going on in there?"

Sure, I go to the meetings, but that doesn't mean that I'm privy to any inside information. And to be quite honest, but I didn't know anymore than what the living unit staff already knew.

I certainly didn't considered myself to be part of the inner circle, nor was I expecting to be issued a key to the executive washroom anytime soon either.

In any event, I guess we'll just have to wait and see how it all shakes out.

Well, just when I thought that staff moral couldn't get any lower, Mr. Wohlers was back at it again. And for the past two weeks, Wohlers has been issuing two to three nasty memos a day. And to be quite honest, but I just don't know how much more the living unit staff can take.

Every morning the staff would huddle together outside their mailboxes, as they would read one explosive memo after the other, such as, "Limited Time Off," or "Upcoming Training Schedule," or "The Dawn of a New Era Is Upon Us."

But the one memo that seemed to have everybody in the Unit chirping was, "The Days of Clients Living on the Back Wards are Finally Over!"

Wohlers insightful reminders, or should I say, "inciteful" reminders, wasn't exactly what the living unit staff wanted to see on the subject line of Wohlers' irritating memos. Especially when the rank and file has been doing their jobs the same exact way since time and memorial.

So when the living unit supervisors finally went back to their respective units and told their staff what the game plan was, the staff simply couldn't believe their ears. Especially since the general consensus among the living unit staff was, "these kids ain't ever gonna learn nothin' anyway, so what's the point in trying to teach them how to do anything at all!"

What's the point?

Uh…, millions of dollars to be made, - that's the point!

Well, as we inched closer to the sixty day deadline, the two Team Leaders were quickly realizing that there simply wasn't enough time to accomplish everything that needed to be done.

Mr. Wohlers could see that his two trusty Lieutenants were under a tremendous amount of duress, so he decided to have Snead shoulder some of the burden for the two Team Leaders.

Even with Snead's help, the two Team Leaders were still putting in some pretty grueling hours, and it would take a miracle to get all of the logistics coordinated by the sixty day deadline.

So while the two Team Leaders were trying to get it all done before zero hour, the living unit staff was spending virtually all of their time bellyaching about Wohlers, and how ridiculous it was that the top brass was now ordering them to start teaching these "kids" some new tricks.

Once again, the living unit staff is extremely closed minded when it comes to change. So the sheer thought of altering their routine was enough to make them scream. And I think it would be safe to say that the living unit staff was quite content in keeping things just the way they were.

With all of these impending changes that were looming, the staff was afraid that they might even lose the luxury of having the "working boys" do all of their grunt work for them. And all for the mere price of a cup of coffee, or a handful of goodies out of the goody cupboard.

I'm sure that Wohlers knew all about the "working boys." And he knew all about the little short cuts that the living unit staff likes to take. But he chose not to do anything about it, because he was afraid that if he stirred the pot too much, then it might get back to the Director.

So that being said, you can only imagine how upset the living unit staff were when Mr. Wohlers fired off his latest spicy memo that read, "All cleaning and housekeeping duties on the living units will now be the sole responsibility of the living unit staff. And if I catch one of the clients doing any of the assigned duties that the staff are expected to do, then heads will roll!"

Yeah, the handwriting was definitely on the wall.

And the days of the staff putting their feet up on the coffee table, while the "working boys" did all of the backbreaking chores around the living unit may soon be coming to an end.

Another irritating memo that was getting under the skin of the living unit staff was, "Effective immediately, there will be no more shoe-shining, back rubs, or clients running errands on the behest of the staff. Just remember, the days of clients being indentured servants are over!"

So is it any wonder why every staff lounge in Wohlers' Unit had an 8X10 glossy of his face pasted to the dart board, or why every staff person on the living unit was heard to say, "That son-of-a-bitch Wohlers wouldn't last one day working on this ward!"

Well, the moment of truth had finally arrived, and the sixty day deadline was upon us.

Today would prove to be a landmark day. And from this day forward, the clients at the State School would be looked upon as an economic windfall, instead of a custodial nightmare.

On the morning of this momentous day, Mr. Wohlers was all smiles. However, I wish I could say the same for his two trusty Lieutenants, who both looked completely nervous as hell.

Wohlers made sure that all hands were on deck this morning, so that everything would go off without a hitch. The last thing that Colonel Wohlers wanted today was for any foul-ups or glitches to occur, which might ruin his red letter day.

It's extremely difficult for me to put into words what this morning was really like. It reminded me of some sort of military exercise. Wohlers and the two Team Leaders were all standing at attention in the hallway, while the staff and the clients slowly paraded by them.

As crazy as it may sound, but Wohlers reminded me of General George S. Patton, pearl-handled revolver and all, as he nodded his head and smiled agreeably as the troops marched by.

Like Patton, Wohlers didn't concern himself with the amount of casualties that might be sustained today, as long as the battle was fought, and victory was attained.

As we marched past Wohlers and the two Team Leaders, I was having a lot of difficulty in justifying what we were doing this morning.

In order for us to qualify for federal funding, then all of the habilitation services that we were hoping to provide to the clients needed to be implemented on a neutral program site, and could not be conducted on or anywhere near the general vicinity of the living units.

So that being said, over two hundred profoundly retarded individuals had to be uprooted from the sanctity of their living unit, which is the only living environment that they have ever known, and then transported to a neutral program site that was completely unfamiliar to them.

Just imagine how you might feel if you were in their shoes. These clients had no idea where they were going or what they were going to do when they got there. And as macabre as this might sound, but it reminded me of cattle being led to the abattoir for slaughter.

Yet, despite it all, the real irony was that these clients were making history today.

Not because they were finally receiving the services that they so richly deserved, but because they were standing on the precipice of generating hundreds of millions of federal dollars for the State coffers.

Well, according to our calculations, we were hoping to have the clients transported to the program areas by 9:30am. And once everyone was situated, it was my job to do roll call.

Roll call was extremely important, because we wanted to make sure that everyone was present and accounted for. The last thing we wanted was to lose any stragglers along the way.

And trust me, - that was a definite and distinct possibility.

By 10:15am, we had all of the clients corralled and situated where they were supposed to be. I'm sure that Colonel Wohlers will be extremely disappointed when Intel notifies him that we wound up overshooting our mark by forty-five minutes.

But hey, - the beachhead was secured, and we didn't sustain any casualties.

Not a bad morning's work, if I do say so myself. But then it suddenly dawned on me that we were going to be doing this little military exercise every day.

Oh, my God! Heaven help us!

It goes without saying, but there was certainly a hint of sarcasm in the air this morning as we caravanned our way from the living units to the program site. Much of what was said by the living unit staff was said in rather poor taste. But it still didn't negate the fact that their scathing remarks were pretty damn funny, and I found myself to be thoroughly amused by what they said.

Of course, the sarcastic comments ended the minute we paraded by Mr. Wohlers and the two Team Leaders. But once safely out of earshot, their racy remarks fired right back up again.

Day, after day, after day, we would transport the clients back and forth from the living units to the program site. We actually looked like a band of gypsies, as we traipsed along keeping a steady eye on the clients, while pulling wagon-loads of surplus and supplies behind us.

The staff kept trying to convince themselves that it was only a matter of time before the top brass would realize the futility of it all. And in their hearts, the living unit staff truly believed that all they had to do was just hang in there for a little while longer and simply ride it out.

Well, little did they know, but we were in it for the long haul. Not because it was the right thing to do, but because there was just too much damn money at stake for the State to pass up.

As time went by, my role in the Unit was changing. Although I was still in charge of vocational services, I was also responsible for coordinating the Adaptive Skills program as well, which were basically habilitation services that dealt with grooming and personal hygiene.

To be perfectly honest, but I had absolutely no expertise in this area whatsoever. And when the living unit staff would ask me a technical question regarding the client's grooming or personal hygiene, I would simply answer them by saying, "Uh, your guess is as good as mine."

Hey, I never took any electives in college pertaining to grooming or personal hygiene. If anything, Snead should've been the one heading up the Adaptive Skills program, not me.

After all, isn't Snead our resident guru?

Thus far, the only contribution that Snead has made regarding off-unit programming was recommending what type of data sheet we should use to document the services that we provide.

So despite the many challenges that we have been facing in off-unit programming, I would have to say that our biggest challenge by far was in the area of toileting the clients.

Now although the topic of toileting can be an extremely awkward subject to talk about, the simple reality was that all of the clients that we worked with in the habilitation program were totally incontinent, and they all needed to be closely monitored and supervised at all times.

And trust me, I'm not talking about some minor oops, mishaps, or near misses either!

From the minute we arrived to the program site, until the minute that we finally left, the only thing we seemed to be doing was shuttling the clients in and out of the bathroom all day.

And the sixty-four thousand dollar question that the living unit staff kept asking me over and over again was, "Why are we dragging these clients back and forth to a program site every day, when all we're doing here is exactly what we would be doing back on the living unit?"

Well, I guess from the staff's perspective, they were making a pretty valid point.

Another comment that I would frequently hear the living unit staff say was, "We'll be tripping these kids until the day we retire."

The term "tripping" is a slang expression that is commonly used among the living unit staff when toileting the clients. And as a rule, the living unit staff usually trips the clients every hour on the hour, whether the clients need to use the bathroom facilities or not.

The living unit staff is very careful never to use the term "tripping" when the top brass is around, because the term is considered to be extremely taboo. And from what I hear, Wohlers has been known to make an example out of anyone he hears using that expression in the Unit.

Now that being said, Wohlers has been known to use the term "tripping" when in the company of his two trusty Lieutenants. And proving once again that a double standard exists.

Well, we've been doing off-unit programming for a year now, and I wish I could say that we've made even the slightest hint of progress in helping the clients to be more independent. But to be quite honest, I really don't think that we've made any headway with the clients whatsoever.

I think it's safe to say that no one here at the State School would have ever imagined that this little crapshoot of ours would've ever lasted this long. And even the living unit staff has finally given up the idea of just riding it out.

Now although I spend the majority of my time overseeing the habilitation program, I'm still in charge of the Work Activity Center.

And yes, - that includes keeping a steady eye on my old buddy Bobby Diggs too.

Bobby has certainly had a very interesting year, and he's gone through more jobs in one year than most people go through in a lifetime.

In retrospect, I was really hoping that Bobby would have learned his lesson the day he lost his truck driver's helper job. But unfortunately, Bobby continues to be his own worst enemy.

Bobby has systematically jeopardized my credibility with every worksite supervisor here at the State School, yet Bobby continues to think that he is nothing but a victim of circumstance.

But what's really most disturbing to me is that worksite supervisors that I consider to be my close and personal friends, won't even return any of my phone calls. And when they happen to see me over at the commissary, they drop their lunch tray and then run straight for the hills.

Bobby seems to think that he can screw up, say I'm sorry, and then all is forgotten.

Quite honestly, but sometimes I wonder why I keep going back to the well with

Bobby Diggs. I want to believe that he has an upside, but I'll be damned if I can figure out what it is.

When Bobby worked as a truck driver's helper, he not only subjected the staff to his constant guff all day, but when you factor in his list of shortcomings too, such as, spilling gas at the gas pumps, banging laundry carts into freshly painted walls, or forgetting to latch the back cargo door, and then having racks of clean laundry come flying right out of the back of the truck.

Well, - is it any wonder why I can't sleep at night, and why I'm also losing my hair?

Oh, and how could I forget the blunder of all blunders. Which was the day that Bobby decided to jump behind the wheel of one of the laundry trucks, and then attempt to move the truck out of the path of an oncoming vehicle.

Although Bobby meant well, and his intentions certainly weren't malicious, but Bobby wound up crashing the truck into the side of a building. Which not only caused serious damage to the front end of the truck, but the unfortunate mishap nearly resulted in several fatalities too.

Sadly, the truck driver who was responsible for supervising Bobby that day wound up being suspended for two weeks without pay. I felt terrible when I heard the disciplinary board's ruling, especially since the guy had a wife and four kids, and he was barely making ends meet.

Despite my efforts in advocating for the truck driver at his disciplinary hearing, the board determined that the truck driver was not only negligent, but he was also derelict in his duties as well. And as a result of his poor judgment that day, then he needed to suffer the consequences.

When I look back on it now, I guess I was pretty lucky that the disciplinary board didn't wind up throwing the book at me as well. And penalize me for being crazy enough to place someone as irresponsible as Bobby Diggs in a dangerous work slot like that in the first place.

The other day, I received a frantic phone call from the supervisor of the Work Activity Center, who was screaming at the top of his lungs, and saying that Bobby Diggs was wreaking all sorts of havoc in the work program.

So after finally calming the Work Activity Center supervisor down, I told him that I would speak with Bobby as soon as I could, and that I would try to get to the bottom of things.

As I headed over to the Work Activity Center, I was thinking that even though I have a master's degree in counseling, none of the counseling techniques that I've learned up to this point has proven to be all that effective in dealing with someone as challenging as Bobby Diggs.

Even Snead, who is a seasoned psychologist with over twenty-five years of experience, has been known to throw his hands up in the air when it comes to dealing with Bobby Diggs.

Quite honestly, but the clients who attend the Work Activity Center are nothing more than a bunch of hooligans, who are all similar to Bobby, but maybe not quite as devious as him.

As a rule, the clients seem to spend more time bickering with one another than actually working. And sometimes I wonder if all of the grief and aggravation that I seem to put up with in operating this little two-bit laundry program of mine is really worth it.

The following week, I happened to bump into Mr. Wohlers on the Building 12 staircase, who then proceeded to ask me how everything was going in the Unit.

Without any hesitation, I was quick to say, "Never better, Mr. Wohlers!"

Wohlers then patted me on the back and said, "That-a-boy, Jack! I've been hearing a lot of good things about you from my two trusty Lieutenants, so just keep up the good work, boy!"

Mr. Wohlers' question was simply rhetorical. Because the last thing that Wohlers or any of the other administrators around here wanted to hear were complaints from their subordinates.

As far as the top brass goes, if there's a problem then they expect you to fix it. And God help you if the problem that you're trying to fix should happen to find its way outside the four walls of the State School, because then you'll have a pack of wolves breathing down your neck.

Later that afternoon, I attended a client case review over in Building 13. And as usual, Wohlers was sitting at the head of the table, with Ms. Fields seated at his immediate right, and a chair that was reserved for the client that we were meeting on to Mr. Wohlers immediate left.

So as we waited for the case review to begin, Wohlers said that he was meeting with the Director right after our case review was over. And although Wohlers wasn't at liberty to discuss any of the details of what the meeting was about, he did tell us that there were some interesting developments that were happening on the horizon, which could seriously impact all of us here at the State School.

As we all tried to absorb the bombshell that Wohlers just dropped on us, the Building 13 social worker entered the room with Johnny, who was the client that we were meeting on today.

When the meeting commenced, Mr. Wohlers began doing his "inspection" of Johnny, while Ms. Fields "spoon-fed" Wohlers pertinent information that was relevant to Johnny's case.

So once Johnny passed inspection, Wohlers then directed Ms. Fields to have each of the clinicians go around the table and give their reports and summaries about Johnny to the group.

While Mr. Wohlers listened to the various reports, he would nod his head periodically, as if he were actually interested in what was being said. But everyone in the room knew that Mr. Wohlers was merely going through the motions, and that his mind was completely elsewhere.

So after the last report was read, Mr. Wohlers capriciously said, "Well, if there's nothing else, then I guess we're all done here. This meeting is adjourned."

As the group was getting up from the table, I kept staring at the top of Johnny's head, specifically his scalp, which was riddled with an irregular pattern of bald spots. And in a strange sort of way, the bald spots resembled that of a small chain of islands, such as an archipelago.

Although the nurse covered Johnny's scalp condition in her report, and also informed the group that his bald spots were a form of alopecia, I was actually curious to know if his condition was permanent or would it improve over time.

As Mr. Wohlers was getting up from his chair, I felt compelled to ask, "Excuse me, Mr. Wohlers. But can you tell me if Johnny's bald spots will grow back?"

Mr. Wohlers, who is completely bald himself, then said while pointing to the top of his head, "Jack, do I look like an expert on baldness to you?"

All of a sudden, the entire room erupted into uncontrollable laughter. And even Mr. Wohlers joined in on all of the knee-slapping hilarity as well.

When all of the laughter subsided, the nurse then explained to me that the doctor thinks that Johnny is having some sort of allergic reaction to one of his medications. However, the doctor will continue to monitor the situation. And barring any further complications, Johnny's hair should grow back again in a few more months.

Well, aside from the fact that I made a complete and utter fool of myself in today's case review, most of the case reviews here at the State School are of the ho-hum variety.

So that being said, if you were to take a straw poll and ask the staff which case review they would absolutely hate to miss, the overwhelming consensus would probably say Tommy Gerard's case review.

Now if you're planning to attend Tommy Gerard's case review, then you better get there early, because Tommy's meeting was usually standing room only. Tommy enjoys performing in front of a packed house, as he entertains the crowd with his incredible savant talents.

Even Wohlers has been known to join in on the fun as well.

Tommy's meeting had a real carnival atmosphere to it. Tommy would not only crank out people's birthdays one after the other, but he would proceed to tell them without fail what day of the week their birthday fell on in any given calendar year as well.

But wait, there's more!

Tommy would then proceed to move on to phase two, - by scintillating the crowd with his uncanny ability to multiply three, four, and even five digit numbers.

The staff sitting around the table would become so spellbound by Tommy's incredible savant talents that they would simply forget why they were all assembled there in the first place.

In the blink of an eye, Tommy would spit out the answer with the greatest of ease. Yet, this computer genius lives right here at the State School, and probably will for the rest of his life.

When it was my turn to update the group on Tommy, my reports were usually less than favorable. And the mood in the room would suddenly shift, and the meeting would go sideways.

As a rule, Tommy was pretty lazy. And he would much rather spend his time in the Work Activity Center entertaining the other clients, then working on any of his assigned laundry tasks.

To be honest, but I always felt like I was a bit of a party-pooper at Tommy's case review, especially since my reports tended to be negative, and never captured Tommy in a positive light.

So after giving my report on Tommy, everyone in the room would start to moan and groan and then flash me the stink eye, as if to say, "Who the heck invited Jack to the meeting?"

Upon hearing how poorly Tommy was doing in the work program, Mr. Wohlers would usually scowl, and then sternly say, "Listen Tommy, you better start shaping up or else!"

Tommy feared confrontation of any kind, especially from someone as intimidating as Mr. Wohlers. So Tommy would reach deep into his bag of tricks, and then pull out the crème-de-la-crème of all of his savant talents by rattling off the entire list of U.S. Presidents in consecutive order, including when they were born, when they died, and their presidential term in office.

Once again, Wohlers would firmly say, "Listen Tommy, you better learn to straighten up! Just remember, you were transferred into this Unit for a reason! And furthermore….,"

Unfortunately, Wohlers efforts to reprimand Tommy fell on deaf ears. Because Tommy was now entering some deep dark and mysterious tunnel, and there was really no hope of turning back, as he recited, "George Washington, - Father of our Country, born February 22, 1732, and died on December 14, 1799, and served as President of the United States from 1789-1797. John Adams, - born October 30, 1735, and died on July 4, 1826, and served as President of the United States from 1797-1801. Thomas Jefferson, - born April 13, 1743, and died on July 4, 1826, and served as President of the United States from 1801-1809. James Madison, - ..."

No one in the room said a word, - what was the point.

Tommy was in such a deep dark trance right now that he couldn't hear a damn thing that anyone would say to him anyway, so why not just sit back and enjoy the history lesson.

By the time Tommy reached Abraham Lincoln, he had really hit his stride. As we all sat there glancing at one another, we all knew that there was absolutely nothing that any of us could say or do in bringing Tommy back to reality, until he exhausted the entire list of U.S. Presidents.

When Tommy was finished reciting the entire list of U.S. Presidents, he was hoping that his little dog and pony show would be just the trick in appeasing Mr. Wohlers.

As Wohlers threw his hands up in the air, he shouted in frustration, "Tommy, I better start hearing some good reports about you the next time that we meet! This meeting is over!"

Lately, there's been a changing of the guard here at the State School. Apparently, several of the top administrators here at the State School have finally decided to pack it in and retire, including Ms. Albright, who is retiring after thirty-five years of service.

In Ms. Albright's honor, we had a small gathering of friends and colleagues at a local pub in town. And it saddens me to say, but not many people attended Ms. Albright's retirement party.

Quite honestly, but you would have thought that after thirty-five years of service that Ms. Albright would've commanded a better turnout for her retirement party. But then I guess that's the price you pay for being such a tough and cantankerous old administrator for so many years.

Kramer wound up being a no show for the party, which really didn't surprise me one bit. But be that as it may, I thought it was still incumbent upon him to attend the gathering anyway.

Now granted, Kramer and Ms. Albright weren't exactly on the best of terms.

But for appearances sake, Mr. Kramer should've at least buried the hatchet for a couple of hours, and made some sort of effort to attend the function.

After all, Mr. Kramer was her immediate supervisor.

Well, on the heels of Ms. Albright's retirement, Wohlers and the rest of the Unit Chiefs are entertaining the notion of retirement too. These five Unit Chiefs are often referred to as the "five families," and Wohlers is considered to be the undisputed "Godfather" of the group.

Despite the fact that the Unit Chiefs do nothing but sit at their desks all day and twiddle their thumbs, they've all decided to pack it in and take advantage of the tremendous incentive package that the State is offering to all of their top level administrators. And from what I hear, these incentives are just too good to pass up.

In addition to the lucrative incentive package that the State was offering, the Unit Chiefs could see that the political landscape of the State School was dramatically changing as well, so why not get out while the getting was still good.

Yes, life as they knew it here at the State School was coming to an abrupt end. It was now a younger man's game, and these old dogs were not about to learn any new tricks.

This exclusive "gentleman's club" that Wohlers and the other Unit Chiefs have been such staunch members of for so many years was now a thing of the past. So I guess it was time for them to butt out their cigars and take one last chug of brandy, because the party was finally over.

Well, there seems to be a rumor floating around that our facility may be selected as a new pilot program for individuals that are dually diagnosed, which is a program that is designed to help people who are both mentally retarded and mentally ill.

Although these reports are unsubstantiated, the federal government has agreed to partner with the state, and appropriate a significant amount of money for this new pilot program to start.

Now if you recall, Wohlers mentioned a couple of months ago that something big was looming on the horizon here at the State School, so this might be what Wohlers was referring to.

Furthermore, the Governor has assembled a special subcommittee to determine if inmates in state prisons and patients in state psychiatric centers are appropriately placed, or should they be transferred to an alternate facility that is more commensurate to their needs.

As it stands right now, there's still some uncertainty as to whether this new pilot program will even get off of the ground, so all of these rumors may be nothing more than pure conjecture.

Well, since there were such a large number of employees taking advantage of the State's incentive package, the Director thought that it might be a good idea to hold one large gala at the banquet hall in town.

The night of the retirement party, the banquet hall was packed to the gills. And as I strolled from one reception room to the other, I can honestly say that I was genuinely happy for the vast majority of retirees.

And for a few of the others, well, all I can say is good riddance!

Apparently, Ms. Neff has decided to cash in her chips and call it a career too. As I look back on my time with Ms. Neff, I can honestly say that she was a pretty good egg. Despite her rather coarse exterior, she really did care about the clients, and she went above and beyond the call of duty to make sure that they were all well-cared for and treated fairly and properly.

As a matter of fact, she even plans on coming back to the State School in her spare time to do some volunteer work, which clearly tells me just how much she loved working here.

During the cocktail hour, I spotted Mr. Wohlers hobnobbing around the room. Wohlers had a glass of Scotch in one hand and a big fat cigar in the other. When Mr. Wohlers caught my eye, he flashed me his million dollar smile, and then sauntered over to where I was standing.

Mr. Wohlers shook my hand, and then proceeded to thank me for all of my fine efforts over the years. And he even encouraged me to take as many civil service exams as I possibly could, so that I could try to shinny my way up the career ladder.

As Wohlers and I chatted, I could tell he was starting to feel the effects of all that Scotch he was knocking back. He wasn't exactly three sheets to the wind, but he was definitely a little tipsy, especially in the way he kept slurring his words and wobbling back and forth on his feet.

Mr. Wohlers then took another slurp of his Scotch. And as he leaned right into me, he accidently spilt some of his drink on my shirt. He then laughed the mishap off by whimsically saying, "Sorry about that Jack, just send me the bill! Hahahaha…!"

Wohlers leaned into me again, and then discretely whispered, "Hey Jack, I heard that the new Unit Chief that's coming on board is a real son-of-a-bitch, so you better watch your back."

I was a bit taken aback by Mr. Wohlers' comment. He then said that the new Unit Chief's name was Alfred Hanson. And according to Mr. Wohlers, he barely passed the Unit Chief exam.

Mr. Wohlers took another hearty belt of his Scotch, and then sarcastically blurted out, "As a matter of fact, I heard that the only reason Hanson got the Unit

Chief job here at the State School was because he has a "rabbi" out at the State Capital."

Suddenly, I had vivid thoughts of Ms. Albright racing through my head, especially the day that she lost her temper, and then let it slip that the reason she was overlooked for promotion here at the State School was because Mr. Kramer had a "rabbi" out at the State Capital too.

I thought to myself, "It sounds like Mr. Hanson's "rabbi" has a lot more clout than Mr. Kramer's "rabbi," especially since Hanson just beat him out for one of the Unit Chief positions."

As I continued to listen to Mr. Wohlers ramble on and on about nothing, it then suddenly dawned on me for the first time that I too had a "rabbi" in the form of Jim Brindamore. Who as you may recall was the Associate Personnel Director at the State Capital, and the guy that Bob Watson put me in touch with three years ago when I landed my state job here at the State School.

Wow! I never pieced that together before.

So that being said, I guess it would be rather hypocritical of me to fault either Hanson or Kramer for having a "rabbi." When I too, an Irish Catholic God fearing altar boy, apparently worships at the same altar as they do.

In parting, Mr. Wohlers shook my hand and thanked me once again for all of my efforts over the years. And then just like that, - Mr. Wohlers magically disappear back into the crowd.

As the evening wore on, I found myself strolling down memory lane with each passing face that I saw. But for some reason, my mind kept reverting back to thoughts of Ms. Albright.

Actually, I was a little disappointed that I didn't get the chance to see her tonight. I really would've enjoyed catching up with her, and having her tell me how wonderful retirement was.

I was also curious to know if Ms. Albright was enjoying this new chapter in her life, or was she simply sitting at home by the telephone and waiting for it to ring.

When it was time to leave, I grabbed my jacket from the coat check counter, and then made my way towards the door. As I happen to glance to my left, I noticed that Ms. Albright was sitting in a corner chair all by herself, as if she had magically appeared out of nowhere.

It was sad seeing Ms. Albright sitting there all by herself. She didn't seem to notice me as I approached her, because her mind looked to be a million miles away.

When I gently tapped her on the shoulder she flinched, and almost jumped completely out of her chair.

"Hello, Ms. Albright. I'm sorry, if I startled you."

"Oh, my word, I guess you did. It's good to see you, Jack."

"It's nice to see you too, Ms. Albright. I was hoping that you'd be here tonight."

"Well, I've known most of the people in this room for over thirty-five years, and I wanted to wish them well in their new endeavors."

"Certainly, so are you enjoying retirement?"

"Yes, very much so, and I'm considering writing my memoirs as well."

"Ah, well, I'm sure that will make for some interesting reading."

"Thank you, but enough about an old war horse like me. Is your wife here tonight?"

"Um, no, she wasn't feeling up to it tonight. My wife and I are expecting our first child, and she's been experiencing some nausea and fatigue lately."

"I see, well, that's a pity, because I would've liked to have told her what a wonderful man that she's married to. Oh, and congratulations on the upcoming birth of your first child, I'm sure you'll make a wonderful father." Ms. Albright said, with much sincerity.

"Thank you, Ms. Albright. Well, I better get home and see how my wife is doing. It was very nice seeing you." I then gave Ms. Albright a warm embrace.

Ms. Albright seemed to appreciate my heartfelt sentiments, and then said with a rare burst of enthusiasm, "It was so wonderful to see you again, Jack. Just remember, stay the course!"

At that moment, I had thoughts of Dr. Stevens swimming through my head, because he too would always encourage me to "stay the course."

As I was driving home, I was thinking what a coincidence it was that two of the most influential people in my professional life would both express the same words of wisdom to me.

But then realizing that there are no coincidences in life, and that things happen for a reason.

CHAPTER FIVE

MEMORANDUM

To: All Building 12 and Building 13 Clinical Staff

From: Ms. Barbara Fields, Team Leader, Building 13

Re: Introduction to the New Unit Chief, and Building 12 Team Leader

"There will be a mandatory meeting for all Building 12 and Building 13 clinical staff on Friday afternoon at 2pm in the upstairs conference room of Building 12. The purpose of the meeting is to welcome aboard our new Team Leader for Building 12, Mr. Dick Henderson, and our new Unit Chief for Buildings 12 and 13, Mr. Alfred Hanson. I look forward to seeing all of you there on Friday.

Thank you very much, and have a wonderful day."

As I crumbled up the memo, I had a passing thought of Mr. Wohlers the night of his retirement party, when he said, "Hey Jack, watch your back with regards to the new Unit Chief."

Needless to say, but the Unit has been buzzing all week long in anticipation of meeting the new Unit Chief and the new Team Leader for Building 12. And even though the rumor mill is usually pretty reliable in digging up some real juicy gossip, no one seems to know too much about the new Team Leader or the new Unit Chief.

So on Friday afternoon, you can only imagine how intense the atmosphere was when the clinical staff all met in the Building 12 conference room to welcome aboard the new top brass.

As I sat there waiting for the meeting to begin, I was wondering if Mr. Wohlers had let the cat out of the bag to anyone else in the Unit regarding the new Unit Chief Alfred Hanson, or was Mr. Wohlers so inebriated that night that he simply had an inadvertent slip of the tongue.

Just then two well-dressed men entered the room and walked directly over to where Ms. Fields was standing, and then engaged her in some casual chitchat.

Although the crowd continued to talk amongst themselves, everyone in the room seemed to be keeping a pretty steady eye on the front of the room. And what's more, they were all tilting their heads forward a bit, so that they could try to hear what was being discussed by the bosses.

Ms. Fields saw that everyone was assembled for the meeting, so she addressed the group by saying, "Good afternoon, everybody. May I please have your attention. It's my pleasure to welcome aboard Mr. Alfred Hanson, who is our new Unit Chief for Buildings 12 and 13, and Mr. Dick Henderson, who will be replacing Ms. Neff as the new Team Leader for Building 12. Can we please give each of them a nice round of applause?"

So after all of the applause subsided, Ms. Fields then turned towards the two gentlemen and said, "Mr. Hanson, would you like to say a few words to the group?"

At that moment, the younger of the two men stepped forward, which took everyone in the room by complete surprise, especially since we all thought that the older man was Mr. Hanson.

Mr. Hanson was probably in his late twenties, and he didn't look that much older than me. He then addressed the group by saying, "Well, thank you for that warm introduction. I'm looking forward to working with each of you very closely. I must say that Mr. Wohlers has spoken very highly of you all, especially Jack O'Leary. Jack would you mind standing up?"

"Holy shit…," I mumbled to myself.

The last thing that I wanted right now was to be singled out by the new boss. And even though I take great pride in doing my job to the best of my abilities, I try to make it a point to fly completely under the radar as much as possible, so as not to draw any undue attention to myself.

I then stood up and awkwardly said, "Um, hi Mr. Hanson, it's very nice to meet you."

Mr. Hanson walked straight over to me, and then firmly shook my hand and said, "Jack, the pleasure is all mine! And I'm really looking forward to working with you here in the Unit!"

As I took my seat, I was looking for some deep dark hole to crawl into. I then heard my good friend Morrie comically whisper, "brown nose," which prompted me to quietly chuckle.

Hanson kept his comments brief, and although he seemed quite friendly on the surface, I kept hearing Mr. Wohlers' emphatic warning of "watch your back" resonating through my head.

Ms. Fields then turned towards Mr. Henderson, and asked him if he would like to say a few words to the group.

Mr. Henderson seemed a bit bashful, and kept his comments short and sweet by saying, "Well, it's nice to be here, and uh…, I look forward to the challenges that lay ahead, thank you."

Mr. Hanson then concluded the meeting by saying, "In the coming weeks, the two Team Leaders and I would like to meet with each of you individually. And not only get to know you on a more personal basis, but have a fluid exchange of ideas as well. Okay, well, that's it for now, and I look forward to chatting with each of you real soon. Enjoy your weekend, everybody!"

As I was heading towards my car, I turned to my friend Morrie and asked him what his impressions were of the meeting. Morrie isn't one to pull any punches, so he candidly said, "Well, Henderson seems okay, but I'm not too sure about Hanson."

I curiously replied, "Really? Well, Hanson seems okay to me."

Morrie slightly chuckled, and as he was getting into his car, he sarcastically blurted out, "Whatever you say Jack, but just make sure that you watch your back, okay."

"Whoa!" I thought to myself. Of all the expressions that Morrie could have said, he used the same exact phrase as Mr. Wohlers.

Could fate be giving me a gentle nudge, and trying to tell me something?

A couple of days later, I met with Mr. Hanson and the two Team Leaders to discuss my role in the Unit. Upon entering the room, Mr. Hanson jumped right out of his chair, shook my hand, and then offered me a nice hot cup of coffee, as if we were long lost pals.

As Mr. Hanson reached for the coffeepot, I simply couldn't get over how young he was. Mr. Hanson really wasn't that much older than me, yet he's managed to leapfrog his way right up the career ladder in a relatively short amount of time.

Meanwhile, the rest of us poor dumb schmucks are all struggling to shinny our way past the first rung.

As the meeting got underway, I found Mr. Hanson to be quite articulate and professional, and he had a definite command of the room. He had the looks of a Hollywood movie star, and the charm of a snake oil salesman. Yet despite his stunning good looks and silvery tongue, he seemed to exude a noticeable arrogance about him, which smelled as rancid as three day old fish.

Hanson struck me as a real go-getter, and someone who was clearly on the rise. Although most people would give their eye teeth to have Hanson's job as Unit Chief, he merely viewed his current position as a stepping-stone to something bigger and better. And I wouldn't be surprised to see Hanson as the Director of a facility someday, and maybe even the State Commissioner.

Well, if he plays his cards right anyway.

So after dispensing with a few formalities, Hanson got right down to business by asking me to bring him up to speed on what types of vocational services we were providing in the Unit.

I was anticipating this line of questioning, so I took the liberty of preparing a handout so that Mr. Hanson and Mr. Henderson could follow along as I presented the information to them.

So after bringing Hanson and Henderson up to speed on what types of services that we offered in the Unit, Hanson flippantly remarked, "Okay, but how can we make things better."

Quite honestly, I wasn't expecting such a lukewarm reaction like that from Mr. Hanson, especially since the clients here at the State School aren't exactly the easiest clients to work with.

And what's more, but I think the handouts alone should've at least warranted me a "that-a-boy, Jack."

Anyway, as I pondered what to say next, Ms. Fields rushed to my defense and staunchly said, "Well Mr. Hanson, Jack has done an outstanding job of not only organizing our vocational programs, but our habilitation programs as well."

Ms. Fields then glanced in my direction and smiled appreciatively.

Hanson just nodded his head, as he continued to study the handouts that I gave him.

Meanwhile, Mr. Henderson remained as quiet as a church mouse, as he aimlessly gazed out the window, and seemed to be a million miles away from any of us.

As I sat there waiting for Mr. Hanson to say something, I had a quick thought of Mr. Kramer, and then wondered if Hanson and Kramer have had the opportunity to cross paths yet.

Although Kramer is not as powerful as he once was, he still manages to grab some front page headlines. Kramer really thought that he'd be a shoe-in for one of the Unit Chief positions when the good ole' boys decided to pack it in and retire, especially with five vacancies to be had.

Kramer not only has a "rabbi" at the State Capital, but he also had one of the top scores on the Unit Chief exam too, so he thought his chances for getting one of the jobs was real good.

Oh yeah, and did I happen to mention that Kramer is halfway up the Director's ass too!

But at the end of the day, Kramer was once again passed over for promotion.

So when Kramer heard that he wasn't being promoted to Unit Chief, he was absolutely livid, and spouted off by saying, "I have twice as much experience than Hanson! And the only reason Hanson got the Unit Chief position was because he has a "rabbi" out at the State Capital!"

Kramer's backhanded swipe at Mr. Hanson was similar to the pot calling the kettle black, especially since the only reason Kramer got his promotion as Director of Rehabilitation Services here at the State School was because he has a "rabbi" out at the State Capital too.

After all, what's good for the goose, is also good for the gander.

It seems like everybody in State service has a "rabbi," even an Irish Catholic altar boy like me!

In fact, that reminds me, I'll have to remember to send my "rabbi" a Christmas card for the holidays. Oh, wait a minute, I better make that a Hanukkah card instead.

So after Hanson finished perusing the handouts, he looked me straight in the eye and then cunningly asked, "Okay Jack, so how can we make the vocational programs in our Unit better?"

I simply replied, "Well, frankly Mr. Hanson, I think we need to establish better ties with the Central Rehab Department. And in my opinion, we need to aggressively lobby for more work slots from Mr. Kramer, who is the Director of Rehabilitation Services."

Ms. Fields then interjected, "That's the gentleman I was telling you about earlier, Mr. Hanson."

Mr. Henderson then suddenly perked up and said, "Hey Jack, I bumped into a client on the behavioral unit yesterday named Bobby. So what can you do for him?"

I quietly chuckled, and then replied, "Well, the client that you're referring to is named Bobby Diggs. Bobby thrives on telling people his tale of woe, especially people in authority. So, uh…, did Bobby happen to mention to you that he's had five different jobs over the past year and a half, and that he's been fired from every job that he's ever had?"

Mr. Henderson replied, "No, he never mentioned that. He just said that he would like the chance to earn some money, instead of sitting on the lock up ward all day twiddling his thumbs."

As I listened to Dick Henderson describe his brief encounter with Bobby, I didn't want to come across as sounding too negative, so I just simply said, "Well, Bobby is a very complicated individual, and he'll probably be your most problematic client in Building 12."

Ms. Fields then chimed in and said, "I would have to agree with Jack. Bobby spent several years under my watch, and it might sound harsh to say, but he was in and out of trouble so many times that the living unit staff would often refer to Bobby as a frequent flyer."

Mr. Hanson then interrupted our impromptu sidebar, as he snidely said, "Excuse me, but can we please get back to the subject at hand? I'm sure we'll have ample opportunities to discuss Mr. Diggs in the future. But for right now, I'm just trying to focus on the big picture, okay?"

So after being scolded by Mr. Hanson, the room became noticeably awkward.

Mr. Hanson then asked me to elaborate more on the Central Rehab component, to which I replied, "Well, in my opinion Mr. Hanson, I think relations with the Central Rehab Department are somewhat strained at the moment, and have been for a while now. Perhaps you may have some better luck, or maybe even wield more influence with Mr. Kramer than Mr. Wohlers did."

Hanson nodded his head, and then jotted down Kramer's name on the notepad that was in front of him. Mr. Hanson then thanked me for coming in today, and said that he'd be in touch.

Well, it was probably two weeks later when I bumped into Mr. Kramer on the Building 12 staircase. Kramer informed me that he just wrapped up a two hour meeting with Mr. Hanson.

Apparently, the purpose of the meeting was to discuss the possibility of Mr. Kramer allocating more work slots from the Central Rehab Department to Mr. Hanson's Unit.

As Mr. Kramer proceeded to fill me in on all of the particulars of his meeting with Mr. Hanson, he seemed rather pleased in telling me that he was unable to provide Mr. Hanson with anymore additional work slots. And by the smug look on Kramer's face, I'm guessing that the decision to deny Mr. Hanson anymore additional work slots was based more on settling some old scores than it was on anything else.

I'm sure that Kramer is still fuming over the fact that he didn't get one of the Unit Chief positions, especially Wohlers' position, which was considered to be the crown jewel of all of the Unit Chief jobs.

Quite honestly, but I think Kramer's unwillingness to give Hanson anymore additional work slots was nothing more than a pissing contest, and Kramer's way of showing Hanson that he was a formidable adversary.

About a week later, Mr. Hanson approached me after a case review and asked me to compile a list of names that I thought would be suitable candidates for work programs in the Central Rehab Department. Hanson informed me that he was just granted five additional work slots from Mr. Kramer, and needed the list by the end of the week.

Upon hearing Mr. Hanson's request, I was rather perplexed. I then spoke up and said, "Excuse me, Mr. Hanson. But when I bumped into Mr. Kramer last week, he told me that there were no available work slots to be had for our Unit. Have there been some new developments?"

Hanson quietly chuckled, and then said with a coy smile, "Well, let's just say that Mr. Kramer forced my hand. After speaking with the Director about it, he instructed Mr. Kramer to allocate an additional five work slots for our Unit, which was actually two more slots than I had originally bargained for."

So after hearing Mr. Hanson's reply, I then realized that he was a force to be reckoned with. And from that moment on, I would privately refer to Mr. Hanson as the "road grader."

Since Mr. Wohlers' retirement, I would have to say that the overall tenor in the Unit has drastically changed. People seem to be busier, and there's a lot less sitting around going on.

Mr. Wohlers was the type of boss who enjoyed being camped out in his office all day, and the only thing that would pry him loose from the friendly confines of his surroundings were either meetings or some type of administrative obligation. The staff knew Mr. Wohlers' schedule like the back of their hand, and they certainly took full advantage of it.

Hanson on the other hand was this young and energetic go-getter, who was constantly roaming the Unit, and the staff never knew from one minute to the next when he'd pop up.

In fact, Hanson will even roll up his sleeves and help out the staff with some of their day-to-day chores. Which for a boss was highly unusual, and something that Mr. Wohlers never did.

Up until now, the living unit staff had never seen an administrator of Hanson's ilk before. Yet despite Hanson's repeated attempts at trying to win the staff over, they were still quite leery of him, and didn't trust him as far as they could throw him. They felt that Hanson's motives were nothing more than a cunning ploy, or a shifty way of lulling them into a false sense of security.

Thus far, I've been able to stay on Mr. Hanson's good side. However, the new Building 12 Team Leader, Dick Henderson, has become Mr. Hanson's personal whipping boy. And there isn't a day that goes by that Dick Henderson isn't summoned into Mr. Hanson's office and verbally browbeaten by Hanson, and whatever pet peeve that may be irritating Hanson that day.

It's quite apparent to me that Hanson has some sort of anger management problem. And if you happen to walk by Hanson's office on any given day, then you'll certainly get an earful.

In all honesty, I think that Hanson suffers from some type of bipolar disorder. In public, he seems to be calm, cool, and collected. But behind closed doors, he can be a raving lunatic.

When it comes to handling the staff, Hanson could certainly learn a thing or two from Dick Henderson. Dick treats everyone in the building with dignity and respect. And even on those rare occasions when Dick is forced to drop the hammer on his subordinates, he does it in a way so that he gets his point across, yet you don't feel like you were just raked over the coals.

I'm not really sure why Hanson has it in for Dick Henderson. But if I had to guess, it's probably due to some sort of petty jealousy that Hanson has for Dick. Hanson realizes that the living unit staff totally despises him, yet when it comes to Dick Henderson the staff is behind him one hundred percent.

Although Hanson continues to roam the living units with regularity, we've noticed lately that he's not as quick to roll up his sleeves and help out the living unit staff as he once did.

But when the Director is touring the living units with Hanson, then Hanson can't roll up his sleeves fast enough, so that he can pitch right in and help out the staff wherever needed.

Obviously, Hanson is only putting on this staged performance to impress the Director, and his motives at winning the staff over are as phony as a three dollar bill. But I guess it's all part of the game if you wanna make it to the top of the career ladder like Hanson is trying to do.

Lately, every time I bump into Dick Henderson, he seems to go out of his way to butter me up by saying, "Hey, nice haircut Jack," or "Hey Jack, have you lost some weight lately?"

Of course, what Dick is really trying to say is, "Hey Jack, can you find Bobby Diggs a job, so that he won't harass the hell out of me every time he sees me on the lock up ward?"

Bobby Diggs hasn't worked in over nine months now. And as a result, Bobby continues to be stuck on the lock up ward all day, harassing the staff and getting into all sorts of trouble.

Now ordinarily, Bobby will only consider top notch jobs. But at this point, Bobby is so desperate to earn some money that he's actually begging to work in the Work Activity Center.

I'm really not surprised that Dick Henderson has taken such a shine to Bobby. Dick is a very kind and gentle soul. But due to the fact that Bobby has such a cockeyed view of the world, he seems to equate kindness for weakness. So in Bobby's mind, why not try to capitalize on the situation, and take full advantage of Dick Henderson's extreme good-naturedness.

So that being said, it's only a matter of time until Bobby has Dick firmly wrapped around his little finger, and very similar to the way that Bobby reeled me in when I first met him too.

The other day, one of the living unit staff on the lock up ward told me that Bobby Diggs was spouting off at the mouth by saying, "When I get off this fuckin' unit, Jack O'Leary is gonna find me a good paying job, because Dick Henderson is a very good friend of mine!"

Gee, does that mean that Dick Henderson might wind up being Bobby Diggs' "rabbi?"

Well, Bobby hasn't worked in almost a year now. And as long as Bobby continues to live on the lock up ward, then he's plum out of luck in making any money.

Bobby can't seem to get it through his head that in order for him to be eligible to get a job and make some money, then he needs to satisfy all of the terms of his behavioral contract, so that he can earn his way back onto the open unit again.

Once again, Bobby's borderline personality disorder continues to rear its ugly head, and hold Bobby hostage on the lock up ward.

Sometimes I wonder if we're expecting a little too much out of Bobby by asking him to be good. And even though what we're asking Bobby to accomplish is a relatively simple thing to do, I really think that the bar we're setting for Bobby is still way too high for him to jump over.

At Bobby's last case review, Dick Henderson stated that Bobby's behavioral contract was written in such a way that his chances for getting off of the locked ward was virtually impossible.

Snead didn't like the fact that Dick was questioning the terms of his behavioral contract. So in an effort to neutralize Dick's criticism, Snead raised a very interesting point, and said that Bobby may finally be showing signs of organic brain damage, due to the amount of psychotropic medication that has washed over his gray matter for the past forty years. And this might explain why Bobby continues to spin his wheels, and why he just can't move forward in life.

Well, I guess no one in the room could argue with that that theory anyway.

Although Snead can certainly rub me the wrong way at times, I found his assessment of Bobby to be quite illuminating. And for the first time since knowing Snead, I actually think he may be onto something with regards to Bobby Diggs.

In summarizing his analysis of Bobby, Snead paraphrased the thought provoking essay of Albert Camus's, Myth of Sisyphus. By inferring that Bobby, like Sisyphus, is condemned to a lifetime of torment. And that every day of his life, Bobby sets out to roll the massive boulder up the hill, only to have the boulder roll back down the hill by day's end, so that Bobby can start the grueling and monumental task of rolling the massive boulder back up the hill again the next day.

Snead's powerful metaphor seemed to epitomized Bobby's life to a tee, and everyone in the room could see some definite parallels between Sisyphus' plight and Bobby Diggs' misery.

As we all continued to reflect on Snead's thought provoking words, Hanson then broke the silence by saying that he is seriously toying with the idea of transferring Bobby to a special forensic unit, which is designed to treat individuals that possess severe problematic behaviors.

Upon hearing Hanson's stunning announcement, I was expecting either Dick Henderson or Snead to comment on Hanson's bold recommendation on Bobby, but neither one said a word.

Mr. Hanson then went on to say that a transfer of this magnitude would be contingent upon the Director's approval, and that he will keep us posted if anything further should develop.

So it would seem that after all these years, Bobby Diggs may finally be getting his wish to leave the State School.

But it may not necessarily be the dream destination that he was hoping for.

I've learned that when Mr. Hanson gets something in his head, then he usually follows through with it. So it might be safe to say that the chances of Bobby spending his next birthday, or maybe even the Christmas holidays here at the State School may be dwindling by the minute.

The rumors seem to be intensifying that our facility is still in the running as the prime test site for the new pilot program. And from everything that we've heard thus far, it sounds like the State will be making an official announcement within the next two to three months.

Not only has the Governor ordered all statewide prisons and psychiatric centers to review their current census, but the Governor has also asked all of the developmental centers across the state to review their current client census as well.

So that being said, the Director has instructed all of the Unit Chiefs to take a real hard look at which clients in their respective Units might be possible candidates for the new pilot program. And the two names being kicked around so far are Bobby Diggs and Tommy Gerard.

When Dick Henderson heard that Bobby's name was being mentioned as a possibility for the new pilot program, he decided to meet with the Director and put a good word in for Bobby.

Dick was hoping that he could convince the Director that the new pilot program would be a much better fit for Bobby Diggs than the state forensic unit, especially since the State School is the only real home that Bobby has ever known.

Well, apparently Dick must have presented a pretty compelling argument. Because the next day the Director met with Hanson, and told him that after speaking with Dick Henderson about Bobby that he has decided to hold off on transferring Bobby to the state forensic unit.

When Hanson found out that Dick went crawling to the Director behind his back, he was absolutely furious. Hanson demanded that the Director fire Dick immediately on the grounds of subordination, and for being derelict in his duties in not following the proper chain of command.

Although the Director understood Hanson's frustration, he felt that Dick Henderson was only acting on Bobby's behalf, and that disciplinary measures were not warranted at this time.

Of course, it should also be noted that Dick Henderson and the Director are actually first cousins, and proving once again that nepotism and state employment often go hand-in-hand.

Well, last night I received a phone call from a very close friend of mine from back home whose name is Murphy Doherty. And Murphy and I have been best friends since grade school.

Now to the casual observer, Murphy and I may seem to be the most unlikely pair of kids to strike up a friendship. Especially since Murphy was a three sport all-star in high school, and I was simply an uncoordinated kid with a severe weight problem and extremely poor eyesight.

Although I can't say for sure, but sometimes I think Murphy took me under his wing because he felt sorry for me. Especially since I couldn't play on any of the sports teams in high school, and I was constantly being ridiculed and bullied by the other kids in my neighborhood.

Nevertheless, being best friends with the most popular kid in school made life a lot easier for me, and certainly opened up a few social doors that might've otherwise remained closed.

Every morning at the bus stop, I would give Murphy the rundown on all the scores and highlights from the night before. And he'd always shake his head in amazement that I was able to remember every sparkling play and dazzling detail from every single game that was played.

Back in high school, whenever Murphy made a sensational play, whether it be out on the basketball court or on the athletic field, I would enthusiastically cheer him on from the bleachers. And he would often point in my direction, and then flash me his patented million dollar smile.

It might sound strange to say, but I always felt like Murphy was out there playing for the both of us. And when the game was over, he would immediately seek me out, instead of heading straight over to the popular "in crowd," and hanging out with them for the rest of the night.

So when speaking with Murphy last night, he told me that he was quite disillusioned in his current job, and wished that he could put his hard earned college degree to better use.

I then mentioned to Murphy that our facility is always looking to hire people, and that he might be qualified for some of the positions that we were hoping to fill here at the State School.

At that point, I suggested that he send me a copy of his resume, and that I would forward it on to a friend of mine who works in the Personnel Office. Murphy seemed quite receptive to my suggestion, and indicated that he would mail out his resume to me first thing in the morning.

Well, Bobby Diggs is once again in the news.

Apparently, the afternoon shift on the lock up ward told Bobby to pack up his duffle bag, because he was being transferred over to the open unit effective tomorrow morning at 9:00am.

So I guess that means that the staff party on the lock up ward will begin precisely at 9:01am, because none of the staff on the lock up ward will be missing Bobby Diggs one bit.

When I first heard that Bobby Diggs was being transferred to the open unit, I thought that the staff was simply pulling my leg. The last I heard, Bobby was wreaking all sorts of havoc on the lock up ward, and he was nothing but a constant thorn in the side of the living unit staff.

So in light of this new development, I thought I would talk to Snead and ask him why Bobby Diggs was being transferred over to the open unit.

When I finally tracked down Snead, he was sitting down to a toasted bagel smothered in cream cheese, while leisurely reading the newspaper in the staff lounge. We exchanged a few pleasantries, and then I asked him why Bobby Diggs was being transferred over to the open unit.

As Snead nonchalantly perused the morning newspaper, he said that it wasn't his call, it was an executive decision made by Dick Henderson. Which was surprising to hear, because it's hard to believe that Hanson would've signed off on an administrative move like that for Bobby.

It's certainly no secret that Snead and Dick have been bumping heads over Bobby since Dick came on board as Team Leader. And I could tell by the tone in Snead's voice that he didn't agree with the decision to have Bobby transferred to the open unit, especially since Bobby hadn't even come close to meeting any of the terms of his behavioral contract to warrant consideration.

Once again, I found myself siding with Snead. Because it was pretty obvious to me that Bobby was playing the role of the puppet master, and knowing which strings to pull on Dick.

Anyway, I thanked Snead for explaining the situation to me, and then I headed over to the open unit so that I could talk to Bobby.

Before speaking with Bobby, I thought I would swing by Dick Henderson's office first, and ask him why he approved the transfer for Bobby. Especially when Bobby hadn't even come close to meeting any of the terms or stipulations of his behavioral contract yet.

When I knocked on Dick Henderson's office door he wasn't there, so I decided to head over to the open unit and speak with Bobby Diggs for a few minutes in private.

As I walked onto the open unit, I saw Dick Henderson sitting on one of the couches in the dayroom, and he was chatting with Bobby Diggs.

I walked over to where Bobby and Dick were both sitting, and then casually greeted them by saying, "Good morning, men. How's it going?"

Bobby Diggs piped right up and excitedly said, "Hey Jack, isn't it great, I finally made it off of the lock up ward! So when can I start my new job, oh boy, oh boy, oh boy!"

In typical Bobby style, he began to feverishly scratch the back of his head with both of his hands, which prompted Dick Henderson to smile and then quietly chuckle.

So after Bobby settled down, I turned to Dick Henderson and casually asked, "Hey Dick, when you finish talking to Bobby, I'd like to speak with you for a few minutes, okay?"

Dick nodded his head, and then softly replied, "Yeah, sure, I think Bobby and I are all through here anyway."

As Dick was getting up from the couch, he reminded Bobby to stay out of trouble and to keep his nose clean.

Bobby excitedly answered, "Don't worry Dick, I will, oh boy, oh boy, oh boy!"

Just as I was about to speak, Dick beat me to the punch and said, "Jack, I already know what you're gonna say, but I think the time has come to give Bobby a chance to prove himself."

"Hey Dick, I've known Bobby for a long time, and I think he's playing you like a fiddle."

"Maybe so, but sometimes you just have to rely on your own instincts." Dick quietly said.

I quickly countered, "Dick, nobody has tried harder with Bobby Diggs than me. I'm not saying that Bobby is a lost cause, but he's as close to the apocalypse as you're ever gonna get."

Dick laughed heartily, but then took a moment to be serious by saying, "Well, perhaps, but look at it from my perspective Jack, the whole time that I've been here Bobby has resided on the locked unit, so maybe it's time for us to cut him a little slack and see what materializes."

"Well Dick, it's only a matter of time until Bobby turns the open unit upside down."

Dick smiled, and then calmly said, "Jack, you know how much I value your opinion. But I feel very strongly about this, and I would really appreciate your support on the matter."

I paused a moment, and then asked, "So how much leeway do you intend to give Bobby? Are there going to be any consequences to his actions, or does he simply have carte blanche?"

Dick lightly chuckled, but then staunchly replied, "Well, I made it quite clear to Bobby that he needs to keep his nose clean, or else he'll be back on the lock up ward, tout de suite."

"Unh-uh, and I've got your word on that, right Dick?"

"Yep, you've got my solemn word, Jack." Dick said, smiling.

"Okay Dick, we'll play it your way. I'll make all of the necessary arrangements for Bobby to start back in the Work Activity Center tomorrow. Hey, still friends, right?"

Dick softly replied, "Never better! And if I were in your shoes, I probably would've reacted the same way. I'll see ya later, I've got a meeting with the Commandant."

As Dick left for his meeting with Mr. Hanson, I strolled over to where Bobby was sitting, so that I could have a little heart-to-heart talk with him.

When Bobby saw me approaching him, he casually asked, "Hey Jack, what were you and Dick Henderson talking about over there?"

"Well, we were talking about you Bobby. But I think you already knew that, right?"

Bobby could barely control himself, as he screeched, "Really..., oh boy, oh boy, oh boy!"

He then impetuously asked, "So when can I start my new job? Hey, I wouldn't mind working back on the trucks again."

I quietly chuckled, and then sarcastically said, "Uh, you gotta be kidding me, right? Listen Bobby, the only job offer that's on the table right now is the Work Activity Center."

"What! Why...? C'mon Jack, you know that I'm the smartest kid at the State School. I haven't worked in a really long time, and I need to make some money!" Bobby pleaded.

"Sorry Bobby, but you're gonna have to start at the bottom and then work your way back up the ladder again, before I'll even consider giving you a better paying job, ya got it?"

"But how long is that gonna take? Ah, forget it! I'm just gonna go talk to Dick Henderson about it, he'll fix everything for me, you'll see!" Bobby viciously snarled.

"Listen Bobby, Dick may have pulled a few strings in getting you off of the lock up ward, but I'm the guy who's in charge of the work program. So it's either the Work Activity Center, or else you can sit on the living unit all day and twiddle your thumbs, it's your choice."

"But, uh..., what if I'm good for say one week? Can I get a better paying job then?" Bobby asked, with his usual conniving charm.

"One week! C'mon Bobby, get real!"

Bobby then blurted out, "Alright, but if that Tommy Gerard starts bugging me...,"

I interrupted Bobby in midsentence, and then sternly said, "Listen Bobby, you better learn to get along with Tommy Gerard and everyone else down in the Work Activity Center if you wanna make any money. And if I hear that you're up to your old tricks again, then you'll be back on the lock up ward faster than you can say Rumpelstiltskin. Do I make myself clear?"

"Yes Jack...," Bobby muttered, as he bowed his head in disappointment.

So after speaking with Bobby, I headed straight over to the Work Activity Center so that I could update the staff on Bobby. When the staff heard that Bobby Diggs was being reinstated back into the work program again, they weren't very happy. I tried to explain to them that it was an administrative decision, and that the matter was completely out of my hands.

The following day, I discovered a large manila envelope sitting in my mailbox. When I looked at the return address, I was pleased to see that the envelope was from my old pal Murphy Doherty. Murphy finally got around to sending me a copy of his resume, so that he could apply for one of the recreation therapist positions that the facility was hoping to fill.

Since I had a few minutes to kill before heading over to Tommy Gerard's case review, I thought I would swing by the Human Resources Office, so that I could hand deliver Murphy's resume to Rita Spinelli. And while I'm over there, maybe put in a good word for Murphy too.

When I went by Rita Spinelli's office, the receptionist said that Rita was all tied-up in a meeting. However, she would be happy to place the envelope on Rita's desk, and attach a note asking Rita to get back to me as soon as possible.

By the time I made it over to Tommy Gerard's case review, it was already standing room only, and we actually had to borrow a couple of chairs from an adjacent office so that we could accommodate everyone for Tommy's meeting.

As I've mentioned before, none of the staff here at the State School are all that enthused about attending case reviews, and will go to whatever lengths possible to avoid them at all costs.

But when it comes to Tommy Gerard's case review, it's still the hottest ticket in town.

Well, it didn't take long for everyone in the meeting to go around the table and present their reports on Tommy. So I guess that means that the live show will be starting momentarily.

Once again, no one seems to take Tommy Gerard's meeting too seriously, because we're all here today for one reason and one reason only, - to be thoroughly entertained by Tommy.

It's kinda like skipping dinner and going straight to dessert!

As I sat there marveling at Tommy's incredible savant talents, I had a sudden thought of Murphy. And if Murphy is lucky enough to land a job here, then I know he'll get a big kick out of Tommy, along with the rest of the cast of characters that are here at the State School as well.

So as Tommy continued to entertain the crowd with his one-in-a-million mind-bending routine, the case review had essentially been reduced to nothing more than a sideshow.

Even Hanson found Tommy's shtick to be just as captivating as we did.

It's funny, but just when you think you have Hanson pegged as being a stickler for the rules, here he is laughing and whooping it up with the rest of us, as he permits the staff to exploit Tommy's inexplicable savant talents, and all for nothing more than just a few cheap laughs.

Tommy then asked Mr. Hanson when his birthday was.

Hanson quietly replied, "February 5th."

"What year…?" Tommy impatiently asked.

"1994," Hanson replied, with a slight chuckle in his voice.

Tommy quickly answered, "You were born on a Wednesday that year!"

"Wow! You're right, Tommy. I was born on a Wednesday that year. Hey Tommy, do you happen to know what the weather forecast was that day?" Hanson sarcastically quipped.

Tommy thought a minute, and then replied, "Well, uh…, it was probably thundering and lightning that day, because the staff around here says that you're really mean."

All of a sudden, the entire room burst out into hysterical laughter. And even Mr. Hanson got a big chuckle out of what Tommy just said.

Although I'm not wild about Hanson, he did show me today that he has the capacity to laugh at himself. And that maybe buried deep beneath that cold harsh exterior of his lies a sense of humor, and a willingness to lower his guard a bit, so that he can try to be one of the boys.

So after Tommy's meeting was over, I headed over to the commissary to get a quick bite to eat. And as luck would have it, I saw Rita Spinelli sitting at a corner table eating lunch.

As I approached Rita, she asked me to sit down and join her. I no sooner sat down, when I inquisitively asked, "So Rita, have you had a chance to review Murphy Doherty's resume yet?"

Rita pleasantly replied, "Yes, and from what I can see, your friend Murphy certainly looks good on paper. So what else can you tell me about him?"

Well, at that point, I couldn't get the words out fast enough in describing my good friend Murphy Doherty.

Although Rita was certainly impressed with what she heard, she was more interested in knowing why Murphy wanted to change jobs, and take a position with the State for less money.

I then explained to Rita that Murphy wasn't happy in his current position, and that he was really hoping to better utilize his college degree, which is in the field of special education. So when I mentioned to Murphy that our facility was looking to fill some job vacancies, he thought that working at a state developmental center might be just the ticket that he was looking for.

Rita then said, with a coy smile, "Boy, you just pitched a pretty convincing argument for your friend Murphy. Maybe you should be working with me, instead of in Mr. Hanson's Unit."

I quietly chuckled at Rita's quipping remark, and then amusingly replied, "Well, thanks, Rita. But let's forget that I'm an Irishman, and God blessed the Irish with the gift of gab."

Rita then wrapped up our conversation by saying that she would contact Murphy this week, and see if he was interested in setting up an interview. She also mentioned that our facility was just approved as the test site for the new pilot program for dually diagnosed individuals, and that Murphy is more than qualified for several of the positions that the facility is hoping to fill.

So Bobby Diggs has been back in the Work Activity Center for a few weeks now. And according to Bobby, he's been doing so well in the work program that he deserves a promotion.

Now if you should happen to ask the Work Activity Center staff how Bobby Diggs is doing, then they might have a slightly different opinion than Bobby.

Unfortunately, Bobby is a legend in his own mind, and he refuses to believe that he should be lumped in with all of the other hooligans that work down in the Work Activity Center.

In Bobby's defense, due to the fact that he has been a lifelong working boy, he may have adopted a false sense of entitlement. Because Bobby truly believes that he is an extension of the staff, especially since Bobby has performed every staff duty on the living unit that there is to do.

So from Bobby's perspective, he seems to think that he has the authority to boss the other clients around whenever he wants, and to do it without any fear of punishment or reprimand.

Well, it's been roughly a week now, and I still haven't heard a word from Murphy as to whether Rita Spinelli has contacted him regarding a job interview here at the State School.

To tell you the truth, I'm beginning to get a little nervous. Especially since the clock is ticking on the new pilot program that's opening up, and I don't want Murphy to run out of time.

Of course, news about the new pilot program has been sweeping through the State School like a canyon fire, and it seems to be the only thing that people are talking about around here.

Construction crews are working around the clock, so that the building renovations for the new pilot program can be completed on schedule. The Director is hoping that the renovations can be finalized as soon as possible, especially since there is so much federal money at stake.

On Friday, I ran into Dick Henderson on the Building 12 staircase, and he looked like a beaten man. Dick wouldn't say what was troubling him, but I had a sneaking suspicion that it had something to do with Mr. Hanson.

The word around the water cooler is that Hanson has been riding Dick harder than usual, and that Dick was beginning to crack under the pressure. Despite the fact that Dick is a pretty laid back guy, there's just so much that a person can take.

As Dick and I parted ways, I proceeded to head down the staircase, but then heard Dick call out to me, "Hey Jack, any chance that we could talk for a few minutes down in my office?"

I quickly replied, "Sure, Dick. I've got a few minutes for ya."

We walked down to Dick's office. And as Dick closed the door behind me, I immediately asked him, "Is everything okay, Dick? You don't look well."

Dick replied, "Uh, it's Hanson, you know how much he likes to micromanage."

There was a momentary pause, and then Dick continued by saying, "Listen Jack, the reason that I wanted to talk to you is because the job postings for the new pilot program are coming out today. And between you and me, I'm putting in for the Team Leader position."

"Really…," I said, with utter surprise.

"Yeah, that's right. The time has finally come for me to part ways with Hanson. He's too much of a control freak for me, and his constant micromanaging is driving me absolutely crazy. So, uh…, how would you like to be my Rehabilitation Counselor for the new pilot program?"

I then replied, "Uh, don't take this the wrong way Dick, but before you start cleaning out your desk, isn't there the little matter of a job interview that needs to be conducted first?"

Dick lightly chuckled, and then quietly said, "Hey, just let me worry about that, okay."

"Gee Dick, you sound rather confident that you'll be selected as the Team Leader for the new pilot program. Personally, I think you're the obvious choice. But I'm sure there will be quite a few candidates throwing their hat in the ring for the new Team Leader position as well, right?"

"Well, off the record, but the Director told me that the job is mine if I want it."

"Ah, the plot thickens." I humorously replied.

Dick quietly chuckled, and then said with a sly grin, "Thus, as the new Team Leader for the new pilot program, I will be conducting all of the interviews and selecting whomever I want. So, uh…, do you see where I'm going with this Jack?"

"In other words, the game is rigged. Is that what you're really telling me, Dick?"

We both laughed heartily, and then Dick replied, "Well, I guess that's one way of looking at it. Listen Jack, I think this new pilot program has the potential for being a really dynamic program, especially if I can convince enough of the right people to come on board with me."

"Okay, well, I'll certainly keep it in mind. Thanks, Dick."

Well, it looks like the honeymoon period for Bobby Diggs is over. And the beleaguered staff in the Work Activity Center has given me an ultimatum, "Either Bobby goes, or they go!"

Once again, Bobby's borderline personality disorder continues to rear its ugly head, as Bobby single-handedly wreaks nothing but havoc down in the Work Activity Center.

So when I asked Bobby to explain to me what happened down in the work program, he stated that he didn't do anything wrong, and that the workshop staff was simply over-reacting and blowing everything completely out of proportion.

When I finally worked up enough courage to talk to Dick Henderson about Bobby Diggs, Dick just laughed it off by saying, "C'mon Jack, you're the best counselor on grounds, I'm sure you'll find a way to straighten things out with Bobby Diggs and the Work Activity Center staff."

Well, since Dick wasn't an option, then my only other recourse was to rely on my trusty counseling skills, which basically meant that I had to threaten Bobby within an inch of his life.

Of course, this band-aid approach of mine doesn't last very long with Bobby Diggs. And in a day or two, I will probably be having the same conversation with Bobby all over again.

Later that afternoon, I received a phone call from my old pal Murphy Doherty. Murphy called to let me know that he has a job interview scheduled for next week with Rita Spinelli. And when the interview was over, he was hoping to visit with me for a little while, and maybe even grab some dinner.

The following week, as I was working at my desk, I heard a knock on my office door. When I looked up, I was shocked to see Rita Spinelli and Murphy standing in the doorway.

Rita then effervescently said, "Hi Jack, I've got someone here that I think you know."

Upon seeing Murphy, I bolted out of my chair, and then gave him a big bro hug.

I then excitedly exclaimed, "Hey, it's great to see ya, Murphy! But, uh…, I thought your interview was scheduled for tomorrow?"

Rita piped up and said, "Well, that was the original plan, but something came up and Murphy was nice enough to reschedule. We certainly like a lot of flexibility in our interviewees, wouldn't you agree, Jack?"

"Uh, yes, yes…, I would Rita!" I emphatically replied, and we all laughed heartily.

Rita then said, "Well Jack, we're about halfway done with our tour. But if you're free for lunch, we can meet you over at the commissary around noontime. So, whatta ya say to that?"

"Yeah, okay, sounds good, Rita. So I'll see you both over there at noon."

Murphy sheepishly smiled, and then gave me a slight wave of his hand, as he and Rita left my office and then continued on with the balance of their tour.

Around twelve o'clock, I met up with Rita and Murphy over at the commissary.

So after exchanging a few pleasantries, we grabbed our lunch trays and utensils off of the rack, and then stood in line and waited for Becky to take our lunch order.

Becky greeted Rita and I with her usual bubbly charm, and then addressed Murphy by saying, "Hi there, are you a new employee, because I haven't seen you in here before?"

Murphy quickly glanced at Rita, as he awkwardly replied, "Um, no, I'm, uh…, just visiting for the day."

Rita and I lightly chuckled at the absolute innocence of their social exchange.

Becky then asked Murphy what he would like for lunch, and Murphy responded by saying, "Um, I'll have a small garden salad, please."

Rita piped up and said, "Hey Murphy, lunch is my treat, so order whatever you want, okay."

I then chimed in and light-heartedly replied, "Yeah, eat up, Murphy! It's all part of the recruitment process, right Rita?"

While Murphy was deciding on what to have, I ordered up the "blue plate" special.

As Becky handed me my order, Murphy said, "Uh, gimme what he's having," which prompted Becky to giggle, and then she served Murphy up a generous portion of baked lasagna.

So after enjoying a nice leisurely lunch, Murphy and Rita continued on with the rest of their tour.

As we parted ways, I told Murphy to swing by my office when he was all done with Rita. And then afterwards, Christine and I wanted him to join us for dinner over at our apartment.

Around three o'clock, there was a tap on my office door and it was Murphy. He sat down and made himself comfortable, and then humorously said, "So Jackie boy, do you think there's enough room in this office for another desk?"

With a sudden burst of excitement, I exclaimed, "What! You mean, Rita offered you the job already?"

Murphy replied, with a huge grin, "Yeah, can you believe it? I really wasn't expecting a decision to be made so quickly. But then I thought to myself, what the hell. So I called up Colleen and told her to start packing."

"So did Rita happen to mention what your assignment will be?"

Murphy nonchalantly said, "Yeah, she mentioned something about a new pilot program that will be opening up soon. And she thought that I would be perfect for the job."

"Really, 'cause I'm considering the new pilot program too! Hey, wouldn't it be great if you and I could both work there together!"

"Yeah, that would be awesome, Jackie boy!" Murphy replied, with a big smile.

So after chatting for a few more minutes, Murphy and I jumped into our cars and then headed over to the apartment to join Christine for dinner.

When we walked into the apartment, we stopped dead in our tracks, as we both inhaled the heavenly aroma of corned beef and cabbage that was simmering away on top of the stove.

Murphy then said, "Mmm…, something smells real good, Jackie boy!"

I amusingly replied, "Yeah, Christine is finally getting the knack of knowing how to boil up the cabbage," which prompted Murphy to laugh out loud, as he hung up his jacket.

Although my wife Christine is of Italian descent, she actually prefers cooking Irish meals over Italian meals, because there's a lot less clean-up involved.

When cooking up an Italian meal, the Italians seem to use every piece of cookware in the cupboard. Whereas the Irish only require one large pot, so that they can fill the pot up with water and then boil the hell out of the potatoes, the cabbage, and the corn beef all at the same time.

The following day, I decided to swing by Dick Henderson's office, so that I could tell him that I was interested in applying for the Rehabilitation Counselor position that was being posted for the new pilot program. And when I told Dick the news, he was utterly ecstatic.

So while I was on the subject of the new pilot program, I thought I would put in a good word for Murphy, so I mentioned to Dick that Murphy would be absolutely perfect for the new pilot program as well.

At that point, Dick informed me that he spoke to Rita Spinelli late yesterday afternoon, who just so happens to be Dick's niece, and Rita highly recommended Murphy for one of the Recreation Therapist positions for the new pilot program.

Dick then said on the Q.T., "Okay Jack, your boy Murphy is in. But just keep it under your hat for now, okay. Because we haven't officially conducted any of the job interviews yet."

I then replied, with a rather dastardly grin, "Mum's the word, Dick."

As I sat back in Dick's cushiony leather chair, I then thought to myself, "Gee, I guess this means that I'm Murphy's "rabbi" now. Boy, I sure hope that Father O'Malley doesn't find out about this, because he might think that I've decided to switch teams!"

CHAPTER SIX

For the past two weeks, the only time we ever see Dick Henderson is when he darts in and out of the staff lounge for a quick cup of coffee.

Why?

Well, since being selected as Team Leader for the new pilot program, or as its commonly referred to now as the Special Behavioral Unit, or SBU for short, Dick has been burning the midnight oil, so that he can assemble a team of clinicians for when the SBU finally opens up.

If all goes according to plan, the SBU is slated to open up within the month. So that being said, the Director has mandated Dick to complete the staff selection process as soon as possible.

I wish that I could say that all of this urgency to get the SBU up and running is strictly for clinical reasons. But despite all of the lip service and rhetorical bullshit that the top brass likes to spew out to the rank and file, the push to open up the SBU on time simply boils down to money.

For every day that the SBU remains closed, the State loses out on thousands of dollars. And although the politicians would like you to believe that they have an overwhelming desire to help out the poor and less fortunate, the truth is, - the quicker we can get the SBU doors opened up, the quicker the State can start lining their pockets with some cold hard cash.

So that being said, the Director has given strict orders that the staff selection process be a high priority. And that once the staff is assembled and properly trained, then the money train can be cleared to leave the station.

I thought that my "interview" with Dick Henderson went very well the other day. And even though I was a shoe-in for the position, Dick never showed me any preferential treatment.

Murphy wound up being interviewed the same day that I did too. And then afterwards, Murphy and I ate a hearty lunch over at the commissary.

As we devoured our "blue plate special," Murphy and I laughed over the fact that the game was rigged. And in a couple of weeks, Murphy and I will be working side-by-side together.

I have to say that Dick Henderson has done an outstanding job at convincing some of the more top-notch staff that work here at the State School to sign on with the SBU team. And from what I understand, the five Unit Chiefs are already feeling the effects of the new pilot program.

While at lunch the other day, I overheard several of the Unit Chiefs say, "That goddamn pilot program is poaching all of my best people! So how am I supposed to run a quality Unit?"

Oddly enough, but Snead and Askew both declined interviews. I know that Dick lobbied pretty hard to recruit them. But at the end of the day, they simply weren't interested in the SBU.

Apparently, Snead and Askew told Dick that they only had a few more years left until retirement, so they were content to just ride it out the rest of the way in their current positions.

To be honest, but I'm glad that neither one of them will be joining the SBU team. I was never that impressed with them anyway, and I thought that they were simply nothing more than deadwood. I'm not really sure why Dick valued them so much, but I guess Dick had his reasons.

Hanson has been climbing the walls lately, because Dick Henderson has been spending virtually all of his time on the interview process. Hanson expects Dick Henderson to be at his beck and call at all times, so that Dick can attend to whatever pressing matters that Hanson may want him to address in the Unit.

Mr. Hanson is not accustomed to having his hands tied, because he enjoys the luxury of having Dick Henderson at his disposal at all times. But at the moment there's really nothing that Mr. Hanson can do about it, especially since the Director has given Dick strict orders to get the interview process all wrapped up as soon as possible.

Dick Henderson on the other hand is relishing his time away from Mr. Hanson. And despite the fact that the interview process can be an extremely tedious and time consuming ordeal, it's actually been a very healthy diversion for Dick, and he seems to be enjoying the experience immensely.

Murphy telephoned me last night and said that he received his official confirmation letter in the mail, stating that he would be working as a Recreation Therapist in the SBU.

He also decided to take my advice by renting out the same on-grounds apartment that Christine and I resided in when I first started working here at the State School. Murphy's plan is to drive up on Sunday morning with his wife Colleen and his son Sean, and he asked if I could meet him at the on-grounds apartment, so that I could help him unload all of his belongings.

So on Sunday morning, Christine and I went to early Mass and then we drove over to the State School to meet with Murphy and his family at the on-grounds apartment.

When we pulled up in front of the apartment, Christine and I were absolutely ecstatic to see that Murphy's car and trailer was already parked there. While Christine and Colleen caught up on some of the news from back home, Murphy and I unloaded the trailer.

As Murphy slipped the padlock out of the hasp, I decided to have a little fun with him by saying, "Hey Murphy, my psychic instincts are telling me that the key to the apartment is stashed in the flower pot, which is sitting right over there next to the front door."

All of a sudden, Murphy displayed a rather astonished look on his face, as he replied in a totally bewildered tone of voice, "Wow! How the heck did you know that?"

As I burst out into laughter, I then said with a coy smile, "Because that's exactly where Rita hid the key for me three years ago, when I moved into the apartment. I guess some things never change, eh Murphy."

So Murphy reached his hand into the flower pot, and then plucked the key out from under the soil. He then slipped the key into the cylinder, and we all walked into the apartment.

Murphy and Colleen couldn't get over how spacious the apartment was. And even little Sean said with excitement, "Look Mommy, I can ride my three-wheeler forever!"

As we toured the apartment, it brought back some fond and vivid memories for me, and it made me realize just how fast time has flown since working here at the State School.

The following day, Murphy was standing in the hallway outside my office waiting for me to arrive. Upon seeing him, I cheerfully called out, "Morning Doc," which is my nickname for Murphy, because of his initials M.D., for Murphy Doherty.

Murphy then replied, "Morning Rodney," which is Murphy's nickname for me. Murphy has been calling me Rodney as far back as I can remember. The nickname was derived from the legendary comedian Rodney Dangerfield, who was a very popular comedian back in the day.

Rodney Dangerfield is noted for saying in his comedy routines that he never receives any respect, and Murphy was of the opinion that I never received any respect either. Especially from some of the kids in my neighborhood, who would constantly bully me due to my poor eyesight.

As kids, Murphy would always try to look out for me, so that I wouldn't get picked on by any of the other kids in school, or bullies in the neighborhood. And as time went by, Murphy and I grew to become best friends.

So after unlocking the door, I turned to Murphy and eagerly said, "Welcome to your new office, Doc." I then tossed Murphy the key, and he proceeded to give me a high-five.

As Murphy and I chatted over coffee, he said that he was feeling a little bit nervous this morning. I tried to reassure him that whatever jitters he had right now were completely normal, and that I would be right there with him every step of the way to help guide him through it.

So this morning Murphy and I are scheduled to attend a staff meeting at 9:00am. The purpose of the meeting is to welcome aboard all of the new staff that was just hired for the SBU. And from what I hear, the Director will be stopping by to make a cameo appearance as well.

When the staff meeting is over, Murphy and I will be attending a week long training session with all of the new SBU hires, and the training will be conducted by Dick Henderson.

As it stands right now, no one seems to know who the new Unit Chief will be for the SBU. Apparently that little piece to the puzzle seems to be a well-kept secret, and even Dick Henderson is scratching his head as to who his new boss will be.

Quite honestly, I really don't care who the new Unit Chief will be for the SBU, because no one could be any worse than Hanson, so whoever it is will certainly be a welcomed relief.

So after Murphy and I finished our coffee, we took a leisurely stroll over to Building 12 for the 9:00am staff meeting. As we took our seats, I introduced Murphy to some of the staff that he would be working with. And in no time at all, Murphy was feeling like a fish in water.

Just then Dick Henderson dashed into the room, and he had several three-ring binders tucked under his arm. Dick barely said hello, as he plopped the three-ring binders down on the table in the front of the room, and then proceeded to get organized for the staff meeting.

As I panned the room, everyone seemed to be excited about their new assignments, and there was lots of chatter and nervous laughter that was resonating throughout the room as well.

A few moments later, the Director strolled into the room with Mr. Hanson, which deaden the crowd, and put an abrupt halt to all of the various sidebar conversations throughout the room.

The Director then addressed the group by saying, "Good morning, everyone! Well, today is certainly a landmark day. As you all know, the Commissioner has chosen our facility to be the new pilot program for treating individuals with dual diagnoses. And as I look around the room, I can see that Dick Henderson has done an outstanding job at assembling a great team. There's no doubt in my mind that each and every one of you will make this new pilot program a huge success."

So after the Director was all done blowing sunshine up our ass, Hanson decided to be a real brown noser, as he cheered, "Hear! Hear!" Hanson started clapping his hands, and then he motioned for everyone else in the room to stand up and join him in all of the applause as well.

When the fanfare subsided, the Director continued by saying, "Well, I'm sure that many of you already know Al Hanson, and it's my pleasure to announce that Al will be the new Unit Chief for the SBU. Al was actually hand selected by the State Commissioner to head up the new pilot program, and this executive decision has been in the works for over two years now."

I quickly thought to myself, "Wow! Does that mean that the State Commissioner is Hanson's "rabbi?" No wonder why everybody is so afraid of Hanson, including the Director."

As the Director and Mr. Hanson shook hands, the entire room was in complete and utter shock. Especially Dick Henderson, who looked like he just saw a ghost.

I quietly mumbled, "holy shit," under my breath, which seemed to startle the hell out of Murphy, and then prompting him to anxiously whisper, "What's wrong, Rodney."

"Uh, I'll tell ya later, Doc." I replied, as I tried to process what the Director just conveyed to us.

As Mr. Hanson was basking in the spotlight, he just stood there in the front of the room with a big shit-eating grin on his face, as if he were some sort of Hollywood celebrity.

The Director then turned to Mr. Hanson, and cordially said, "So Al, would you like to say a few words to the group?"

"Um, yes, yes I would, thank you, Kevin."

Hanson cleared his voice, and then addressed the group by saying, "Well, as Kevin just mentioned, today is certainly a landmark day, and I'm really looking forward to the challenges that lay ahead. I'm sure that my appointment as Unit Chief for the SBU must come as a complete surprise to all of you, especially to Dick Henderson, right Dick?"

Dick smiled, and just decided to play along with Hanson's two-bit theatrics.

Hanson then wrapped up the meeting by saying, "Well, you all have a lot of work to do this week. And from what Dick tells me, it should not only prove to be educational, but lots of fun as well. Thanks again for joining the team, and I look forward to working with each of you."

So after the Director and Hanson left the room, Dick amusingly said, "Well, I don't think anyone saw that coming," and prompting a smattering of nervous laughter from around the room.

I leaned over to Murphy, and then whispered, "Boy, Dick can't seem to catch a break."

"Why's that, Rodney?" Murphy asked, with considerable interest.

"Because Hanson is a real son-of-a-bitch, that's why. And he has been riding Dick Henderson's ass since day one."

"Huh, really? They both seemed pretty chummy to me." Murphy replied.

"Yeah, well, looks can be deceiving, Doc."

Dick then playfully said, "Remind me never to play poker with Mr. Hanson," prompting another round of nervous laughter, as well as a few choice comments about Hanson as well.

So once the room finally settled down, Dick began the training session by passing out several handouts for the group to read. Although Dick was smiling, I could tell that he was still reeling over the fact that Hanson was selected as the new Unit Chief for the SBU. Dick really thought that he was going to be free and clear of Mr. Hanson once and for all.

But unfortunately, the nightmare continues.

So the first handout that Dick Henderson distributed to the group was the client roster for the SBU, and the corresponding facility that each of the clients was being transferred from.

The list contained sixty names in all. And as I panned down the list, I saw two names that immediately caught my eye, which were Bobby Diggs and Tommy Gerard.

As I continued to peruse the list of names, I overheard one or two of the staff say that they recognized a couple of the names on the list as being former clients of the State School.

From what I understand, these former clients were discharged from the State School years ago. But for one reason or another, they have been kicking around the system for years, and now they have found their way back to the State School again.

Apparently, the recidivism rate with the mentally challenged is extremely high. And anyone who has ever worked in the human services field long enough will definitely tell you, - that you should never throw any of your old case files away, because you never know when one of your former clients may suddenly appear at your doorstep again.

According to the list, most of the clients that were being referred to us were coming from psychiatric centers from across the state, with a handful from some private agencies, and even a sprinkling that were coming to us directly from jail. No one in the room was pleased to see the words STATE PRISON next to someone's name. And I was actually surprised to hear a few people in the room say that maybe signing on with the SBU wasn't such a good idea after all.

Dick could sense the tension in the room, so he suggested that we take a twenty minute break, and then reconvene after we've had a chance to stretch our legs and clear our heads a bit.

While everyone made a mad dash for the door, Murphy and I opted to stay back and chat with Dick for a few minutes, so that we could assess his spirits, especially after hearing the earth-shattering news that Hanson was still going to be his boss.

As Murphy and I approached Dick, the first thing out of his mouth was, "Can you believe that lousy no good son-of-a-bitch Hanson is gonna be the Unit Chief for the SBU?"

I quietly replied, "Yeah, it's unbelievable. But what's even more shocking is how Hanson kept the news so hush-hush. You know how much he loves tooting his own horn."

Dick then sharply said, "Do you know that over the past year, my blood pressure has climbed so high that my doctor is recommending that all of my blood pressure medications be doubled, so that I don't wind up having a stroke. And it's all because of that goddamn Hanson."

Murphy and I just stood there in uncomfortable silence.

So once Dick had a chance to blow off some steam, he seemed a bit more relaxed. Dick then turned toward Murphy and asked, "So Murphy, are you all squared away in a place to live?"

Murphy replied, "Um, yeah, my family and I are living in the on-grounds apartment. Well, until we can find a place of our own anyway."

Dick responded, "Nice! As a matter of fact, I lived in that same on-grounds apartment for almost a year and a half, when I was going through my divorce."

There was another moment of uncomfortable silence, and then I piped up and asked, "So, uh…, what types of training are we in store for this week, Dick?"

Dick replied, "Oh, the usual sort of stuff. But we'll try to jazz it up a bit, so that nobody falls asleep."

Murphy and I lightly chuckled.

Dick reached into his pocket, and then tried handing me a ten dollar bill while saying, "Why don't you guys stretch your legs a bit, and go get something to drink. And on your way back, maybe you can pick me up a large container of black coffee, okay?"

I replied, "Hey, the coffee is on me Dick, but would you prefer that I pick you up a large container of Irish coffee instead?"

Dick laughed, and then said, "Uh, don't tempt me. I've got a class to teach, remember."

When class resumed, we spent the whole day reviewing client histories. Murphy found it to be quite interesting, especially since he's never worked with the mentally challenged before.

Every so often, Murphy would lean over and ask me a question regarding some of the information being discussed, and he seemed very reassured in knowing that he had me to rely on.

By midafternoon, we trudged through half of the client roster. And when Dick brought up Bobby Diggs' name, the crowd definitely perked right up. Just the mere mention of Bobby's name seemed to spark a healthy dose of sarcastic comments from everyone sitting in the room.

At first, Dick let the comments slide. But as the comments persisted, Dick reminded us that we needed to be more professional. And that going forward, he expected all of his staff to display nothing but the utmost dignity and respect for all of the clients that we worked with.

Furthermore, Dick made it quite clear to everyone that if he saw or heard any type of impropriety, or even the slightest hint of questionable behavior whatsoever, then disciplinary action would be taken, including staff suspensions, or maybe even possible termination as well.

Although Dick's candid remarks put a noticeable damper on the room, his point needed to be made, or else the SBU could potentially become as lawless as the Wild Wild West.

The next day, Dick got right down to business and started class at precisely 8:00am. As soon as Dick asked everyone to refer to their handouts, the entire room began to moan and groan.

Suddenly, a voice from the back of the room cried out, "C'mon Dick, we're state workers, we haven't even had our first cup of coffee yet!"

Everyone in the room burst out into laughter, including Dick.

So once the room settled down, Dick picked up from where he left off yesterday. As we delved deeper into the case histories, much of what Dick conveyed to us sounded a little scary.

As I glanced around the room, some of the staff looked like they were having some real second thoughts about signing on with the SBU, and that perhaps they made a terrible mistake in taking a position with the new pilot program.

Several of the case histories were so graphic that it sounded like Jack the Ripper and Attila the Hun would soon be folding towels for me down in the Work Activity Center.

Dick could sense the tension in the air, so he took a moment to reassure us that everyone on the list wasn't as bad as the case histories made them out to be. Which I think we needed to hear, because Dick's reassurances seemed to quiet the crowd, as well as lay our minds to rest too.

As we shuffled into the room on day three, Dick surprised all of us with some coffee and donuts. Thus far, Dick has been pushing us pretty hard, so he wanted to show his appreciation by treating us to some mouthwatering refreshments. Dick has a real knack for gauging his staff, and he's quite adept at knowing when to step on the gas, or when to pump the brakes.

So after wrapping up the last of the case histories, Dick then turned his attentions toward the ever popular subject of staff attire.

Although the State School has no official dress code, Dick was quite adamant in telling us not to wear any type of provocative clothing while on duty. Especially since a large portion of the clients that we would be working with had some sexuality problems, and there were even a few that were classified as being sexual predators too.

So that being said, Dick strongly discouraged the female staff to wear any type of low neckline apparel, tight jeans, open toed shoes, or even dangling jewelry. Dick suggested that we all use a little bit of common sense regarding our appearance. And to be mindful of the fact that we were dressing for work, and not getting all dolled up for a hot night out on the town.

Upon hearing Dick's ultraconservative remarks, everyone in the room began to snicker, and even prompted several of the male staff in the back of the room to make some rather gauche and playful comments as well.

One comment in particular that seemed to tickle the funny bone of everyone in the room was, "Geez Dick, it sounds like you want all of the women in the SBU to dress like librarians."

Suddenly, everyone in the room burst out into laughter.

Dick then countered that whimsical remark with a whimsical remark of his own, as he said, "Well, as long as the women don't dress like naughty librarians, then we should be okay."

Before breaking for lunch, Dick wanted to revisit the topic of social decorum again. Dick made it loud and clear to everyone in the room that he didn't want to hear any inadvertent slips of the tongue, such as, vulgarity, risqué language, or any disparaging remarks toward the clients.

Dick also said that many of the clients that we would be working with were African-American, so he better not hear any types of racial slurs or denigrating language of any kind, especially since our facility has a zero-tolerance policy regarding harassment and discrimination.

After lunch, we focused on some health and safety issues, and also familiarized ourselves with some of the more commonly prescribed medications for treating people that are mentally ill.

Dick was very knowledgeable in this area, especially since he came up through the ranks as a registered nurse, so he was able to present the information to us right off the top of his head.

Around three o'clock, I was surprised to see Snead come waltzing into the room.

Apparently, Dick asked Snead to come by and give us a brief overview on some of the more prevalent psychological diagnoses that we would be encountering in the SBU. And to also recommend the most effective approach to use in dealing with these types of behaviors.

Surprisingly, the information that Snead provided us was very helpful. And for once in his life, Snead actually kept his comments short and sweet and straight to the point.

On the last day of training, Dick wanted to end the week on a fun note. So Dick told us to wear a pair of sneakers and some comfortable clothes today, because we were all going to be boning up on some of our "wrestling" moves.

Of course, Dick was only joking when he used the term "wrestling." What Dick really meant to say was that we would all be practicing some of our behavior management techniques, which are techniques that the staff use when clients become agitated or even violent. And these techniques are often used by the staff to prevent any type of injury from occurring as well.

And in private, the staff often refers to this type of training as, "hand-to-hand combat."

Everyone in the class, with the exception of Murphy, has had some type of training in this area before. So today's training exercise was simply going to be a refresher course for everyone.

Our instructor for this morning's training session was going to be Gerry Decker. Gerry is a real nice guy, and he works in the Education and Training Department here at the State School.

Since Murphy has never had this type of training before, Gerry will be scheduling him later in the month for a full day of training.

But for now, Murphy could just observe all of the techniques that were being employed. However, if at some point during the class that Murphy felt comfortable, then he was certainly welcome to jump in and participate in any of the exercises that were being demonstrated today.

Well, since today was only a refresher course, Gerry began the class by having everyone watch a twenty minute videotape. The video was basically an overview of the various types of techniques that the staff use, and how these techniques are to be utilized in any given situation.

Over the years, these techniques have proven to be a safe and effective way in helping the staff to neutralize potentially dangerous situations from escalating. And these techniques range from simple calming methods to the more intricate maneuvers of wrap-ups and take-downs.

Gerry reminded us that the primary objective when using any of these techniques is to control the situation in the safest way possible, and to prevent any type of injury from occurring.

As Gerry reached for the light switch, we noticed that the classroom door began to swing open, and who of all people should come waltzing into the room but Mr. Hanson. We haven't seen Mr. Hanson all week, so to see him today of all days took us by complete and utter surprise.

The minute we saw Hanson, we knew this wasn't a social call. Hanson was all decked out in an old pair of gym shorts, a washed out tee shirt, and a pair of high top sneakers. No one in the room would've ever seen this coming. Even Dick Henderson's jaw dropped straight to the floor.

It was strange seeing Hanson wearing casual attire, instead of his tailor-made Armani suit and designer Italian shoes, which we've all grown quite accustom to seeing him wear in the Unit.

As Hanson sauntered into the room, he had a real smug look on his face. He then walked straight over to Gerry and asked him, "Hi Gerry, so is there any room in the class for one more?"

Gerry replied, "Why sure, Al. C'mon in and join us!"

As Hanson pulled up a chair next to Dick Henderson, I was wondering what possessed him to be here today. Did Hanson have some sort of hidden agenda in mind, or was he simply here to flaunt his Hollywood good looks and his Adonis-like physique?

Apparently, Hanson is a real health nut. And not only is he an avid long distance runner and cyclist, but he also enjoys playing a friendly game of pick-up basketball two to three times a week at the local YMCA so that he can stay in tip-top shape.

Alfred Hanson was born with a silver spoon in his mouth, and comes from a long line of blue bloods. His father and grandfather were both captains of industry, and they just so happen to be one of the richest and most powerful families in the entire state.

Naturally, everyone just assumed that Hanson would enter the family business. But after attending one of the finest boarding schools in the country, and then completing his studies at the best Ivy League college that money could buy, Hanson decided to forego his corner office and stock options so that he could try his hand in the human services field.

Huh, go figure!

Although Hanson's father was extremely disappointed that his son Alfie didn't want to follow in his footsteps, he respected his son's decision nonetheless.

As a matter of fact, Hanson's father was quite instrumental in paving the way for dear 'ole Alfie to get his foot in the door with the State. By using his money and his influence to convince the Commissioner that his son had the makings to be a fine administrator someday.

It certainly wasn't unusual to see the Hanson limousine parked outside the State Capital steps anywhere from two to three times a week, so that Hanson's old man could wine and dine the State Commissioner at his posh and rather exclusive country club.

Afterwards, both men would then retire to the executive library to enjoy a nice cigar and a snifter of brandy. And as the evening drew to a close, Hanson's daddy would then take out his checkbook and pledge millions of dollars to fund faltering state programs that were in the red.

When Hanson landed his first State job, it certainly wasn't an entry level position. The Commissioner decided to create some cockamamie title out of thin air for dear little Alfie, and have him start his career where 99.9% of the rest of us can only dream of ending our careers at.

Although most of us have been taught that hard work and dedication will get you far in life. In reality, this little pearl of wisdom may be nothing more than a fairy tale. And maybe what parents should really be teaching their kids is, "It's not what you know, but who you know!"

As my Dad often says, "In order to succeed in this world, then you better make sure that you rub elbows with all the right people, or else you'll be serving the steak instead of eating it."

So after watching the videotape, Gerry asked for a volunteer so that he could demonstrate some of the simple touch control techniques that we just learned about in the training module.

Essentially, these touch control techniques allow the staff to enter the client's personal space in a nonthreatening way, and are generally used when a client is agitated but not violent.

Gerry then asked everyone in the group to split up into pairs, so that we could practice some of these basic touch control techniques that he just finished demonstrating to the class.

As everyone found a partner, I was quite surprised to see Dick Henderson pair up with Hanson. I was wondering what prompted Dick to do that, especially since Dick has so much contempt for the man, and Dick can barely tolerate being cooped up in the same room with him.

Then again, perhaps Dick was simply taking the high road, and casting aside whatever bitter feelings he may have for Hanson, so that Hanson could feel more comfortable in the group.

Anyway, as I pondered the question, I detected a rather sinister look in Dick's eye, which indicated to me that perhaps Dick had some ulterior motives. And that maybe he viewed today's training exercise as a way of evening the score with Hanson without making it look too obvious.

Although Dick was a lot older than Hanson, and at least fifty pounds over his ideal body weight, Dick was as strong as an ox. And he could probably hurt Hanson if he really wanted to.

Now I'm not saying that Dick would intentionally try to hurt Hanson, but maybe rough him up enough so that he could alleviate some of the pent-up anger and stress that Hanson has been inflicting on him for years.

Ironically, Hanson seemed quite pleased to be paired up with Dick. And I actually think that Hanson was looking forward to going toe-to-toe with Dick in our little training class today.

Yeah, I'm sure that Mr. Hanson wanted to show Dick who was boss. And maybe even teach Dick a good lesson for all the grief and aggravation that Dick has been causing him of late.

As we waited to get underway, Mr. Hanson kept taunting Dick about his weight. Hanson was telling Dick that his tee shirt looked so tight that it could barely stretch over his big fat belly.

Hanson was absolutely brutal in the way that he was needling Dick about his waistline, and he seemed to think that his bristling remarks were quite clever and just downright funny too.

But as far as I was concerned, Hanson's remarks only confirmed to me just how cruel he can really be. And despite all of his power and influence, his lack of class was certainly evident.

Although Dick took Hanson's insults in stride, I could tell by the look in Dick's eye that he was simply biding his time, and waiting for just the right moment to get even with Hanson.

So in the interest of time, Gerry asked each of the pairs to buddy-up into groups of four, so that we could try to move things along and get through all of the training exercises quicker.

Naturally, Murphy and I were both paired up together, and then we decided to buddy-up with Dick Henderson and Mr. Hanson to round out the foursome.

So after reviewing all of the touch control techniques, we then progressed into the wrap-up phase. A wrap-up is used in the event that a client becomes increasingly more hostile or violent. There are several wrap-up techniques that the staff can use in order to control a situation, and Gerry was extremely thorough in making sure that we ran through each of them correctly.

Dick, Hanson, and I all took turns wrapping-up Murphy, or should I say holding onto Murphy for dear life. Murphy stands 6'5, and weighs close to 250 pounds. So wrapping-up a big guy like Murphy was like trying to jackass a refrigerator around the room without any casters.

In college, Murphy not only played baseball and basketball, but he was also a four-year starter as a lineman on the college football team as well.

At one point, Hanson actually displayed a rare moment of levity, as he amusingly said, "Boy, I'm sure glad that we've got Murphy on our team!"

The last exercise in today's training class dealt with take-downs. Take-downs were by far the most challenging of all the techniques. And if not done correctly, they could result in serious bodily harm. Not only for the client, but to the staff who was performing the take-down as well.

Take-downs are usually required when a client becomes so violent and out of control that there's no hope of reasoning with them whatsoever. So when performing a take-down the staff needs to effectively communicate with each other, and be very decisive in all of their actions.

Some of the ladies in this morning's training class were a bit skittish when performing some of these take-down techniques, and amusingly referred to these techniques as "tackling."

When Gerry glanced at his watch, he saw that we were running a little behind schedule, so Gerry decided to have multiple take-down groups performing the exercises simultaneously.

As I glanced around the room, I saw bodies flying in every direction and then landing on the soft rubber mats that were all laid out on the floor.

It kinda reminded me of a high school wrestling team, as they practiced their wrestling moves, with Gerry serving as the team's head coach.

At any given moment, I was expecting to hear Gerry blow his whistle and then shout at the top of his lungs, "Red, take-down, two points!"

Gerry's head was on a swivel, as he coached us through all of the tricky maneuvers. And laughter abounded, as we all took turns being hog-tied and then thrown right down to the floor.

Yeah, we all knew that we were going to be sore tomorrow. And in all likelihood, we'll be reaching into the medicine cabinet tonight, so that we can pop a couple of aspirin.

As we raced through each of the techniques, Gerry advised us to use our time wisely. So instead of practicing at half speed, Gerry suggested that we put our heart and soul into it, so that when the time came for us to utilize these trusted techniques, then we would be better prepared.

Of course, Gerry's suggestion was all the encouragement that Dick Henderson needed to hear. So when it was Dick's turn to take-down Hanson, he decided to use a little extra mustard.

Hanson never knew what hit him, as Dick grabbed him around his waist and then hoisted him straight up into the air. And like a piledriver, Dick pounded Hanson right down to the floor.

As Hanson went plummeting to the ground, he looked absolutely petrified. And for a split second there, I thought I heard Hanson scream, "Mommy!"

When the take-down was over, Dick helped Hanson up to his feet, and then apologized to Hanson for being a little too enthusiastic. As Hanson shook out the cobwebs, he told Dick that there were no hard feelings, because he knew that it was all part of the training exercise today.

As Hanson staggered over to the water fountain, Dick glanced at me and smiled. I'm sure that body-slamming Hanson to the floor was very cathartic for Dick, and probably helped even the score a bit for all the grief and aggravation that Hanson has imposed on him over the years.

Gerry then took everyone by complete surprise when he said, "Okay, so now that you're all experts in knowing how to use these techniques, then who's ready to take-down Murphy?"

Suddenly, five men stepped forward, and prompting one of them to say, "Yeah, I think five should do the trick," causing the entire room to burst out into laughter, including Gerry.

So after the room quieted down, Gerry confidently said, "Hey, you don't need five people to take-down a big guy like Murphy. In fact, I'll show ya how one person can easily do the job."

Gerry then approached Murphy from the side, and before any of us even realized what was happening, Murphy was lying flat on his back with Gerry in total control of the situation.

The crowd roared with laughter, coupled with a few razzing remarks that were directed toward poor old Murphy as well.

As Gerry helped Murphy up to his feet, he called on Mary Beth, who was the smallest person in the room, to perform the same take-down maneuver on Murphy as Gerry just did.

When Mary Beth stood next to Murphy, it looked like a modern day version of David and Goliath.

Gerry told Mary Beth precisely what to do. And in the blink of an eye, Murphy was once again lying flat on his back, and looking straight up at Mary Beth in a state of total disbelief.

As everyone cheered, Mary Beth just smiled, and then daintily curtsied to the crowd.

In wrapping up the take-down portion of the training, Gerry said that all of the techniques that we worked on today were simply based on leverage, and allowing gravity to be your friend.

We finished up around noontime. Dick thanked Gerry for helping us out today, and then everyone gave Gerry a big round of applause, coupled with a few uncensored remarks as well.

As we all stood around waiting for Hanson to say a few parting words, I noticed that he was nowhere to be found. Hanson must have slipped out of the room without our knowledge.

I guess I just assumed that Hanson would want to stick around and throw his two-cents worth in to Gerry and everyone else in the room. But then knowing Hanson, he was probably so ashamed by his lackluster performance today that he needed to go find a place to hide, so that he could lick his wounds and try to console his incredibly large ego.

As we broke for lunch, Dick reminded everyone to be back in their seats by one o'clock, so that we could try to wrap things up for the week.

Murphy, Dick, and I headed over to the commissary to grab a bite to eat. We all worked up a pretty hearty appetite this morning, so we all decided to order up the "blue plate" special.

Dick didn't have too much on the docket for the afternoon session, because he wanted to keep Friday afternoon wide open in the event that he was falling behind schedule. So Dick just used the remaining time for questions and answers, and to get to know his staff a little bit better.

By three-thirty, Dick decided to call it a day. Before releasing the staff, Dick announced to the group that the first wave of clients were scheduled to start moving into the SBU by next Wednesday, so Dick told everyone to report to their old worksites on Monday and Tuesday.

Murphy then leaned over to me and whispered, "Hey Rodney, I better find out from Dick where he wants me to go on Monday, seeing how I don't have an old worksite to report to."

Which then prompted me to say, "Uh, good thinking, Doc."

As everyone headed for the door, Murphy and I made our way up to the front of the room so that we could chat with Dick for a minute.

Murphy then hastily asked, "Hey Dick, where should I report to on Monday morning?"

Dick told Murphy that he could hang out in Building 12 for the next couple of days and help out the recreation staff, who would certainly welcome having an extra pair of hands.

Over the weekend, Christine and I got together with Murphy and his family for a little barbeque. Nothing fancy, just hamburgers and hot dogs on the grill, and some great company.

During the course of our fun-filled afternoon, I wound up spilling the beans to the wives by telling them that Murphy had been wrestled down to the ground by a middle-aged and under sized woman during our behavior intervention training class on Friday.

Upon hearing the story, the wives were in utter hysterics, and certainly had a few choice comments to make for poor old Murphy.

And if that still wasn't embarrassing enough, Murphy's three year old son Sean threw his arms around his father, and inquisitively asked, "Daddy, did some little old lady beat you up?"

Murphy replied, in a rather hasty tone, "No Sean, daddy let her win!"

As Sean went off to play in the spare bedroom, Murphy then turned towards me and sarcastically said, "Thanks Rodney, now my son thinks that his father is a big sissy."

When I arrived to work on Monday, Murphy was already parked at his desk, and he was killing time by reading some old and outdated policy and procedure manual from ten years ago.

"Mornin' Doc, you're in early this morning." I said, while yawning.

"Yeah, well, I'm only a stone's throw away Rodney." Murphy said, quietly.

"True," I mumbled, as I took a big stretch, and tried to wake up.

"So are you ready for some coffee yet?" Murphy asked.

"Yeah, sure, grab the mugs." I said, still yawning.

En route to the coffee room, Murphy asked me if I would walk over to Building 12 with him this morning, so that I could introduce him to the staff that he would be working with today.

To which I replied, "Yeah, of course, I was planning on it anyway, Doc. We'll head over to Building 12 right after we've had our morning coffee."

"Okay boss," Murphy answered.

So as we headed over to Building 12, I filled Murphy in on some of the recreation staff that he would be working with today.

As fate would have it, I happened to see Bobby Diggs running out of Building 12, and then cutting across the courtyard in the direction of the community store.

I hastily called out, "Hey Bobby, c'mon over here for a minute, okay?"

Bobby glanced over his shoulder, and then shouted, "I can't right now Jack, I gotta go to the store for Mr. Askew!" Bobby then threw it into high gear, and sprinted off into the distance.

Murphy then nonchalantly asked, "Is that one of the clients that you work with Rodney?"

I answered, "Yeah, and someone that you'll be working with too."

"Really…," Murphy replied, as he glanced back over his shoulder to take another quick glimpse at Bobby.

"Yeah, his name is Bobby Diggs. And don't let his friendly disposition fool ya, because Bobby can be a real piece of work. I'm sure that we'll bump into him later today, and then I'll introduce ya." I said, as we reached Building 12.

We walked into Building 12, and then took the staircase down to the basement where the Recreation Office was located. When I tapped on the door, it was slightly ajar, and all of the recreation staff was leisurely sipping their morning coffee and trying to gear up for the day.

As I introduced Murphy to the gang, they all welcomed him with open arms. And in no time at all, Murphy was feeling right at home, as if he's been working with the crew for years.

So after leaving Murphy in the very capable hands of the recreation staff, I then headed over to the Work Activity Center, and prayed that Bobby wasn't wreaking havoc over there.

As I cut across the courtyard, my mind was consumed with thoughts of Mr. Askew. I didn't like the fact that Mr. Askew was still having Bobby Diggs running errands for him.

Apparently, Mr. Askew continues to view Bobby as a working boy.

Well, perhaps Mr. Askew should take a moment to re-examine his files, so that he can refresh his memory a bit by re-reading some of the old memos from Mr. Wohlers, which plainly states that the clients should not be looked upon as "indentured servants" anymore.

When I entered the Work Activity Center, the room was in total shambles, and it looked like a regular three ring circus. As usual, Bobby was bossing all of the other clients around, and he was refusing to listen to a damn thing that any of the workshop staff was telling him to do.

The workshop supervisor was so upset with Bobby that he wound up clocking out for the day, and he actually threatened to kill Bobby if he was forced to stay at work for another minute.

This is exactly the type of affect that Bobby can have on people. Bobby has a real knack for knowing how to press people's buttons, so that he can drive them completely over the edge.

Even Mother Theresa would have a tough time putting up with Bobby Diggs all day.

Bobby just can't understand why most people really don't like him, and why they try to go out of their way to avoid him as much as they possibly can.

And yes, even try to sabotage him whenever possible.

So when I finally got around to asking Bobby what happened between him and the workshop supervisor, he told me that he had absolutely no idea what I was even talking about.

As a matter of fact, Bobby actually had the audacity to ask me when I was going to find him another job, and a job that pays him a lot more than what the

Work Activity Center does.

Bobby seems to think that he can say or do whatever the hell he wants without suffering any of the consequences. And when the staff tries to correct him, he just can't understand why.

Well, I guess that would explain why Bobby Diggs was drafted by the SBU in the first round!

But knowing Bobby, he'll probably think that living in the SBU will bring him one step closer to freedom. When in reality, living in the SBU will only hurt his chances even more.

When I finally got back to the office it was roughly four o'clock, and I was a bit surprised that I didn't see Murphy parked at his desk.

In a way, I was kinda glad not to see Murphy in the office yet, because it probably meant that he was having a pretty good time of it up on the living units. And knowing Murphy, he'll be busting at the seams to tell me all about it tomorrow morning over coffee.

When I arrived at the office the next day, Murphy was already parked at his desk. He was gnawing on an apple, and he had his nose completely buried in one of the client's charts.

As I tossed my backpack off of my shoulder, I greeted Murphy by saying, "Mornin', Doc. So, uh…, what are you doing over there?"

"Morning, Rodney. Oh, I'm just reading up on your old buddy, Bobby Diggs."

"Oh, yeah! So you finally got to meet the infamous Bobby Diggs yesterday, huh?"

"Uh, yeah, I sure did. And he told me that he can't wait to work with me when he moves into the SBU." Murphy replied, as he continued to peruse Bobby's chart with interest.

"Well, that sounds like vintage Bobby to me. Just don't let him pull the wool over your eyes in thinking that you're an easy target, because Bobby is a real pro at that, okay." I stated.

"Yeah, okay, thanks!" Murphy replied, as he continued to be engrossed in Bobby's chart.

"So Doc, do you think you can pull yourself away from that scary novel for a few minutes, so that you and I can go grab some coffee for ourselves?" I asked, humorously.

"What, oh yeah, sure…," Murphy said, as closed Bobby's chart.

As we sipped our morning coffee, Murphy filled me in on his day yesterday.

Murphy said that the recreation staff treated him quite well, and that they were all a bunch of straight-shooters.

But what really surprised Murphy the most yesterday was how comfortable he felt around all of the clients. But to be perfectly honest with you, it really didn't surprise me one bit.

After all, who in their right mind wouldn't love Murphy.

So after finishing our coffee and thoroughly dissecting the sports page, Murphy headed over to Building 12, and I headed over to Building 13.

As we parted ways, I told Murphy that I'd see him later this afternoon over in Building 51 for a mandatory staff meeting.

Apparently, Hanson decided to call an emergency staff meeting this afternoon, because he wanted to bring everyone up to speed on what the game plan was for tomorrow morning, when the SBU officially opens its doors and welcomes aboard the first wave of clients.

When I arrived for the three o'clock staff meeting, Murphy was already there and he saved me a seat. Dick and Hanson were standing in front of the room, and they both had their game faces on.

As Dick and Hanson waited for everyone to get situated in their seats, I leaned over to Murphy and whispered, "Is it me, or does it feel like a military briefing in here to you?"

Murphy just nodded his head, and nervously chuckled.

Hanson saw that everyone was assembled for the meeting, so he addressed the group by saying, "Okay, I think we're all here now. Well, thank you for meeting with us on such short

notice. As of right now, we're still scheduled to open up the SBU doors tomorrow morning, and I just wanted to make sure that we had all of our ducks in a row and all of our bases covered."

Dick then proceeded to hand out a list of clients that were projected to arrive tomorrow morning from Metropolitan Psychiatric Center. The list contained thirty names in all, and the remaining thirty clients for the SBU were all slated to arrive on Thursday and Friday this week.

As I sat there listening to Hanson blow sunshine up our ass, I could tell that his flowery remarks were nothing more than lip service.

Although Hanson made reference to the fact that tomorrow will be a landmark day, I highly doubt that he was referring to the clients, but more in the context of it being a landmark day for himself instead.

Why?

Well, the fact that Hanson was personally hand selected by the State Commissioner to launch a new federally funded pilot program will certainly look darn good on his resume, and it might even land him a Directorship at another state facility somewhere.

So you can bet your bottom dollar that Hanson is going to make damn sure that nothing stands in the way of the SBU being an overwhelming success, so that he can get his "that-a-boy" from the State Commissioner, who will then promptly reward him with a handsome promotion.

When the meeting was over, Hanson wished us "good luck," and then said that he would see us all bright and early tomorrow morning up in the front lobby.

As we all filed out of the room, I turned towards Murphy and quietly said, "So are you all ready for tomorrow, Doc?"

Murphy looked me straight in the eye, and then confidently said, "Rodney, let the games begin!"

CHAPTER SEVEN

Well, it's a little after 9:30am, and the clients that were supposed to be here at 7:00am this morning from Metropolitan Psychiatric Center still haven't arrived yet.

For the past three hours, we've all been twiddling our thumbs and wondering where the hell the clients are, but so far no one seems to know what's going on. And the longer we wait, the more anxious we seem to become.

As I glanced around the room, I noticed that some of the staff was busying themselves by playing cards, and others were trying to figure out the crossword puzzles. But what really caught my eye was that some of the staff was sitting all by themselves in some sort of trance, as if they were hypnotized, and under some sort of bizarre and mysterious spell.

Perhaps some of the staff was letting their imagination get the best of them, especially after hearing some of the case histories that Dick told us about in last week's training class.

Hey, for all we know, but maybe the reason why the clients are so late this morning is because they've seized control of the bus, and have taken the Metro Psychiatric staff hostage.

Thus far, we haven't seen Mr. Hanson yet. Hanson told us that he would see us bright and early this morning, but then Hanson is always making promises that he can't keep.

Well, unless of course, he promises to make your life completely miserable that is.

Actually, I'm a little surprised that Hanson isn't here yet, especially since he's banking on the SBU to be his ticket to fame and fortune. I've come to realize that Mr. Hanson is a very precise and calculating man, and he seldom leaves anything to chance.

As a matter of fact, Hanson instructed Dick not to approve any time off today, because he wanted to make sure that all hands were on deck this morning when the clients arrived.

When I heard Hanson issue that directive to Dick, it brought back vivid memories of Mr. Wohlers, the day that we launched off-unit programming for the habilitation services initiative.

Mr. Wohlers was bound and determined that day not to have any foul-ups or glitches, so that everything would go according to plan. And I think the same can be said for Mr. Hanson today as well.

As I continued to sit there lost in my thoughts, Murphy leaned over to me and asked what time it was, to which I replied, "Uh, its two minutes later than the last time you asked me, Doc."

Murphy quietly nodded his head, and then simply said, "Oh yeah, right. Sorry about that Rodney, I guess I'm having some game day jitters."

Just then the telephone rang, which seemed to ignite the crowd. The building supervisor then announced that a coach bus was spotted down the road and it was heading in our direction.

Upon hearing the update, Dick grabbed his clipboard and then said in a bit of a nervous tone, "Okay everybody, showtime!"

At that moment, everyone seemed to have a terrified look on their face, as they all reluctantly stood up, and then cautiously trailed behind Dick in single file. And although I can't speak for anyone else, but I could feel my autonomic nervous system firing on all cylinders.

The thirty clients that were arriving this morning were all coming from a large inner-city facility known as the Metropolitan Psychiatric Center, and a facility that is notorious for housing some of the most hardcore and psychiatrically impaired individuals in the state.

As the coach bus crested the top of the hill, my heart skipped a beat. The bus then swung into the circular driveway in front of the building, and then came to an abrupt stop. And when I heard the sound of the hydraulic air brakes release, it sent an icy chill right down my spine.

When the retractable door on the coach bus started to open, I quickly panicked.

I then thought to myself, "I wonder if it's too late for me to beat it over to the Human Resources Office right now, so that I can rescind my position for the SBU."

Suddenly, a wiry middle-aged black man hopped off of the bus with a clipboard in his hand. He struck me as a no-nonsense type of guy. Not necessarily a hard ass, but more like a guy who was not going to put up with a lot of unnecessary guff or bullshit.

The man walked straight over to Dick, and then said in a very direct tone of voice, "Good morning! My name is Jefferson, and I was told to see a fella by the name of Dick Henderson."

Dick casually replied, "I'm Dick Henderson, it's nice to make your acquaintance."

The two men shook hands, and then Mr. Jefferson said in a very business-like tone, "So I believe that you're expecting thirty of our clients from Metro Psychiatric Center today, right?"

Dick then jokingly replied, "Yeah, about three hours ago."

Mr. Jefferson lightly chuckled, and then affably said, "Well, we had a couple of glitches along the way, but nothing to get too alarmed about."

"Okay, well, I'm glad that you all arrived here safely." Dick light-heartedly replied.

Jefferson glanced down at his clipboard and said, "Before we unload the bus, why don't we cross-reference the list. Oh, that reminds me, one of the clients on the list didn't make the trip with us today, but we will be transporting him later this week, and his name is Tyrell Freeman."

Dick quietly nodded his head, and then made a notation on his clipboard.

As Dick and Mr. Jefferson were verifying the list of names, we saw Mr. Hanson pull into the parking lot. Hanson hopped right out of his sporty red convertible, and then sprinted straight over to where Dick and Mr. Jefferson were standing so that he could be apprised of the situation.

Hanson was chomping at the bit, as he stood there waiting for Dick to finish conferring with Mr. Jefferson, so that he could be brought up to speed on what the status of the transfer was.

So after cross-referencing the list of names, Dick introduced Hanson to Mr. Jefferson, and then Dick proceeded to brief Hanson on what has transpired thus far regarding the transfer.

Mr. Jefferson then asked, "So how would you gentlemen like to handle the exchange?"

Hanson took immediate charge of the situation, and then exercised his authority by saying, "Let's take everyone into the gym, and then we can sort it all out down there?"

Jefferson nodded his head, and then replied, "Sounds like a plan to me gentlemen."

Mr. Jefferson then hopped back onto the bus, so that he could confer with his staff and bring them up to speed as to what the game plan was for handling the transfer.

A few moments later, the clients began to trickle off the bus. My first impression of the new arrivals was that they all reminded me of a band of refugees. Not only did they looked tired and confused, but they were all wearing the same exact camouflaged jackets. The jackets all looked to be brand new, as if they were just bought yesterday from the local Army-Navy store.

In fact, I'm pretty sure that I saw a price tag hanging off the cuff of one of the client's sleeves, which indicated to me that very little thought or planning went into these purchases.

By now, the clients were starting to pour off of the bus at a steady rate. Murphy and I were waiting our turn to escort one or two of the clients into the building. I was glad that I had Murphy by my side, because I was actually feeling a little bit nervous right now.

As I studied the look on each of the client's faces, they seemed to be as nervous as we were, and I was beginning to wonder what was going through their minds right about now.

Quite honestly, but I've been so wrapped up with my own set of fears and insecurities that I really haven't given any thought as to how the clients must be feeling at this point.

It's not easy to be plucked out of one living situation and then plopped into another. And even though the facility that these clients were being uprooted from wasn't exactly Shangri-La, it was still their home. And on some level, I'd like to believe that these clients enjoyed at least some modicum of comfort or peace-of-mind at their former facility.

All of the clients who were being transferred to us this morning were African-American.

Up until now, but my whole existence in life has been centered around white people, whether it be church, school, or families that I grew up with in my neighborhood.

If the truth be told, but I've never had any black friends or acquaintances before. And although it shames me to admit it, but standing here amongst so many black people right now was starting to make me feel a little bit uncomfortable.

Yeah, I realize that must sound terrible to say. But for some reason, cultural diversity seems to have eluded me.

Well, maybe in time I can strip myself of all of these fears and biases of mine, so that I can find an effective way to relate to these inner-city black clients, who probably have their own set of fears and prejudices towards white people as well.

When it was our turn to escort two of the clients down to the gym, Murphy and I made several attempts to initiate some conversation with them, but neither of the two clients that we were paired up with was too interested in making any small talk with us.

So at that point, Murphy and I decided not to force the issue, so we just walked along in uncomfortable silence, and not a single word was spoken amongst any of us.

Once safely in the gym, Dick instructed Murphy and I to remain there so that we could help supervise the clients that were already gathered.

One of the clients in the gym must've taken note of the basketball hoops that were mounted on the wall, so he decided to ask Murphy for a basketball so that he could shoot some baskets. Murphy then tried to explain to the young man that we couldn't play basketball right now because it would create too much noise and chaos in the room. But maybe later when things settle down, we could come back into the gym and shoot some baskets then.

Needless to say, but that wasn't exactly what the young man wanted to hear. So he just kept badgering Murphy for a basketball, and he simply wouldn't take "no" for an answer.

By now, the gym was beginning to fill up rather quickly, and the noise level was almost deafening. Dick and Hanson seemed to be at wits end, as they tried to make sense out of it all.

The client that was hounding Murphy five minutes ago for a basketball, then decided to up the ante, and began insinuating that the only reason Murphy wouldn't give him a basketball was because Murphy was too afraid to challenge him to a friendly one-on-one basketball game.

As I stood alongside the young man who was pestering Murphy, I actually found him to be quite intimidating, and he looked like he could be a real handful if he didn't get his own way.

This young man's name was Jamal Buchanan, and he had a physique that was chiseled out of pure granite. Jamal stood about 6'7, but the teased out afro-hairstyle that he was rocking made him look almost 7'0 tall.

Jamal then decided to push the envelope a little further, so he got right up into Murphy face and started taunting Murphy with some rather explicit racial slurs. Despite Jamal's efforts to antagonize Murphy, Murphy remained as cool as a cucumber, and he refused to take the bait.

So seeing how none of Jamal's intimidation tactics were working, Jamal then decided to switch gears by telling us that all of his homeboys back in his neighborhood refer to him as Jam.

Naturally, I just assumed that Jam was short for Jamal.

But apparently, Jamal's hommies all refer to him as Jam because Jamal has a reputation for jamming the basketball into the basket whenever he plays in any pick-up basketball games on the playground back in his old neighborhood.

Quite honestly, I'm not really sure if Jamal was trying to impress us with his basketball prowess, or simply scare the hell out of us. But if Jamal thinks that he's going to intimidate Murphy, then he's definitely barking up the wrong tree.

At that moment, Mr. Jefferson walked into the gym and began surveying the room. When Mr. Jefferson heard some of the vulgar and indignant remarks that Jamal Buchanan was directing towards Murphy, he got right up into Jamal's face and then sternly said, "Hey boy, haven't I told you about that foul mouth of yours. Now get your ass over there with all of your other little hommie friends, and leave these two fine gentlemen alone, ya got me boy!"

To say that Murphy and I were totally stunned by Mr. Jefferson's sharp tone would be an understatement, as we just stood there like two statues listening to him lay wood into Jamal.

Obviously, Mr. Jefferson has been down this road before. And from the looks of things, Jamal wanted nothing to do with Mr. Jefferson, as he obediently said, "Yessir, Mr. Jefferson."

Jamal then slinked away with his tail between his legs. But as he got closer to all of his hommies, he began acting all cool and cocky again, and strutting like a rooster in a henhouse.

Mr. Jefferson then turned to us in a more relaxed tone, and quietly said, "I'm sorry that you gentlemen had to be subjected to that. Jamal really isn't a bad kid, but sometimes he needs to be reminded as to who's in charge."

So before making any room assignments, Dick decided to confer with Mr. Jefferson first, so that he could ask his opinion as to who should bunk with whom. The last thing that we wanted right now was to have two sworn enemies sharing the same bedroom together.

The SBU was comprised of three living units, L.U. 511, L.U. 512, and L.U. 513, and each unit had a capacity for twenty clients. The clients who were being processed today would be filling up L.U. 512 first, and then the remaining clients would all be assigned to L.U. 513.

So after consulting with Mr. Jefferson, Dick was now ready to make all of the living unit assignments. In a loud and distinct voice, Dick then said, "When I call your name, please step over to where Mr. Jefferson is standing."

Dick then rattled off twenty names. And after the twentieth name, he decisively said, "Okay, all of you guys will be heading over to L.U. 512. The staff will escort you over there now, so that you can get your room assignments and then settle all of your belongings."

So after the first twenty clients left the gym, Dick turned to the remaining clients and said, "Okay, the rest of you guys will be assigned to L.U. 513. So why don't you grab your stuff and head over to L.U. 513 with the staff, so that you can all get situated in your rooms as well."

Murphy and I wound up tagging along with the first group. As we made the short walk over to L.U. 512, Jamal Buchanan was still spittin' and sputterin' about not getting his own way down in the gym. Not to mention, the tongue lashing that he just took from Mr. Jefferson too.

Jamal then said to his friend Jerome, "Yo' bro, I'm sick and tired of taking shit from Mr. Jefferson. That old dude is nothin' but an Uncle Tom. And if he thinks I'm gonna be some kinda house nigger to a bunch of uppity white folk, then that Oreo cookie is outside his mind, man."

So after hearing Jamal's extremely racist remark, I was almost tempted to say something.

But then thought better of it, because I was afraid it might incite a riot.

If this is how Jamal reacts when he hears the word "no," then he is certainly in for a rude awakening. Jamal might not realize it yet, but the staff around here is not that easily intimidated.

And if Jamal thinks that the clients are going to be running the show, then he's sadly mistaken.

So once all of the clients were safely escorted onto L.U. 512, the unit charge then asked everyone to take a seat in the dayroom, so that he could go over a few housekeeping items with them, and to also review the rules of the living unit as well.

Before reviewing the rules, the unit charge made it quite clear that infractions would not be tolerated. And if anyone was caught violating the rules, then there would be consequences.

With absolutely no exceptions!

So after reviewing the rules, the unit charge was ready to make the room assignments. The plan was to settle one bedroom at a time, and each bedroom accommodated two clients.

While Murphy and I waited for our turn to escort two clients down to their bedroom, we sat and chatted with the clients in the dayroom, and tried to get to know them a little bit better.

Well, as luck would have it, but when it was our turn to escort two clients down to their room, one of the clients that we escorted was Jamal Buchanan. Jamal had a big grin on his face when he saw that Murphy was one of the staff who was escorting him down to his bedroom.

As we headed towards the bedroom area, Jamal started right up again by telling us what a terrific basketball player he was. And to paraphrase Jamal, "He can't wait to play Murphy in a one-on-one basketball game later, so that he can kick Murphy's lily-white ass all over the gym."

For a minute there, I was wondering just how good of a basketball player Jamal really was, or was he only spewing hot air. I would love to see Murphy kick Jamal's ass in a game, so that Murphy could finally shut him up once and for all and teach Jamal a real good lesson.

Yeah, I know that sounds terrible to say. But sometimes the clients have a way of getting under your skin, and then you wind up saying things that you wouldn't ordinarily say.

So in an effort to appease Jamal, Murphy agreed to play him in a friendly one-on-one game later, but only if Jamal followed the rules and kept his nose clean for the rest of the day.

When we entered the bedroom, Jamal quickly decided to take the bed that was closest to the window. He then tossed his duffle bag to the floor, and then launched himself onto the bed so that he could see for himself just how firm his new mattress was.

As Jamal was all stretched out on his bed and making himself comfortable, he suddenly realized that there was no television set in his bedroom, so he brashly said, "Hey man, where's the television at? I wanna be able to watch basketball games on television in my bet'room."

Murphy replied, "Hey man, the only television set on this unit is out in the dayroom. So unless you brought one with you from Metro, then I guess you're just plum out of luck Jamal."

Like a shot, Jamal jumped off of his bed and then got right up into Murphy's face, and in a very intimidating tone of voice he shouted, "Oh yeah, well, we'll just see about that cracker! I want a television set for my bet'room, and I'm gonna make damn sure that I get one, aight!"

Murphy then calmly said, "Well, then you better start saving up your pennies Jamal, because that's the only way that you're ever gonna get a television set in your bedroom."

Jamal then indignantly shouted, "Hey, I ain't gonna waste my time talking to you fool! I'm gonna go talk to your boss down in the gym! He'll fix it for me, you'll see!"

At that point, Jamal pushed Murphy to one side and began strutting up the hallway, so that he could go plead his case to Dick Henderson or to someone in authority.

Jamal got about halfway up the hallway, when all of a sudden Murphy came up from behind and grabbed Jamal around his midsection. Apparently, Murphy was attempting to do one of the wrap-up techniques that he learned about in last week's training class.

And even though Murphy's technique may have been technically incorrect, it certainly proved to be quite effective in wrapping-up someone who is as big and strong as Jamal.

Although Murphy seemed to have the situation well under control, I on the other hand was an absolute nervous wreck. And at that point, I was ready to call out the National Guard.

As Jamal struggled to set himself free, he was calling Murphy every dirty name in the book, and I was utterly appalled by the filthy language that was gushing out of Jamal's mouth.

Yet, Murphy didn't seem fazed in the least.

Murphy then quietly said, "Jamal, you've got two choices, you can either calm down and I'll let you go, or else I'm gonna have to wrestled you down to the floor. It's your choice, bro."

So realizing that his chances of breaking loose from Murphy's grasp was somewhere between slim and none, Jamal cunningly replied, "Okay man, I'll calm down, I promise, aight!"

Murphy took Jamal at his word, and then relaxed his hold from around Jamal's waist. Once free, Jamal turned towards Murphy. And as Jamal stood toe-to-toe with Murphy, he had his fists clenched in fighting position, and he had a look of absolute rage on his face as well.

Although my gut was telling me that Jamal was getting ready to attack, Murphy never flinched a muscle, as he simply stood his ground and waited for Jamal to make the first move.

As the Mexican standoff continued, Jamal suddenly snapped out of his temporary state of insanity, and then said with a smile, "Hey man, do you play basketball as good as you fight?"

Murphy laughed out loud, and then good-naturedly replied, "Well, I'm pretty good at both Jamal, but I'd rather play basketball."

"Phew, crisis averted!" I thought to myself.

I gotta say that I was really impressed with Murphy this morning. Murphy was able to single-handedly defuse a potentially dangerous situation by using his wits instead of his brawn.

Gee, maybe I'll be the one who will be learning a few things from Murphy, instead of Murphy learning a few things from me.

For the rest of the morning, Murphy and I hung out on L.U. 512, so that we could get to know some of the clients a little bit better.

Later that afternoon, Murphy made good on his promise and challenged Jamal to a one-on-one basketball game. And as it turns out, Jamal wasn't the player that he professed to be.

Although Jamal possesses some raw talent, his overall game leaves a lot to be desired. He seems to enjoy playing a very physical brand of basketball, such as, pushing, shoving, throwing elbows, and using whatever intimidation tactics he has at his disposal to defeat his opponent.

Then again, let's not forget that Jamal is a product of the playground, where playing by the rules doesn't necessarily apply, and the only thing that really matters is winning at all costs.

So while Murphy was playing basketball down in the gym, I decided to take some clients into the laundry workshop, so that I could assess what types of work skills they had.

Some of the records from Metro Psychiatric Center indicated that several of the clients had some prior work experience, and were hoping to earn some money here at the State School.

Well, based on what I saw, the vocational talent that I just inherited left a lot to be desired. And even the clients who I thought were capable were actually quite marginal at best.

But then this shouldn't come as any big surprise, especially when all of the reports were written by a bunch of bleeding-heart social workers, who seem to have an affinity to exaggerate the positives and downplay the negatives, and often look at life through rose-colored glasses.

So as Murphy and I were leaving for the day, we swapped a few war stories regarding our day. I told Murphy that the pickings in the laundry workshop were pretty slim, whereas Murphy surprised me by saying that he is actually toying with the idea of organizing a client basketball team, and maybe even challenging some of the local agencies around town to a friendly game.

As I listened to all of Murphy's lofty ideas with regards to organizing a client basketball team, I then amusingly said, "Well Doc, I think that coaching a client basketball team here at the State School has all the earmarks of a "White Shadow" episode."

When Murphy heard me referencing "The White Shadow," he let out a hearty laugh, especially since "The White Shadow" was Murphy's favorite TV program growing up as a kid.

"The White Shadow" was a popular TV show that was aired back in the late

1970's. The show was about a white high school basketball coach named Ken Reeves, who after playing ten years as a professional basketball player, was offered a job to coach the boys varsity basketball team at Carver High School, which was a predominately black inner-city school in Chicago.

Now even though Reeves has never had any experience coaching teenage kids before, he agrees to take the head coaching position, but then quickly realizes that he's spending more time bailing his players out of trouble than actually teaching the boys the game of basketball.

Although the players consider Reeves to be their coach, they also view him as a social worker and a surrogate father figure all rolled up into one. And I'm sure this will certainly be the case for Murphy, when he starts working with the clients on a regular basis here at the SBU.

The next day, Murphy and I spent some time getting to know the clients that resided on L.U. 513. Before stepping onto the living unit, Murphy turned to me and amusingly quipped, "Well Rodney, let's see what kinda basketball talent we'll find on this living unit today, eh."

When we walked onto L.U. 513, the atmosphere was friendly and upbeat, and everyone on the unit seemed to be in exceptionally good spirits. We asked several of the living unit staff what their impressions were of the new recruits. And not only were their comments informative and straight to the point, but as you can only imagine they were also quite funny to say the least.

The one name that seems to be on the tip of everybody's tongue right now was Terrence Morehouse, who apparently views himself as being the undisputed "kingpin" of L.U. 513.

Although Terrence can certainly be quite charming, his records indicate that his behavior can turn on a dime, and he has been known to be pretty violent when he doesn't get his own way.

Around three o'clock, Bobby Diggs and Tommy Gerard were admitted to L.U. 513, along with a third client who is a long time resident of the State School named Johnny Mayfield.

Bobby was all smiles as he walked onto L.U. 513. And if you didn't know any better, you'd almost think that he just won the grand prize for an all-paid vacation to a five-star resort.

Tommy was in his glory too, and it didn't take long for Tommy to start showcasing his incredible savant talents to a brand new live audience.

And then there was Johnny Mayfield, who was guilty of breaking every rule in the book. Johnny has been a constant thorn in the side of every administrator here at the State School for the past thirty years, and his notorious reputation is almost equal to that of Bobby Diggs.

Although I have never had the "pleasure" of working with Johnny Mayfield before, Johnny has compiled a rap sheet a mile long, consisting of a string of petty larcenies and a slew of misguided deeds and wrongdoings that are just too numerous to mention.

Well, today we're scheduled to receive twenty-five new clients. We are expecting twenty female clients for L.U. 511, along with five male clients who will be residing on L.U. 513.

So after Murphy and I snagged our morning coffee, we swung by Dick Henderson's office to see what the game plan was for today.

When we saw Dick, he looked absolutely exhausted. Dick told us that he was called into work around nine o'clock last night, and wound up working into the wee hours of the morning.

Apparently, the female clients who were all scheduled to arrive at 9:00am this morning, actually arrived at 9:00pm last night instead.

When the evening supervisor saw the coach bus pull up in front of the building, he didn't know what to do. So in a state of extreme panic, he wound up calling Dick Henderson at home, so that Dick could come in and try to straighten everything out for him.

So after getting the update from Dick, he asked us to head over to L.U. 511, so that we could introduce ourselves to the new female clients, and to get to know them a little bit better.

As soon as Murphy and I stepped onto L.U. 511, we came upon a rather petite middle-aged woman, who was pacing nervously back and forth inside the front foyer of the living unit.

So at that point, Murphy and I made several attempts at saying "hello" to the woman, but she appeared to be so consumed in her thoughts that she acted as if we weren't even there.

As we started to walk away from her, she seemed to snap out of her apparent funk. She then wanted to know if Murphy or I were either psychiatrists, or just plain old medical doctors.

Before I could even respond, she then asked us if we knew the name of a good lawyer, so that she could retain their services in hopes of taking some sort of legal action against the State.

She then screamed, "I'm being held against my will, and I wanna get the hell out of here right away, so that I can go back to the psychiatric center and be with all of my friends again!"

As we parted company, we wished the woman "good luck" in her quest of finding a good lawyer. And then moments later, we came upon a young lady who appeared to be quite pleasant, and even remarked how handsome Murphy and I both were.

Murphy then whispered on the Q.T., "Why is she here, she seems awfully sweet to me? And, I might add, a fine judge of character too. So far these women seem okay to me, Rodney."

Well, the words no sooner left Murphy's mouth, when out of the shadows appeared this middle-aged black woman, who began pestering us for a cigarette. We then proceeded to tell the woman that neither of us smoked. But even if we did, we weren't allowed to dispense cigarettes to any of the clients, only the living unit staff were permitted to do that.

Needless to say, but that wasn't the response that she wanted to hear, so she started screaming at the top of her lungs, "I want a cigarette, I want a cigarette, I want a cigarette…!"

As Murphy and I scurried away from this extremely disturbed woman, Murphy then turned to me and humorously quipped, "Well, I guess two out of three ain't bad, eh Rodney."

So after having our fill with the ladies on L.U. 511, we then headed over to L.U. 512, so that we could assess the situation over there, and to also find out how the clients fared overnight.

When we spoke with the unit charge for L.U. 512, he was happy to report that the clients were doing fine, and that thus far they have all been well behaved and extremely cooperative.

Well…, with the exception of Jamal Buchanan anyway.

Apparently, Jamal Buchanan is demanding to see his lawyer, so that he can be transferred back to Metro Psychiatric Center because he feels that all of his civil rights are being violated.

So in an attempt to be funny, I then mentioned to the unit charge that one of the female clients on L.U. 511 is shopping around for a lawyer too. So when Jamal is all wrapped up with all of his legal problems, then maybe he can pass his lawyer's phone number along to her.

Around nine-thirty, the clients began to file in to the laundry workshop. Although I wasn't overly impressed with what I saw yesterday, I was hoping that maybe yesterday was nothing more than some first day jitters. What we were asking the clients to do in the Work Activity Center really wasn't all that difficult to do. We simply wanted them to sort and fold laundry in a cooperative manner. And in return, they would be compensated for their efforts.

At this point, I wasn't too worried about how many towels someone could fold, or how proficient they were at sorting or folding laundry. But more interested in knowing if they could all get along with each other without killing one another.

As the clients began working, I walked around the room making some observations and jotting down some notes on my clipboard. Jamal Buchanan was in attendance this morning, and he was working in the back corner of the room next to several of his hommies.

Since day one, Jamal has been hounding me for a job, and telling me that he needs to earn enough money so that he can buy himself a brand new color television set for his bedroom.

As I observed Jamal, he was actually doing a pretty decent job on folding his towels. A little mouthy. But all in all, he was working at a pretty steady pace and not being too disruptive.

When Jamal saw me pass by him, he nonchalantly asked, "Hey Mr. O'Really, what does this job pay, about a hunnert dollars a week?"

I quietly chuckled to myself, as I heard Jamal mispronounce my name. I then corrected him by saying, "Uh Jamal, the name is O'Leary, not O'Really. And as far as your pay goes, but a hundred dollars a week doesn't even close to what you'll be making in this work program."

"Okay, well, how much we gettin' then, fitty dollars?" Jamal impatiently asked.

"Well, uh…, it's kinda complicated Jamal." I said, vaguely.

"Complicated, whatcha you mean complicated. C'mon, man! How much damn money am I gonna get to fold these raggedy-ass towels?"

I then replied, "Well, your pay is based on what's called a time study. Which is then calculated by some kinda formula, and then converted to a percentage of the minimum wage."

Although Jamal was trying very hard to understand what I was saying, I could tell he had no idea what I was talking about. And to be honest, I wasn't 100% sure what I was saying either.

Basically, I was doing a little tap dance around Jamal's question. Because I thought if I could double talk him enough then it might satisfy his curiosity, and prevent him from asking me anymore additional questions about how much money he'll be making in the laundry program.

Although I've had some success in using this tactic before, I was starting to realize that Jamal was smarter than your average bear, and trying to outfox him was not going to be easy.

Once again, Jamal defiantly asked, "C'mon man, I just wanna know how much damn money I'm gonna make, 'cause I wanna buy myself a new color television set for my bet'room!"

Bobby Diggs then decided to open up his big mouth and say, "Hey Jamal, we don't make enough money in this workshop to buy something as nice as a new television set, right Jack?"

Before I could even respond to Bobby's unsolicited comment, Jamal lashed out at me and yelled, "Whatcha talkin' about, fool! This is a bunch of bullshit! I ain't gonna work on no punk-ass job for chump change! And if you think I am, then you're crazier than me, cracker!"

Jamal then balled up the towel that he was folding, and flung it halfway across the room. He then high-tailed it out of the laundry workshop faster than a Wyoming jackrabbit, and the two male staff that were assigned to the work program ran after him in hot pursuit.

Bobby Diggs then had the audacity to say, "Hey Jack, what the heck got into Jamal?"

I just stared at Bobby for a moment, and then said, "Bobby, can you just fold your towels and not say another word please, I think you've already done enough damage for one day, okay."

Obviously, I wish things could've gone better with Jamal this morning, but part of me was relieved that he ran for the hills. I'm beginning to realize that working with these types of clients is like sitting on a powder keg that is ready to explode. Because not only do these clients have a warped sense of reality, but they seem to possess a false sense of entitlement as well.

Now take Terrence Morehouse for example. Although he proclaims to be the undisputed "kingpin" of L.U. 513, the guy can't even fold a halfway decent towel to save his own life.

Yet, despite the fact that Terrence continues to fold one sorry ass towel after the next, he keeps telling everyone that he can't wait to spend all of his cold hard cash on either a brand new color television set, or maybe even a "superfly" stereo boom box.

Uh, Terrence, are you kidding me?

With the measly amount of money that you'll be earning in this work program, you'll be lucky if you can scrape enough pennies together to buy yourself a stale box of Cracker Jack's!

When Terrence finds out how much money he'll actually be making, then he'll probably quit his job, and wind up sitting on the couch right next to Jamal watching TV in the dayroom.

Sad to say, but at this point in the game, I was more interested in keeping a lid on the joint than I was on providing a rich and wholesome work environment for the clients to thrive in.

Around twelve o'clock, Murphy and I met for lunch over at the commissary. As we devoured the "blue plate" special, I filled Murphy in on Jamal Buchanan's Oscar winning performance down in the laundry workshop this morning.

Meanwhile, Murphy had a few entertaining stories of his own. But his morning sounded a heck of a lot more enjoyable than the Greek tragedy that I had to endure.

In the afternoon, I evaluated all of the women on L.U. 511 to see if any of the ladies were suitable for the work program. And based on what I saw, I found the pickings to be mighty slim.

To be fair, I would have to say that there were a couple of women that had some definite potential, and were certainly worthy of consideration for inclusion into the work program. But to be perfectly honest, I found the women to be a lot more difficult to work with than the men.

Apparently, the towel folding technique that I had instructed the ladies to use was totally wrong and completely unacceptable. And at one point, I overheard one of the ladies actually say, "Huh, men, what do they know about doing laundry anyway."

At three-thirty, Murphy and I went over to L.U. 513, so that we could visit with the new batch of clients that arrived this morning. From what the living unit charge conveyed to us, all of the new clients were settling in quite nicely. However, they were still waiting for one more client to arrive this afternoon from Western Psychiatric Center, whose name was Russell Turner.

So when we asked the living unit charge if we could visit with some of the new arrivals, he told us that they were all down at the nurse's station right now having their physicals done.

However, the unit charge did say that Tyrell Freeman, who was the client that we were expecting from Metro Psychiatric Center the other day, was relaxing comfortably down in his room right now if we wanted to visit with him. So Murphy and I decided to take a little stroll down the hallway and introduce ourselves to Tyrell, and to get to know him a little bit better.

When we reached Tyrell's room, we saw that the window shades were drawn and that the room was completely dark. Tyrell's bedroom door was ajar, so we lightly tapped on the door and poked our heads into the room while saying, "Hello Tyrell, do you mind if we come in?"

We then heard a very deep and muffled voice quietly say, "Yessir, c'mon in."

As we entered the bedroom, we saw the figure of a man lying down on his bed with his back completely towards us, and he was all curled up in a ball.

At first, Murphy and I didn't think much of it. But as Tyrell slowly rose to his feet and began to straighten out his frame, we were absolutely shocked by the enormity of his stature.

I quietly mumbled to myself, "Holy shit, look at the size of this guy."

Tyrell stood roughly 7'0 tall, and his massive frame was built out of tungsten steel. Even Murphy, who is a pretty big guy in his own right, looked relatively small standing next to Tyrell.

And in comparison to me, well, let's not even go there.

Quite honestly, but I was totally petrified at that moment. And I was counting my lucky stars that I had Murphy standing right next to me, just in case something went awry.

As I studied Tyrell, I remember reading his case history. Tyrell was a twenty-five year old African-American man, who was born in the deep South. And according to his records, his family decided to move north so that they could pursue a better way of life for themselves.

Tyrell was the youngest of thirteen children. And due to some complications at birth, he developed a slight learning disability, which has prevented him from living a more fruitful life.

When Tyrell was eight years old, he inadvertently set fire to an apartment house, and it resulted in ten people being tragically killed.

Due to the severity of the incident, Tyrell's family was forced to relinquish him into the care of Child Protective Services. And from that point on, Tyrell became a ward of the State.

So there we were, - standing in the middle of Tyrell's bedroom engaged in nothing more than a staring match. And at that point, neither Murphy nor I knew exactly what to do next.

Suddenly, I found the courage to say, "So, uh…, how ya doin', Tyrell? My name is Jack O'Leary, and this man's name is Murphy Doherty." We then proceeded to shake Tyrell's hand.

I then asked Tyrell, "So Tyrell, I was just wondering if you might be interested in having a job here in the building and earning some money?"

Tyrell replied, in his soft southern drawl, "Yessir, I'd like that very much."

Murphy then piped up, and excitedly said, "Hey Tyrell, have you ever played any basketball?"

I quickly glanced at Murphy, and then cracked an appreciative smile.

"Uh, yeah, some…," Tyrell quietly said.

"Great, 'cause I'm seriously thinking of organizing a basketball team here in the building. Hey, would you like to play on our team, Tyrell?" Murphy asked, with bated breath.

As I listened to Murphy pose the question to Tyrell, Murphy reminded me of a college scout, who was trying to recruit the most highly coveted and sought after player in the country. And needless to say, but a "blue chip" player that every coach was dying to get their hands on.

Tyrell replied, with a quiet smile, "Um, yeah, sure, I'll play. It sounds like a lotta fun."

I then curiously asked, "So Tyrell, do you work out with weights or barbells at all?"

"Um, no sir." Tyrell replied, in a very matter-of-fact way.

Quite honestly, but if you didn't know any better, you'd almost think that Tyrell was an avid bodybuilder. Not only did Tyrell have massive size, but he had incredible definition as well.

I shudder to think what would happen if Tyrell ever lost his temper and became violent, because the only way we would ever be able to subdue him is by using a high powered dart gun.

"Well, it was nice chatting with ya, Tyrell. And maybe tomorrow we can see what kinda work skills you have down in the laundry program." I said, optimistically.

Murphy then chimed in and spiritedly said, "Yeah, and maybe tomorrow we'll get you down in the gym and see what kinda game you got too, Tyrell."

"Yessir, thank you, sir." Tyrell said, humbly.

As we left Tyrell's room, I was thinking that he may possibly be one of the kindest and most gentle human beings that I have ever met. There was a certain pureness about Tyrell, and I was really looking forward to working with him tomorrow in the Work Activity Center.

When Murphy and I exited L.U. 513, we bumped into Mary Beth, who is the building social worker. Mary Beth was standing outside the living unit door conversing with two men.

One of the men she was speaking with was wearing a fancy three piece suit, and the other man was casually dressed in a flannel shirt with some faded blue jeans and worn leather boots.

Upon seeing us, Mary Beth interrupted her conversation with the two men, so that she could introduce them to us. Mary Beth then proceeded to say, "Hi Jack, hi Murphy, hey, I'd like you both to meet Russell Turner, who will be residing on L.U. 513."

Murphy and I both smiled, and then I extended my hand to the man who was dressed in the flannel shirt and faded blue jeans. I then cordially said, "It's very nice to meet ya, Russell. My name is Jack O'Leary, and I'm in charge of the work program here in the building."

As we shook hands, I couldn't help notice how strangely the guy was looking at me.

I then heard the other man, who was dressed in the three piece suit, sarcastically say, "Hey buddy, whatta ya stupid or somethin'? He's not Russell Turner, I am!"

All of a sudden, Murphy and Mary Beth began laughing hysterically. However, the man that I was shaking hands with wasn't the least bit amused, especially since I just mistook him for being a client.

As I apologized to the man in the flannel shirt, I could hear Russell Turner laughing his ass off in the background, and he seemed to be taking a great deal of pleasure in mocking me.

The following day, Jamal Buchanan decided to join us for the morning work session. I haven't spoken to Jamal since yesterday's incident, so I'm not really sure why he decided to give the work program another try.

But if I had to guess, I would probably say that the living unit staff made him an offer that he couldn't refuse, so that they wouldn't have to be stuck with him all morning on the unit.

As I watched Jamal hamming it up with all of his hommies in the back corner of the room, he had a real cocky look on his face, which indicated to me that he probably didn't learn a damn thing from yesterday's drama.

When our eyes crossed paths there was no sign of remorse, or even the slightest attempt on his part to extend the olive branch. Well, I'm sure that Jamal blames me for what happened yesterday anyway, and he probably thinks that he's doing me a big favor by being here today.

Oh well, let's just see where the morning takes us. And let's hope that yesterday's mishap was nothing more than a minor misunderstanding, or a mere bump in the road.

Thus far, Bobby and Jamal seem to be my two biggest challenges in the morning work group.

Or should I say, - my two biggest headaches!

Bobby and Jamal both have very strong personalities, and neither one of them is willing to give the other an inch. It seems like all they want to do when they walk through the door is bicker with one another, - from the moment they arrive, to the moment that they finally leave.

On a more positive note, Tyrell Freeman seems to have made a very smooth transition into the work program. And I can definitely see him as being the stabilizing force of the group.

In terms of the afternoon work group, it was shaping up to be just as animated as the morning group, with Russell Turner starring as our featured headliner for the afternoon matinee.

Every afternoon when Russell arrives to work, he waltzes into the room as if he owns the joint. He's loud and obnoxious, and enjoys barking out orders to everyone working around him.

He'll even order me around too!

Russell actually worked five years in the laundry plant at Western Psychiatric Center, so I guess Russell considers himself to be an expert on laundry, and my unofficial right hand man.

Wow, lucky me!

Whenever one of the clients has a question, Russell will drop whatever he's doing and run straight over to me, so that he can assess the situation and then give me his two-cents worth.

Quite frankly, but the more I get to know Russell Turner, the more glaring his sociopathic personality disorder seems to be. On the surface, Russell appears to be quite capable. But as you slowly peel back the layers of his personality, I'm finding that he's crazier than a shithouse rat.

While at Western Psychiatric Center, Russell was responsible for operating some heavy-duty machinery, such as, fork lifts, laundry presses, and industrial washer machines and dryers.

Now as impressive as that might be, it should also be noted that Russell has some major anger management problems as well. And he has been known to put the fear of God into people.

And even people that he considers to be his closest friends too!

While at Western Psychiatric Center, Russell was charged with several felonies, such as, assault and battery, lewd sexual misconduct, and wielding a dangerous weapon with the explicit intent to do serious bodily harm, which wound up buying Russell six months in the county jail.

So having said all of that, I actually approached Russell one afternoon and asked him if he would entertain the idea of teaching Terrence Morehouse how to fold a neater looking towel.

Russell and Terrence reside on the same living unit, and they have actually grown to become pretty good friends. Naturally, I just assumed that Russell would want to jump at the chance to help out his bosom buddy Terrence. After all, friends enjoy helping out friends, right?

So after floating the idea by Russell, I was a bit surprised when I heard him say, "Okay, I'll help Terrence out. But, uh…, what's in it for me?"

I told Russell that if he agreed to help me out with Terrence Morehouse, then I would treat him to lunch. So after giving it some thought, Russell replied, "Okay Jack, you got a deal."

Initially, Terrence was thrilled with the idea that Russell was willing to help him out with his towel folding problems. But after two minutes of putting up with Russell's constant criticism, Terrence wound up blowing his stack, and simply unloaded on Russell as he shouted, "Hey, white boy, I ain't your nigger! Who the hell do you think you are talking to me like that, boy!"

Suddenly, the entire room came to a screeching halt. Terrence was so angry at Russell that his eyes were bulging right out of his head, and he was actually snorting like a Brahma bull.

Terrence then hauled off and punched Russell right in the jaw, causing Russell to stagger momentarily, and then collapsing to the floor. The staff was quick to intervene, and then whisked Terrence Morehouse right out of the laundry workshop and escorted him back to his living unit.

As Terrence exited the room, he kept shouting at the top of his lungs, "Keep that fuckin' white boy away from me! Keep that fuckin' white boy away from me! Keep that fuckin'…!"

When I glanced over at Russell Turner, he was lying flat on his back with his arms and legs completely sprawled out on the floor. And from the glassy look in his eye, I could tell that he was still feeling the effects of that haymaker that Terrence Morehouse just landed on his jaw.

As I helped Russell up to his feet, he actually had the audacity to ask me what day I was taking him out to lunch, and what type of punishment I was intending to dole out to Terrence.

I just stared at Russell, and then said in utter disbelief, "Russell, are you kidding me? Do you realize how belittling you were to Terrence? You should be totally ashamed of yourself."

Russell just looked at me in a rather dumbfounded way, and he had absolutely no idea what I was referring to. He then shrugged his shoulders, and said with a big smirk on his face, "Hey, I don't know why you're so mad at me, especially since I'm the one who got punched. I was only trying to help the guy out. I can't help it if Terrence is dumber than a box of rocks!"

As Murphy and I were leaving for the day, he asked me how my day was. Before I could even answer him, Murphy blurted out, "Boy Rodney, I can't believe that I'm getting paid to play basketball, floor hockey, and kick ball every day. This job is absolutely amazing!"

I then seemed to take some self-pity on myself, as I quietly mumbled, "Well, I got to referee a fight in the workshop this afternoon."

Obviously, I was happy for Murphy. But I guess when it came right down to it, I was feeling a little bit sorry for myself too.

On the drive home, I knew that I had to figure out a way to make this job work for me, or else I was headed straight for the loony bin.

And with the way my luck has been running lately, I might even wind up working right next to Jamal Buchanan, and folding some raggedy-ass towels for some lousy "chump change."

Huh, now wouldn't that be poetic justice!

CHAPTER EIGHT

Well, it's the start of a brand new week. And as I was driving into work this morning, my mind was totally consumed in thinking about the zany cast of characters that I have working for me down in the laundry workshop.

This unusual array of personalities then prompted me to think about a TV show back in the late 1970's that I would religiously watch as a kid called, "The Bowery Boys."

"The Bowery Boys" was a slapstick comedy about a gang of street-wise teenage punks, who all lived in the same neighborhood. This precocious band of hoodlums were basically good kids by nature. But for some reason, trouble always seemed to follow them wherever they went.

One minute the boys would be linked to a suspicious crime in the neighborhood, and then moments later, you'd see them helping a little old lady with a bagful of groceries crossing the street.

Yeah, "The Bowery Boys," that pretty much describes who I have working for me down in the laundry workshop.

So is it any wonder why I'm losing my hair, or why I can't get a good night's sleep?

As I headed down to my office, I prayed that this week wouldn't be a repeat performance of last week.

Last week, the clients argued more than they actually worked. And if I allow this type of chaos to continue, then my days of working here in the SBU will certainly be numbered.

Although there were some real positives to draw upon from last week, my mind kept reverting back to the constant turmoil that seemed to occur. In order for me to survive in this job, then I better find a way to minimize all of these disruptive behaviors that keep happening over and over again, so that I can attempt to cultivate a more stable and conducive work environment.

To be honest, but I didn't think that any of my expectations were all that unreasonable. I simply wanted the clients to follow a few rules, and to work to the best of their abilities.

Oh yeah, - and try not to kill each other!

So seeing how I was at a total impasse on how to proceed, I decided to bounce a few ideas off of Cameron, who is the building psychologist. Perhaps getting a different perspective on things might help remedy the situation, so that I would be less tempted to take the bridge.

Cameron, who is a really nice guy and one of the smartest people that I know, has a PhD in cognitive behavioral psychology. And although his methods in shaping behavior may seem a bit unorthodox, his track record for achieving positive results was simply off the charts.

So after explaining the situation to Cameron, he suggested a few ideas that might help level the playing field, so that I could deal more effectively with the clients in the work program.

One of the ideas that Cameron suggested was to jot down some general rules, and then post them on the grease board that was mounted on the front wall of the Work Activity Center.

Cameron thought that a visual aid may help eliminate some confusion on the part of the clients, and provide them with a better understanding of what my expectations of them were.

So when the clients filed in for the morning work session, they quickly took note of the list of rules that were posted on the grease board in the front of the room.

Before commencing with the morning's work, I took a few minutes to review the rules, so that the clients had a better understanding as to what the expectations of the program were.

So after reading each rule aloud, I then asked all of the clients if they had any questions. Although no one said a word, I could hear the wheels in the back of their heads slowly grinding.

At that point, I strongly urged everyone in the room to learn the rules and to abide by them. Because infractions would not be tolerated, and could possibly result in privilege loss.

As the clients proceeded to get down to work, my eye seemed to be drawn to the back corner of the room where Jamal Buchanan was working. I noticed that Jamal had a big smirk on his face, and I could hear him making some rather insidious remarks about Bobby Diggs and Russell Turner to some of his hommies that were all working in close proximity to him.

It's certainly no secret that Bobby and Russell rub Jamal the wrong way. Mainly because they're white, but also because Bobby and Russell are two of the alpha dogs in the building who are constantly competing with Jamal for top dog honors.

As I inched closer to Jamal, the disparaging remarks that he was making towards Bobby and Russell were riddled with racially charged overtones, which were just too vile to mention.

Although this is typical behavior for Jamal, I'm not really sure if he knew that he was violating any of the rules that I had just posted on the grease board in the front of the room.

Then again, maybe Jamal doesn't care about the rules, and he was simply challenging my authority, so that he could see just how far I would permit him to go before I had to step in.

By now, the whole back corner of the room had stopped working. Jamal had managed to amass a captive audience. And as he played to the crowd, he was spewing nothing but hatred and bigotry towards Bobby Diggs and Russell Turner, and for all white people for that matter.

Well, I guess Jamal's distain for white people shouldn't come as any big surprise to me.

After all, Jamal came from a facility that was 99.9% black, and any mention of white people in the black community was usually referenced in an extremely negative context.

Well, maybe in time I'll be able to break through the color barrier, and change Jamal's way of thinking about white people. But for now, I'll just need to put my Pollyanna thoughts on the back burner, so that I can deal with the problem at hand, and put an immediate halt to all of this hateful rhetoric that is being tossed around the back corner of the room by Jamal Buchanan.

As Jamal continued to speak ill of Bobby and Russell, he was tossing around words and phrases that I had never heard before, and language that was exclusive to the black community.

Jamal sounded like he was back in his old neighborhood, hanging with his hommies, and blaming white people for all of the atrocities and injustices that existed in the black community.

As the back corner of the room continued to hang on Jamal's every word, Jamal then cried out, "Yo, that white boy Bobby won't be messin' with me no mo'. And neither will any of his other white honky friends, 'cause I'll kick all of their bitch ass vanilla behinds, aight!"

"Damn straight, Jamal!" Jerome shouted, as he laughed heartily.

Well, at that point, I had just about enough of Jamal's wiseass racist remarks. And when Jamal saw me walking towards him, his cocky smile quickly vanished.

I then calmly said, "Gee, it sounds like you guys are having a little party back here. Hey Jamal, do me a favor, will ya. Can you please tell me what Rule #3 says up on the grease board?"

Jamal looked directly up at the grease board that was mounted on the front wall of the room, and in a slow and deliberate tone of voice, he then read aloud, "Rule #3, - There will be no harsh words toward others."

I quietly answered, "Uh-huh, yeah, that's right, Jamal. Now wouldn't you say that you were speaking harshly about Bobby Diggs a few minutes ago?"

Jamal thought a moment, and then said with a straight face, "Well, yeah, I guess so. But that cracker Bobby ain't even here right now. So then why you trippin' about it, Mr. O'Really?"

"Listen Jamal, whether someone is here or not shouldn't make any difference. I don't wanna hear you talking smack at all, especially when I'm paying you to fold towels, okay?"

"Yeah, okay, that's cool! Hey, we're sorry Mr. O'Really, we didn't know." Jamal said, in a real wiseass tone.

"Uh Jamal, the name is O'Leary, not O'Really, okay."

"Aight!" Jamal answered, with his usual cocky grin.

"Alright, now let's get back to work. And if I have to come back over here again and talk to you about this, then you'll find yourself on privilege loss, got it?" I said, rather sharply.

As I turned to walk away, I wasn't sure if Jamal would try to sucker punch me or not. Jamal is diagnosed as having an antisocial personality disorder, and people who suffer from this type of mental illness are usually prone to violent outbursts, especially when they are confronted.

Actually, I was almost tempted to glance back at Jamal. But then thought better of it, because Jamal might think that it was a sign of weakness, and that maybe I was afraid of him.

Anyway, Jamal just decided to let the matter go. So he went back to folding his towels again, as if the entire incident had never happened.

As the clients were filing into the workshop for the afternoon work session, Bobby and Russell were already bickering with one another, and they were literally at each other's throats.

Before commencing with the afternoon's work, I asked everyone in the room to take note of the grease board that was mounted on the wall in the front of the room, so that I could review the rules of the workshop with them.

So after reading each rule aloud, I then made it perfectly clear to everyone in the room that infractions to the rules would not be tolerated, and could even result in privilege loss.

I then looked directly at Bobby Diggs and Russell Turner, and in a quiet but stern voice, I said, "Uh, Bobby, Russell, do either of you have any questions regarding the rules? Because in the five minutes that you've been here, you've already broken at least three of them, okay?"

Neither Bobby nor Russell uttered a single word, because the last thing they wanted right now was to dig themselves an even deeper hole than the one that they were already standing in.

Well, it's been a couple of months now since the SBU opened its doors. And aside from a few brush fires, everything seems to be going along quite well. Dick couldn't be happier with what he has seen thus far, and even Mr. Hanson threw us a compliment at our last staff meeting.

Murphy and I still manage to eat lunch together every day, and we're never at a loss for words in swapping stories regarding some of the wild and crazy things that the clients say or do.

In terms of organizing a client basketball team, Murphy seems to be keeping his promise, and he's already contacted some of the local agencies in town, such as the ARC and Catholic Charities, in hopes of scheduling a few friendly games with them in the not so distant future.

As a matter of fact, Murphy is even toying with the idea of organizing a client softball team this summer as well. And he's already asked Dick Henderson to requisition him some new softball equipment, so that Murphy can start practicing with the guys out on the softball field.

Although the field hasn't been used in years, Dick has given us his solemn word that the field will be up and running by Spring, and Murphy says that the guys are pretty excited about it.

Now that I've established some semblance of law and order in the Work Activity Center, I've recently discovered some dissention in the ranks. It seems as though Bobby, Jamal, Russell, and Terrence are all sick and tired of doing laundry, and they would prefer to do something else.

Initially, when the four horseman approached me on the subject, I thought they had some pretty legitimate grips. But after listening to some of their ideas on what they would prefer to do instead of laundry, I found their work alternatives to be a little far-fetched and totally unrealistic.

As a matter of fact, I was almost tempted to suggest to the four amigos that maybe they should schedule a counseling session with Cameron, so that he could remind them that they all suffer from delusions of grandeur, and that perhaps they were setting their sights a little too high regarding the types of work that they envisioned themselves doing in the Work Activity Center.

Now ordinarily when the clients have a complaint, they'll usually spit and sputter about it for a couple of days or so. But then as time goes by, they eventually seem to forget all about it.

However, the SBU clients are not exactly taking this same type of approach. And for the past three months, the clients have been hounding me every day to provide them with something else to do besides laundry. And quite honestly, but I don't know if I can put them off any longer.

Jamal, Bobby, Russell, and Terrence can be utterly relentless when it comes to badgering the staff to get what they want. And now that they've elected Bobby as their spokesman, I guess you could say that they were pulling out all the stops, and trying to play every angle in the book.

There's certainly no doubt in my mind that Bobby probably told his fellow compadres that he could talk me into just about anything, especially since Bobby and I have "enjoyed" a prior working relationship together.

The day that I met with Bobby, I thought he made a pretty compelling argument. Bobby said that only working on laundry every day was stunting his vocational growth. And if he's ever lucky enough to leave the State School someday, then his chances for living a more fruitful life would be greatly enhanced if he had a broader range of vocational opportunities to choose from.

Well, I guess I really couldn't argue with that line of thinking.

In wrapping up my meeting with Bobby, he decided to lay it on thick by saying that I was the best counselor that he has ever had here at the State School. And that the next time he sees the Director, he is going to tell him that I should be nominated for employee of the year.

As I listened to Bobby sweet talk the hell out of me, he sounded slicker than a used car salesman. But I guess if I were in Bobby's shoes, then I probably would've done the same thing.

Bobby learned a long time ago, - that when it comes to getting what you want, then you usually catch more flies with honey than you do with vinegar. But Bobby has become such a good bullshit artist over the years, that one never knows if he's being truthful, or if he's simply telling you what you want to hear.

Anyway, despite the Oscar winning performance that Bobby just gave me, I finally had to tell him that the only type of work that I could offer in the Work Activity Center was laundry.

And why you may ask?

Well, because Kramer would much rather settle for mediocrity, then take a chance on developing any work programs here at the State School that were cutting edge, especially if it meant that he might have to use his precious operating certificates from the DOL as collateral.

Kramer's motto has always been, - "status quo is the way to go!"

And take it from me, but the last thing that Kramer wants to do is to kick up any dust with the Department of Labor, or draw any undue attention to himself or any of the vocational programs that we have in operation here at the State School.

As far as I'm concerned, Kramer is quite content to just sit back and fly under the radar, so that he doesn't have to explain himself or his actions to any of the federal watchdog agencies.

Lest we forget, but Kramer's operating certificates from the Department of Labor is the only thing that's keeping him in a job around here.

So as long as Kramer can tread lightly, and try not to stir the pot too much, then his first-class ticket on the gravy train will continue to be punched.

In the meantime, Kramer expects all of his subordinates to be as loyal as the family dog. And to not burden him with any innovative or radical ideas that might arouse the suspicions of the Department of Labor, and possibly place his precious operating certificates in jeopardy.

Well, the work week was finally over and I was happy to be walking out the door. It was time for me to head home and spend a relaxing weekend with my wife Christine, and to forget all about the Bowery Boys for a few days and all of the craziness that the State School has to offer.

As I walked into the apartment, I couldn't wait to pop open a beer, prop my feet up on the coffee table, and just chill out for a little while before dinner. As I reached into the refrigerator, I heard Christine's voice frantically call out, "Jack, come quick! There's water all over the floor!"

Upon hearing Christine's pleas for help, my immediate thought was, "Shit! A broken water pipe, - that's not exactly the way that I wanted to start my weekend off."

Christine shouted again, "Jack, where are you! I need you to come in here right away!"

I ran towards the bathroom, but Christine wasn't there.

Christine kept shouting, "Jack! Jack! Jack!"

The only other place in the apartment to look was in the bedroom. As I darted towards the bedroom, I kept scratching my head as to what possible water problems we could be having in there. Especially since it was a bright sunny day, and there wasn't a single cloud in the sky.

When I entered the bedroom, I saw Christine hunched over the bed with a towel draped around her midsection and she was crying inconsolably. She was standing over a puddle of water that had pooled on the floor below her.

Christine turned to me, and with a great deal of anguish in her voice she sobbed, "You better call the doctor, because we need to get to the hospital right away! My water just broke!"

"Oh, my God!" I hysterically replied.

Christine wasn't due to have the baby for at least another week, so you can only imagine how frantic I was at that point. I quickly ran towards the kitchen and dialed the number for the obstetrician's office. When the receptionist answered the phone, I told her that I was Christine O'Leary's husband, and that Christine's water just broke and we were on our way to the hospital.

To which she replied, "Okay Mr. O'Leary, I'll notify the doctor right away!"

When we pulled up to the emergency room, an orderly was already waiting for us outside the entranceway with a wheelchair, so that he could transport Christine up to the maternity floor.

As we stepped into the elevator, I was shaking like a leaf. However, Christine was calm, cool, and collected, and she kept reassuring me that everything was going to be alright.

Christine reached for my hand, and then gently said, "C'mon Jack, you gotta try and pull yourself together, okay. You're a trained counselor, remember."

I anxiously replied, "Yeah, I know, but I'm only good at helping other people," which prompted the hospital orderly who was in the elevator with us to quietly chuckle to himself.

Suddenly, the elevator doors flew wide open, and two nurses then whisked Christine towards the delivery room. Although Christine was in quite a bit of discomfort, she still managed to bring the two nurses up to speed on her current medical condition.

She even told the nurses how far apart her contractions were too!

Christine actually works as a registered nurse right here on the maternity unit, so I knew that she would be well-cared for and in very capable hands.

One of the nurses then instructed me to put on a hospital gown, so that I could join Christine in the delivery room, and assist with the birth of the baby.

Quite honestly, but I was so rattled at that point that I couldn't figure out how to put the damn hospital gown on correctly, so the nurse had to put the hospital gown on for me.

As I entered the delivery room, it suddenly dawned on me that I had completely forgotten all of my Lamaze training. But as General Custer valiantly said to the brave and courageous men of the 7th Cavalry, as he ordered the bugler to sound the charge at the Battle of the Little Big Horn, "There's no turning back now men!"

So keeping that in mind, I was fully resigned to the fact that I essentially had to wing it, so I took my place right next to Christine, and tried to coach her through the delivery to the best of my abilities.

Despite all of Christine's hard work in trying to push the baby down the birth canal, her efforts were in vain, and you could feel the tension that was mounting in the room.

Christine's voice then rose above the clamor and commotion, as she kept calling out to the doctor, "What's wrong! What's wrong! Why won't the baby come out?"

In a calm and gentle voice, the doctor then explained to Christine that her pelvis was too narrow for the baby to slide down the birth canal. And that in order for him to deliver the baby, then he would need to perform a Caesarian section.

Obviously, that wasn't the answer that Christine wanted to hear. And as Christine began to sob, it thoroughly shook me to the core, especially since this was the first time in our marriage that I was unable to help the one person in my life who meant so much to me.

The doctor then turned towards me, and in a quiet and soothing voice he said, "I'm sorry Jack, but you'll need to step out into the waiting room now, so that we can prep Christine for surgery. But don't worry, because everything is going to be just fine."

As I turned to leave the delivery room, Christine grabbed my arm and nervously pleaded, "Jack, say a prayer that the baby will be all right, okay."

One of the scrub nurses then escorted me out into the waiting area. But before she headed back into the delivery room again, she confidently said, "Don't worry Mr. O'Leary, we'll make damn sure that nothing happens to Christine or the baby. After all, she's one of ours."

I can't remember how long I sat in the waiting room. The only thing I do remember was reciting the rosary a couple of times, and praying to God that everything would turn out alright.

Suddenly, I looked up and saw the waiting room door swing wide open, and a pleasant sounding voice then eagerly say, "Hello, Mr. O'Leary, would you like to meet your son now?"

"A boy! Is the baby okay? And how is Christine doing?" I asked, alarmingly.

The surgical nurse smiled, and then replied, "Both mother and child are doing just fine."

So after slipping on a new hospital gown, we then headed down to the nursery.

As I nervously inched toward the bassinette, I couldn't believe my eyes. Because what I saw laying right there in front of me was nothing short of a miracle.

The nurse gently picked up my son, who was wrapped snugly in a warm blue blanket. She then turned towards me, and proudly remarked, "He's absolutely perfect. Congratulations, dad! So have you thought of a name yet?"

"Um, yes, his name is Rory." I quietly said, as I couldn't stop taking my eyes off of him.

As the nurse placed Rory in my arms, I was still trying to process the fact that this tiny little human was actually ours. I then asked the nurse, "So when can I see Christine?"

She replied, "Well, Christine is still a bit groggy at the moment. Tell ya what, why don't you hang out here in the nursery with Rory for a few minutes, and I'll go down to the Recovery Room and check on how she's doing."

When the nurses finally wheeled Christine down to the nursery, she looked absolutely exhausted. Her face was all puffy and swollen, and completely covered with red splotches of petechiae, due to the excessive strain that she endured during childbirth.

Although Christine was still woozy, she seemed to perk up a bit the minute she saw me holding Rory in my arms, as she smiled and then lovingly said, "Jack, isn't he beautiful?"

At that moment, I was so overcome with emotion that I was simply unable to speak. So I just quietly nodded my head and smiled, as I continued to hold little Rory gently in my arms.

Christine then told the nurses that she was feeling really tired, and that she would like to go back to her room now so that she could lie down and hold Rory for a little while.

While Christine was getting situated down in her room, I decided to make a few phone calls, and proudly announce to the world that there was a new sprig on the O'Leary family tree.

So after making my phone calls, I headed down to Christine's room to see her and the baby. Christine was caressing Rory in her arms, and stroking the top of his head ever so gently.

I could tell that Christine was starting to feel the effects from all of the analgesics that were pumping through her body. Christine was fighting to stay awake so that she could savor the moment, but her efforts in thwarting the Sandman were seemingly in vain.

Before succumbing to inescapable slumber, she joyously mumbled under her

breath over and over again, "Jack, isn't he beautiful, isn't he beautiful, isn't he beau…
…"

As Christine lay sleeping, I sat in the chair next to her bed with Rory fast asleep in my arms. As I gazed at Rory, I still couldn't believe that this tiny little miracle was actually ours.

Christine kept drifting in and out of consciousness. And when she stirred, she would ask me over and over again if the baby was okay. The nurses kept popping into the room every five minutes to check on Christine, and they doted on her as if she were the only patient on the unit.

Around midnight, the charge nurse suggested that I go home and get some rest. She gave me her solemn word that she would call me if any unforeseen developments arose. But as far as she was concerned, Christine and the baby were doing just fine and that things couldn't be better.

When I arrived at the hospital the next day, Christine was sitting up in her chair cuddling with Rory, and she looked dramatically better today than she did yesterday. Christine remarked how well Rory did overnight with his breast feeding, and she couldn't get over what a voracious appetite her little man had, which then prompted me to say, "Well, I'm not surprised to hear that in the least, because the O'Leary men love to eat!"

Christine then handed Rory over to me, so that I could hold him for a little while. As I held Rory in my arms, I began chuckling at all of the funny little faces that he was making as he squirmed to get comfortable.

A few moments later, we heard some loud crackling noises, as if popcorn was popping in the microwave. Christine and I began to laugh, because these crackling noises could only mean one thing and one thing only, - that Rory was filling up his diaper.

Christine then asked, with a bit of a sly grin, "So Dad, are you ready to change your first diaper now?"

I hesitantly replied, "Well, I guess now is as good a time as any, right?"

Christine then patted me on the back, as she good-humoredly said, "Don't worry rookie, I'll coach you through it. The baby wipes are on the shelf, and there's a package of diapers over on the night stand."

As I gently placed Rory down on the bed, his chubby little arms and legs were flailing in every direction. I took a deep breath, and then carefully peeled back the sticky plastic tabs that held the disposable diaper in place.

When I lowered the front flap of the diaper, I was shocked by the enormous amount of pasty brown soil and debris that was confined in that little space. I glanced at Christine, and then said in total disbelief, "Whoa…! I had no idea that it would be this messy, and smelly!"

Christine chuckled, and then teased me by saying, "Oh yeah, so what did you think, - that it was all going to be rolled up into a nice little ball, and smell just like a bouquet of roses?"

As I attempted to clean up Rory, I seemed to be doing more dabbing than wiping. I could hear Christine snickering in the background, especially since I had no idea what I was doing.

Christine was coaching me by humorously saying, "C'mon, ya big sissy, you don't need to be so dainty about it. Just get right in there and clean him up. Oh, and make sure that you get in all of his little tiny cracks and crevices too."

"Like this?" I asked.

"Yeah, kinda...," she replied, with a bit of a sarcastic grin.

When I was finally done cleaning up Rory, I must've gone through at least a half a box of baby wipes. Which from my perspective wasn't too bad, especially since it was my first time in the batter's box.

As the day wore on, I wound up changing Rory's diaper at least five or six more times. And by nightfall, I was getting to be a real expert at it.

In the afternoon, Murphy and Colleen came up to the hospital to congratulate us on the birth of the baby. Rory looked so tiny in Murphy's massive arms. Murphy and Colleen didn't stay too long because Christine was starting to fade, and Rory was getting a little fussy.

Nevertheless, it was good to see our dear friends, even if only for a short while anyway.

So for the next couple of days, I was spending virtually every waking moment up at the hospital with Christine and Rory. Christine was getting stronger and stronger every day, and Rory looked like he had already doubled in size.

Despite the fact that I've thoroughly enjoyed every minute up at the hospital, I was still quite eager to bring Christine and Rory home with me. And if everything goes according to plan, then the doctor will probably discharge Christine and the baby sometime tomorrow morning.

The following day, Christine asked me to swing by the bakery and pick up three large platters of cookies for each of the three shifts on the maternity unit. I must say that the maternity staff really went above and beyond the call of duty for us these past few days, and Christine and I will always be eternally grateful and forever in their debt.

Around ten-thirty, Christine's obstetrician stopped by the room to see how she was doing, and to address any questions or concerns that she might have. So after reviewing Christine's chart and then talking with her for a few minutes, he decided to discharge Christine and the baby.

On the ride home from the hospital, I kept thinking of ways that I could be a good father and a positive role model for Rory.

At one point, I started to burst out into laughter, which then prompted Christine to curiously ask, "What's so funny?"

I casually replied, "Oh nothing, I was just thinking that I need to clean up my act a bit, that's all."

Christine seemed somewhat surprised by my unexpected remark, and then inquisitively asked, "So what's that supposed to mean?"

I answered, "Well, I need to make more of a conscious effort to start improving on things, such as my eating habits, my grooming, and my occasional crude language."

Christine chuckled, and then asked in an astounded tone, "So what brought this on?"

I replied, "Well, we're parents now, and I need to set a good example for Rory."

Christine paused a moment, and then humorously quipped, "Gee, if I knew you were going to have an epiphany like this, then I would've lobbied to have a baby a long time ago."

Later that afternoon, Murphy and his family came by the apartment to welcome us home. Not only did they bring us a lovely dinner, but they brought us a mouthwatering dessert as well.

So while the girls were busy "oohing and ahhing" over the baby, Murphy and I were doing what we do best, which was adjourning to the living room with an ice cold drink and a hearty plate of food, as we watched the ballgame on TV.

As Murphy and I enjoyed each other's company, I casually asked him how things were going at work. Murphy conveyed to me that yesterday was a bit of a ticklish day, because Jamal Buchanan was involved in a behavioral episode in the laundry workshop. And due to the severity of the incident, Murphy wound up suspending him from the basketball team.

Apparently, Jamal must've overheard one of the living unit staff refer to him as a jigaboo. And upon hearing the scathing remark, Jamal decided to flip over one of the laundry carts in the Work Activity Center, and the cart narrowly came within inches of seriously injuring someone.

Needless to say, but the incident caused the entire work program to come to a screeching halt, as everyone stopped what they were doing, and then stood there listening to Jamal unleash a barrage of verbal threats and accusations towards the staff person who just disrespected him.

At that point, Tyrell Freeman became so upset at Jamal that he began shouting at the top of his lungs, "Jamal, you bess shut your mouth, or else I'll put a whoopin' on your black ass!"

Obviously, Jamal didn't like the fact that Tyrell Freeman was defending the person who just insulted him with a racist remark. So Jamal got right up into Tyrell's face and called him an "Uncle Tom," which ignited the room even more, and turned the place into a three ring circus.

Murphy said that the Work Activity Center was so loud that he could actually hear all of the yelling and screaming that was going on in there from inside the gym.

And when the building staff heard all of the noise and commotion that was coming from the Work Activity Center, then everyone in the building came running from every direction, so that they could try to prevent a riot from breaking out.

So in the wake of what happened, the incident has now sparked an official investigation by the Director. And the staff person who was allegedly accused of making that despicable racial slur towards Jamal is currently suspended, and he may be in jeopardy of losing his job as well.

And rightly so!

So after filling me in on all of the unsettling news that unfolded yesterday in the Work Activity Center, Murphy then decided to switch gears by telling me a funny story involving Cameron, and the new behavioral program that Cameron is trying to institute in the building.

As I've stated before, Cameron is a real whiz when it comes to shaping behavior. And he's definitely someone who is always trying to build a better mousetrap, so that the clients can learn to display more socially acceptable behavior.

So that being said, Cameron decided to implement a behavioral program that was based on a point system, which was actually a variation on theme to the old Token Economy Program that behavioral psychologists routinely practiced throughout the1970's and 1980's.

The basic premise of Cameron's new behavioral program was that every time the clients did something of a positive nature, then they would have the chance to earn some points. And these points were then recorded on a data sheet, and reviewed by Cameron on a weekly basis.

So once the points were all tallied up, the client would then have the option to either cash in their points at the end of the week, or bank their points for future use.

Rewards were based on the amount of points that the client earned. And rewards could range from a simple cup of coffee, to as much as dinner and a movie in town with Cameron.

Now as clever as Cameron's new behavioral program might be, there does seem to be one minor glitch however, - the clients aren't exactly sure what constitutes a legitimate point.

For instance, if a client should hold the door open for someone, then they feel that should warrant a point. Or if someone says "God bless you" after someone sneezes, then that too should earn them a point as well. And the list of incidental good deeds just goes on and on and on.

As a matter of fact, one of the clients actually told Cameron in their weekly counseling session that he went around the building saying "thank you" exactly one hundred times, so that he could bank enough points to be the top point-getter for the week.

But as soon as he had enough points to win top dog honors, then he immediately stopped saying "thank you" to everyone, and then went back to being his usual shifty and conniving self.

So I think it would be safe to say that some of the clients don't exactly have a good handle on what the new behavioral program was intended for. And that they are merely using the program to satisfy their own selfish needs, instead of as a tool to become much better people.

In fact, Cameron's new behavioral program has become such a logistical nightmare for him that he's not really sure if the program is worth all of his time and aggravation. And at this point, he's seriously thinking of scrapping the whole idea altogether.

When I asked Murphy how the client basketball team was shaping up, he seemed to hesitate for a moment. But then said with some cautious optimism that the guys are showing some real signs of improvement, and that maybe in time they can all come together as a team.

Although their shooting, dribbling, and passing skills may leave a lot to be desired, the enthusiasm that they bring to the gym every day makes up for any lack of skill they may have.

Murphy then went on to say that even though Jamal was his most talented player, he wasn't necessarily his best player. And when the game was on the line, Murphy would much rather see the ball in Francis Watson's hands than in the hands of any of his other players.

Apparently, Jamal seems to think that the ball should be in his hands at all times. And when the other players don't pass him the ball, he will either threaten them within an inch of their life, or literally chase them around the court, and try to wrestle the ball out of their hands.

In Jamal's mind, he is the designated shooter for the team. And as far as he is concerned, any shot that he takes on the court is a good shot, no matter where he decides to shoot it from.

Often times, Jamal has teammates that are wide open under the basket, and they actually have a much better chance of scoring a basket than Jamal does. But Jamal is so intent on shooting the basketball that he simply ignores their pleas, and winds up taking the shot anyway.

It shouldn't come as any big surprise, but most of the players on the team are intimidated by Jamal, and several of them have actually approached Murphy and expressed their concerns.

Murphy is in a real quandary as to how he will address the issue. But for now it seems to be a moot point, especially since Jamal is currently suspended from the team indefinitely.

As I continued to listen to Murphy rattle on about how rough and tumble his basketball team was, I then had an amusing thought pop into my head. Perhaps Murphy should consider replacing all of the athletic tape, ice packs, and bandages that are stored in the team's medical kit, and restock it with strait jackets, riot gear, and a full assortment of psychotropic medications.

For some reason, I've got a funny feeling that when Murphy and the Bowery Boys take the court for their first official basketball game, it should prove to be a very memorable event.

And in all likelihood, - it will give the phrase "sports entertainment" a whole new meaning.

CHAPTER NINE

Well, for the past two weeks, it's been nothing but changing dirty diapers, 2AM feedings, and hauling mounds of smelly laundry to the laundromat every day.

And even though I told Christine that I'd rather stay home with her and the baby instead of going back to work, the truth is, - I'm happy to be heading out the door today.

Hey, don't get me wrong, I wouldn't trade the last two weeks with Christine and Rory for the world. But I've actually worked harder these past two weeks than I have ever worked before in my entire life, so heading back to work today will certainly be a welcomed relief.

When I arrived to work this morning, everyone was thrilled to see me and quite interested to know how Christine and the baby were coming along.

So after maneuvering my way through the gauntlet of inquisitive staff, I then headed down to my office, so that I could catch up on two weeks' worth of mail and phone messages.

As I glanced up from my desk, I saw Murphy standing in the doorway with a big smile plastered on his face. He was holding two large containers of coffee and a box of gooey glazed donuts, which he had tucked securely under his arm like a football.

I then excitedly said, "Hi Doc, it's good to see ya! Hey, sorry I didn't get a chance to talk to ya too much these past two weeks, but life in the O'Leary household has been pretty hectic."

As Murphy handed me a container of coffee, he nonchalantly replied, "Hey, don't worry about it Rodney, I know how crazy it can be when there's a new baby in the house."

Murphy pulled up a chair next to my desk, and then opened up the box of donuts. As he helped himself to a donut, he casually asked, "So have you had a chance to talk to Dick yet?"

"No, not yet," I replied, as I nabbed one of the gooey glazed donuts out of the box.

Just then Dick appeared in the doorway of my office, and then greeted Murphy and I by saying, "Morning, men! Jack, you're a sight for sore eyes, welcome back!"

"Thanks Dick, so what's going on?" I asked, as Murphy passed the box of glazed donuts over to Dick.

"Ugh, don't ask," Dick replied, as he helped himself to a donut.

"So, uh…, Murphy told me all about the incident that happened down in the Work Activity Center last week." I said, with considerable concern.

Dick replied, "Yeah, it was pretty bad. But what really infuriates the hell out of me is that I specifically pointed out in our staff training class to treat the clients with the utmost dignity and respect, especially since our facility has a zero-tolerance policy for inappropriate language. Now it looks like I might have to fire a guy that I've known for over twenty-five years. Hell, I've been to his house a million times, and now I might have to put him on the unemployment line."

"So what's gonna happen now, Dick?" I quietly asked.

Dick replied, "Well, Hanson and I are both heading over to Personnel this morning for a disciplinary hearing. The Director feels that the comment directed towards Jamal is clearly a form of client abuse, so don't be surprised if you see a few heads roll on this one. It's the dawn of a new era boys, and the State School that we once knew is now a thing of the past."

"Well, if that's the case, then some of these old dogs around here better start learning some new tricks." I adamantly said.

Murphy then decided to change the subject by saying, "Oh, by the way Rodney, we have our first official basketball game on Thursday night down in the School Building gym. So, uh…, can I count on you to be my assistant head coach that night?"

I then replied, "Uh, tell ya what Doc, why don't you draw up the contract and I'll have my lawyer look it over. But just to let you know, I won't consider anything less than a six figure salary, limousine service to and from the game, and of course a very generous expense account."

Murphy paused a moment, and then said with a sly grin, "Well, the best that I can do is to provide you with a few good laughs, and possibly pizza and chicken wings right after the game."

"Okay, it's a deal!" I quickly replied, prompting Dick and Murphy to laugh out loud.

When the clients filed in for the morning work session, they seemed genuinely happy to see me, and many of them even congratulated me on being a first-time father.

Of course, Jamal Buchanan took center stage by directing a few unnecessary wisecracks towards me, as he sarcastically said, "Hey Mr. O'Really, ain't you too old to be makin' a baby."

Terrence Morehouse burst out into laughter, and commented, "Damn straight, Jamal!"

Bobby Diggs then rushed to my defense by saying, "Hey Jamal, just because Jack is kinda fat and losing most of his hair doesn't mean that he's too old to make a baby, right Jack."

I just stared at Bobby for a moment, and then exhaustedly said, "That's right, Bobby."

Jamal then asked, in a real cocky sort of way, "So how old are you Mr. O'Really, about fitty?"

Although I'm only two years older than Jamal, he seems to think that I'm a lot older than him, probably because he views me as an authority figure.

Jamal then decided to take it up a notch, as he impetuously asked, "So how do you make a baby anyway, Mr. O'Really?"

All of a sudden, a burst of nervous laughter resonated throughout the entire room.

So realizing that he had captive audience, Jamal cracked a big smile and then posed the question to me once again, as he asked, "C'mon Mr. O'Really, tell us how you make a baby?"

Russell Turner, who just so happened to be standing out in the hallway, then stuck his head into the workshop and shouted, "Hey Jamal, you make a baby by having sex, you moron!"

As Russell continued to have a pretty good laugh at Jamal's expense, he then decided to make a rather lewd gesture, as he demonstrated the sex act by using both of his two hands.

Jamal didn't like being the punchline to Russell's humiliating wisecrack, so he scoffed at Russell by saying, "You better shut your mouth white boy, or else I'll make you my bitch!"

Russell quickly countered, "Oh yeah, well, we'll see who the bitch is bitch!"

Jamal dropped the towel that he was folding, and then stormed directly towards Russell in a very threatening manner. As I attempted to intercede, Murphy suddenly appeared out of nowhere, and then shouted, "Russell, aren't you supposed to be down in the gym right now?"

Russell stopped dead in his tracks, and then replied, "Yes, Murphy." Russell then made an about-face, and beat it straight down the hallway towards the gym as fast as he possibly could.

Jamal then shouted, in an arrogant tone of voice, "That's right, get-to-steppin', bitch!"

When the room settled down, I was thinking how relieved I was that Murphy showed up when he did. Murphy has a real knack for showing up at the right time. And an uncanny ability to turn a potentially dangerous situation into nothing more than just a minor misunderstanding.

As I've stated before, I think I'm the one who will be learning a few things from Murphy, instead of Murphy learning a few things from me.

So as I walked around the room making my observations, I noticed that several of the clients have developed a few bad habits since I've been gone. Not only has the quality of their work suffered, but there was a certain level of lackadaisicalness throughout the room as well.

Out of the corner of my eye, I spotted two clients who were sitting down. And instead of focusing on their work assignment, they were engrossed in a lively conversation with each other.

When I asked these two smart-alecks to stand up and get back to work, they said that they were not done talking yet, and that they would get back to work when they were good and ready.

So seeing how the nice approach wasn't getting me anywhere, I decided to get tough by saying, "If you guys don't stand up and get back to work, then you'll both be on privilege loss."

Which prompted one of them to say, "Hey, you can't do that, we've got rights!"

I quickly countered, "Yes, you do have rights, but I'm talking about privileges. And if you don't get up and start working, then I'll be giving Cameron a call to revoke your privileges."

As the two clients reluctantly stood up and started working on their assignments, I heard one of them say to the other, "Remind me to call my lawyer later, and my Congressman too!"

Around noontime, I decided to head down to the gym to see if Murphy had any plans for lunch. When I walked into the gym, Murphy was just finishing up the morning session.

As I watched Murphy interact with the clients, I simply marveled at what a natural born teacher he was. Although Murphy was disappointed that he didn't land a teaching position right out of college, I actually think he found his true calling working right here at the State School.

For my money, Murphy was the whole package, - he was kind, thoughtful, and extremely fair.

But tough when he had to be!

During lunch Murphy couldn't stop talking about the upcoming basketball game on Thursday night. He even said that he designed a few set plays for the guys to use in the game.

Murphy still wasn't sure if Jamal was going to play Thursday night. Although Jamal was certainly wrong in what he did, Murphy feels that he really wasn't to blame for what happened.

Let's face it, if the staff person that day could've just exercised a little bit more restraint, then Jamal wouldn't have lost his temper, and this whole incident could've been easily avoided.

But knowing Murphy, I'm sure that he will ultimately make the right decision regarding Jamal, and do whatever is in the best interest for everyone on the team as well.

Later that afternoon, Murphy wound up running a two hour basketball practice, and he worked the guys pretty hard. We don't usually hold practice for that length of time. But seeing how it was our last practice before tomorrow night's game, Murphy wanted to make sure that the boys were good and ready for the big showdown.

Now even though Murphy has the patience of a saint, even his limits are sometimes put to the test every once in a while, especially in teaching the guys the three new set plays that he has designed for them to use in tomorrow night's basketball game.

In addition to learning the three new set plays, we also focused on practicing our pre-game warm-up drills as well. And believe me when I tell you, but watching the boys practice their pre-game warm-up drills was like watching an old episode of the "Three Stooges" on TV.

Throughout the entire practice, Murphy seemed to be blowing his whistle nonstop, as he would repeatedly say over and over again, "Okay guys, let's try it again!"

Personally, I think Murphy was setting the bar a little too high in thinking that the guys could master these set plays. But at the end of the day, Murphy loves a challenge. And come hell or high water, he'll make sure that the guys know these plays like the back of their hand.

On Thursday morning, Murphy and I sat down to a big pot of coffee and then went over our strategy for tonight's basketball game. In the midst of our discussion, the telephone rang and it was Coach Peterson, who is the head basketball coach for Mitchell Psychiatric Center, which is the team that we are slated to play tonight.

Unfortunately, Coach Peterson called Murphy to cancel tonight's game. The reason for the cancellation was because two of Mitchell's players had succumbed to severe panic attacks.

Apparently, when Coach Peterson told his players that they were going to be playing a game against a team that they have never played before, then two of his players had severe panic attacks, and needed to be admitted to the Mitchell Crisis Center for counseling and observation.

In wrapping up their conversation, Coach Peterson apologized for cancelling the game on such short notice, and told Murphy that he'd call him again next week to reschedule the game.

The following week, Coach Peterson telephoned Murphy and wanted to know if Murphy was still interested in setting up a day to reschedule the game that was cancelled last week.

Needless to say, but Murphy was up for the challenge. But then asked Coach Peterson how his two players were feeling, and if they were fully recovered from their panic attacks. Coach Peterson then began to laugh. And then quickly reassured Murphy that his two players were doing much better, and that these types of setbacks happen with his players all the time.

Peterson then used a very clever analogy to make his point by saying, "Well Murphy, let me put it to ya this way, anxiety attacks at the psych center are as frequent as the common cold."

For the past several days, Murphy has been subjecting his players to some pretty rigorous practices, so that they will be in tip-top condition for Thursday night's contest against Mitchell Psychiatric Center.

Murphy has been ending each of his basketball practices by having the guys run wind sprints and laps around the gym, so that he can build up their stamina and try to make sure that they won't run out of gas by the fourth quarter.

In addition to that, Murphy has also been conducting some classroom instruction in the evening, so that he can diagram different offensive and defensive strategies on the blackboard.

I guess you could say that Murphy was doing everything in his power to make sure that the boys were good and ready for tomorrow night's contest, and not leaving anything to chance.

The day before the big game, Murphy decided to have a little fun with the boys. So right before practice was over, Murphy instructed everyone to line up on the baseline, so that they could finish up practice with a few hard wind sprints and four or five easy laps around the gym.

As the boys were lining up on the baseline, they were all complaining to Murphy how exhausted they were. As the boys continued to whinge and whine, they pleaded with Murphy to take pity on them, so that they didn't have to be subjected to running any wind sprints or laps.

After listening to their incessant bellyaching, Murphy decided to make a deal with them by saying, "Okay guys, we'll flip a coin for it, - heads I win, tails you lose."

So after hearing Murphy's proposition, the guys all agreed to flip a coin for the wind sprints and laps, especially since they figured that they had a 50/50 chance of coming out on top.

Murphy took a quarter out of his pocket and then flipped it up into the air.

I quietly chuckled to myself, as I watched the coin tumble effortlessly through the air, because the boys had absolutely no idea that Murphy was playing a practical joke on them.

When the coin hit the ground it came up tails, which then prompted Bobby Diggs to let out a disappointing sigh, as he groaned, "Darn it, it's tails, we lose!"

Murphy then quickly shouted, "Alright guys, on my whistle, I want you to run as hard as you possibly can to the far baseline on the other side of the gym!"

So after blowing the whistle, the boys took off running. Murphy then glanced over at me and gave me a subtle wink of his eye, which prompted both of us to quietly snicker to ourselves.

Well, just when Murphy thought that he had successfully pulled the wool over their eyes, doesn't Russell Turner stop dead in his tracks, and on the very last lap of the wind sprint Russell yells, "Wait a minute, heads you win, tails we lose, - that ain't right! You cheated us, Murphy!"

All of a sudden, Murphy and I started howling with laughter.

Murphy then good-naturedly said, "Hey, you got me Russell. Tell ya what, when we win tomorrow night's game, I promise that I'll make it up to ya. Now c'mon, let's finish up the drill."

Well, tonight is the big game, and Murphy has been a nervous wreck all day. Not only is Murphy worried about the guys playing well, but he's also hoping that there won't be any assault and battery charges filed against any of his players tonight by the other team as well.

Murphy is still not sure who his starting lineup will be tonight. In terms of sheer talent he knew, but talent isn't always the deciding factor as to who will play and who will sit the bench.

What seems to be weighing most heavily on Murphy's mind right now is how well the boys will respond to playing in front of a packed house tonight, and whether they can maintain their composure. As much as Murphy would love to win tonight, he would much rather lose with dignity, then win by embarrassment.

When we rounded up the guys for the game, I saw Murphy hand Jamal a game uniform. Apparently, Murphy has decided to let Jamal play tonight. Murphy still feels that Jamal was a victim of circumstance, and that Jamal simply reacted to what was an unfortunate situation.

As the boys were slipping on their uniforms, I asked Murphy if he knew anything about the team that we were playing tonight. Murphy wasn't sure what caliber of team Mitchell was, and he had no idea if they played more like the New York Knicks, or the Sisters of the Poor.

To play it safe, we decided to head over to the School Building gym a little earlier than planned, so that we could get a quick practice in before the other team arrived for the game.

On the ride over to the gym, I asked Murphy who was refereeing tonight's game, and he told me that Dick was able to line up two guys that both work midnights here at the State School.

Apparently, the two guys that Dick was able to commandeer for tonight's contest were full-fledged referees, and actually referee local high school and college games in their spare time.

I then amusingly quipped, "Well Doc, since both of the referees work here at the State School, then let's just hope that they're both up to date on all of their wrap-ups and take-downs, especially if any of our players gets upset with one or two of their calls."

As the boys walked into the gym, they all looked pretty snazzy in their new uniforms, which were royal blue with gold trim. And the word Grizzlies that was embossed in gold lettering on the front of their jerseys was a real eye-catcher too.

Apparently, Murphy was able to contact his former college basketball coach, and asked him if he had any old uniforms that were lying around in the equipment locker. And as luck would have it, the coach said that he just received a brand new shipment of uniforms for their upcoming season, and then told Murphy that he would be happy to donate the old ones to him.

When Murphy first showed me the uniforms, I thought they were nothing but a big pile of rags. They were old and grungy, and the lettering on the front of the jerseys were in tatters.

But fear not!

Because Murphy was able to reach out to the head seamstress in the Central Clothes Room, and he asked her if she wouldn't mind giving the uniforms a little sprucing up.

Initially, when the head seamstress saw the condition of the uniforms, she told Murphy that the uniforms were simply beyond repair, and that they needed a lot more attention than just a few simple stiches or a good starching.

Furthermore, she told Murphy that she didn't have the time or the manpower to devote to such a large undertaking like this, and that she was very sorry that she couldn't help him out.

But the story didn't end there.

Because Murphy decided to give the head seamstress a little dose of his impeccable Irish charm. And in a matter of minutes, Murphy had the head seamstress eating right out of the palm of his hand. She then became as giddy as a schoolgirl, and told Murphy to leave the uniforms with her and that she would see what she could do to help him out.

Well, about a week later, Murphy received a phone call from the head seamstress, who then told Murphy that the uniforms were all set and ready for pick up.

When Murphy and I went over to the Central Clothes Room to pick up the uniforms, we couldn't believe our eyes. Because this dingy pile of rags that we had dropped off about a week ago, were now miraculously transformed into showroom condition apparel.

Murphy was so grateful that he gave the head seamstress a big hug and a kiss, which then prompted her to say, "Now I'll expect you boys to drop these uniforms off after every game, and we'll make sure that they are washed and ready to go for the kids to wear in their next ballgame."

Before breaking out the basketballs, Murphy had the guys do a few light stretches. Which was probably a good thing, because the last thing that we needed was to have one of our starting players pull a muscle and be forced to leave the game. Especially since all of our bench players were absolutely horrible, and they were more likely to score points for the other team than for us.

So once the guys were all loosened up, Murphy instructed the boys to form two lines, so that we could start practicing our pre-game warm-up drills.

Murphy then asked Lance Coppenger, who was our designated water boy and equipment manager, to toss out the basketballs from the equipment bag and then fill-up the water bottles.

Initially, Murphy wasn't sold on the idea of having Lance be part of the team, especially since Lance can sometimes be more trouble than he's worth. But seeing how none of the other clients were willing to help us out, then Lance was given the team manager job by default.

Although Murphy can usually find the good in people, for some reason he just couldn't seem to warm up to Lance Coppenger at all. Personally, I found Lance to be an absolute joy to be around. Yet, Murphy didn't seem to share the same sentiments as I did, and felt that Lance was nothing more than a royal pain in the ass.

Now I'm not saying that Lance was absolutely perfect in every way, and he certainly had his shortcomings. But there was just something about him that really struck a chord in me.

Lance was actually a lot brighter than Bobby Diggs, - although some people might say that's really not saying too much.

Despite Lance's usual happy-go-lucky disposition, he does possess a bit of a dark side too. And on occasion, it can certainly rear its ugly head, especially when you least expect it.

As a matter of fact, at one time Lance was actually considered to be the prime suspect in a murder investigation that happened about twenty-five years ago. But the charges against Lance were eventually dropped, because the District Attorney wasn't able to mount much of a case against him, due to a lack of evidence.

Of course, it should be noted that Lance's uncle was the Chief of Police. And during the course of the investigation, the DA had a sneaking suspicion that the evidence against Lance may have been tampered with, so the judge had no other choice but to dismiss the case altogether.

Oh, and just in case you were wondering, but the murder was never solved. And to this day, it still remains a cold case.

As Murphy and I watched the guys warm up, they looked a little shaky. Their passing and dribbling skills were pretty sloppy, and there seemed to be more finger pointing than high fives.

During the shooting drills, the ball would either fly completely over the basket, or carom so hard off of the wooden backboard that I was afraid that the wood might suddenly crack.

Murphy and I were both keeping a pretty steady eye on Jamal Buchanan, who was so wired that he was barely hanging on by a thread. Jamal kept demanding the ball, and when the other players didn't pass him the ball, he would viciously glare at them and make some rather nasty and threatening remarks towards them.

Every so often, Murphy would pull Jamal aside and try to talk to him. But each time that Jamal returned to the court, he would then revert back to his antagonistic and intimidating ways.

If this is how Jamal behaves during the pre-game warm-up drills, then how the hell is he going to be when he's out on the court playing against his opponent in front of a packed house.

About twenty minutes later, the opposing team walked into the gym. Murphy then asked me to keep an eye on things, so that he could go over and introduce himself to Coach Peterson.

As Murphy headed toward the Mitchell bench, the two referees for tonight's game then strolled into the gym. I must say that the referees looked rather professional, as they donned their stripes, and had nice shiny whistles hanging around their necks.

Both of the head coaches then walked over to the referees and introduced themselves, and then reviewed a few ground rules for tonight's game.

By now, people were pouring into the gym at a pretty steady pace. Apparently, the flyers that Murphy had posted all over the State School this week really paid off. And from the looks of things, tonight's contest was going to be standing room only.

Even the Director showed up!

As the Director made his way through the crowd, he shook hands with everyone he met. The vibe inside the gym had a real carnival atmosphere to it, with music blaring overhead, and an irresistible aroma of popcorn and cotton candy that filtered through the air as well.

So after making the rounds, the Director sat down next to Hanson and Dick Henderson. And by the look on their faces, they seemed to be quite pleased with the number of spectators that came out tonight to support the hometown Grizzlies.

As I watched the Mitchell team warm up, they looked extremely polished and precise in their pre-game warm-up drills. We on the other hand looked a little iffy, and if our pre-game warm-up drills were any indication on how well we would play tonight, then I would have to say that we were certainly in for a long evening.

While Murphy and Coach Peterson continued to chat at half-court with the two referees, I was on the verge of pulling my hair out, as I was busy breaking up one argument after the other, and trying to manage all of the chaos and bickering that kept popping up all around me.

The referee then blew his whistle, and signaled for both teams to take the court.

As Murphy came back over to the bench, he suddenly realized that he had forgotten to do the player introductions. So Murphy then asked the referee to indulge him for another minute or two, so that the players from both teams could be properly introduced to the crowd.

The referee glanced at his watch, and then hesitantly said, "Uh, sure coach, but let's try to make it snappy, okay. I'm scheduled to work the midnight shift tonight."

Murphy hustled over to the scorer's table, so that the public address announcer could cue up the music, and then proceed to make the player introductions.

With a look of sheer excitement in his eye, Murphy then turned to me and exuberantly said, "Wait until you see this, Rodney!"

As it turns out, the guy doing the public address announcing for tonight's game is a disc jockey that works at one of the local radio stations right here in town. And as fate would have it, Murphy just happened to bump into this guy one day while standing in line at the coffee shop.

During the course of their conversation, one thing led to another, and Murphy wound up asking the guy if he wouldn't mind lending his talents at the State School sometime. The guy said that he would be happy to oblige, especially since his younger brother is Down-syndrome.

So without any further ado, the public address announcer cued up the music, and then addressed the crowd in his perfectly pitched radio voice by saying, "Good evening, ladies and gentlemen! And welcome to the School Building Sports Complex tonight!"

I glanced at Murphy, and then said with a tinge of sarcasm, "This is a Sports Complex?"

Murphy just smiled and nodded his head, as he soaked up the moment.

The public address announcer continued by saying, "Tonight, the SBU Grizzlies will be taking on the Spartans of Mitchell Psychiatric Center. Now here are tonight's starting lineups, - for the Spartans......"

So after introducing the starting lineup for the Spartans, the public address announcer then threw it into high gear, as he dimmed the house lights, and then turned up the volume of the music, while saying in rare animated style, "And now here are your SBU Grizzliessssssssssssss!"

Suddenly, colorful strobe lights began flashing all around the room, along with some toe-tapping music that was streaming overhead on the high-fidelity sound system. The atmosphere inside the gym was simply electric, and it was just the ticket in igniting the crowd for tonight's contest between the hometown Grizzlies and the Spartans of Mitchell Psychiatric Center.

The public address announcer then addressed the crowd by saying, "And now here is the starting lineup for your SBU Grizzlies. At guard, 6'7, #23, Jamal Buchanan, at guard, 5'5, #1, Francis Watson, at forward, 6'4, #12, Eddie Johnson, at forward, 6'5, #13, Russell Turner, and at center, the big dawg, at 7'0 foot tall, #19, Tyrell Freemannnnnnn!"

If you didn't know any better, you'd almost think that you were attending a professional sporting event. And trust me, - the music and lighting alone was worth the price of admission.

As I glanced down the player bench, I noticed that all of the Grizzly players were literally sitting on the edge of their seat, and they all seemed to be just as thrilled and excited as I was.

Well, with the exception of Bobby Diggs anyway.

Bobby was seething in anger. Because in Bobby's mind, he felt slighted that he wasn't one of the five starting players out on the court right now that was being introduced to the crowd.

I then heard Bobby grumbling under his breath, "This is nothing but a bunch of bullshit, I should be starting the fuckin' game."

As I studied the disappointment on Bobby's face, I really felt sorry for him. Bobby has endured a lifetime of adversity, and although he feels that he should be out on the court right now, he's simply not good enough to crack the starting lineup as one of our five best players.

But knowing Murphy, he'll make sure that Bobby and the rest of the guys that are riding the bench will get into the game at some point tonight. Especially if the game gets too lopsided, and there's really no chance that our team will come away with a victory tonight.

Before taking the court, Tyrell Freeman turned to me and excitedly asked, "Hey Mr. Jack, how do I look in my fancy new uniform?"

As I gazed up at Tyrell and his massive 7'0 frame, I confidently said, "Tyrell, you look like a real Grizzly in that uniform, so just go out there and play like one tonight, okay buddy."

The Mitchell Psychiatric team was by no means stout, nor did they have any players on their roster that stood over six feet tall. All of the Mitchell players were lean and lanky. And what they lacked in size, they certainly made up for in skill and athleticism.

When our team took the court, we looked extremely nervous. Whereas our opponent appeared to be calm and relaxed, and they seemed to exude an undeniable air of confidence.

As a show of good sportsmanship, the referee asked all of the players on the court to shake hands with each other before starting the game. So everyone proceeded to shake hands.

Well, with the exception of Jamal Buchanan anyway.

Jamal decided to have one of his usual meltdowns, as he strutted around the court, while viciously mumbling under his breath, "I ain't shakin' no hands with the enemy, fuck that shit."

Tyrell, who was voted team captain, begged Jamal to be a good sport and shake hands with the opposing team. But Jamal simply snarled, "Unh-uh, no way, Tyrell. I ain't shakin' no punk-ass hands," as he just kept strutting around half court, trapped in his own crazy little world.

Murphy realized that it was simply futile to convince Jamal to shake hands with the other team, so Murphy instructed Tyrell to just let the matter go, and to line up for the opening tip-off.

The referee blew his whistle, and then alertly said, "Ready, men!"

As the players took their positions on the court, Murphy shouted, "Alright Grizzlies, let's show 'em what ya got! And don't forget that we're playing a tight man-to-man defense!"

The referee tossed the ball straight up in the air, signifying the start of the game. Mitchell Psychiatric Center took immediate possession of the ball, mainly because Tyrell forgot to jump.

Murphy shouted, "Tyrell, next time you gotta jump in the air for the ball, okay buddy!"

Tyrell glanced over at Murphy, and then softly said, "Yessir, I'm sorry, Mr. Murphy."

As the Mitchell player dribbled the ball down the court, all five of the Grizzly players were chasing after him, which was certainly a far cry from the tight man-to-man defense that Murphy had just instructed his players to employ.

Just as all five Grizzlies were about to converge on the Mitchell player, he then lofted the ball high up into the air to one of his teammates, who was positioned directly under the Mitchell basket for an easy two points. Mitchell was now on the scoreboard, and they had a 2-0 lead.

Murphy turned to me, and then quietly said, "Well, let's just hope that we look a little better on offense than we do on defense, eh Rodney."

It was now our turn to take possession of the ball.

Francis Watson tossed the inbounds pass into Jamal Buchanan. As Jamal dribbled the ball up the court with his right hand, he was displaying a raised clenched fist with his left. And from where I was sitting, it looked like Jamal was ready to punch the daylights out of the first Mitchell player who was crazy enough to try to steal the ball away from him.

To tell you the truth, but I was a little surprised that the referee didn't blow his whistle and stop play, so that he could at least talk to Jamal, or perhaps even give him a stern warning.

Especially since Jamal was exhibiting such a flagrant display of unsportsmanlike conduct.

In any event, Jamal dribbled the ball past the half court stripe, and then launched an ill-advised shot that wound up missing the basket by a mile. The ball hit the backboard so hard that it sounded like a cast iron safe being dropped out of a 3rd floor window.

One of the Mitchell players then snatched up the loose ball, and made a crisp pass to an open man that was positioned directly under the basket for another easy score for Mitchell.

Francis tossed the inbounds pass to Jamal. As soon as Jamal crossed over the half court stripe, he took another ill-advised shot, which once again hit the backboard like a ton of bricks.

The Mitchell player then gobbled up the loose ball. And with pinpoint accuracy, he passed the ball over to his teammate, who was perched directly under the basket for a 6-0 run.

By now, Murphy was getting a little hot under the collar, so he instructed Francis Watson to inbound the ball to anyone other than Jamal.

As Francis was getting ready to inbound the ball, Jamal demanded that Francis pass the ball to him. But when Francis refused, Jamal began to threaten Francis within an inch of his life.

Although Francis was quite intimidated by Jamal's threatening words and accusations, I think Francis was even more afraid of what would happen to him if he disobeyed a direct order from Murphy.

So in a bit of a panic, Francis passed the ball to Eddie Johnson, who managed to catch the ball, but then had no idea what to do with the ball once he received it. Eddie was not accustomed to receiving the inbounds pass, because that was Francis and Jamal's job.

Eddie was so distraught that he started shouting, "What should I do? What should I do?"

Russell Turner, who we often refer to as Mr. Sensitive, then sarcastically blurted out, "You need to dribble the ball, nitwit!"

So instead of dribbling the ball, Eddie decided to run up the court with it, so that he could hand the ball to one of his teammates. The referee blew his whistle, because Eddie was guilty of committing a traveling violation. And by rule, we were forced to give the ball back to Mitchell.

As the Grizzlies all stood around looking at each other, the referee blew his whistle and then handed the ball to the Mitchell player, who heaved the inbounds pass the entire length of the court to one of his teammates for an uncontested basket, and giving the Spartans an 8-0 run.

At that point, Murphy had seen enough, as he shouted, "Timeout, ref!"

In a fit of frustration, Murphy called his team over to the bench so that he could give them a much needed pep talk.

As Lance Coppenger was busy passing out the water bottles, Murphy pondered what to say to his beleaguered team. Murphy knew that his players were much better than this, so maybe a few words of encouragement might just be the ticket in getting them on track.

Well, as soon as Murphy looked at Jamal, the thought of saying anything positive went straight out the window, as Murphy yelled, "Jamal, what the hell are ya doin' out there man?"

Jamal replied, "Whatcha mean, fool! I'm tryin' to score points for this punk-ass team! Tyrell needs to do a better job at clearing out the middle, so that I can score some easy hoops!"

Tyrell quickly chimed in and said, "Hey, don't be pointing your finger at me, Jamal!"

Jamal then decided to take a potshot at Murphy by saying, "Hey man, if you wanna win this punk-ass game, then you better tell all of these other dumb-asses to pass me the damn ball!"

Murphy could feel the tension in the air, and the last thing that his players needed to hear right now was criticism. So Murphy took a deep breath, and then calmly said, "Hey guys, what is the one thing that we have been emphasizing all week in practice?"

Francis Watson piped up and said, "To work as a team, and to always pass the ball to the open man. But every time Jamal touches the ball, he winds up taking a shot at the basket."

Jamal snarled, "Whatcha talkin' 'bout, fool! None of you damn punk-asses can shoot the ball as good as me! So if you wanna win this game, then you bess feed me the damn ball, aight!"

Murphy then sternly said, "Hey Jamal, if you don't start passing the basketball to the open man, then you'll be sitting on the bench right next to me for the rest of the game, got it?"

Jamal glared at Murphy, but opted not to say a word, because he knew that he couldn't intimidate Murphy one bit.

The referee then blew his whistle and shouted, "Let's play ball, coach!"

Both teams broke their respective huddles and then took the court. Francis Watson inbounded the ball to Jamal, who then dribbled the ball up the court.

Once over the half court stripe, Jamal passed the ball over to Tyrell Freeman. For a split second, Tyrell thought about shooting the basketball, but then decided not to.

Tyrell then hoisted the ball straight up over his head, and the only way that any of the Mitchell players could ever try to snatch the ball out of Tyrell's hand was by dragging a stepladder out onto the court with them.

Jamal kept calling for the ball, but Tyrell just simply said, "Unh-uh, no way, Jamal."

Tyrell then spotted Francis Watson, who was standing all by himself at the top of the key.

With the flick of his wrist, Tyrell passed the ball over to Francis Watson, who caught the pass, and then lined up the shot and swish! The ball went straight into the basket.

The crowd roared!

And everyone in the gym, with the exception of Jamal, was clapping their hands and cheering at the top of their lungs, because the hometown Grizzlies were now on the scoreboard.

As Jamal strutted down the court, he had a big scowl on his face. And I could hear him mumbling a string of profanities under his breath, because the spotlight wasn't shining on him.

Mitchell took the inbounds pass and then dribbled the ball up court. The Mitchell squad made their patented three passes, but when the Mitchell player who was lurking underneath the basket went to shoot the ball, Tyrell Freeman came out of nowhere to swat the ball out of midair.

Francis Watson then gobbled up the loose ball and dribbled it down the court. Francis weaved in and out of the Mitchell players, as if they were stationary cones. He then found his usual spot at the top of the key, and launched his shot and swish! The ball went into the basket.

Once again, the crowd cheered because the hometown Grizzlies were on the scoreboard again, and the score was now 8-4 in favor of Mitchell Psychiatric Center.

As Mitchell dribbled the ball up the court, they continued to be very slick in the way that they distributed the ball. Be that as it may, our team was beginning to figure them out, because Mitchell was starting to tip their hand a bit, and revealing some noticeable chinks in their armor.

Somehow we had managed to knock Mitchell completely off of their game. And in doing so, we had taken them so far out of their comfort zone that they were now being forced to take shots at the basket that they don't ordinarily take.

Although we were still behind on the scoreboard, we had mighty Mitchell on the ropes, and our pesky man-to-man defense was doing a pretty good job of keeping Mitchell at bay.

Well, the most exciting play of the first half was watching Tyrell snag a rebound, and then spotting Jamal streaking down the court, as he shouted, "Tyrell, pass me the damn ball!"

Tyrell then threw the ball the entire length of the court, which Jamal was able to catch in perfect stride. Jamal then soared into the air and slam-dunked the ball with both of his hands, which gave the upstart Grizzlies the lead by two points over the beleaguered Mitchell Spartans.

Jamal's electrifying basket brought the house down, and forced Coach Peterson to call a much needed timeout, so that he could talk to his players and try to restore their confidence.

As both teams went to their respective benches, the Mitchell players were all squabbling amongst themselves and engaging in some rather flagrant finger pointing. Whereas the Grizzlies were all smiling and whooping it up, and giving each other some well-deserved high fives.

Jamal was simply in his glory, and as he strutted off of the court, he was boogying down to the rhythm of the music that was playing directly overhead on the high-fidelity sound system.

As Jamal gazed up at the exuberant crowd, he began to showboat a bit by chanting, "Yo', yo', that's why they call me Jam! Yo', yo', that's why they call me Jam! Yo', yo'…!

Although Murphy was thrilled by his team's turnaround, he was still a bit concerned that his players might become a little too over confident. The tide had definitely shifted in our favor. And from the looks of it, mighty Mitchell might be on the verge of totally unravelling tonight.

As Murphy corralled his five starting players around him, he said with quiet enthusiasm, "Guys, you're playing fantastic, and you're finally playing like a team out there. Tyrell that was a real nice pass to Jamal, and I need you to keep pounding the backboards for me, okay buddy."

So while Murphy continued to provide his team with some last minute instructions, Lance Coppenger went around to each of the Grizzly players and gave them a squirt of water.

The referee then blew his whistle and shouted, "Let's play ball, gentlemen!"

Before taking the court, Murphy reminded the boys to continue to play as a team. And as they broke the huddle, they all stacked their hands and shouted, "One, Two, Three, Grizzlies!"

As the boys walked back onto the hardwoods, Murphy was smiling like a proud papa. But as the clock slowly ticked down toward halftime, Murphy's radiant smile quickly vanished.

The timeout that Coach Peterson called for his team seemed to do wonders for the Spartans. And the adjustments that he made proved to be quite effective, as mighty Mitchell imposed their will on the upstart Grizzlies by reeling off ten consecutive baskets in a row.

This sudden burst by Mitchell seemed to take all of the starch out of the Grizzlies. And as the boys walked off the court at halftime, they hung their heads low and felt utterly demoralized.

The poor play on the part of the Grizzlies seemed to carry over into the second half, as the boys wound up losing the game by thirty points. Murphy was completely dumbfounded as to why his team had suddenly bottomed out. After Jamal electrified the crowd with his sensational slam-dunk to take the lead, everyone in the gym thought that a Grizzly victory was in the bag.

But as so often is the case, momentum can be fleeting. One minute you're sitting pretty, and then moments later, you're scratching your head and wondering what the hell went wrong.

When the game was over, both teams lined up at half court and shook hands.

Well, with the exception of Jamal Buchanan anyway.

Murphy didn't say too much to the guys after the game, and opted to keep his comments short and sweet. Murphy did say that he saw some positives to build on, and that the team we played against tonight hasn't lost a single game to an opponent in over three years.

While Murphy gave his post-game comments, Lance Coppenger was busy collecting all of the uniforms and placing them into a laundry bag, so that they could be brought over to the Central Clothes Room tomorrow to be washed and ready to go for the next basketball game.

Murphy then finished up his post-game comments by telling the guys to stay positive and get a good night's sleep, and that he'd see them all tomorrow afternoon for basketball practice.

As Murphy and I were walking toward our cars, he turned to me and dejectedly said, "Boy, we really played awful tonight, Rodney. We had more turnovers than a day old bakery."

I laughed at Murphy's humorous metaphor, and then tried to pick up his spirits by saying, "Yeah, but for their first game, I think it went pretty well tonight, Doc. Hey, just look at it this way, no one got hurt, and we didn't need to dial 911, so I think that's a pretty good night."

Murphy just nodded his head, and then half-heartedly chuckled.

I then casually asked, "Hey Doc, you really didn't think that we were gonna win tonight, did ya?"

With a straight face, Murphy then replied, "Well, I thought we had a pretty good chance, especially when Coach Peterson told me that two of his players were hyperventilating before the game, and they were almost on the verge of having a panic attack," which prompted me to laugh.

The following day, the entire building was buzzing about last night's game. From what the living unit staff was telling me, Jamal was bad-mouthing Murphy all night long, and he even insinuated that the reason we lost last night's game was because Murphy wasn't allowing him to showcase any of his basketball talents.

Jamal also said that if Murphy doesn't start making some wholesale changes right away, and allow him to start shooting the basketball more, then he's seriously thinking of quitting the team altogether.

Later that morning, Jamal was working down in the laundry workshop, and I heard him making some rather scathing remarks about some of his teammates on the basketball team.

And what's more, Jamal was even saying a few nasty things about Murphy too!

Jamal basically said that Murphy wasn't allowing him to shoot the basketball enough last night, which was the main reason why the Grizzlies wound up losing the game by thirty points.

Unfortunately, Jamal doesn't seem to realize that he was just as much to blame for last night's loss as any of his teammates were.

As I listened to Jamal spout off about the team, I was trying very hard to put everything that he was saying into perspective. Especially since Jamal is not only developmentally disabled, but he's also burdened with a number of severe psychiatric disorders as well.

Jamal's inability to take ownership in last night's loss speaks volumes as to the type of person that Jamal really is. But more importantly, - the fact that Jamal blames everyone else in life for all of his misfortunes is something that will probably keep him squarely behind the eight ball for the rest of his days.

In Jamal's mind, we lost the game last night because of our inability to get him the ball, so that he could light up the scoreboard, and be the one who would lead us to victory.

But in actuality, we lost the game last night because Jamal's narcissistic personality disorder prevented him from being what we really needed him to be, - which was a team player.

As Jamal continued to take potshots at the team, I could see that Tyrell was getting a little annoyed at him. But as soon as Jamal started to bad-mouth Murphy, that's when Tyrell became totally unglued, and then shouted, "Jamal, you bess shut your mouth, or else I'll shut it for ya!"

Jamal then got real cocky by saying, "Oh yeah, well, if you try any of your shit with me Tyrell, then I'll have these white honkies put your black ass on privilege loss, aight!"

As I watched Tyrell and Jamal glare at one another, I quickly charged over to where they were standing and said, "Hey Jamal, enough with the idle threats and racist remarks. Now why don't you do yourself a big favor and get back to work, or else you'll be on privilege loss, got it."

Jamal came within inches of me, and then viciously snarled, "Oh yeah, so whatcha gonna do about it Mr. Pillsbury's dough boy? You better slow ya roll old man, or else I'll kick your lily white ass all over this room! Ya got me, boy!"

The look in Jamal's eye was downright scary, and I'd be lying if I told you that I wasn't frightened.

I then turned to one of the male staff that was assigned to the room, and nervously said, "Hey John, you better call the living unit for some backup."

Jamal then shouted, in a very belligerent tone, "Damn straight, white boy! You gonna need a whole lotta backup if you wanna mess with a cat like me, 'cause I'll fuck you up bad!"

Suddenly, Tyrell Freeman grabbed Jamal Buchanan by the throat, and then picked Jamal up off of the floor with one hand and began punching the daylights out of him.

As Jamal struggled to set himself free from Tyrell Freeman's grasp, Jamal began yelping like a wounded animal. And although Jamal managed to land a few glancing blows of his own, he just couldn't shake himself loose of the vice-like grip that Tyrell had on him at that point.

Despite our best efforts to separate the two combatants, Tyrell was just too big and too strong for any of the staff in the Work Activity Center to restrain him.

Then, call it what you want, luck, kismet, or divine intervention, but Murphy just so happened to be walking into the laundry workshop at that exact moment. And when Murphy saw what was happening in the far corner of the room, he managed to sneak up from behind, and then grab Tyrell firmly around his waist before Tyrell had the chance to knock Jamal into submission.

I'm not really sure if Murphy's wrap-up technique was technically correct. Or for that matter, if it was even a legally sanctioned or approved method. But at that point, who cares.

Because sometimes in the heat of the battle, - you just gotta do, what you just gotta do.

Well, as soon as Tyrell Freeman realized that it was Murphy who had a hold of him, then his entire body went completely limp. As Murphy held Tyrell in his arms, he said to Tyrell in a calm and reassuring voice, "It's all over now Tyrell, so just try to relax, okay buddy."

With tears in his eyes, Tyrell said in his deep and gentle Southern drawl, "I'm so sorry, Mr. Murphy. Please try and forgive me for what I did to Jamal."

Murphy loosened his hold on Tyrell, and then calmly said, "C'mon Tyrell, let's you and me head back to the living unit now, okay."

As I glanced over at Jamal, he was lying flat on his back and he was completely sprawled out on the floor. Jamal was all covered in blood, and he appeared to be in a great deal of pain.

Jamal's face was badly bruised and swollen. And although I'm not a doctor, it looked like he had sustained a possible broken nose, and maybe even a fractured cheekbone as well.

At that point, I grabbed an ice pack out of the freezer, and then wrapped it in a hand towel and gently placed it on Jamal's swollen face. As Jamal held the ice pack in place, I then ran for the telephone and called the nurse's station, so that one of the nurses could come down to the laundry workshop and assess Jamal's medical condition.

When the nurse arrived, I explained to her what had happened, and the circumstances that led up to Jamal's injury. She then instructed me to dial 911, because Jamal's face was beginning to swell up like a grapefruit, and it was obvious that he was going to need an ambulance to take him to the emergency room to get a full set of x-rays and to be thoroughly examined by a doctor.

As I was filling out Jamal's accident report, I was thinking that this entire incident could have been easily avoided if Jamal had simply kept his big mouth shut about last night's game.

But once again, Jamal's borderline personality disorder got in the way, just like it does for Bobby Diggs, and the rest of the misguided castaways that inhabit the Island of Misfit Toys.

It's funny, but the clients are always complaining that the staff is constantly preventing them from living the life that they've always dreamed about. And I guess if I were in their shoes, then I'd probably be blaming the staff as well.

But what the clients fail to realize however is that often times they are their own worst enemy. And until these square pegs can find a square world to fit into, then their hopes of living a more productive and fruitful life may be nothing more than a well-constructed fairytale.

As my dad often says, "It's tough to make chicken salad when there's no chicken in the house."

Later that afternoon, Jamal came back from the hospital and the x-rays revealed that he had sustained a broken nose, along with a hairline fracture to his right cheekbone.

When I went onto the living unit to check on Jamal, he looked like he just went fifteen rounds with the heavyweight champion of the world. His face was all black and blue and it was completely swollen, and his nose was heavily taped and bandaged.

Some of the staff actually felt sorry for Jamal, but the lion's share really didn't have any sympathy for him whatsoever.

And what's more, they honestly felt that Jamal got what he deserved.

As for me, well…, I guess I had a foot in both camps.

On the one hand, I felt bad that Jamal had the stuffing knocked out of him. But on the other hand, if you keep poking a bear with a stick, then sooner or later you're gonna get hurt.

And God help you if the bear that you're poking is the size of Tyrell Freeman!

Well, I guess we can theorize all we want. But one thing is for sure, Jamal Buchanan won't be playing in anymore basketball games for the Grizzlies this season.

And maybe the same can be said for Tyrell Freeman as well.

CHAPTER TEN

Well, for the past two weeks, Murphy has been completely down in the dumps. And in all the years that I've known him, I've never seen him look so glum.

The altercation between Jamal Buchanan and Tyrell Freeman has thrown Murphy into such a tailspin that he's actually lost his appetite. Which is really saying a lot, especially since Murphy can eat like a horse.

I can't even entice him with the "blue plate" special!

The day that Murphy informed Tyrell that he was suspended from the basketball team, Murphy could barely get the words out. Upon hearing the news, Tyrell actually broke down and cried, and then he dropped to his knees and prayed for God's forgiveness.

Tyrell's suspension has been so gut-wrenching for Murphy that there's been no talk of basketball in the building since the altercation happened.

Which is pretty ironic, especially since Murphy had agreed to challenge the ARC to a friendly game just minutes before the unfortunate incident occurred.

So I guess the season could potentially be over, even before it ever really got started.

It's actually too bad that it's had to come down to this, because Murphy heard through the grapevine that the ARC has a pretty weak basketball team. So playing the ARC might have afforded us the opportunity for not only a win, but maybe help soothe a few fragile egos too.

Well, it's been roughly three weeks now since we've had any mention of basketball in the building, and Murphy has been doing a lot of soul searching regarding the status of the team.

So that being said, I was a little surprised this morning when Murphy asked me if I was available to help him out with running basketball practice this afternoon down in the gym.

Although I had a burning desire to ask Murphy why he decided to resume practicing with the boys again, I just let the matter go and told him that I would be happy to help him out.

Around three-thirty, Murphy and I went onto the units to gather up the guys for practice. When we entered L.U. 512, we saw Tyrell sitting quietly on one of the dayroom couches reading his Bible. And on the other side of the room, we saw

Jamal Buchanan watching cartoons on TV.

Since the incident occurred, neither Jamal nor Tyrell have been allowed to participate in any off unit activities. And although it shames me to admit it, but it's been pretty nice not having to put up with Jamal or any of his annoying antics down in the Work Activity Center every day.

When Tyrell saw us enter the living unit, he smiled and gave us a slight wave of his hand. As Tyrell watched us gather up the boys for practice, I could detect a deep sense of sorrow in his eyes. He then decided to put down his Bible for a moment, and walk over and say hello to us.

As Tyrell approached us, Murphy placed his hand comfortingly on Tyrell's broad shoulder, and then gently asked, "So how ya doin', Tyrell?"

Tyrell replied, in his distinct Southern drawl, "I'm doin' real good, Mr. Murphy. I've been reading a lot of scripture passages from the Bible, and it really seems to relax me."

Murphy smiled, and then said, "That's good to hear, Tyrell. Just stay positive, okay."

As we were exiting the living unit, we could hear Jamal Buchanan mumbling a few nasty comments under his breath, as he viciously sneered, "Yeah, go on, take your raggedy-asses to practice. But you ain't gonna win no punk-ass games without me, fools!"

Neither Murphy nor I paid any attention to Jamal's inflammatory remarks.

But the minute we left the living unit, Murphy turned to me and nervously whispered, "Boy Rodney, I sure hope that the ARC team is as weak as everybody says they are, especially since two of my starting players for next week's game are both sitting on the shelf."

I lightly chuckled, and then patted Murphy on the back, as I spiritedly said, "Hey, don't worry Doc, our bench players are just gonna have to step up and show ya what they can do."

Murphy groaned a bit, as he sarcastically replied, "Well Rodney, I think I already have a pretty good idea as to what our bench players can do, which is why they're bench players."

As we headed over to L.U. 513 to round up the rest of guys for basketball practice, I was thinking how nice it was to see Murphy back to being his old self again.

Anyway, Murphy worked the boys pretty hard in practice all week, because he was bound and determined that his players would have a much better showing against the ARC than the one that they had against Mitchell Psychiatric Center.

When Murphy spoke with the ARC coach, she stated that her main reason for organizing a team was purely for social reasons. And that being a part of a team is an ideal way of building strong interpersonal relationships with one another, and allows her clients to meet new people.

Well, as admirable as that thinking might be, I don't think that Murphy necessarily shares those same exact sentiments. Because to Murphy's way of thinking, nothing is going to stand in the way of his team beating the ARC on Tuesday night.

As we all know by now, Murphy is a highly competitive individual, and he has stated to me on more than one occasion, "Rodney, warm fuzzies may be good for the soul, but they are generally not reflected in the box score."

Since Jamal and Tyrell were scratched from tonight's contest, Murphy has decided to insert Bobby Diggs and Jerome Harrison into the starting lineup as their replacements.

As I've stated before, the talent level on our basketball team drops off significantly once you get past our usual five starting players. So only God knows what surprises may be in store for us tonight if one or more of our starting players should happen to foul out of tonight's game.

In fact, Murphy told me that he even lit a candle after Mass last Sunday, so that God would watch over his five starting players, and not allow any of them to get into foul trouble.

Uh, geez Murphy, as if God didn't have enough to worry about!

So before gathering up the guys for tonight's contest, Murphy and I decided to grab a quick bite to eat over at the commissary.

Our strategy for tonight's game was to rely heavily on Francis Watson, who Murphy often refers to as our "floor general." Francis will not only provide us with some solid perimeter shooting, but he possesses a very high basketball acumen as well, and we're really counting on him to distribute the ball and help direct all of our other players out on the court.

As we were passing out the game uniforms, Bobby Diggs approached Murphy and asked, "Excuse me, Coach Murphy. But since Jamal isn't on the basketball team anymore, would it be okay if I switched my uniform number for his, because twenty-three is my lucky number."

Murphy chuckled at Bobby's innocent request, and then replied, "Okay Bobby, but on one condition, you'll have to promise me to step up your game by wearing your lucky number."

Bobby then excitedly said, "Okay, I promise, I promise, oh boy, oh boy, oh boy!" And in typical Bobby style, he began to feverishly scratch the back of his head with both of his hands.

As we boarded the van to take the short ride over to the School Building gym, Lance Coppenger approached Murphy, and then said with a real serious look on his face, "Hey coach, I know we're down some players tonight, so I'm available to play in the game if you need me."

Murphy quietly nodded his head, and then tried to keep a straight face, especially since Murphy knows that Lance doesn't possess a single ounce of basketball talent whatsoever.

So after a slight pause, Murphy then tactfully said, "Okay, thanks Lance, but you're much more valuable to me as the team's water boy and equipment manager than just a mere player."

Lance replied, "Okey-dokey, you're the coach," and then Lance hopped onto the van.

When we walked into the gym, it was already bustling with activity, and it had a definite carnival atmosphere to it. There was an irresistible aroma of popcorn and cotton candy that was swirling through the air, and it smelled so good that it actually made my mouth water.

Murphy had the guys limber up a bit by doing a few stretching exercises. And then once the boys were all loosened up, we formed two lines and began our pre-game warm-up drills.

As the guys ran through all of their warm-up drills, they looked pretty rusty. Their ball-handling skills were sloppy, and their passing and dribbling skills were lackluster to say the least.

During our shooting drills, no one other than Francis Watson even came close to hitting the basket. Some of the shots soared right over the backboard, and others were shot with such force that they actually made little scuff marks into the wood. Murphy and I simply couldn't believe our eyes. And even though Murphy was shouting out gentle words of encouragement, every so often, he would look in my direction and just shake his head in utter disbelief.

When the opposing team walk into the gym, they were led by a young and very attractive woman, who presumably was Coach Ferguson, and an older man that was her assistant coach. All of the ARC players were small in stature, and they appeared to be docile and quite harmless.

Murphy then asked me to keep an eye on things, so that he could go over and introduce himself to Coach Ferguson.

As Murphy made his way over to the ARC bench, he looked back to me and said, "Hey Rodney, have the guys work on the pick-and-roll play, and I'll be back in a few minutes, okay."

The pick-and-roll is one of the most fundamental plays in basketball. And if executed properly, it will afford a player the opportunity to take a totally uncontested shot at the basket.

Well, at least in theory anyway.

Now even though we've been practicing the pick-and-roll play for weeks, the guys were still struggling to understand the underlying concept of the play, and how to execute it correctly. It just seemed like every time we ran the play, the guys were finding a new way to louse it up.

Quite honestly, but I hope that Murphy isn't relying on the pick-and-roll play to be the linchpin for our offense tonight. Because if that's the case, then we will definitely be in trouble.

The only two players out on the court that had even the slightest inkling of understanding the pick-and-roll play were Francis Watson and Russell Turner. And even then, it was a stretch to say that either one of them knew precisely what to do.

As far as I was concerned, the pick-and-roll play was just too complicated for any of our players to comprehend. And every time we tried to execute the play, it was like watching an old re-run episode of the "Three Stooges" on TV.

We had players zigging when they should be zagging, or passing the ball to someone who wasn't even looking, which would then cause tempers to flare and arguments to ensue.

As we kept running through the pick-and-roll play, the guys were making a complete and utter spectacle of themselves out on the court. There was some flagrant finger pointing going on, as well as some colorful and descriptive language too. Especially from Russell Turner, who certainly wasn't shy when it came to voicing his opinion.

I kept asking myself over and over again, "Do these guys have any idea what the term social decorum means? And in approximately fifteen minutes from now, they will be playing in front of hundreds of people. And in doing so, they will essentially be representing the facility?"

When Murphy finally joined me back on the bench, he enthusiastically asked, "So how are we looking tonight, Rodney?"

To which I sarcastically replied, "Uh, do you really wanna know, Doc?"

Murphy quietly nodded his head, and just simply said, "Huh, maybe not."

By now, the gym was filled to capacity, and the referees were looking a little antsy to start the game. Murphy was able to commandeer the same two referees that we had last time.

Before taking the court, Murphy huddled all five of his starting players around him, so that he could give them a few words of encouragement and some last minute instructions.

As Murphy finished up his pre-game comments, Bobby Diggs then excitedly asked him, "Coach Murphy, are we still gonna have pizza and chicken wings right after the game tonight?"

Murphy just stared at Bobby for a moment, and then replied, "C'mon Bobby, don't worry about after the game. You need to focus all of your energy on your opponent right now, okay?"

The referee blew his whistle, and then motioned for both teams to take the court. Before getting into position, the referee had both teams shake hands and wish each other good luck.

So after all the players were squarely in position, the referee blew his whistle again and then tossed the ball up in the air, signifying the start of the game.

Eddie Johnson, who was almost a foot taller than the ARC player that he was matched up against, then tipped the ball over to Francis Watson. Francis dribbled the ball down the court and then launched a fifteen foot shot from the top of the key, and swish! Two points for the Grizzlies.

As the hometown cheered, I immediately glanced at Murphy, and then said with absolute astonishment, "Wow! Is that really our team out there?"

Murphy proudly replied, "Yep, it sure is, now let's just hope it continues." Murphy began clapping his hands, and shouting out words of encouragement to his players from the sidelines.

As the Grizzlies ran up the court, I could hear Russell Turner absolutely bellowing to the crowd, "The ARC team stinks! And our team is number one!"

I gave Murphy a gentle nudge, and then quietly said, "Yeah, that's our team."

It was now our turn to play defense. The ARC team took the inbounds pass and then began dribbling the ball up the court.

The ARC was not a very skilled team, and this was certainly quite evident in how poorly they were dribbling the ball. The ARC player was dribbling the ball with both hands, which is technically an infraction of the rules, and something that Russell Turner was quick to point to the referee, as he brashly shouted, "Hey ref, whatta ya blind, he's double dribbling the basketball!"

At that point, the referee turned in Russell's direction, and I could tell by the look in the referee's eye that he didn't appreciate Russell's wiseass remark one bit. The referee then glanced over at Murphy, as if to say, "Hey coach, how 'bout controlling your players."

Murphy seemed to pick up on what the referee was laying down, so Murphy promptly shouted from the sidelines, "Hey Russell, shut your mouth and let the referee call the game!"

Well, it didn't take a genius to figure out that Murphy was a little hot under the collar at Russell. Murphy demanded excellence from his players, both on and off the court. And dollars to donuts, but I'm sure that Murphy will be giving Russell an earful at the next stoppage of play.

So when the ARC player stopped dribbling the basketball, he looked for someone on his team to pass the ball to. The young man appeared to be very indecisive on what he should do with the basketball. And with each passing second, he was becoming increasingly more anxious.

The young man then frantically shouted to one of his teammates, "Here Joey, catch!"

Francis Watson, who was Johnny on the spot, saw that the ARC player was telegraphing his pass, so Francis managed to step into the passing lane and intercept the ball. Francis then threw the ball up the court to Russell Turner, who then scored an easy basket under the hoop.

As the Grizzly players proudly ran up the court, the crowd continued to cheer. Not only were the Grizzlies scoring points on offense, but they were scoring points on defense as well.

The ARC players looked completely rattled. And at that point, I was beginning to feel sorry for them, because we were basically doing to them what Mitchell Psychiatric Center had done to us only a few short weeks ago. Coach Ferguson could see that her players were a little flustered, so in an effort to get her team back on track she decided to ask the referee for timeout.

As Russell Turner trotted off the court, he was all shits and giggles, especially since he just scored the last basket. Not only was Russell acting like a real hotshot, but he was also being quite rude and obnoxious to some of the ARC players as they were walking off of the court too.

Yeah, Russell thought that he was being a real comedian. But in reality, he was nothing but an absolute embarrassment. Not only to Murphy and me, but to all of his teammates as well.

As Russell got closer to Murphy, he blurted out, "Hey Murphy, those ARC guys play like a bunch of bums! So what did ya think of the basket that I just scored, pretty good, huh?"

Russell was expecting Murphy to pat him on the back and tell him what a tremendous job he was doing. So you can only imagine how surprised Russell was when Murphy lit into him by saying, "Russell, if I ever see you act like that again, then you'll be thrown off this team faster than you can shake a stick. Now go grab some water, and get the hell out of my sight right now!"

Once again, Russell had no idea why Murphy just yelled at him. As far as Russell was concerned, he just scored two points for the team, so why wasn't Murphy happy with him.

Quite honestly, but sociopaths like Russell Turner are simply unable to look at the world through the same corrective lens as you and I do. Their critical thinking tends to be somewhat askew, which is one of the reasons why Russell is on a full scholarship here at the State School.

As Russell Turner snatched the water bottle out of Lance Coppenger's hand, he snidely mumbled to himself, "What the hell is Murphy's problem? For crissakes, I just scored two points for this lousy team, so why the hell is Murphy so mad at me for?"

The referee then blew his whistle and shouted, "Let's play ball, gentlemen!"

Well, the timeout that Coach Ferguson called seemed to do wonders for her team. And even though we were still dominating our opponent, we were keeping the score relatively close, because we were guilty of committing a comedy of errors of our own, as well as missing a bunch of real easy shots underneath the basket too.

In hindsight, but I think our lackluster performance was probably a blessing in disguise. Especially since Murphy and I didn't want the score to get too lopsided, or have the guys fool themselves into believing that they were a lot better than they really were.

The highlight of the first half was watching Eddie Johnson trying to steal the ball away from one of the ARC players at half court. As both players wrestled for of the ball, neither one of them was willing to give the other an inch. The two players were so intent on possessing the ball that they were literally spinning around in circles fighting for it.

Eddie Johnson finally managed to gain control of the ball, and then began dribbling the ball up the court in the direction that he was facing. What Eddie failed to realize was that he was dribbling the ball towards the wrong basket, and wound up scoring two points for the other team.

Poor Eddie, he was so determined on scoring a basket for the hometown Grizzlies, that he never heard Murphy shouting from the sidelines that he was heading in the wrong direction.

When Eddie finally realized his blunder, he began apologizing to anyone who was willing to listen to him. He even climbed up into the bleachers, so that he could plead his case to the Director. It was pretty funny, and even the referees got a big laugh out of the mishap as well.

In the second half, Murphy decided to play his bench. We were actually winning the game by a pretty comfortable margin, and for all intents and purposes the game was over, so Murphy wanted some of his weaker players to get some playing time.

So in an effort to keep things from getting too willy-nilly out on the court, Murphy decided to keep three of his starting players in the game at all times, and platoon two bench players in and out of the lineup. Murphy's game plan seemed to be working out quite well, until halfway through the fourth quarter, when the referee decided to call a foul on Russell Turner.

Apparently, Russell didn't agree with the referee's call, and certainly let the referee know about it, as he shouted at the top of his lungs, "Hey ref, what are you crazy, that wasn't a foul! You better change that call right now, or else you're gonna have a big problem on your hands!"

The referee walked straight over to Russell Turner, and in a calm and relaxed tone of voice the referee then asked Russell, "Excuse me, but are you threatening me, #13?"

Russell replied, in an antagonistic tone, "Maybe, so what are you gonna do about it, ref?"

At that point, the referee walked over to the scorer's table and decisively said, "We have a personal foul on #13, as well as a technical foul on #13 for unsportsmanlike conduct."

The referee walked directly over to Murphy, and then bluntly said, "Listen coach, if I have another outburst like that, then not only will #13 be ejected from the game, but you'll also be in jeopardy of forfeiting the game as well."

Upon hearing the referee's staunch warning, Murphy motioned Russell off the court, so that Russell could take a seat on the bench. Murphy then inserted Bobby Diggs into the lineup.

As Russell Turner stormed off the court, he viciously shouted, "Hey ref, I'll see you out in the parking lot after the game, and it won't be for an ice cold beer either!"

To this day, I still don't know how Murphy managed to keep his composure in check.

As Russell sat down on the far end of the bench, he began pleading his case to whomever would listen to him. Russell then shouted, "Hey Murphy, that referee doesn't know his ass from his elbow, and he shouldn't be allowed to officiate anymore of our basketball games either!"

Murphy got up from his seat and walked down to the far end of the bench where Russell Turner was sitting, and then quietly but sternly said, "Russell, did you forget all about our little conversation earlier, when I told you to keep your mouth shut and to not argue with the referee."

"But Murphy...," Russell exclaimed.

Murphy replied, "No buts! I don't want to hear it, Russell. I'm very disappointed in you. You're supposed to be one of the leaders on this team. We'll talk more about this later, trust me."

As Murphy made his way back to the other end of the bench, Russell hung his head low and then draped a towel over his head. Russell knew that he was in Murphy's doghouse, so now he needed to come up with a way to get back into Murphy's good graces again.

So after weighing his options, Russell decided to turn on the waterworks and start crying. Not because he was sad, but because he was hoping that Murphy would feel sorry for him.

Just for the record, but Russell Turner is an extremely dangerous individual. And as cruel as that may sound, but if it wasn't for the fact that Russell was already under lock and key, then his photograph would be posted on the bulletin board of every state and federal law enforcement agency in the country.

As I've gotten to know Russell Turner a little bit better, I would have to say that he is one of the most cunning individuals that I've ever known, and there is absolutely nothing that he wouldn't do to save his own neck.

So as Russell continued to hide under his towel, he was crying loud enough to wake the dead. And this Oscar winning performance of his was staged solely for Murphy's benefit.

But unfortunately, Murphy wasn't buying it.

Every time that I glanced in Russell's direction, he was peeking out from under his towel in hopes of getting Murphy's attention. Or should I say, trying to tug at Murphy's heartstrings.

So as Russell's little Greek tragedy continued to drag on, Russell wasn't even crying any real tears, they were merely crocodile tears.

But then Russell isn't capable of generating any real tears. Because Russell is a textbook sociopath, who lacks the capacity to possess any genuine feelings for anyone other than himself.

Like Bobby, Russell equates kindness for weakness. So Russell preys on people that he can take advantage of, - because Russell views kindhearted people as nothing but easy targets.

When I glanced over at Murphy, he looked totally disillusioned and completely at the end of his rope. Although Murphy had his eyes fixed on the game, I could tell that his mind was a million miles away.

Murphy then quietly asked, "So whatta ya think Rodney, should we end the game?"

I simply replied, "Hey, you're the head coach, Doc. So it's your call."

Murphy stood up and shouted, "Timeout, ref!"

The referee blew his whistle, signifying a stoppage in play.

Murphy then motioned for the two referees and Coach Ferguson to join him at the scorer's table, so that he could confer with them.

Before the game, Murphy and Coach Ferguson both agreed on the "Mercy rule," which basically means that if the score becomes too lopsided, or if the game should get too out of hand, then both coaches would consider shortening the game by having the clock run continuously.

So after much deliberation, the coaches and the referees agreed to invoke the Mercy rule. And then instructed the timekeeper to keep the clock running, except for any injuries or timeouts.

With the clock winding down, Coach Ferguson decided to call her final timeout, so that she could draw up one last play for her team to execute. The referee blew his whistle, signifying a stoppage in play, and then both teams left the court and went over to their respective benches.

As the Grizzly players all huddled around Murphy, he proceeded to tell them that in the event that they should gain possession of the ball, then he absolutely and positively did not want anyone to take a shot at the basket. But to just simply run out the clock and let the game end.

Lest we forget, but Murphy is a gentleman of the game. And win, lose, or draw, he fully expects his players to exercise good sportsmanship at all times towards their opponent.

The referee then blew his whistle and shouted, "Let's play ball, gentlemen!"

So with twenty seconds remaining in the game, the ARC team threw the ball inbounds and then attempted to execute one last play.

As the clock ticked down, the ARC team seemed to be rather unsure of themselves, and it looked as though they were going to run out of time before they could actually get a shot off.

So with five seconds remaining in the game, the ARC player then inadvertently dribbled the ball off of his foot, and the ball just so happened to carom directly over to Bobby Diggs.

As Bobby stood at half-court with the basketball, he was so caught up in the moment that he didn't know what to do. As the clock was ticking down toward zero, Bobby's teammates were all clamoring for the ball, but Bobby seemed rather hesitant in passing the ball to any of them.

Bobby then made a split second decision, so he heaved the basketball straight up into the air with all his might, and hoped that the basketball wouldn't come down until the clock hit zero.

As I watched the ball float through the air, it was a pretty safe bet that the ball didn't have a prayer of coming anywhere near the backboard, let alone hitting the basket, or even scoring.

That being said, I noticed that the atmosphere inside the gym was beginning to shift, and that all eyes were now riveted on the flight of the ball in anticipation of what might happen next.

As crazy as it may sound, but the ball seemed to take a dramatic shift in its trajectory, as if some sort of tractor-beam had just locked on to it, and steered it in the direction of the basket.

When the buzzer sounded, signifying the end of the game, the crowd continued to watch the flight of the basketball, and wondering if Bobby Diggs was somehow flirting with destiny.

As the ball began its downward arc, I suddenly realized that the ball had a pretty good chance of hitting the backboard. And dare I say, - a remote possibility of going into the basket.

Swish!

Oh, my God!

The shot that Bobby Diggs just took from the half-court stripe went straight into the basket. And if I hadn't of seen it with my own two eyes, then I never would've believed it.

Pandemonium swept through the crowd, as everyone jumped out of their seat and started to applaud Bobby, and his utterly spectacular feat of sinking a half-court shot right at the buzzer.

As the crowd continued to cheer, everyone in the gym began chanting in unison, "Bobby! Bobby! Bobby…!"

Bobby was so excited that he started running around the court in circles, as he feverishly scratched the back of his head, while shrieking over and over again, "Oh boy, oh boy, oh boy!"

Suddenly both teams started chasing after Bobby, so that they could congratulate him on his utterly sensational accomplishment. For the first time in his life, Bobby had attained celebrity status, and everyone in the gym couldn't stop chanting his name or taking their eyes off of him.

When all of the excitement finally died down, both teams lined up at half-court and shook hands. Dick Henderson jumped out of the bleachers and went straight over to Bobby Diggs, so that he could shake Bobby's hand, and congratulate him on his one-in-a-million basketball shot.

As I watched the look of complete joy on Bobby's face, I was thinking that this might be the happiest moment that Bobby has ever had in his entire life. I felt honored to be here tonight, so that I could witness this epic event, and share in this unforgettable moment with Bobby Diggs.

Murphy then walked over to Bobby, and said with a big smile, "Nice shot, Bobby! But I thought we all agreed during the timeout that we weren't going to take any shots at the basket."

Bobby then innocently replied, "But Coach Murphy, I wasn't trying to score a basket, I was only trying to run out the clock by throwing the ball up in the air, and I guess the basket just got in the way. Hey, I told you that wearing the #23 uniform was lucky, oh boy, oh boy, oh boy!"

As we were packing up the gear, the Director and Mr. Hanson came over to the bench so that they could commend the boys on their hard fought victory. The Director then shook Bobby's hand, and congratulated him on his buzzer beating shot. Hanson shook Bobby's hand too, and then hastily asked Bobby if he would teach him how to make a basket from half-court sometime.

As Hanson was busy lapping it up with Bobby, I started to wonder if Hanson would've been this chummy with Bobby if the Director wasn't standing there right next to him.

Lest we forget, but Hanson was ready to pull the trigger on transferring Bobby Diggs to the forensic unit only a few months ago, and now he's acting like he and Bobby are best friends.

So as Bobby recounted his golden moment with Hanson, the Director then turned toward Murphy, and proudly said, "Murphy, I'm very impressed with the job that you're doing thus far here at the facility. I know how challenging these clients can be. As a matter of fact, I've actually mentioned your name several times in my reports to the Commissioner. Hey, thanks for making me look good in front of the big boss!"

As we shut off the lights and made our way out of the gym, I was glad to see that Murphy was finally getting the recognition that he so richly deserved.

And maybe, in some small way, the fact that the Director acknowledged him tonight on the outstanding job that he was doing here at the State School, just might help take some of the sting out of the embarrassment that Russell Turner caused him during the basketball game.

CHAPTER ELEVEN

"Good morning, coaches! Hey, congratulations on last night's victory!" The building supervisor said, as Murphy and I walked onto the unit.

Apparently, everyone in the building is buzzing about last night's basketball game. And despite the fact that the game was totally one-sided, a win is still a win. And at the end of the day, I guess that's all that really matters.

As I fired up the morning work session, I noticed that some of the boys on the basketball team weren't exactly giving it their all this morning. And they seemed to be more interested in resting on their laurels than they were on completing any of their assigned laundry tasks.

Now ordinarily, I frown on goldbricking. But in this case, I decided to cut the boys a little slack, and permit them to enjoy their fifteen minutes of fame, especially since this could possibly be their only victory of the season.

Jamal Buchanan and Tyrell Freeman started back in the laundry workshop this morning. Dick and Cameron both felt that it was time for Jamal and Tyrell to resume their normal routines again, and I would certainly have to agree with that.

But to be perfectly honest with you, it's been nice not having to deal with Jamal and all of his silly antics every day. But as the old adage says, "All good things must come to an end."

As Jamal strutted into the Work Activity Center, his face remains badly bruised, and his nose was still heavily bandaged. But all in all, Jamal seemed to be in relatively good spirits and eager to be back to work again, and to have the chance to earn some pocket money.

When the boys on the basketball team starting talking about last night's game, I noticed that Jamal Buchanan had a very disgusted look on his face, and I'm sure that it must've bothered the hell out of Jamal that he wasn't part of the excitement of last night's victory.

Now under normal circumstances, Jamal would've had a few choice comments to make regarding last night's game. But seeing how it was his first day back to work, he didn't want to rock the boat too much, so he just decided to keep his thoughts and comments strictly to himself.

Tyrell Freeman on the other hand was his usual gracious self. And the first thing that Tyrell did when he walked through the door of the Work Activity

Center was to congratulate the boys on their hard fought victory last night.

When Murphy arrived to work this morning, he found a sealed envelope sitting on top of his desk. When he opened up the envelope, he saw that it was a letter of commendation from Mr. Hanson. Apparently, Mr. Hanson wrote the letter because he wanted to express his appreciation for all of the hard work and dedication that Murphy has demonstrated thus far in the SBU.

I must admit that it was a very thoughtful gesture on Hanson's part to write the letter. Although given his unsavory reputation, it seemed completely out of character for him to do.

Let's just hope that Hanson doesn't try to use this noble deed of his as leverage against Murphy, and trick Murphy into believing that he has him safely tucked away in his back pocket.

At lunch the other day, Murphy mentioned to me that he plans on having a rematch with the ARC. Upon hearing the news, I was quick to ask Murphy if he was scheduling the rematch as a courtesy to Coach Ferguson, or because he was looking to bolster his win/lost record.

Before responding to my rather ominous question, Murphy seemed to hesitate a bit, but then pointed out to me that scheduling a rematch with the ARC was simply the right thing to do.

But that devilish grin on Murphy's face told me otherwise.

In addition to scheduling a rematch with the ARC, Murphy also said that Coach Ferguson furnished him with a list of teams that might be willing to play us in the future. So Murphy plans on contacting some of the teams on the list later this week to see if he can generate any interest.

So after jotting down the list of names that Coach Ferguson gave him, the first thing out of Murphy's mouth was, "Are any of these teams as good as Mitchell Psychiatric Center?"

Coach Ferguson laughed, but then quickly reassured Murphy that none of the teams on the list even comes close to beating Mitchell, which made Murphy breathe a huge sigh of relief.

So after contacting each of the teams on the list, Murphy was able to schedule five basketball games for the upcoming month. Four of the games were scheduled to be home games, and one of the games was slated to be on the road.

Lately, the guys have been really gelling as a team. And even though I have a tendency to be somewhat cynical at times, I must admit that the boys have really surpassed my expectations.

Not only are the boys executing the pick-and-roll play with much more efficiency, but they are becoming more adept in learning several other basic plays that Murphy has incorporated into their arsenal as well.

By month's end, Murphy and the boys had managed to win all five of their basketball games, and they were currently riding a six game winning streak.

Each of the wins were won by a comfortable margin, except for one which turned out to be a real barn burner, as Francis Watson threw up a desperation shot with only one second remaining on the clock, and he wound up sinking the winning basket right at the buzzer.

At lunch the other day, Murphy surprised me by saying that he was entertaining the idea of scheduling a rematch with Mitchell Psychiatric Center. I'm sure this burning desire to play mighty Mitchell again is based on the fact that we are currently riding a six game winning streak.

Now even though we've enjoyed some recent success, I really didn't think that we had a snowballs chance in hell of beating an explosive team like Mitchell. Mitchell not only had more firepower than us, but they were significantly more skilled and athletic than we were as well.

So despite having the deck stacked against us, Murphy decided to give Coach Peterson a call over at Mitchell Psychiatric, so that he could schedule a rematch with the mighty Spartans.

When Coach Peterson heard that Murphy was interested in a rematch, he was absolutely thrilled, especially since not many teams are willing to go up against Mitchell for a second time.

As a friendly gesture, Murphy offered to play the game in Mitchell's home gym, which is situated right on the grounds of the main campus, and the game is slated for next Tuesday night.

For the past week, Murphy has been running basketball practice day and night, so that his scrappy bunch of Grizzlies will be good and ready to face the challenge from mighty Mitchell.

As a matter of fact, Murphy even decided to hold basketball practice on the weekend, because he was afraid that the boys might forget everything that they learned during the week.

No joke!

Now although we looked pretty good in practice, Murphy knew that game situations were a horse of a different color. And to make matters even tougher, but this time the game was going to be played on Mitchell's home court, and not in the friendly confines of the State School gym.

In addition to that, Murphy still wasn't sure how the guys would react to playing mighty Mitchell again, especially after the drubbing we took the last time that we played against them.

Well, I guess we can speculate all that we want. But we really won't know how well the boys will do until we lace 'em up tomorrow night, and look mighty Mitchell square in the eye.

So tonight is the big game, and as Murphy and I were finishing up our pre-game strategy session, I noticed that Murphy seemed a bit on edge and that he had a real bad case of the jitters.

In an effort to ease Murphy's mind, I casually said, "Listen Doc, this is our last game of the season. So why don't we just go out there tonight and try to have some fun, and let the chips fall where they may. So whatta ya think of that idea?"

Murphy replied, "Yeah, you're right, Rodney. But I'd really like to beat Mitchell tonight. No one has beaten Mitchell in over three years, and I'd really like to be the team that snaps their three year consecutive winning streak."

As we were rounding up the boys for the game, Lance Coppenger pulled Murphy aside, and said on the Q.T., "Hey coach, if you need a scouting report on any of the Mitchell players tonight, then I'm your man. Because I know most of the guys on the team."

Murphy paused momentarily, and then said, "Okay, but I thought you came to us from Western Psychiatric Center?"

Lance replied, "I did come from Western Psychiatric, but I also spent time at Mitchell too. And the last time we played those guys, I recognized some of the players on their team."

Murphy nodded his head, and quietly said, "Okay, well, I'll keep that in mind. Thanks, Lance."

"Okey-dokey," Lance replied, as he gathered up all of the towels and the water bottles.

As the guys were changing into their game uniforms, Murphy leaned over to me and whispered, "Hey Rodney, Lance just told me that if I need a scouting report on Mitchell tonight, then he'll be happy to give me the rundown on all of their players."

I quietly chuckled, and then replied, "Well, I think that was very considerate of Lance, but what he fails to realize is that a scouting report is only useful in the event that you haven't played someone before. And based on the beating that we took from Mitchell the last time that we played them, I think we already have a pretty good idea on what their players can do."

"Exactly…," Murphy groaned.

On the ride over to Mitchell Psychiatric Center, the guys seemed awfully quiet to me. Usually, the clients are pretty loud and boisterous whenever they're on the van, and you can barely hear yourself think. But tonight you could almost hear a pin drop. And for some strange reason, my psychic instincts were telling me that tonight may possibly be a night to remember.

As we drove along, Murphy seemed to be keeping one eye on the road and one eye glued in the rearview mirror. He appeared to be quite concerned about his players. And every so often, he would glance in my direction, as if to say, "I've got a real bad feeling about tonight, Rodney."

In all my years of working here at the State School, I have never experienced this type of sensation come over me before. The only sounds that you could hear on the van were the sounds of rhythmic breathing. It kinda reminded me of how soldiers must feel right before stepping into battle, as they prayed to God to keep them safe, so that they could make it back home to see their family and loved ones again.

When we walked into the Mitchell gym, it was buzzing with activity. The Mitchell faithful really came out in droves tonight, so that they could cheer on their hometown Spartans.

Quite honestly, but no one in their wildest dreams would've ever imagined six months ago that we'd be playing an official basketball game on the road in front of a packed house, with matching uniforms and real referees. Yet, here we are tonight, and it's all because of Murphy.

For tonight's final game, Murphy designated Francis Watson to be our team captain. Tyrell decided to step down as team captain, because he felt that his egregious actions toward Jamal Buchanan were unbecoming of wearing the heralded C on the front of his uniform.

Although Murphy tried to convince Tyrell to reconsider his decision, Tyrell is a man of principle, and nothing that Murphy could say or do was going to sway this gentle giant's mind.

When the Mitchell team walked into the gym, they had the swagger of a champion.

The Mitchell players were all business, as they ran through their pre-game warm-up drills like a well-oiled machine. Their bulls-eye shooting and pinpoint passing was utterly impeccable.

As I stood there marveling at the skill and athleticism that all of these talented young Mitchell players had, it was difficult for me to fathom that all of these players were actually inpatients at a state-run psychiatric hospital, and the mere thought of it saddened me greatly.

Murphy wanted to visit with Coach Peterson for a few minutes, so he asked me to keep an eye on things while he went over and chatted. As Murphy headed over to the Mitchell bench, he asked me to have the guys work on the three set plays that we have been practicing all week.

As I was getting the guys into position, Lance Coppenger asked me if he could say "hi" to some of his Mitchell friends that were sitting in the bleachers on the other side of the gym.

Although my initial thought was to say "no," I reluctantly agreed to permit Lance to go over and say "hi" to his friends, but then made it a point to say that I wanted him back on the team bench sitting right next to me as soon as the referee blew his whistle to start the game.

Lance then flashed me his million dollar smile, and excitedly replied, "Okey-dokey!"

By now, the referees had arrived and they were engaged in a lively conversation with Murphy and Coach Peterson.

I then motioned all of our players over to the bench for a quick water break. And since Lance wasn't around, I instructed each of the guys to help themselves to a squirt of water.

The referee blew his whistle, and then motioned for both teams to take the court.

Murphy and Coach Peterson shook hands, and then they hustled over to their respective benches, so that they could give their players a little pep talk and some last minute instructions.

As Murphy addressed the boys, they all had that deer in the headlights look in their eye.

And even though they kept nodding their heads "yes" to everything that Murphy was telling them, I could tell that they simply weren't processing a single word that Murphy was saying.

The referee blew his whistle again, and then shouted, "Let's play ball, gentlemen!"

As a show of good sportsmanship, the referee had all of the players shake hands with each other, and then he reminded both teams that he expected to see a nice clean game, with no foul language, or no unnecessary wisecracks or name calling.

While addressing the players, the referee seemed to be looking directly at Russell Turner the whole time. Russell didn't like the fact that the referee was singling him out, so in a rather defiant tone of voice Russell then said, "Hey ref, what the hell are you looking at me for?"

It would seem that Russell Turner has built up quite a reputation around the league, and that news travels fast that Russell has a pretty short fuse and a really bad temper. It was quite apparent to me that the referee was not about to put up with any of Russell's guff or nonsense tonight, and he certainly let Russell know about it right from the get-go.

So after making sure that the players were all set and squarely into position, the referee blew his whistle, and then tossed the ball up into the air, signifying that the game was underway.

Well, it certainly didn't take long for Mitchell to get on the scoreboard. The Mitchell point guard dribbled the ball right down the court, and then orchestrated three nifty passes, which led to mighty Mitchell taking an uncontested shot under the basket for a 2-0 lead.

Russell Turner immediately pointed the finger at Tyrell Freeman, and accused Tyrell for allowing the Mitchell player to score such an easy basket. Murphy could see that his players were a little flustered, so he shouted out some gentle words of encouragement from the sidelines.

It was now our turn to play offense. Francis Watson took the inbounds pass and then dribbled the ball up the court. Murphy instructed Francis to run play #2 once he crossed over the half-court stripe, so Francis raised two fingers in the air to indicate the play that Murphy wanted.

As soon as Francis raised his two fingers in the air, Tyrell cut straight to the basket. But in doing so, Tyrell ran smack into Russell Turner, who fell to the floor like a sack of potatoes.

Russell looked up at Tyrell, and then viciously snarled, "Tyrell, you stupid numbskull, you're running play #3. Murphy wants us to run play #2, which means that you gotta set a pick at the foul line, so that Francis can shoot the goddamn ball at the basket, you big dummy!"

Murphy then quickly shouted, "Timeout, ref!"

Both teams trotted off the court and then went directly over to their respective benches.

As Murphy corralled all five of his starting players onto the bench, he then instructed them to take a couple of slow deep breaths, and just try to relax.

Russell Turner then spouted off by saying, "Hey Murphy, you better talk to your boy Tyrell, because that big lunkhead is screwing up all the plays!"

Murphy scowled at Russell, and then sternly said, "Russell, I don't wanna hear another word out of you, or else you'll be sitting on the bench right next to me for the rest of the game!"

"Yes Murphy…," Russell replied.

Murphy took a moment to collect his thoughts, and then addressed the team by saying, "Listen guys, I know it gets a little confusing out there trying to remember which play is what, so let's go through it one more time. Play #1 is the pick-and-roll, play #2 is the back door play, and play #3 is setting the pick at the foul line, so that Francis can take a wide open shot at the top of the key. Now c'mon, let's start playing some good basketball out there. We can beat these guys!"

The referee blew his whistle and shouted, "Let's play ball, gentlemen."

As our team broke the huddle, Murphy quickly said, "Listen guys, we're gonna run play #3, which is what again, Tyrell?"

Tyrell thought about it for a moment, and then said in his deep and deliberate Southern drawl, "Um, I set a pick at the foul line, so that Francis can shoot the ball at the top of the key."

"Yes, that's right! Very good, Tyrell!" Murphy said, with a satisfying smile.

Both teams then took the court. The referee handed the ball to Eddie Johnson, who then tossed the inbounds pass into Francis Watson. As soon as Francis dribbled the ball over the half-court stripe, then that was Tyrell's cue to cut to the foul line, so he could set a pick for Francis.

When Francis saw that Tyrell was in position, he dribbled the ball directly toward him. The Mitchell player that was defending Francis never saw Tyrell standing at the foul line, and the Mitchell player ran smack into Tyrell. The impact between the two players was so violent that the Mitchell player went flying into the air, and almost landed directly into the bleachers.

Meanwhile, Tyrell never budged an inch.

When Tyrell saw that the Mitchell player was lying flat on his back, and completely sprawled out on the floor, he quickly bent down and picked him up, while saying in a very gentle and contrite tone of voice, "I'm awfully sorry, sir. Please accept my sincere apologies."

In the midst of all the confusion, Francis found a wide open spot next to the foul line, and then launched a fifteen foot shot at the basket and swish! The ball sailed right through the hoop.

The Grizzlies were now on the scoreboard, and the game was all tied up at 2-2.

As the boys ran up the court, Murphy was clapping his hands and cheering from the sidelines, and encouraging his Grizzlies to "bear" down and play a stingy man-to-man defense.

Mitchell inbounded the ball, and then dribbled the ball up the court.

Once again, Mitchell employed their signature move, which consisted of three crisp passes, and then finding a wide open man standing under the basket for an uncontested score.

Eddie then tossed the inbounds pass into Francis, who then dribbled the ball up the court.

Murphy shouted from the sidelines, "Francis, let's run play #1!"

Francis nodded his head, and then quickly raised one finger in the air, signifying the play that Murphy wanted the boys to run, which just so happened to be the pick-and-roll play.

As soon as Francis Watson raised one finger in the air, then that was Russell Turner's cue to run directly to the foul line, so that Russell could set a pick for Francis.

Francis then dribbled the ball towards Russell. As soon as Francis dribbled past Russell, Russell quickly cut to the basket, and Francis passed him the ball. Russell managed to catch the nifty pass from Francis Watson, and then banked the ball off of the backboard for an easy score.

Murphy and I couldn't believe our eyes, the play actually worked to perfection. And I was now beginning to buy into Murphy's theory, - that on any given day miracles can happen.

I then asked myself, "Could this possibly be the night that mighty Mitchell goes down in defeat?"

Mitchell inbounded the ball and then dribbled it decisively up the court. Once again, Murphy was imploring his Grizzlies to "bear" down and play a stingy man-to-man defense.

To our credit, our guys were a bunch of scrappy players. And even though the pesky man-to-man defense that we employed could technically be construed as a form of assault and battery, the referees were allowing us to play a physical brand of basketball tonight. This really played to our advantage, and might very well be the difference in leading us to victory tonight.

Despite our grit and determination, we just couldn't match the speed and the athleticism of the mighty Spartans, who were also quite adept at dribbling and passing the basketball too.

Mitchell passed the ball around the court as if it were a hot potato!

The Mitchell squad was starting to wear us down. But when the first quarter was over we were only down by two points, which from our standpoint was like playing with house money.

As the boys staggered over to the bench, Murphy was patting each of them on the back, and giving them some well-deserved high fives. The boys were completely dehydrated, so it was crucial for them to get some water into their system before heading back out onto the court again.

Before addressing his players, Murphy cried out, "Let's go, Lance! I need you to get over here right now, so that you can give these guys some water, because they're all dying of thirst!"

Murphy didn't waste any time in talking to his players. But then in the middle of his pep talk, Murphy realized that none of the guys were drinking any water, so he shouted for Lance again, "C'mon Lance, let's go, the referee is gonna blow the whistle any second now!"

It suddenly dawned on me that Lance Coppenger was not on the bench. I guess I was so caught up in the game that it completely slipped my mind that Lance didn't make it back from visiting with his friends over on the far bleachers.

Murphy then hastily asked, "Hey Rodney, where the hell is Lance Coppenger?"

I anxiously replied, "Um, I think he's on the other side of the gym visiting with some of his Mitchell friends. But don't worry Doc, I'll go get him right now!"

As I dashed across the gym, my adrenal glands were operating on overdrive. When I reached the far bleachers, I quickly surveyed the crowd, but Lance was nowhere to be found.

In a state of extreme and utter panic, I began to frantically ask willy-nilly if anyone knew Lance Coppenger. And if so, when was the last time that anyone may have seen him.

One of the Mitchell staff then spoke right up and said that she saw Lance a few minutes ago, and that he was heading towards the restroom area with his friend Melissa.

When I entered the restroom, it was completely dark and empty, and there was no sign of Lance whatsoever. I then sprinted out into the parking lot to see if Lance and Melissa were both outside enjoying a little bit of the moonlight air, but there wasn't a soul in sight out there either.

At that point, I was so frazzled that I didn't know what to do. In all my years of working here at the State School, I have never been in this type of a predicament before.

I then asked myself, "Could Lance have possibly flown the coop?"

Suddenly, my imagination started to run wild, and it was beginning to get the best of me, so I decided to head back into the gym and inform Murphy of the situation.

As I approached Murphy, he nervously asked, "So where's Lance, did you find him?"

I quickly replied, "Doc, I don't know where he is, I can't find him anywhere. I think he may have taken off with some girl named Melissa."

"What!" Murphy exclaimed.

Murphy thought a moment, and then continued by saying, "Okay, well, let's try not to panic. Lance couldn't have gotten very far, so we're gonna have to stop the game and go look for him. Why don't you stay here with the guys, while I go break the news to Coach Peterson."

I quietly mumbled, "Okay Doc, I'll try not to lose anyone else while you're gone."

Murphy requested timeout, and then explained the situation to the two referees.

Coach Peterson joined Murphy and the two referees at half-court, and then they all proceeded over to the scorer's table, so that they could officially end the game.

Meanwhile, there was a lot of confusion on the faces of the Grizzly players.

When the guys finally realized that Lance was missing, Tyrell began to pray, Bobby was laughing his head off, and cold-hearted Russell Turner started crying like a baby.

However, the most disturbing reaction of all came from Francis Watson, who is not only our team captain, but someone that is supposed to be our most level-headed player as well, as he sadistically mumbled, "When they find Lance, I hope they bring him back in a body bag."

When Murphy came back to the bench, he looked as white as a ghost.

Apparently, Coach Peterson informed Murphy that he just got off the phone with the Mitchell Security Office, and the dispatcher said that he would issue a code red right away, and notify every patrol car and security officer to start searching the grounds immediately for Lance.

In addition to searching the grounds, an APB has also been issued, so that state and local authorities can be on the lookout for anyone matching Lance's description.

So after giving me the update on Lance, Murphy then asked me to stay with the guys for a few more minutes, so that he could give Dick Henderson a call and apprise him of the situation.

As I sat there waiting for Murphy to return, I kept asking myself over and over again why I permitted Lance to go over to the other side of the gym all by himself. Especially when Lance has a well-documented history of poor impulse control and highly questionable decision making.

Well, I guess I just deluded myself into thinking that Lance and I had an extraordinary relationship, and that he would never do something that might jeopardize this incredible bond that existed between us.

But apparently, I was wrong about that one. Obviously, Lance was sent to the State School for a reason, - he's not exactly here on a scholarship.

Let's face it, there's really no excuse for what I did. I simply let my guard down, and I wound up placing my faith in someone, who even on a good day, - is a wild card at best.

I wonder if Lance flew the coop on purpose, or was it simply opportunity knocking?

But the one question that kept gnawing at me was, "Why would I let someone who was once charged on suspicion of murder, head over to the other side of the gym all by himself, so that he could associate with people who were just as cunning and unscrupulous as he was?"

On the ride back to the State School, Murphy and I barely said a word to each other. We were both a nervous wreck, and extremely worried about what Mr. Hanson would say when he finds out that Lance Coppenger took off from the basketball game.

When we pulled up in front of the SBU, Dick Henderson was standing outside the building waiting for us. And by the look on Dick's face, I could tell that he was very troubled.

Bobby Diggs couldn't wait to hop off of the van first, so that he could spill the beans to Dick Henderson about Lance running away. Although Dick tried to reassure Bobby that everything was going to be okay, I could tell by the look in Dick's eye that he didn't believe a word that he was telling Bobby, and that Dick was very concerned about Lance's well-being.

So after escorting the guys back to their living units, Murphy and I stopped by Dick Henderson's office to see if there was any news on Lance. But unfortunately, Dick said that Mitchell Psychiatric Center still hasn't gotten back to him yet with any additional updates.

Dick tried to jog our memory's a bit by asking us a few questions regarding the incident, but nothing of any real significance was accomplished in our little question and answer session.

Due to the severity of the situation, Dick said that he had to notify Mr. Hanson regarding Lance's disappearance. And when Dick told Hanson the news, Hanson went totally ballistic.

If you ask me, Hanson probably blew his stack because he was more concerned about his precious reputation being tarnished than he was for any real concern for

Lance's safety.

So with nothing else to say, Dick told Murphy and I to go home and try to get some rest. And that maybe in the morning, we'll hear some news about Lance.

Or better yet, - that Lance will be found.

So the following day, I stopped by the building supervisor's office to see if there was any news or additional updates on Lance. The building supervisor informed me that Lance was still missing, and at the present time there were no new leads to follow up on.

The building supervisor also said that when he walked by Dick Henderson's office a little while ago, Dick and Mr. Hanson were arguing, and Hanson sounded like he was on the warpath.

Apparently, he must've heard Mr. Hanson screaming at the top of his lungs, "If Lance Coppenger isn't found within the next twenty-four hours, then heads will definitely roll!"

Well, that wasn't exactly the update that I was hoping to hear.

As I left the building supervisor's office, it certainly confirmed my suspicions, - that if Murphy and I were hoping to keep our jobs, then a few Hail Mary's might be in order.

I then headed down to Murphy's office, so that he and I could commiserate over a hot cup of coffee. When I tapped on Murphy's door, he looked mentally and physically drained. He told me that he couldn't sleep a wink last night, and he wound up tossing and turning all night.

As I listened to the pain and anguish in Murphy's voice, it seemed to bring back vivid memories of Henry Josephson, when I found out that he was missing from the psych center back in my days of working at WEALTH Industries. Henry was eventually found, and thank God he was no worse for the wear either, so let's just hope that the same can be said for Lance as well.

Obviously, Murphy doesn't want any harm to come to Lance Coppenger. But at the same time, Murphy can't wait to wrap his hands around Lance's scrawny neck for all the grief and aggravation that Lance has caused him. Especially since Lance's little Houdini act wound up costing Murphy his big chance at beating mighty Mitchell the other night, and snapping their impressive three year consecutive winning streak.

Before leaving for the day, Murphy and I stopped by Dick's office to see if there was any additional news or updates about Lance. But unfortunately, Dick had nothing new to tell us.

The following day, Murphy told me that he had a very lengthy telephone conversation with Coach Peterson last night. Peterson conveyed to Murphy that the girl Lance rendezvoused with the other night at the basketball game was a very troubled young lady, and that she's been a patient at Mitchell Psychiatric Center for almost twenty-five years.

Peterson said that she is diagnosed as being bipolar, and also having a severe antisocial personality disorder as well. And that over the years, she has had several brushes with the law.

Murphy also said that the young lady apparently likes to use sex as a way of enticing unsuspecting men to perform a variety of unscrupulous and dastardly deeds for her, and the quicker the authorities can locate her the better.

On a much lighter note, Murphy said that Coach Peterson was quite impressed with the quality of play that our team displayed the other night. And if the game had continued to be played, then his three year consecutive winning streak may have been in jeopardy.

As I was getting ready to head down to the workshop for the morning session, Murphy wanted to know if I would be interested in helping him out with softball practice this afternoon.

Apparently, Mitchell Psychiatric Center has a client softball team. And during the course of Murphy's telephone conversation last night, Coach Peterson asked him if he was interested in scheduling a friendly game sometime, and Murphy said that he would welcome the challenge.

Murphy then said, with a look of sheer panic on his face, "Gee Rodney, I hope Mitchell's softball team isn't as good as there basketball team," which then prompted me to laugh out loud.

As I was wrapping up the afternoon work session, I was surprised to see Murphy and Dick Henderson walk into the laundry workshop. Dick and Murphy both had a very serious look on their face, and I could tell that this wasn't exactly a social call.

Dick then pulled me aside, and quietly said, "Hey, guess who just popped up on the radar."

"Lance…?" I quickly answered.

"Uh-huh, and he's down at the Social Security Office right now too." Dick quietly said.

"Really…!" I hastily replied.

"Yeah, so I'd like you, Murphy, and Cameron to go down there and pick him up. And I told the Social Security Office that we could be there in about ten minutes." Dick decisively said.

As we headed over to the Social Security Office, Cameron pointed out that we needed to stay on our toes with Lance. Because he could be a bit squirrelly, or maybe even dangerous, especially since he hasn't taken any of his psychotropic medications for the past couple of days.

We were also curious to know why Lance was over at the Social Security Office in the first place. Did he go of his own volition, or did his friend Melissa put him up to it?

As we reached the main entrance of the Social Security Office, there was a young lady standing outside the doorway smoking a cigarette, who then took it upon herself to ask, "Are you gentlemen here for Mr. Coppenger?"

Cameron piped right up and said, "Uh yes, we are. Is Lance still here?"

She quickly replied, "Oh yeah, he's still here. He's sitting in the back cubicle with Mr. Harvey, who is our branch manager."

The young lady butted out her cigarette, and then eagerly said, "Please, follow me."

As we followed the young woman into the building she seemed very excited, almost giddy, as she stated, "When I entered Mr. Coppenger's social security number into our system, my computer red-flagged him as being a fugitive."

I quickly interjected, "Well, I wouldn't classify Mr. Coppenger as a fugitive, but we're certainly grateful that you contacted us. Is Mr. Coppenger alright?"

She nervously replied, "Well, to tell you the truth, he's been a bit odd. And at one point, he got a little testy with Mr. Harvey, and demanded that we cut him a check in the amount of five thousand dollars, so that he could find himself an apartment and stock up on some groceries."

Cameron then said, "Well, Mr. Coppenger has been off of his prescribed medications for the past three days, so I'm sure that he's not thinking too clearly right now."

As we drew nearer to Mr. Harvey's cubicle, I could feel my heart beginning to pound, and I was praying that we wouldn't wind up having an ugly scene on our hands with Lance.

I then turned to Murphy, who quietly whispered, "Let's get ready to rock'n roll, Rodney."

Just then I could hear Lance's voice faintly in the distance. I couldn't make out what he was saying, but the pitch of his voice was very shrill and his speech was rapid fire.

As we turned the corner, Lance was sitting across from Mr. Harvey. Lance was drinking a cup of coffee and he looked very disheveled. His hair was all matted and greasy. And not only could he use a fresh change of clothes, but he was in dire need of a shower and a shave as well.

When Mr. Harvey saw us approaching his cubicle, he looked utterly relieved, as if to say, "Thank God, the cavalry just arrived!"

Yet, strangely enough, but when Lance discovered that we were standing directly behind him, he never flinched, nor was he even the least bit surprised to see us. And if you didn't know any better, you'd almost think that nothing was wrong, just an ordinary day, business as usual.

As Lance nonchalantly glanced over his shoulder, he spoke to us in a very matter-of-fact way by saying, "Hi guys, so are you here to pick up your social security money too? Well, I hope you're not in too much of a hurry, because this guy is as slow as molasses."

Obviously, it never occurred to Lance that we were down at the Social Security Office for one reason and one reason only, - which was to drag his sorry ass back to the State School.

Cameron then calmly said, "C'mon Lance, we're here to bring ya back home now, okay."

Lance hesitated a bit, so that he could try to process what Cameron just said to him.

In a somewhat confused tone of voice, Lance replied, "Okay, well, I guess they can mail me my check. Hey, do you think we can stop somewhere and get something to eat, 'cause I'm pretty hungry."

I quickly said, "Sure, we can do that, but I heard that they're having your favorite dinner down in the dining room tonight. Hey, you wouldn't wanna miss out on that, would ya?"

Lance then excitedly replied, "Really! You mean we're having meatloaf with mashed potatoes and gravy tonight?"

"Yep, that's right." I said, with a big smile.

Cameron leaned over to Murphy, and then quietly whispered, "Lance is so hungry that he'd eat a bowl of dog food right now if you were to put it in front of him."

We thanked Mr. Harvey for all of his help, and then we left the Social Security Office.

The minute the van pulled away from the curb, Lance fell right to sleep. I'm sure that Lance hasn't slept a wink since this little escapade of his started, probably because he wanted to squeeze as much excitement into his day as he possibly could before we eventually found him.

As we headed back to the State School, we had to roll the windows down all the way, because the stench that was coming off of Lance was pretty bad. Lance will definitely need a good scrubbing before he has any ideas about sitting down to dinner tonight, that's for sure.

Anyway, the main thing was that Lance was safe and sound. So now the only thing left for us to worry about was to figure out a way to smooth things over with Mr. Hanson, so that Murphy and I can keep our jobs, and try to avoid having our heads placed on the chopping block.

When we arrived back at the SBU, Lance was still out like a light, and we actually had to shake him a few times so that we could get him to wake up.

Dick was waiting for us at the curb when we pulled up. And as soon as Dick spotted Lance in the vehicle, it looked as if a thousand pounds had just been lifted off of his shoulders.

As Lance stumbled off of the van, he greeted Dick in a bit of a groggy voice by saying, "Hi Dick, I'm back from my vacation. So did you miss me?"

Dick replied, "Boy, I sure did, it's good to have you back home again, Lance."

Lance gave Dick Henderson a big hug, and then tenderly said, "Yeah, I missed you too. Hey, I'll talk to you later, because I gotta get down to the dining room right now and grab some meatloaf with mashed potatoes and gravy before it's all gone."

Dick asked Murphy to escort Lance down to his living unit, so that Lance could get all washed up for dinner. As Murphy and Lance headed toward the building, Dick asked us if we had any problems down at the Social Security Office. We told Dick that everything went off without a hitch, and that Lance was extremely cooperative.

Dick then curiously asked, "So did Lance happen to mention why he decided to take off from the basketball game with that girl Melissa?"

Cameron grinned, and then sheepishly said, "Well, not in so many words, but I think I have a pretty good idea as to why he did it. Uh, that is, if you catch my drift, Dick."

In a chuckling voice, Dick then replied, "Yeah, I catch your drift, but how the heck am I supposed to word that in my report to Mr. Hanson," which prompted all of us to laugh out loud.

As we headed toward the building, Dick turned to me and commented, "Oh, by the way Jack, I don't remember seeing meatloaf with mashed potatoes and gravy on the menu tonight. I think it's quite a coincidence that Lance would mention his all-time favorite dinner on the same day that he returned back from his little getaway vacation, wouldn't you agree?"

I awkwardly replied, "Um, yeah, well, it must be wishful thinking on his part Dick."

Dick stared at me for a moment, and with a sly grin he quietly said, "Yeah, right, wishful thinking, I'm sure that's exactly what it was Jack."

Chapter Twelve

Well, now that basketball season is officially over, we've decided to shift gears, and try our luck at playing a little softball.

But to tell you the truth, I think managing a softball team is twice the nightmare that basketball is. And for my money, it's like jumping from the frying pan directly into the fire.

Why?

Well, for starters, in the game of basketball, you only need to manage five players at a time. Whereas in softball, you need to manage ten.

In basketball, the players have only one moving object to contend with. Whereas in softball, you have a lot more moving parts, such as players swinging hard wooden bats, balls traveling at excessive speeds, and players running around the base paths totally unsupervised.

Hey, don't get me wrong, nobody is a bigger sports nut than me. But I really don't understand why Murphy wants to start up a softball team this quickly, especially after all of the grief and aggravation that we just put up with in managing the basketball team.

Anyway, despite having the deck stacked against us, I agreed to give up my Saturday morning, so that I could help Murphy out with the softball team.

When I arrived at the field, Murphy was busy passing out the new softball equipment that Dick Henderson just requisitioned for him.

Initially, Dick was very excited about the prospects of having a client softball team. But in the wake of what just happened in the whole Lance Coppenger fiasco, Dick's enthusiasm for having a client softball team has certainly waned.

Although Hanson has given Murphy the green light for organizing a softball team, this little venture of ours comes at a pretty hefty price. And in order for Murphy to proceed with the softball team, then he needs to follow a few ground rules.

First and foremost, - when it comes to all matters regarding the softball team, then Murphy must run every decision by Mr. Hanson first!

Secondly, - absolutely no away games!

And last, but certainly not least, - to designate someone to watch the clients at all times!

When Murphy told me what the conditions were for having a softball team, it prompted me to sarcastically say, "Well Doc, you better ask Dick Henderson to requisition you some handcuffs and ankle bracelets, because that's the only way we're ever gonna corral this bunch!"

Upon hearing my quipping remark, Murphy relied on his incredible Irish wit by saying, "Well, just look at it this way Rodney, if something goes wrong and they wind up firing us, then at least you and I will be able to keep each other company on the unemployment line."

To start off practice, Murphy had the guys do some light stretching exercises. Once the guys were all limbered up, Murphy had the boys pair up into two's, so that they could toss the ball back and forth to each other and work on some of their catching and throwing skills.

Needless to say, but as the guys tossed the ball around the diamond there were a lot more misses than catches. And the only clients out on the field that had even the slightest bit of raw talent were Russell Turner, Francis Watson, and Jamal Buchanan.

As we watched the guys warm-up, I turned to Murphy and playfully said, "So, uh…, where's Lance Coppenger, I thought you had him penciled in to be our batboy this season?"

Murphy slightly chuckled, but then he became a bit more serious by telling me that Mr. Hanson made it quite clear to him that he doesn't want Lance involved with the softball team in any way, shape, or form. And what's more, but if he hears that Lance attended a single game or even helped out with one lousy practice, then pink slips would be issued to both of us forthwith.

In other words, Hanson was essentially placing Lance on house arrest.

We also heard through the grapevine that Hanson is toying with the idea of transferring Lance to the state forensic unit, which of course is the same facility that he wanted to transfer Bobby Diggs to six months ago. The state forensic unit deals exclusively with individuals that are considered to be chronic offenders, and often portray an unwillingness to follow the rules.

Or as the Nuns would often say back in parochial school, students who are "incorrigible."

In layman terms, the forensic unit was the equivalent to jail for the mentally challenged. So I guess it would be safe to say that Hanson doesn't believe in second chances. And for some reason, Hanson can't seem to get it through his head that the clients who live here at the State School are prone to poor decision making, and that it's only a matter of time until they screw up.

Well, all I can say is, God help you if you should happen to make a mistake on Hanson's watch. Because that mistake will ultimately buy you a one-way ticket to Palookaville, as payback for blemishing Hanson's impeccable reputation, or even tarnishing his exemplary track record.

So after watching about ten minutes of "catch," well..., if that's what you want to call it anyway, Murphy had the guys come over to the bench so that he could review the team rules.

As the boys all huddled around Murphy, he made it quite clear to them that he wasn't going to put up with the same types of shenanigans that he put up with during basketball season.

Murphy emphatically stated, "I expect all of you to be a cohesive team, a phalanx!"

At that point, the clients all seemed to glance at one another in a rather dumbfounded way, as they all quietly mumbled under their breath, "A phalanx, what the heck is a phalanx?"

None of the boys had any idea what Murphy's obscure metaphor even meant.

And to be perfectly honest with you, but I was scratching my head too with regards to the point that Murphy was trying to make to the boys as well.

Bobby Diggs then broke the silence, as he spiritedly shouted, "Hey, we won't let you down Coach Murphy!"

Murphy just nodded his head and grunted, "Yeah, okay, we'll see."

So once the ground rules were established, Murphy was now ready to make his player assignments. Like anything else, some of the boys were happy with their assigned positions on the field, and others, well, not so much.

As Murphy was getting ready to announce who was playing right field, I heard Russell Turner sarcastically mumble, "Huh, right field sucks, only the lousy players play right field."

Although I didn't particularly care for Russell's snide remark, his assessment of right field was pretty much accurate. Often times, coaches hide their weakest player out in right field because not many balls are hit to that side of the field. And more times than not, but the right fielder doesn't usually play a key or significant role in deciding the outcome of a game.

So without any further ado, Murphy announced that Bobby Diggs would be playing right field. Which caused Bobby to grumble, and Russell Turner to start laughing his head off.

As Russell continued to poke fun at Bobby, Murphy looked at Russell and shouted, "Hey Russell, if you keep it up then you'll be watching practice from your bedroom window, got it!"

"Yes Murphy…," Russell replied.

When making his player assignments, Murphy's strategy was to stack all of his strong players in the infield, and stick all of his weaker players out in the outfield.

Of course, manning the infield requires six players, but Murphy only had three players that were actually worth their salt. And the rest, well…, they were all pretty sketchy at best.

So in an effort to maximize all of his resources, Murphy needed to choose his positions wisely, so he decided to have Russell Turner play first base, Jamal Buchanan play shortstop, and Francis Watson be his pitcher.

To round out the infield, Murphy had Joe Conrad play second base, who could catch but he couldn't throw, and Dan Christoff play third base, who could throw but he couldn't catch.

The only other position in the infield that was up for grabs was catcher, but Murphy still wasn't sure as to whom he was going to stick behind home plate.

In terms of the rest of the guys on the team, well, they were nothing but a bunch of ragtag stumblebums, who couldn't catch or throw even if their lives depended on it. But despite their obvious lack of talent, they were all enthusiastic about playing and being part of the SBU team.

Murphy thought he would begin practice by concentrating on some fielding skills, so Murphy worked with the infielders, and I was stuck with all of the ragtags out in the outfield.

Obviously, the guys would have preferred to do some batting practice first, but Murphy reassured everyone that they would all get a chance to hit after we finished our fielding practice.

So after positioning everyone in the infield, Murphy looked at Dan Christoff who was playing third base, and then shouted, "Okay Dan, get ready, 'cause the ball is coming to you!"

Murphy tossed the ball up in the air, and then hit a slow ground ball to Dan Christoff. Dan bobbled the ball momentarily, but then snatched up the loose ball and rifled it across the diamond to Russell Turner. Russell caught the ball, but it was thrown with such velocity that he wound up catching it squarely in the palm of his glove, which caused Russell's hand to sting.

In dramatic style, Russell fell to his knees and started screaming like a baby. He then took off his glove and threw it down in disgust. Russell began rubbing the palm of his hand, so that he could try to soothe the pain, and help ease some of the agony and discomfort that he was feeling.

As Russell's Oscar winning performance continued, Dan Christoff wasn't the least bit sympathetic to Russell. And if anything, Dan found the entire incident to be quite funny, and he was even mocking Russell in front of the whole team for carrying on in such a juvenile way.

Russell Turner was absolutely livid at Dan Christoff, so Russell started screaming at the top of his lungs, "Are you fuckin' crazy! You threw the goddamn ball too hard, asshole!"

At that point, Dan Christoff and Russell Turner started jawing back and forth at each other, and trading insults that were so disgusting that it would even make a longshoreman cringe.

Obviously, Dan Christoff could've displayed a little bit more compassion toward Russell. But then I guess you could say that Dan was giving Russell a little dose of his own medicine too.

As I watched the drama unfold, I was thinking how psychiatrically impaired these two guys really were, especially Russell Turner, who has a list of psychiatric diagnoses a mile long.

Although Russell is diagnosed as having eight separate psychiatric disorders, the one psychiatric disorder that best describes him to a tee would probably be "glass jaw syndrome."

What...? You mean you've never heard of that diagnosis before?

Well, technically, "glass jaw syndrome" may not officially be listed in the DSM-V handbook, or appear in any double-blind studies in the American Psychiatric Journal. But I assure you that it does exist, and it certainly checks all of the boxes in describing Russell Turner.

In layman's terms, "glass jaw syndrome" simply means that Russell can dish it out but he can't take it. Russell seems to think that he can say or do whatever the hell he wants. But the minute that Russell hears something that he doesn't like, then Russell goes completely haywire.

By now, everyone on the ballfield was having a pretty good laugh at Russell's expense. Not only was Russell embarrassed, but his hand was throbbing like hell too. Russell was so mad that he threatened to punch Dan Christoff square in the mouth if Dan didn't stop laughing at him.

Despite the fact that Dan Christoff only stands 5'4, and weighs a measly one hundred and twenty pounds soaking wet, he's not one to back down from anyone. So when Dan took off his glove and started walking toward Russell Turner, who stands 6'5, I wasn't surprised in the least.

As Russell Turner and Dan Christoff came within inches of each other, Murphy decided to step in and put an end to their little pissing match before it escalated into a full-fledged brawl.

Murphy then shouted, "Hey, did you guys already forget about the team rules!"

Russell Turner and Dan Christoff stopped dead in their tracks. And from the tone of Murphy's voice, Russell and Dan both knew that Murphy meant business.

Murphy then asked Russell Turner how his hand was feeling, and if he needed an ice pack out of the first-aid kit to help ease the pain and prevent it from swelling up like a grapefruit.

Russell flippantly remarked, "Nah, it's okay now, it doesn't sting anymore."

Murphy then had Russell Turner and Dan Christoff shake hands with each other, and then he instructed both of them to return to their respective positions on the infield.

As Russell headed back over to first base, he looked over his shoulder at Dan Christoff, and then said in a chuckling voice, "Hey Dan, try not to throw it so hard next time, okay buddy!"

Dan Christoff then replied, in a rather playful and jocular tone, "Okay, buddy!

As Russell and Dan settled back into their respective positions, they were both giggling and hamming it up with each other as if they were a couple of drunken sailors on shore leave.

Murphy was now ready to resume infield practice again, so he looked at Jamal who was playing shortstop, and then shouted, "Okay Jamal, get ready, 'cause the ball is coming to you!"

I noticed that Jamal wasn't paying any attention at all to Murphy. Although Murphy tried calling his name several times, Jamal was too engrossed in the conversation that he was having with himself, and he seemed to be quite oblivious to everything that was happening around him.

Jamal kept strutting around the shortstop position arguing with himself. And to be honest with you, I wasn't quite sure who was winning the argument, Jamal or his imaginary friend.

Murphy then yelled at the top of his lungs, "C'mon Jamal, let's look alive out there!"

Suddenly, Jamal snapped out of his apparent funk. And in a real cocky tone of voice, he then shouted, "Chill out man, why you buggin'? Don't be screamin' at me like that cracker!"

As Jamal crouched down into position, he brashly said to Murphy, "Alright man, hit me a real hard one this time, and not some candy-ass grounder like you just gave Christoff, aight!"

Dan Christoff glanced over at Jamal, and then flashed Jamal a real nasty look.

As Murphy tossed the ball up in the air, I noticed that he had a real sinister smile on his face. With the crack of the bat, Murphy unleashed a howitzer directly towards Jamal Buchanan.

Murphy hit the ball so hard that it sounded like a bullet piercing through the air.

At first, it looked as though Jamal was in perfect position to handle the spicy ground ball. But due to the incredible velocity that the ball was traveling, Jamal just couldn't react in time, and the ball wound up scooting right through his legs and rolling straight out into the outfield.

Upon witnessing Jamal's mishandling of the steamy ground ball, all of the players on the field began to laugh out loud.

Jamal then muttered, "Damn! That ball took a bad-ass hop! You saw it, right Jerome!"

Jerome then shouted from his centerfield position, "Yeah man, the ball kinda skidded on ya. Ain't nobody catchin' any ground balls on this raggedy-ass field, nigger!"

Jamal replied, "Yeah, you're right, man! That's exactly what I'm talking about too, nigger! There are just too many bad-ass bumps on this crumby-ass field, dawg! Aight!"

Murphy shouted. "Hey Jamal, watch your language! I don't wanna hear that kinda talk out on the ballfield! Let's talk to each other with dignity and respect! Are we clear about that?"

Jamal flippantly replied, "Yeah, okay, whatever, man!"

Murphy then turned his attention toward Joe Conrad, who was our second baseman. For the most part, Joe wasn't a bad guy. And although Joe has a variety of psychiatric problems, the one problem that seems to haunt him from sun up to sun down are auditory hallucinations.

And trust me, - when these voices start talking to Joe, he usually listens!

So while Murphy continued to work with the infield, I was stuck with all of the ragtags out in the outfield. Every time that I hit a fly ball, someone would either misjudge the flight of the ball, or be so afraid that the ball would hit them that they would literally run away from it.

Although this comes as no big surprise to me, I shudder to think what will happen when we play our first official game. Not only do our outfielders have trouble catching the ball, but once they chase it down, they haven't the slightest idea as to whom they should throw the ball to.

As I continued to watch the comedy of errors unfold in front of me, I was thinking that Murphy may have bitten off more than he could chew with regards to organizing a softball team.

So after about an hour of "miss," I told the guys to take a little water break so that I could chat with Murphy. As I approached Murphy at home plate, he looked just as saturated as I was. So maybe it was time for us to break out the lumber, and have the boys practice a little hitting.

As Murphy dumped out the bag of bats, he asked me how we were looking out in the outfield. I just gave Murphy one of my patented stares, and quietly replied, "Don't ask, Doc."

Murphy grimaced, and then squeamishly said, "Uh, that bad, huh."

I then amusingly quipped, "Well Doc, I'm just glad that you didn't ask me to help you coach an archery team," which prompted Murphy to burst out into laughter.

So after the boys had a quick water break, Murphy announced to the team that we were going to do some batting practice now. Everyone cheered, and then all of the guys began to swarm around Murphy and started pleading with him if they could bat first. Murphy's voice then rose above the clamor, as he reassured everyone that they would all get a turn to swing the bat.

To make it easy on everyone, Murphy decided to have the guys bat according to their position. So that meant that Russell Turner would bat first, and that Bobby Diggs would bat last.

Russell Turner grabbed a bat, while everyone else took their respective positions on the field. Since first base was vacated, I manned the position while Russell was taking his turn at bat.

Before stepping into the batter's box, Russell took a couple of practice swings. And to no one's surprise, Russell was now taking centerstage and being his usual cocky and obnoxious self.

As Francis Watson took the mound to pitch batting practice, Murphy then realized that he needed a catcher. As Murphy scratched his head as to what to do, Bobby Diggs then shouted from his right field position, "Coach, Murphy! Coach, Murphy! I'll be catcher, please, please!"

Murphy hesitated a moment, as he tried to weigh all of his options. Murphy then rolled his eyes a bit, and with a noticeable sigh he groaned, "Alright Bobby, you can play catcher."

As Bobby strapped on the catcher's gear, I saw Francis Watson giving Murphy the stink eye. Francis knew that Bobby couldn't catch worth a row of beans, and he couldn't understand why Murphy was sticking someone as dreadful as Bobby Diggs behind home plate to be catcher.

Unfortunately, Murphy was between a rock and a hard place when it came to choosing a catcher. As I've stated before, the only players on the team that could catch worth a lick were Russell, Jamal, and Francis. And Murphy was already utilizing all three of them at key positions.

Before crouching down into position, Bobby turned towards Murphy, and then excitedly asked, "Hey Coach Murphy, how do I look in my catcher's outfit?"

Murphy flashed Bobby a half-hearted smile, and then simply said, "Well, you look like a real big leaguer Bobby, so show me that you can play like one, okay?"

Bobby could barely control himself, as he jubilantly replied, "Oh boy, oh boy, oh boy!"

Russell Turner then stepped up into the batting box. Russell tapped his bat on home plate a couple of times, and then brashly shouted, "Alright Francis, gimme a good one, so that I can knock it right out of the park!"

Francis Watson went into his wind-up and then tossed a real beauty right over the plate, but Russell decided not to swing at the pitch. As the ball sailed over home plate, it caromed off of Bobby Diggs' glove, and then rolled all the way back to the far corner of the backstop.

As Bobby Diggs went to retrieve the ball, Francis Watson curiously asked, "So what was wrong with that pitch, Russell?"

Russell replied, "Uh, it was too low, so gimme something that I can hit this time, okay?"

So Francis Watson went into his wind-up and then pitched another beauty right over the plate, but once again Russell Turner decided not to swing at the ball.

Francis then asked again, "So what was wrong with that pitch, Russell?"

As Russell explained why he didn't swing at the pitch, Bobby Diggs was in hot pursuit of retrieving the ball, which had once again ricocheted off of his glove and rolled to the backstop.

When I glanced at Murphy, he looked like he was ready to explode. But instead of losing his temper, Murphy just calmly said, "Hey Russell, why are you being so particular at the plate? This is batting practice. So start swinging the bat, so that we can try to move things along, okay."

Russell was absolutely dumbfounded by Murphy's comment. And in a real snide tone of voice, Russell replied, "Well, why the hell didn't you say so in the first place Murphy? I thought you wanted me to pretend like we were in a game situation!"

As Murphy tried to keep his composure in check, he quietly said, "Okay, well, that's my fault Russell, I guess I should've explained things better to you. So let's try it again, shall we."

Francis went into his wind-up and then threw a real beauty right over the plate. Russell took a vicious swing, but wound up missing the ball entirely. Everyone on the field burst out into laughter, except for Bobby, who was too busy chasing after the ball that he just missed again.

Russell didn't like the fact that everyone on the field was laughing at him, so he began screaming like a raving lunatic. For a split second there, I thought Russell might do something rash. Especially since he had a bat in his hands, which could have easily been used as a weapon.

Murphy then shouted from the sidelines, "Hey, no laughing out there! We're supposed to be a team, remember!"

I then humorously thought to myself, "You mean a phalanx, right Doc."

As Russell stepped back into the batter's box, he took a deep breath, tapped his bat a few times on home plate, and then carefully repositioned himself as he awaited Francis' next pitch.

Murphy then exhaustedly said, "Alright guys, can we please try it again?"

So Francis went into his wind-up and threw a perfect pitch right over the plate. But this time, Russell hit the ball right on the sweet spot of the bat, and smacked it deep into centerfield.

Jerome, who was playing centerfield, began charging the ball, but then realized that he had misjudged the flight of the ball entirely, and that the ball was sailing clear over his head.

As Jerome chased after the ball, Russell began taunting Francis by saying, "Hey Francis, is that all you got? Boy, you're a lousy pitcher! Hahahaha...!"

Francis didn't say a word, he just stood there on the pitcher's mound glaring at Russell.

Despite Francis' quiet disposition, he may arguably be the most dangerous client that we have living here at the State School.

Before coming to us, Francis was examined by a team of psychiatrists, who diagnosed him as having one of the worst sociopathic personality disorders that they have ever encountered.

In fact, one of the psychiatrist's actually wrote in his report, "In my professional opinion, I wouldn't recommend looking at Mr. Watson sideways, because he just might slit your throat."

Essentially, what makes Francis so dangerous is that he's not only smarter than the other clients here at the State School, but he's also far more devious as well. And the more you get to know him, the better you understand just how dark and sinister his thought processes really are.

According to Cameron, Francis exemplifies all of the personality traits of a serial killer.

Yet, here he is, our team captain, and the one guy that we seem to rely on the most in crucial situations. Which when you really think about it, is a pretty scary thought in itself.

As Russell continued to gloat, Francis quietly said to him in a very calculating and cold-blooded manner, "You got lucky this time Russell, but next time you might not be so lucky."

Russell didn't take Francis' comment too seriously, and felt that it was nothing more an idle threat, so he began taunting Francis by chanting, "We want a pitcher, not a glass of water!"

Francis didn't say a word, he just smiled at Russell and quietly nodded his head.

Murphy then shouted, "C'mon Russell, let's go, batter up!"

As Russell dug his feet back into the batter's box, he had a real big smirk on his face. He tapped home plate a few times with his bat, and then took his batting stance for the next pitch.

Francis went into his wind-up and then threw the ball as hard as he could at Russell's head, which caused Russell to drop his bat, and then fall to the ground like a sack of potatoes.

Believe it or not, but Bobby actually caught the ball this time. Bobby was so proud of himself that he began to laugh. Russell started yelling at Bobby, because Russell thought that Bobby was laughing at him, due to the fact that Francis just threw the ball directly at his head.

Meanwhile, Francis was smiling like a Cheshire cat. And I could tell that Francis was really savoring the moment, especially since Russell just saw his life flash right before his eyes.

As Russell stood up and brushed himself off, he vehemently shouted, "Hey Murphy, Francis just threw the goddamn ball at my head! So what the hell are ya gonna do about it?"

Murphy then asked Francis, "Hey Francis, did you throw the ball at Russell on purpose?"

Francis innocently replied, "No Murphy, I'd never do something like that."

Murphy then said, "Yeah, well, I still think that you owe Russell an apology anyway."

Francis looked directly at Russell, and with little to no expression in his voice, Francis said, "Oops, sorry about that Russell, I guess the ball must've slipped right out of my hand."

Well, at that point, Russell Turner was simply outraged, and he wasn't buying Francis' half-baked apology one bit. Especially when just a few minutes ago, Francis was making some rather subtle threats and inuendoes of his own towards Russell.

So feeling a bit frustrated, Russell began screaming at the top of his lungs, "For crissakes, Murphy! I'm telling you that Francis threw the goddamn ball at me on purpose!"

Murphy replied, "Listen Russell, since the ball didn't technically hit you, then there's really nothing that I can do. Francis said that he didn't do it on purpose, and I tend to believe him. Now go grab your glove and take the field, so that Joe Conrad can have a turn at bat now."

So for the next hour or so, everyone had a chance to "hit."

Well, if that's what you wanna call it anyway.

The majority of the time was spent watching the guys step up to the plate, swing and miss at the ball, and then waiting for Bobby Diggs to retrieve the ball from the edge of the backstop.

So after everyone had a chance to "hit," Murphy decided that he had enough softball for one day, so we wrapped up practice by having the guys run a few easy laps around the ballfield.

We then gathered up all of the softball equipment and threw it into the storage locker, which was situated right next to the field, and then brought the guys back to their living units.

Well, it's another Monday morning. And as Murphy and I were enjoying our morning coffee and donuts, we heard a quiet knock at the door and it was Dick Henderson, who playfully said, "Morning boys, I see that you're both working hard!"

"What's up, Dick?" Murphy replied, as he passed the box of donuts over to Dick.

As Dick helped himself to a donut, he pulled up a chair and then quietly said, "Well, I just thought I'd give you boys the heads up before you heard it from the rumor mill. Its official, Lance Coppenger is slated to be transferred to the state forensic unit within the month."

"Dammit! Why the hell can't Hanson cut Lance a little slack?" I grumbled.

"Because it's payback for Lance running away, that's why." Dick quietly said.

"It's just not right, Dick." Murphy replied.

"Well, from what I hear, Hanson and the Director took a little road trip out to the State Capital the other day and met with the State Commissioner, so that they could get a little more clarification regarding the new recidivism policy." Dick stated.

"Recidivism policy, what's that?" I curiously asked.

"Well, it seems to be the new buzzword that's sweeping through the State Capital. And it basically means that if a client screws up, then the powers to be have the authority to transfer them to a more secure setting, and a setting that is more commensurate to their needs." Dick said.

"Wow! It sounds rather punitive to me, Dick." Murphy stated.

"Well, maybe so, but the top brass wants to make an example out of Lance." Dick said.

Which then prompted me to say, "Well, I think Lance deserves a mulligan."

Dick quietly chuckled, and then replied, "Uh, mulligans only count on the golf course, Jack. So just remember one thing, if a client screws up inside the four walls of the State School, then that's one thing. But if a client should happen to screw up outside the four walls of the State School, then it's a whole different ballgame."

There was a brief moment of silence, and then Dick piped up and said, "In any event, I heard you guys had your first official softball practice on Saturday. So how does the team look?"

Murphy smirked, and then humorously replied, "Well, uh…, let's just say that we kinda resemble an expansion team in their first year of existence," which prompted Dick to laugh.

"Uh, that bad, huh." Dick said, chuckling.

"Yeah, but uh…, we look real good in our uniforms." I said, and we all laughed again.

Around three o'clock, I went by Murphy's office to see if he was planning on having softball practice today. When I tapped on Murphy's door, I saw him hanging up the telephone, and he was grinning from ear to ear.

I then nonchalantly asked, "Hey Doc, are we gonna have softball practice today?"

Murphy nervously replied, "Um, yeah, definitely. Hey, don't get mad at me Rodney, but I just scheduled a softball game with the psych center tomorrow afternoon at four o'clock."

"Uh, you're kidding me, right? Doc, our guys aren't ready to play in a real game yet. We still need a lotta work, such as running the bases, hitting the cutoff man, and throwing out the lead runner. Oh yeah, and did I happen to mention that we can barely catch or throw either."

Murphy quietly chuckled, and then calmly said, "Hey Rodney, aren't you the one who is always telling me to just live in the moment. Well, that's exactly what I'm intending to do, when we play Mitchell Psychiatric Center in a friendly game tomorrow afternoon here at the field."

As Murphy and I were getting ready to round up the boys for softball practice, there was a knock at the door. And to our complete surprise, it was Mr. Hanson standing in the doorway.

Hanson seemed unusually chipper, as he stood there gazing at us.

As Hanson stepped into Murphy's office, he said in a rather upbeat sort of way, "Hi guys, so how's it going?"

"Great!" We both said, in unison.

Murphy and I were at a complete loss for words. We haven't seen Hanson trolling the low rent district in a very long time. Usually when Hanson stops by the building, he goes directly down to Dick's office, and he's not one to sashay around the building making any social calls.

Hanson then continued by saying, "Hey Jack, could you excuse us for a few minutes, because I'd like to speak to Murphy in private."

"Yeah, sure, no problem, Mr. Hanson. I was just on my way out anyway." I replied.

As I walked out the door, I was wondering why Hanson would want to speak to Murphy in private, especially when all he had to do was just pick up the phone and give Murphy a call.

Did Hanson drop by to give Murphy the axe? Or to tell him that his services here at the State School are no longer required, because of what happened the night of the basketball game?

Hanson loves to make an example out of people, especially the ones who cause him to get egg on his face. Murphy didn't do anything wrong that night, I did. And if anyone is to blame for Lance's little Houdini act, it's me. I should be the one packing up my desk, not Murphy.

About twenty minutes later, Murphy joined me out on the softball field. When I asked him how his little powwow went with Mr. Hanson, he just snickered. Murphy then told me that Hanson just recommended him for a promotion. And that the Director has already signed off on all of the paperwork, and that Murphy should be seeing a salary increase in his next paycheck.

Obviously, I was quite elated for Murphy. But at the same time, I was shocked beyond belief. Because I didn't think that Hanson gave out promotions, - just took them away!

Especially since everyone around here refers to Hanson as the "Grim Reaper."

So after Murphy told me the good news, I then humorously quipped, "Gee Doc, maybe we should think about losing clients more often," which prompted Murphy to laugh out loud.

The following day, as I waltzed into Murphy's office, I placed a large container of coffee on his desk, and then casually asked, "So are you all ready for this afternoon's big game, Doc?"

Murphy replied, "Yeah, I think so...," but Murphy didn't sound very convincing to me.

As Murphy took a sip of his coffee, he quietly said, "Hey Rodney, I'm seriously thinking of putting Bobby Diggs out in right field, and having Eddie Johnson behind the plate. So, uh..., whatta ya think of that idea?"

I thought a moment, and then amusingly interjected, "Well Doc, given the fact that Eddie is diagnosed as being a paranoid schizophrenic, how are you going to convince him to crouch down behind home plate, while someone is swinging a wooden bat within inches of his head?"

Murphy quietly chuckled, and then replied, "Yeah, you're right, that never even crossed my mind. Uh, on second thought, maybe catcher isn't the right position for Eddie after all."

Later that afternoon, I met up with Murphy down in his office, so that we could go over some last minute strategy for this afternoon's softball game against Mitchell Psychiatric Center.

As we reviewed the lineup, I asked Murphy if he decided on who will play catcher today. And after giving it some thought, Murphy has decided to go with Bobby as his catcher after all.

Before I could even voice my opinion on the matter, Murphy said with a sly grin, "Don't worry, Rodney, I have a trick up my sleeve that just might solve all of Bobby's catching woes."

I then playfully asked, "Oh yeah, and what pray tell might that be, Doc?"

Murphy flashed me a rather sinister smile, as he cunningly replied, "Uh, you'll see."

Around three-thirty, we rounded up the guys and then headed down to the ballfield, so that we could get a quick practice in before Mitchell Psychiatric Center showed up for the game.

Murphy had the guys loosen up a bit by having them do a few light stretching exercises, and then he instructed them to take their respective positions on the field. As usual, Murphy worked with the infielders, and I wound up being stuck with all of the ragtags out in the outfield.

As Bobby Diggs crouched down behind home plate, he looked like he was still having a lot of trouble catching the ball, and I was wondering when Murphy was going to spring his big master plan into action in solving all of Bobby's catching woes.

Thus far, every time I glanced in Bobby's direction all I saw was the back of his uniform. Because every time that Francis Watson threw Bobby the ball, Bobby would wind up missing it, and then Bobby would have to chase after the ball and retrieve it from the edge of the backstop.

In the distance, I could see Hanson and Dick Henderson making their way toward us. When the clients saw them approaching the field, they all started jockeying for their attention, and asking Hanson and Dick how good they all looked in their brand new softball uniforms.

To tell you the truth, I was a little surprised to see Hanson being as animated as he was. Hanson was all smiles, as he shouted out words of encouragement to the boys out on the field. Especially to Bobby, who kept missing every ball that Francis Watson was throwing to him.

Apparently, Hanson was quite the athlete in his day, and he even played some collegiate baseball at the fancy Ivy League college that he attended.

As Hanson sat up in the bleachers, he was barking out the usual run-of-the-mill baseball lingo to the boys. And if you ask me, he was trying a little too hard to be the center of attention.

While I continued to work with the guys in the outfield, I spotted several state vehicles coming up the road, so I shouted over to Murphy, "Hey Murphy, Mitchell's here!"

As Murphy motioned his players off of the field, they all seemed pretty charged up and raring to go, and extremely excited about playing Mitchell Psychiatric Center in the game today.

While Hanson and Dick chatted with the guys, I leaned over to Murphy and asked him if he solved Bobby's catching woes yet, to which he replied, "Not yet, but don't worry, you'll see."

As the Mitchell contingency pulled up to the field, Murphy turned to me and said, "Hey Rodney…,"

I interrupted Murphy in midsentence, and then sarcastically said, "Yeah, I know, I know, you want me to stay with the guys, while you go over and introduce yourself to Coach Goodman. And in the meantime, you want the guys to warm-up and play catch until you come back, right?"

With a chuckle in his voice, Murphy flashed me his million dollar smile, as he replied, "Rodney, that's why you and I work so well together, you always know what I'm thinking!"

So while Murphy went over to the other side of the field to chat with Coach Goodman, I remained with the guys and had them play "miss," uh…, I mean, catch.

As I watched the boys tossed the ball around, I seemed to be keeping a pretty steady eye on Bobby Diggs, who kept missing every ball that Francis Watson was throwing to him.

Every time Bobby Diggs missed the ball, I could see the frustration building on Francis Watson's face. And with each passing miss by Bobby, I was becoming more and more intrigued as to what Murphy's foolproof plan was in rectifying Bobby's catching woes.

It's funny, but in a perverse sort of way, I actually enjoyed watching Bobby and Francis play "miss." I guess what really tickled my funny bone the most was listening to some of the off color comments that Francis was making to Bobby, especially when Bobby chased after the ball.

As I've alluded to before, Francis is a very dangerous individual, yet he seems to possess a certain je ne sais quoi, that none of the other clients in the building even comes close to having.

In my opinion, Francis shouldn't be living here at the State School, but there's really no other place for him to go. Francis is basically a square peg that's being forced into a round hole.

Murphy and I always try to cut Francis a little slack whenever we can. And when the top brass isn't around, we often refer to Francis as Popeye. Because not only is Francis the spitting image of Popeye the Sailor Man, but it just so happens to be his favorite cartoon show on TV.

By now, I could tell that Francis had reached the end of his rope. Bobby was missing every ball that Francis was throwing to him, and Francis' comments were now becoming a little more jagged.

Francis then glanced over at me, and with a look of total exasperation on his face he said, "Hey Jack, I need someone behind the plate who can catch the damn ball!"

I calmly replied, "Don't worry, Popeye. Murphy is working on a plan to fix it, okay."

Francis replied, in his own unique brand of humor, "Oh yeah, well, I hope Murphy's plan is to throw Bobby down a mine shaft, and then find me someone who can catch the damn ball!"

So after chatting with Coach Goodman for a few minutes, Murphy came back over to our side of the field, and asked me how the guys did in tossing the ball back and forth to each other.

I just gave Murphy one of my patented stares, and then amusingly quipped, "Well Doc, I don't envision us making a serious run at the pennant this year, that's for sure."

Murphy chuckled a bit, and then said with a great deal of confidence, "Well, I don't think we have to worry about Mitchell giving us too much of a challenge today anyway, Rodney."

"Oh, really! So, uh…, are you psychic, or do you have some inside information that you'd like to share with me, Doc?" I asked, with a tinge of sarcasm.

"Hey Rodney, you know I don't subscribe to that psychic energy stuff. That's strictly your department, remember." Murphy said, with an appreciative smile.

"Uh-huh, well Doc, my psychic instincts are telling me that Coach Goodman may be slightly downplaying the situation, and possibly instilling a false sense of security in you."

"Hmm, well, that's quite the analysis, Rodney. And who knows, you might be right. But she did say that half of her team can barely catch the ball." Murphy said, with a glowing smile.

"Well Doc, under normal circumstances, I might find that little tidbit of information to be quite encouraging to hear. But if I were you, I wouldn't get my hopes up. Because three-quarters of our team can barely catch, throw, or hit the ball at all," which prompted Murphy to laugh.

Murphy glanced at Bobby, and then motioned for Bobby to come over to him.

Bobby hustled straight over to Murphy, and then replied, "Yeah, what is it, coach?"

Murphy then asked Bobby, "So tell me something Bobby, what is your most favorite thing to eat in the whole wide world?"

Without blinking an eye, Bobby excitedly said, "Oh, that's easy, a triple scoop strawberry ice cream cone. Am I right?"

Murphy and I both chuckled at Bobby's innocent reply, and then Murphy quietly said, "Uh, well Bobby, there's really no right or wrong answer to my question. So a triple scoop strawberry ice cream cone is your most favorite thing to eat in the whole wide world, right?"

"Yep, it sure is!" Bobby said, eagerly.

"Okay, now, I just want you to imagine that every time Francis throws you the ball, he's actually throwing you a triple scoop strawberry ice cream cone instead. But just remember, if you miss the ball, then it's like dropping that delicious ice cream cone in the dirt, and it won't be any good to eat. Do you understand what I'm telling you, Bobby?" Murphy explained.

"Yeah, I see what you mean. Thanks, coach!" Bobby said, with a glowing smile.

"Okay, good! Now why don't you head back over there and practice catching the ball with Francis, and every time that Francis throws you the ball, I want you to imagine that he's throwing you a delicious triple scoop strawberry ice cream cone instead, okay buddy."

Bobby's face lit up like a Christmas tree, as he excitedly said, "Okay coach, oh boy, oh boy, oh boy!"

As Bobby hightailed it back over to Francis, I just stared at Murphy for a moment, and then sarcastically said, "So, uh…, that's your big plan in getting Bobby to catch the ball better."

"Yep, it sure is, and I think it's gonna work too." Murphy replied, with a sly grin.

Murphy strolled over to the other side of the field, so that he could ask Coach Goodman if she wanted to take some infield practice with her team before the game got underway. Coach Goodman was quite receptive to Murphy's suggestion, so she waved her players onto the field.

As Murphy turned to walk away, Coach Goodman inquisitively asked, "Excuse me, Murphy. But is one of the players on your team named Dan Christoff?"

Murphy replied, "Why yes, he's our third baseman. Do you know, Dan?"

Coach Goodman answered, "Yes, I actually worked with Dan about three years ago. But due to his recurrent violent outbursts, he was usually confined to a strait jacket almost every day. Yet, here he is today, playing in an interagency softball game. Huh, will wonders never cease."

As Murphy reflected on what Coach Goodman just said, it made him realize that what he does here at the State School really matters. And that all the time and effort he puts into these clients every day is well worth it, and it seems to be paying him some valuable dividends as well.

So after about ten minutes of infield practice, Coach Goodman signaled to Murphy that her team was all warmed up and ready to go for the game.

Murphy and Coach Goodman then met with the umpire at home plate, so that they could go over a few ground rules for today's contest, and to also exchange their lineup cards as well.

As the coaches shook hands and then headed over to their respective benches, the umpire brushed off home plate, and then shouted in a deep and well-seasoned tone of voice, "Play ball!"

Before taking the field, Murphy huddled all of his players around him and encouraged them to play well today, and to try to have some fun as well. But above all, he wanted them to demonstrate good sportsmanship towards their opponent, and to respect all of the umpire's calls.

At that point, Murphy seemed to be casting a broad shadow over Russell Turner, who didn't appreciate being singled out one bit, as he bluntly remarked, "Hey, what the hell are you looking at me for Murphy?"

Murphy sternly replied, "Why, because your track record isn't very good when it comes to respecting others Russell, especially authority figures. So why don't you go out on that field today and prove me wrong, okay?"

As the guys took their respective positions on the field, I was admiring how sharp they all looked in their uniforms. Murphy was able to reach out to his former college baseball coach, who just so happened to have some old uniforms lying around in the bottom of his equipment locker, and said that he would be happy to donate the old baseball uniforms to Murphy's cause.

Once again, Murphy managed to use his impeccable Irish charm in persuading the head seamstress to do her magic, who then was able to completely transform an old pile of rags into showroom condition uniforms. And if you didn't know any better, you'd almost think that the uniforms were just bought today at the local sports shop in town.

When I glanced over my shoulder, I spotted Hanson sitting up in the bleachers. Hanson was all smiles as he sat there looking out onto the field. I'm sure Hanson was probably thinking that he was getting a pretty good return on his investment today by promoting Murphy.

Obviously, Murphy deserved the promotion. But I've come to realize that Hanson doesn't do anything out of the goodness of his heart, because he seems to think that if he throws a dog a bone every once in a while, then the dog will do whatever tricks that he's commanded to do.

Francis took the mound, while Bobby crouched down behind home plate. Francis then called out to Bobby, "Hey Bobby, are you ready for me to throw you a few warm-up pitches."

Bobby replied, "Yeah, I'm already Francis, oh boy, oh boy, oh boy!"

Despite the fact that Francis Watson was throwing every ball directly over the plate, Bobby was still missing every ball that Francis was throwing to him.

Time after time, Bobby kept scampering to the rear of the backstop to retrieve the ball that Francis just threw. And every time that the ball bounced off of the chain-linked fence, it would send an icy chill right down my spine, like fingernails scraping across a blackboard.

As the umpire watched Bobby miss every ball that was being thrown to him, he glanced at Murphy and said, "Hey Coach, is this what I have to look forward to for the entire game?"

Murphy just stood there with a real sheepish look on his face, as if to say, "Good luck today, ump! Oh, and I hope that all of your medical premiums are currently paid up to date too!"

The umpire strapped on his facemask, and then shouted in an agitated tone, "Batter up!"

As I observed Francis out on the pitcher's mound, he had a very disgusted look on his face, and I could hear him mumbling a string of expletives under his breath.

Francis then called over to Murphy, "Hey Murphy, I thought you talked to Bobby about catching the ball."

Murphy requested a timeout from the umpire, and then waved Bobby over to the bench.

Hanson then shouted from the bleachers, and loud enough for everyone to hear, "Tell 'em how it's done, coach!"

Although Murphy chuckled at Hanson's corny remark, I could tell that he really didn't appreciate hearing any comments coming from the peanut gallery. So Murphy just decided to play along with Hanson's shtick, especially since Hanson just gave him a nice big promotion.

As Bobby trotted over to the bench, Murphy then quietly asked him, "Hey Bobby, what's wrong? I thought we had this whole catching the ball thing figured out. Don't you remember the conversation that we had about the ball being a triple scoop strawberry ice cream cone?"

Bobby replied, "Oh yeah, that's right, I forgot all about that."

Murphy shook his head in disbelief, but still managed to keep his composure by saying, "C'mon Bobby, we're all counting on you to catch the ball. Just remember, the catcher is the most important position on the field, and that's why I chose you to be my catcher, okay."

Bobby could barely control himself, as he quietly screeched, "Oh boy, oh boy, oh boy!"

"C'mon coach, let's go, wrap it up!" The umpire barked.

"Okay, ump." Murphy replied, as Bobby smiled from behind his facemask.

"Batter up!" The umpire shouted.

The leadoff batter for Mitchell then stepped up to the plate. Francis had his game face on as he went into his wind-up and then threw the pitch. The ball sailed right over the plate, and the Mitchell batter swung at the pitch and managed to catch a piece of the ball on the end of his bat.

As Bobby tried to catch the foul tip, the ball glanced off of his glove and then ricocheted off of the umpire's facemask. Upon being struck by the ball, the umpire looked a bit dazed. He shook his head slightly, and then blinked his eyes a couple of times to try to collect his thoughts.

Murphy quickly cried out, "Are you okay, ump?"

The umpire appeared to be a bit disoriented. And as he continued to shake out the cobwebs, he quietly mumbled to Murphy, "Yeah, I'm okay. Let's play ball, coach."

Murphy then shouted over to Bobby, "C'mon Bobby, make sure you squeeze that triple scoop strawberry ice cream cone real tight next time, okay buddy!"

Bobby smiled at Murphy and attentively nodded his head.

Francis went into his wind-up and then pitched the ball right over the plate. The Mitchell batter swung at the ball and managed to get a piece of it, which wound up catching the umpire squarely on the back of his hand, and then causing the umpire to jump in the air and yell, "ouch!"

As the umpire attempted to shake off the pain, he grumbled, "Goddammit! Is this the thanks I get for volunteering my time to do some community service?"

Murphy grabbed an ice pack out of the first-aid kit, and then dashed out to home plate.

As Murphy reached home plate, the umpire snarled at Murphy by saying, "I'm getting killed back here, coach!"

The umpire snatched the ice pack from Murphy, and then placed it on the back of his throbbing hand, so that he could prevent his hand from swelling up like a grapefruit.

"Are you gonna be okay, ump?" Murphy asked, with a great deal of concern.

"Yeah, yeah, I'll be alright. Let's play ball, coach." The umpire groaned.

The umpire snapped on his facemask, and then crouched down into position behind Bobby Diggs. Francis went into his wind-up and then hurled another beauty right over the plate.

As the Mitchell batter swung at the pitch, the umpire seemed to flinch, probably because he was afraid of being hit by the ball again.

In any event, the Mitchell batter hit a slow ground ball down the third base line towards Dan Christoff. As the Mitchell player took off running for first base, Dan gobbled up the easy ground ball and then threw a bullet over to Russell Turner, who managed to catch the ball, while keeping his foot securely planted on the bag for the first out of the game.

Murphy shouted, "Yeah, now that's what I'm talking about! Nice play out there guys!"

Coach Goodman was so impressed by Dan Christoff's nifty play at third base that she started clapping her hands, and then she jubilantly cheered, "Yay..., way to go, Dan!"

Dan Christoff smiled, and then bashfully replied, "Thank you, Ms. Goodman."

The next batter for Mitchell swung at the first pitch that Francis threw, and wound up hitting the ball sharply on the ground to Jamal Buchanan. Jamal bobbled the ball momentarily, but then picked up the loose ball and threw it across the diamond to Russell Turner at first base.

In dramatic style, the ball arrived a split second before the Mitchell player was able to step on the bag. And low and behold, the upstart Grizzlies had just recorded out number two.

Murphy was thrilled beyond belief, and as he looked at me in total astonishment, he then excitedly said, "Hey, all we need is just one more out for the inning to be over Rodney!"

The next batter for Mitchell stepped up to the plate, and hit a screaming line drive directly at Francis Watson. Francis jumped in the air as high as he possibly could, and managed to snag the ball on the tip of his glove. As Francis' feet hit the deck, he stumbled, and then fell head over heels to the ground. Yet, somehow Francis was able to hang onto the ball, and his utterly sensational catch resulted in out number three for Murphy's scrappy bunch of Grizzlies.

As the boys ran off of the field, we could hear Hanson and Dick Henderson singing their praises. We actually looked like the New York Yankees out there, - three up and three down!

When the boys came over to the bench, they were all hooting and hollering, and slapping each other on the back and giving each other high fives.

Bobby Diggs ran straight over to Murphy, and then excitedly said, "Hey coach, are you proud of me because I haven't missed one ball that Francis has thrown to me yet?"

Murphy replied, "Yeah, I sure am Bobby, so just keep up the good work, okay buddy!"

As Bobby made his way over to the bench so that he could take off his catcher's gear, I leaned over to Murphy, and said on the Q.T., "Hey Doc, I don't think Bobby realizes it yet, but the Mitchell batters have been hitting every pitch that Francis has thrown to them so far."

Murphy quietly chuckled, and then simply replied, "Yeah, I know, but mum's the word Rodney, because I don't wanna say something to Bobby that might shake his confidence."

It was now our turn to bat. Murphy decided to start things off by having Francis "Popeye" Watson be our leadoff hitter.

Before positioning himself in the batter's box, Francis bent down and grabbed a handful of dirt, and then rubbed it into his hands. He then took a couple of practice swings, tapped the dust off of his shoes with his bat, and then with laser focus he stared down the Mitchell pitcher.

Murphy was clapping his hands and shouting out words of encouragement from the third base coach's box, "Alright Popeye, how 'bout starting us off with a base hit!"

As I watched Popeye go through all of his antics, he reminded me of an old-time baseball player, such as the kind of player that you might see back in the days of Babe Ruth or Ty Cobb. Popeye had a real gritty edge, and someone who embodied a win-at-all-cost type of mentality.

And despite the fact that Popeye possesses all of the dark and unsavory characteristics of a cold-blooded serial killer, Murphy and I still found him to be an absolute pleasure to be around.

As Popeye eased himself into the batter's box, he bent his knees, squeezed the bat tightly in his hands, and in a scratchy tone of voice, he then muttered to the opposing pitcher, "Alright bub, how 'bout you put one right over the plate, just like I've been doing for your team so far?"

Popeye decided to lay off the first two pitches that the Mitchell pitcher threw. Murphy was getting a bit antsy, because he felt that Popeye was being a little too particular at the plate.

Murphy then shouted, "C'mon Popeye, swing that lumber while we're still young!"

The umpire then glanced over at Murphy, and quietly chuckled to himself from behind his facemask, because he thought that Murphy's colorful remark was pretty amusing.

Popeye took a few practice swings, and then repositioned himself in the batter's box.

The Mitchell pitcher went into his wind-up and threw a real beauty right over the plate. Popeye swung at the pitch, and then hit the ball right on the nose to the second baseman. As the second baseman bent down to make a play on the ball, the ball seemed to take a funny hop on him, and then the ball squirted right through his legs and rolled straight out into the outfield.

As Popeye stood on first base, he acknowledged the roar of the crowd by tipping the bill of his cap, and quite similar to how an old-time ballplayer would tip his cap to the crowd as well.

It was now Jamal Buchanan's turn to step up to the plate. Jamal strutted into the batter's box with his usual cocky charm. As I observed Jamal at home plate, he looked downright scary, with his 6'7 frame and totally chiseled physique. Jamal kept staring down the Mitchell pitcher, and he seemed to be doing a pretty good job at thoroughly intimidating him.

In typical Jamal style, he was wearing his ball cap sideways, which looked absolutely ridiculous. And if you ask me, Jamal looked more like a street thug than he did a ballplayer.

As Jamal stood in the batter's box, he was becoming increasingly more agitated. And as he continued to stare down the Mitchell pitcher, he was mumbling a string of expletives under his breath, and language that was just too vile and filthy to even mention.

It's as if Jamal just got off the bus from crazyville!

Jamal was making a complete spectacle of himself, and giving the term gamesmanship a whole new meaning. Murphy and I were praying that Jamal wouldn't do anything rash, or God forbid, something that might land us on the eleven o'clock news tonight.

In an extremely vicious tone of voice, Jamal shouted, "Hey, you, white boy, don't even think about trying to get me out today fool! Not today, or any other day, cracker!"

Jamal had nothing but pure rage seething out of every pore of his body. And if I had to guess, I would say that Jamal was on the verge of having a complete psychotic breakdown.

So in an effort to break the tension, the umpire called timeout. The umpire then took off his facemask, and looked up at Jamal and said, "Hey batter, let's try and keep it friendly, okay?"

Jamal looked straight down at the umpire, and in an extremely threatening tone of voice, Jamal indignantly replied, "Uh, you better chill out ump, if you know what's good for ya, aight!"

The umpire didn't say a word, he simply readjusted his facemask, and then gave Murphy a real nasty look, as he shouted, "Batter up!"

Although the Mitchell pitcher was quaking in his boots, he managed to overcome his fears and throw a perfect pitch right over the plate. Jamal took a mighty swing. And with the crack of the bat, he smacked a towering fly ball deep into centerfield.

Upon seeing the ball sail completely over the centerfielder's head, Popeye took off running for second base. As Popeye rounded second and then headed for third, Murphy was shouting from the third base coach's box, "C'mon Popeye, run like your life depended on it!"

Jamal took off out of the batter's box like a jackrabbit, and he scampered around the base paths so fast that he came within a whisker of almost catching up to Popeye at home plate.

The Grizzlies were now on the scoreboard, and we were enjoying a 2-0 lead.

When Jamal crossed home plate, a resounding cheer echoed through the crowd. All of the Grizzlies then stormed the field to congratulate Jamal on hitting such an impressive homerun.

Unfortunately, Jamal was in such a detached state of mind that he was totally oblivious to the cheers of the crowd. His conscious mind seemed to be trapped in some deep dark world. And in order for him to find his way back to reality, then we would've had to dispatch a search party.

As we all waited for Jamal to join us back on planet Earth, we just watched him parade back and forth along the player's bench, as he quietly mumbled to himself over and over again, "Unh-uh, not today fool, this is my house! Unh-uh, not today fool, this is my house! Unh-uh,…"

Well, it was now time for Russell Turner to bat. Russell was all shits and giggles as he sauntered into the batter's box, and he was acting like he was some sort of Hollywood celebrity.

Then again, maybe some sort of half-assed clown in a traveling sideshow might be a better way to describe how Russell was acting.

In any event, it was time for Russell Turner to step up to the plate and take center stage, so that he could bask in the spotlight, and have all eyes riveted exclusively on him now.

As Russell dug his feet into the batter's box, he began to sling some rather snide remarks toward several of the Mitchell players. Russell thought that his comments were pretty clever. But his idiotic one-liners reminded me of some sort of washed-up comedian, who's shtick was so bad that he couldn't even land a gig at a two-bit comedy club out in the middle of nowhere.

I was kinda hoping that one of the Mitchell players would speak up and say something really nasty to Russell, so that they could give Russell a little taste of his own medicine. But the Mitchell players simply had too much class to climb down into the gutter with Russell Turner.

Russell then turned toward the umpire, and flippantly said, "So how ya doin' today, ump? It's a great day for a ballgame, wouldn't ya say!"

The umpire seemed rather surprised by Russell's casual remark. And so the umpire just nodded his head agreeably, and then waited for Russell to get all situated into the batter's box.

As Russell was busy sizing up the opposing pitcher, he then took it upon himself to say, "Hey ump, if I were you I would seriously think about losing a few pounds around that belly of yours, or else the elastic straps on your chest protector may suddenly decide to pop off."

All of a sudden, Russell began laughing his head off, and he apparently thought that his wiseass remark was pretty damn funny. Murphy and I couldn't believe what Russell just said to the umpire, and we were both bracing ourselves for what the umpire might say to Russell next.

Strangely enough, but the umpire never said a word to Russell. Instead, he lifted up his facemask, and then glanced down at his rather large pot belly and let out a tremendous sigh.

Although Russell should have kept his big mouth shut, I must admit that what he said about the umpire's waistline was not only accurate, but it was pretty darn funny as well.

As the Mitchell pitcher went into his wind-up, Russell yelled over to all of his Grizzly teammates, "Hey guys, watch me hit a homerun off of this crummy pitcher, just like Jamal did!"

Once again, Russell's complete lack of grace and social etiquette was simply appalling. Especially since good sportsmanship is something that Murphy and I are constantly preaching to all of our players, and has always been the cornerstone that this team was intended to be built on.

In hindsight, I guess we probably should have yanked Russell right out of the game the minute he started in with his two-bit shenanigans. But like the old adage says, hindsight is 20/20.

As Russell swung at the pitch, he took a vicious swing at the ball, but only grazed it. But he grazed the ball just enough, so that the ball popped straight up into the air and then landed squarely into the catcher's glove, which was positioned perfectly right over home plate.

When the umpire realized that the ball had popped sufficiently high enough into the air for it to be considered as an official out, the umpire simply couldn't believe his good fortune.

The umpire then hoisted his right arm straight up into the air, and with a look of sheer satisfaction on his face, the umpire jubilantly shouted, "The batter is out!"

Upon hearing the umpire's call, Russell was completely dumbstruck. Russell thought that the umpire was only joking with him, so Russell started laughing hysterically.

As Russell continued to laugh out loud, he nonchalantly turned toward the umpire, and then casually asked, "So, uh…, you were only kidding me about being out, right ump?"

When Russell saw the stern look on the umpire's face, he realized that the umpire wasn't joking. So Russell started begging the umpire to reverse his call, but the umpire refused to listen.

In a last ditch effort to have the umpire reverse his ruling, Russell got down on his hands and knees, and pleaded with the umpire to give him a second chance, but the umpire wasn't interested in listening to any of Russell's two-bit theatrics.

So realizing that the nice approach wasn't getting him anywhere, Russell decided to take a different tact, so he got right up into the umpire's face and started blistering him with a string of profanities, which were so filthy that it would even make a longshoreman blush.

Despite the hailstorm of expletives that Russell was raining down on the umpire, the umpire remained as cool as a cucumber. And in a quiet and subdued voice, the umpire calmly said, "Coach, I need your next hitter in the lineup to step up to the plate, please."

Russell got right back into the umpire's face, and then vehemently shouted, "Listen ump, if you think that was an out, then you're crazier than I am, you fat tub of lard! And I'll bet your mother is a fat tub of lard too!"

Well, as soon as the umpire heard Russell taking potshots at his mother, then the umpire completely lost his temper.

The umpire then took off his facemask and bellowed, "Alright batter, I've heard just about enough of your goddamn bullshit, so now I'm tossing your ass right out of the game!"

The umpire then looked over at Murphy, and with absolute fire in his eye, he said to Murphy, "Coach, your player needs to be escorted off of the field right now, because he's been ejected from the ballgame!"

As Murphy and I ushered Russell Turner off of the field, Russell continued to squawk at the umpire, and Russell certainly wasn't shy in calling the umpire every dirty name in the book.

Dick Henderson and Mr. Hanson then hopped off of the bleachers and came right over to the bench so that they could be of some assistance. Mr. Hanson then suggested that it might be a good idea to bring Russell back to his living unit to prevent any further incident from occurring.

Mr. Hanson asked Murphy for the keys to the van. And as Murphy handed him the keys, Hanson sarcastically said, "Uh, just make sure that nobody wanders off while I'm gone, got it."

Murphy quietly nodded his head, but I could tell that he didn't appreciate Hanson's cheap shot one bit. And it reinforced to me just how spiteful and vindictive a man Hanson can really be.

The umpire then shouted, "Let's go, coach! I need a batter to step up to the plate right now, or else you'll be in jeopardy of forfeiting the game!"

Well, from that point on the rest of the game seemed rather meaningless. With Russell Turner out of the game our team fell completely apart. Russell was our best all-around player, and someone who I would categorize as being high-risk/high-reward.

When Russell was hitting on all cylinders, then the sky was the limit. But the minute that things don't go Russell's way, then you better make sure that you hide the women and children.

Russell was actually the glue that held our softball team together. Which when you think about it, was a pretty scary thought in itself.

When Murphy lost the services of Russell Turner at first base, then he had no other choice but to replace him with Eddie Johnson, who normally plays right field.

So that in itself should tell you the caliber of player that Eddie Johnson was!

Eddie was nowhere near the player that Russell Turner was. And in private, Murphy and I would often refer to Eddie as "unsteady Eddie."

With Russell Turner out of the game, we went from playing like the New York Yankees, to playing like the Bad News Bears.

The 2-0 lead that we carried into the second inning quickly evaporated as soon as the Mitchell team came up to bat. The Mitchell batters were whacking every pitch that Francis Watson was throwing to them.

But I guess the one silver lining to all of this was that we didn't have to worry about watching Bobby Diggs chase after the ball every time that Francis Watson threw it to him.

Sad to say, but our team was getting thoroughly trounced.

Every time that Mitchell hit the ball, one of their players would wind up crossing over home plate. It was like watching the carousel at the amusement park spinning round, and round, and round, as mighty Mitchell asserted their will over the beleaguered and war-torn Grizzlies.

Even when we were lucky enough to catch a ground ball, we still had to throw the ball over to Eddie Johnson at first base, who would either miss the ball, or forgot to step on the bag.

In a humorous sort of way, I was thinking that Murphy should've used the same coaching strategy on Eddie Johnson that he used on Bobby Diggs, and I was almost tempted to mention it to Murphy. But every time I glanced in Murphy's direction, he looked like he was having a bad case of food poisoning, so I just decided to keep my thoughts and comments strictly to myself.

As a matter of fact, at one point during the game we were so desperate for an out that Popeye literally chased after the Mitchell player so that he could try and tag him out, instead of taking a chance on throwing the ball over to Eddie Johnson at first base.

By now, we were so far behind on the scoreboard that I turned to Murphy and quietly said, "Hey Doc, we're getting completely annihilated. So whatta ya say that we wave the white flag, and invoke the Mercy Rule."

Murphy thought long and hard, and then replied, "Yeah, I think you're right, Rodney."

So at that point, Murphy signaled for timeout and then motioned for Coach Goodman to join him at home plate with the umpire.

As Murphy conferred with Coach Goodman and the umpire at home plate, all of the Grizzly players were wondering what all of the discussions were about. Although the guys were getting thoroughly trounced by Mitchell, they were still in favor of continuing on with the game.

So after talking things over with Coach Goodman and the umpire, it was all agreed upon that the Mercy Rule would be invoked, and that the game would officially be over.

Of course, with the discussions being held right there at home plate, Bobby Diggs was privy to the whole conversation. And when Bobby heard that the game was officially over, he was madder than a hornet.

In a fit of frustration, Bobby threw his catcher's glove to the ground, and then started to complain by saying, "Wait a minute, you can't stop the game, I didn't get a chance to bat yet!"

Although Murphy was extremely disappointed, he set his feelings aside and shook hands with Coach Goodman, and congratulated her on the victory. Murphy then walked over to the umpire and thanked him for his time, and also apologized for all the grief and aggravation that he had to put up with from some of our players, most notably, Russell Turner and Jamal Buchanan.

In the spirit of good sportsmanship, Murphy had his players line up on the third base line, so that they could shake hands and congratulate the Mitchell squad on their hard fought victory.

When the players returned to their respective benches, Bobby was still pissing and moaning about the game being over, and the fact that he didn't get a chance to step up to the plate and crack some lumber.

As Bobby took off his shin guards and then shoved them into the equipment bag, I could hear his surly mouth say, "That umpire is a fuckin' asshole, he didn't give me a chance to bat."

CHAPTER THIRTEEN

Well, it doesn't look like we'll be playing anymore softball games this season. Late yesterday afternoon, Mr. Hanson summoned Murphy into his office and told him to cancel whatever remaining games were left on the schedule effective immediately.

From what Murphy conveyed to me, Hanson appeared to be rather sympathetic about cancelling the season. But at the end of the day, Hanson was simply following orders himself, and the decision to pull the plug on the rest of season came directly from the top.

So now that we've tried our hand at basketball and softball, what's next, - starting up a client bowling team perhaps, or maybe even choosing up sides for a little game of tiddlywinks.

Our attempts in organizing a client softball and basketball team was certainly a noble gesture. And at times, it was really a lot of fun. But at the end of the day, it proved to be nothing more than just an exercise in futility.

Well, at least we can say that we gave it our best shot. But unfortunately, we just didn't achieve the results that we were really hoping for.

Despite the fact that the top brass encourages the rank and file to be progressive in their thinking, I've discovered that these Pollyanna thoughts of theirs seems to go straight out the window at the first sign of trouble.

And what might sound like a brilliant idea one minute, can quickly transform into, "what the hell were you thinking," the next.

In wrapping up yesterday's meeting, Mr. Hanson strongly suggested to Murphy that he refrain from having anymore involvement with affiliating agencies, especially since our track record with these agencies has been less than stellar, and certainly nothing to write home about.

Hanson also said that even though the Director appreciates the fact that we try to provide the clients with some unique opportunities, he feels that the risks far outweigh the rewards. And since the clients that we work with are usually prone to rash and unpredictable behaviors, then let's not try to place ourselves in any awkward or precarious situations in the future.

The last thing that the Director wants is to have the State School's reputation jeopardized, or be involved in an incident that might generate some negative notoriety. Especially since the Director has been trying to establish a better relationship with our local community for years.

Once again, spilling the milk inside the four walls of the State School is one thing, but spilling the milk outside the four walls of the State School is certainly another.

As the Director often says, "John Q Public is watching our every move, so let's try to be mindful of the fact that their hard earned tax dollars are what's being used to pay our salaries."

So going forward, the Director has made it quite clear that he is not willing to roll the dice on approving anymore outside ventures with affiliating agencies. Especially when these endeavors could potentially give our facility a black eye, and besmirch our public reputation.

That being said, is it any wonder why mediocracy reigns supreme in the state system. And why most state workers usually take the path of least resistance, by checking their brains at the gate, and providing the same old humdrum work mentality day, after day, after day.

Now although we've enjoyed a great deal of success so far here in the SBU, there are still some naysayers out there who feel that federally funded programs like ours might pose a security risk to the community.

As a matter of fact, I read a very interesting newspaper article the other day, stating that a group of concerned citizens have petitioned their local politicians to put an immediate halt to all federal funding involving individuals that are considered to be dually diagnosed.

Now on the flip side, we've heard through the grapevine that there are a number of state-run facilities that are entertaining the notion of opening up their own Special Behavioral Unit. And despite all of the controversy that might exist, facilities would much rather line their pockets with some cold hard cash from federally funded programs, then worry about some petty concerns that the general public may have regarding potential safety risks in their respective communities.

In the meantime, I guess we'll just have to wait and see which way the wind is blowing before the politicians decide on which horse to back. Because at the end of the day, it all boils down to votes and money. And doing the right thing is not always in a politician's best interest.

It's been a couple of weeks now since the softball team was dismantled, and from what I can tell the guys seem to have a lot of free time on their hands. They all seem to be biding their time and waiting to see what types of new things that Murphy has in store for them to do next.

Well, little do they know, but Murphy has nothing new looming on the horizon. Which is probably a good thing, because up until now these little ventures of ours have actually been more trouble than they're worth, and have made our jobs here at the State School a lot more difficult.

Initially, when Murphy and I first set out to organize a team, we did it mainly to have fun. Murphy realized that he had lightning in a bottle the minute the clients came waltzing through the door. And even though we knew that there would be some potential risks, we took these risks in stride, and dealt with whatever challenges might present themselves along the way.

For my money, Murphy has done more with these clients over the past year than anyone has ever done for them in their entire life. Murphy has instilled a tremendous sense of pride and self-worth into their otherwise dreary existence, and they are darn lucky to have him in their life.

It's funny, but even though the State School has been in existence for well over a hundred years, no one outside the four walls of this place has even the slightest idea of what goes on here.

And despite the fact that our facility has had three major name changes within the past twenty-five years, everyone you talk to still refers to us as the State School. And to tell you the truth, but I really don't see that changing anytime soon.

But as long as we stay out of the newspapers, and avoid being the lead story on the six o'clock news every night, then I guess it's safe to say that we're all doing our jobs around here.

And even though most people would lead you to believe that the State School is more like the Island of Misfit Toys than it is the Land of Milk and Honey, I still believe that what we do here really matters, and that all of our efforts can make a real difference in the client's lives.

Well, it sounds like Lance Coppenger will heading out the door come close of business tomorrow. And when Dick informed me of the news, I was thoroughly disappointed. It would seem that Hanson is not one to drag his feet when it comes to paybacks or evening the score.

In fact, Hanson is so vindictive that there were several facilities around the State that were willing to take Lance off of our hands, and with no strings attached. But Hanson declined their offers, - because he wanted to wait until the state forensic unit had an available opening.

When Dick questioned the decision, Hanson snidely remarked, "Mr. Coppenger needs to learn a valuable lesson for all the grief and aggravation that he has caused us, and sending him to some "country club" facility is not an option that I'm willing to entertain."

As I've stated before, the state forensic unit houses some of the most hardcore individuals in the state. And although it's classified as a treatment facility, it's barely a notch above Alcatraz.

Later that afternoon, the clinical staff was summoned into the conference room for an emergency staff meeting. Murphy was already seated when I entered the room. And as I pulled up a chair next to Murphy, I casually asked him what the meeting was about.

Murphy shrugged his shoulders, and simply replied, "No one seems to know, Rodney."

A few moments later, Dick Henderson entered the room along with Mr. Hanson and the Director.

Hanson then piped up and said, "Good afternoon everyone, and thank you for attending the meeting on such short notice. Before we get underway, I just wanted to take a moment and extend my appreciation for all of the outstanding work that each of you has done. I realize that we work with a very difficult population, and seeing the wonderful success that we've enjoyed here so far only reinforces why all of you were selected for the SBU team in the first place."

The Director then interjected, "Yes, bravo everyone! And I would also like to echo Al's sentiments as well, and commend all of you for the outstanding job that you do every day."

So after Hanson and the Director finished blowing sunshine up our ass, Hanson continued by saying, "Well, despite the tremendous progress that we have made over the past year, there is still one or two clients here at the SBU who may be better served elsewhere."

Right there and then I knew exactly where this conversation was headed, and why the top brass summoned us all together this afternoon for this impromptu emergency staff meeting.

So for the next forty-five minutes, Hanson climbed on top of his soapbox and began bending our ears with some long-winded explanations as to why some clients succeed in a particular clinical setting and why others fail.

He then segued his way onto the topic of recidivism, and began filling our heads with all sorts of statistical data, and also citing some high priced clinical studies to support his argument.

Although Hanson never specifically mentioned Lance Coppenger by name, everyone in the room knew where this convoluted dissertation of his was ultimately headed.

I then quietly leaned over to Murphy and whispered, "Well Doc, I guess you can kiss Lance Coppenger good-bye."

Now on the surface, Mr. Hanson may come across as being a champion of client rights. But the better you get to know him, the more apparent it is just how narcissistic he can be. And he will do everything in his power to make sure that all of his selfish needs are being met.

For instance, instead of trying to help Lance learn from his mistakes, Hanson would much rather go for the jugular, and send Lance to a facility that will inevitably break his spirit.

Hanson can cite all of the clinical mumbo-jumbo that he wants. But everyone in the room knew that Hanson had an axe to grind regarding Lance, and his decision to have him transferred to the state forensic unit was based solely on a personal vendetta and not for any clinical reasons.

Doesn't Hanson realize that these clients are here for a reason? And that all of the clients living here at the SBU are prone to impulsive acts, and highly questionable decision making?

Well, if perfection is what Hanson is looking for, then he's definitely in the wrong line of work. And maybe he should reconsider taking that corner office at his daddy's company after all.

So after laying the groundwork with all of his statistical bullshit and rationales, Hanson announced that Lance Coppenger was being transferred to the forensic unit tomorrow afternoon.

Hanson actually had the audacity to say that the transfer was in Lance's best interest, and that the forensic unit could provide Lance with all of the services that he so desperately needed.

So after making his big announcement, Hanson looked quite pleased with himself. And although he pulled the wool over the Director's eyes, he wasn't fooling the rest of us one bit.

Now if you had told me a year ago that Lance would be the first client transferred out of the SBU, then I probably would've laughed in your face and said that you were crazy, especially with the likes of Jamal Buchanan, Russell Turner, or Terrence Morehouse to choose from.

But unfortunately, Lance broke the cardinal rule, which was screwing up outside the four walls of the State School. So now the powers to be will wind up making an example out of him.

No one likes to have their dirty laundry aired in public. But banishing Lance to a facility that houses a bunch of rapists and murderers is not only wrong, but it's completely unethical too.

I wonder if Hanson would've gone to these same lengths if he actually liked Lance, or would he have quietly swept the whole matter under the rug, and told Lance never to do it again.

Well, I guess we'll never know the answer to that one, will we?

When the meeting was over, Hanson told us to keep up the good work, and then he and the Director both ducked out of the room. Hanson didn't even stick around to field any questions.

As I was getting up from the table, I turned to Murphy and whispered, "Well Doc, you better learn to play nice with Hanson, or else he'll buy you a one-way ticket to Siberia."

Murphy and I then headed down to the gym, so that we could shoot a few baskets and rehash the meeting. A few moments later, Dick Henderson strolled into the gym and said with a coy smile, "Yeah, I had a pretty good hunch that I'd find both of you guys in here."

Dick took off his sports jacket, and then Murphy passed Dick the basketball. As Dick was lining up his shot, he casually asked, "So what did you guys think of the meeting?"

Murphy quipped, "What meeting? It felt more like a military briefing to me."

Dick quietly chuckled.

Murphy continued by saying, "Hey Dick, I'm kinda surprised that the Director went along with Hanson's recommendation to have Lance transferred to the state forensic unit."

"Yeah, well, it's politics...," Dick said, as he passed the basketball over to me.

Murphy replied, "Ya know, sometimes I think that the clients are nothing more than pawns on a chess board."

Dick chuckled a bit, and then quietly said, "Yeah, well, that's a pretty good analogy, Murphy."

I then curiously asked, "Hey Dick, the fact that Lance was once charged on suspicion of murder, do you think that had anything to do with him being transferred to the forensic unit?"

Dick replied, "Who knows, the case against Lance was pretty sketchy. There were no material witnesses, no murder weapon was ever found, and not a single trace of DNA evidence whatsoever. Why they even pointed the finger at Lance in the first place is totally beyond me."

Murphy then chimed in and said, "Yeah, it sounds pretty fishy to me too. And I highly doubt that Lance is capable of committing the perfect crime," which prompted all of us to laugh.

As Dick reached for his sports jacket, he quietly said, "Listen fellas, let me give you a little piece of advice. Choose your battles wisely, and learn to accept what you cannot change."

Murphy piped up and said, "In other words, you can't fight city hall, right Dick."

Dick quietly chuckled, and then replied, "Exactly! Oh, by the way, I've got a good friend who works out at the forensic unit, and I'll be talking to him tomorrow about Lance. In fact, if you guys don't have anything planned for tomorrow, then I'd like you both to accompany me out to the forensic unit. Just let me know what your decision is in the morning."

The next day, I swung by Dick Henderson's office to let him know that I was available to accompany him out to the forensic unit. But when I met with Dick, he informed me that due to some unforeseen circumstances, Lance's transfer has been postponed until tomorrow.

I then decided to seize the moment by asking Dick if I could spend the day with Lance, and perhaps take him out to lunch and maybe even grab a movie in town.

Upon hearing my request, Dick hesitated for a moment, but then realized that allowing Lance to enjoy his last day here at the State School was probably the right thing for us to do.

Dick said, "Okay, but there's only one catch, Hanson wants two staff assigned to Lance whenever he's out of the building. So you'll need to find someone to go with you on the outing."

I quickly asked, "Okay, well, uh…, would it be alright if Murphy went with me?"

Dick smirked, and then humorously said, "Gee, now how did I know you were gonna ask me that question? Yeah, okay, Murphy can go with you. But just make sure that you guys don't let Lance out of your sight, or else it'll be the unemployment line for all of us, okay?"

When I entered the gym, Murphy was setting up the room for a little game of kickball. So after exchanging a few pleasantries, I asked Murphy what he had on tap for the day, and he said that he really had nothing special planned. I then asked Murphy if he would like to spend the day with me and Lance Coppenger by going out to lunch and then catching a movie in town.

Murphy, who is usually game for anything, then took me completely off guard by saying, "Um, well, I think I'm gonna pass on the outing, Rodney."

"Really! You're not interested in going with me?"

"Uh, not really…," Murphy replied, in a somewhat deflated tone.

"Okay, I just thought we'd get a few laughs out of it, that's all." I said, disappointedly.

"Well, to tell you the truth Rodney, I don't find Lance nearly as entertaining as you do."

"Yeah, I know. Well, what can I say, I seem to have a soft spot for the guy. Alright, well, I guess I'll just have to find someone else in the building to go with me. See ya later, Doc."

As I walked out of the gym, I was a little disappointed that Murphy wasn't going on the outing with me. Especially since Murphy rarely turns me down, and I can always count on him for just about anything.

Well, since I couldn't talk Murphy into going on the outing with me, I thought I'd go ask Cameron if he was interested in going on the outing with me instead.

So when I finally tracked down Cameron, he was finishing up with a group counseling session on L.U. 512. I've really come to appreciate Cameron. He's not like most of the other psychologists around here, who seem to barricade themselves in their office all day, and the only time that you ever see them is at meetings, or when they dash in and out of the coffee room.

When I asked Cameron if he was interested in going on an all-day outing with me, he had to decline, because he said that he was all tied up for the day with staff training and meetings.

As I was exiting the living unit, Cameron took a moment to thank me for making Lance's last day here at the State School a memorable one. And for what it was worth, Cameron also felt that Lance Coppenger was being railroaded by Hanson too.

Well, since option A and option B were both off the table, then my only other recourse now was to ask the living unit charge if he had any extra staff that he was willing to spare, so that I could take Lance on the all-day outing into town.

When I asked the unit charge if he could provide me a staff person, he told me that he was a little shorthanded today, and that he barely had enough staff to run the living unit himself.

So seeing how nothing was really panning out for me, I decided to scrap the idea of an outing altogether, and simply order up a couple of submarine sandwiches so that Lance and I could enjoy a nice quiet lunch up in the front lobby together.

As I was getting ready to call the sub shop, Murphy ducked his head into my office and casually asked, "So Rodney, were you able to find someone to go on the outing with ya today?"

I quietly replied, "Nah, no takers. But that's okay, I think I'm just gonna order up a couple of subs, and then bring them back to the building. Hey, I'll order you up a sub too, okay?"

Murphy quietly nodded his head, and then hesitantly said, "Well, uh…, I guess I'm available to go on the outing with ya. That is, if you still wanna go."

"Really, hey thanks, Doc! Ya know, somehow I knew you'd come through for me. Tell ya what, why don't you pull the van around front, and I'll go grab Lance off of the living unit."

"Okay Rodney, sounds good."

Before grabbing Lance off of the living unit, I swung by Dick Henderson's office first so that I could apprise him of the situation. Dick was happy that I was able to find someone to go on the outing with me, but the look on his face told me that he was a little bit nervous about it too.

As I was leaving Dick's office, he anxiously said, "Hey, have a great time. But whatever you do, please don't let Lance out of your sight, or else it'll be curtains for all of us, okay?"

I then whimsically replied, "Don't worry, Dick. I've got a pair of handcuffs in my back pocket, just in case I need 'em."

As Lance climbed into the van, he excitedly said, "Hi, Uncle Murphy! Hey, isn't it great that we're all going out to lunch together!"

Murphy quietly nodded his head, and then groaned, "Yeah, fabulous."

As I closed the side door of the van, Lance exclaimed, "Woohoo! I can't believe that I'm going out to lunch with my two most favorite uncles in the whole wide world!"

Hey, what can I say, Lance is quite a character, and he seems to think that we're all one big happy family here at the State School.

Lance considers Murphy and I to be his two most favorite uncles, - probably because we're the only two dumb schmucks around here that pays him even the slightest bit of attention.

To say that Lance has an active imagination might be stretching things a bit. Because Lance's psychiatric problems run much deeper than a few simple quirks, or an offbeat sense of humor.

And trying to figure out Lance is like searching for a light switch in a very dark room.

Despite the fact that Lance may arguably be the craziest person that we have here in the building, I find him to be thoroughly captivating, and someone that I really enjoy being around.

As a boy, Lance had a very dysfunctional upbringing, and he was subjected to all sorts of physical and sexual abuse in his household. So in order for Lance to survive, he constructed an elaborate fantasy world for himself, so that he could try to escape the bane of his existence.

During his teenage years, Lance was beginning to show signs of mental decomposition, and his dissociative disorder was becoming so pervasive that it was controlling his entire world.

As an adult, Lance had numerous brushes with the law. And it got to the point where the county judge was so sick and tired of seeing Lance in his courtroom every week that he finally had Lance committed to a psychiatric hospital, so that he didn't have to deal with him anymore.

Over the course of time, Lance has managed to suppress the pain and suffering of his biological family by systematically deleting them from his memory banks. And replacing them with a whole new subset of people, who he now considers to be his one and only family.

For the past thirty years, Lance has bounced around from one state psychiatric center to another. And during that time he has undergone some extensive psychotherapy, as well as being subjected to some pretty hefty doses of antipsychotic medications and electric shock therapy.

Yet, despite it all, Lance still hasn't gotten any better.

Lance's whole existence has been built on a foundation of delusional thinking. And in this alternate universe that he has constructed for himself, fantasy has now become his reality.

Although Murphy doesn't particularly like it when Lance refers to him as Uncle Murphy, I on the other hand find it to be a term of endearment when he refers to me as his Uncle Jack.

As a matter of fact, Lance often refers to me as his "most favorite" uncle. Which I realize is nothing but a bunch of malarkey, especially since Lance is a pretty good bullshit artist, and he seems to have a propensity at telling people what they really want to hear.

But despite it all, I genuinely like him, and thoroughly enjoy his company.

Yeah, I know that Lance is completely off his rocker. But I'd be off of my rocker too, if I had to deal with the amount of pain and adversity that he's had to contend with for his entire life.

So I guess the one question that I keep asking myself is, "Why does Lance mean so much to me?"

Well, the only answer that I can come up with is, - Lance saved me from the abyss!

Now I know that might sound a bit dramatic to say, but Lance was my only salvation back in the early days of the SBU, when I was ready to pull my hair out with the likes of Jamal Buchanan, Russell Turner, and the rest of the Bowery Boys working in the laundry workshop.

Lance had a real knack for picking up my spirits, with his timely one-liners and his zany anecdotal tales. Despite the fact that most people can only tolerate Lance in small doses, I seem to go out of my way to seek him out, so that I can spend as much time with him as I possibly can.

Yes, he can be annoying, and yes, he can sometimes be more trouble than he's worth. But I've actually become quite fond of him, and I'm going to miss him terribly when I finally have to say "good-bye" to him tomorrow morning.

As we drove over to the sub shop, Lance was talking a mile a minute, and he kept telling us over and over again that he couldn't wait to sink his teeth into his giant submarine sandwich.

Every time Lance opened up his mouth to say something, I noticed that poor old Murphy couldn't stop rolling his eyes and then quietly mumbling, "oh brother," under his breath.

Quite honestly, but I think Murphy would've preferred going to the dentist today to have a root canal done, instead of being cooped up on the van listening to Lance's nonstop gibberish.

When we walked into sub shop, Lance approached the young girl behind the counter and immediately began to pour on the charm. Lance told the young girl that she was as pretty as a picture, and that her dazzling blue eyes twinkled like the midnight star.

Although Lance has a flair for telling people what they really want to hear, one never knows if he's being genuine or deceptive, especially given his track record and checkered past.

Due to the types of clients that we work with, it's sometimes difficult to know if they are demonstrating any progress with their social abilities, or simply sharpening their predatory skills.

So when it was time for Lance to place his lunch order, he knew exactly what he wanted. Lance told the young girl behind the counter, "I'll take two roast beef subs with everything on it, two orders of french fries, and an extra-large soda with no ice, please. Thanks, honey!"

Murphy leaned over to me and whispered, "Hey Rodney, you're not gonna let him order all of that food, are ya?"

I quietly chuckled, and then answered Murphy by saying, "Nah, I'm just letting him get it out of his system first, that's all."

At that point, I asked the young girl behind the counter if she would please cut Lance's order in half, which prompted her to slightly giggle, and then simply replied, "Sure, no problem."

She then turned to Murphy, and pleasantly asked, "So what can I get ya, sir?"

Murphy replied, "Um, roast beef sounds pretty good, I'll take what he's having."

She then glanced at me, and even before she could utter a single word, I quickly said, "Why don't ya make it three of the same order, thanks!"

The young girl behind the counter then asked us to take a seat out in the lobby, and that she would bring out our food as soon as it was ready.

As we waited for our lunch to arrive, Lance was awful fidgety. Lance kept glancing over his shoulder, and wondering what was taking the young girl so long in bringing us our order.

Lance then impetuously asked, "Hey Uncle Jack, do you think we can come back here again tomorrow?"

Murphy and I quickly glanced at each other, and then realized that Lance had no idea that he was being transferred to the state forensic unit tomorrow. So when Lance climbs onto the van tomorrow morning, he'll probably think that he's going on another special outing again.

As I searched for the right words to say, the young girl from behind the counter brought us our order. When Lance saw the amount of food that was sitting on the tray in front of him, he said in dramatic style, "Oh, my God! Today is the greatest day of my life!"

And then prompting me to think, "Maybe so, but tomorrow could possibly be the worst day of your life, - and maybe mine too."

As Lance was getting ready to sink his teeth into his mouthwatering submarine sandwich, he realized that the girl behind the counter forgot to put ketchup on his roast beef sandwich.

Lance then excitedly asked, "Hey Uncle Jack, can you please pass me the ketchup?"

Murphy mumbled, "Ugh…! Ketchup, on a roast beef sandwich."

I lightly chuckled, and then affably said, "Here ya go, Lance. But try not to use the whole bottle, okay?"

So when lunch was over, we discarded our trash in the bin, and then waved good-bye to the young girl who was working behind the counter.

The minute we left the sub shop, Lance started pestering me for some ice cream, which prompted Murphy to sarcastically whine, "Yeah, ice cream! Can we

Uncle Jack, please, please!"

As I chuckled at Murphy's grade school theatrics, I then explained to Lance that we were on a bit of a tight schedule this afternoon. But if we had enough time after the movie, then maybe we could stop and get some ice cream later.

En route to the movie theater, I told Lance that we were going to see a John Wayne double-feature today, who just so happens to be Lance's all-time favorite Hollywood actor.

Lance was so excited about seeing his favorite matinee idol that he began to do his own little impersonation of the "Duke," which is John Wayne's nickname in most Hollywood circles.

Although Murphy cringes every time Lance does his impersonation of John Wayne, I on the other hand think that Lance's colorful rendition of the Hollywood icon is absolutely fabulous.

When we entered the lobby of the movie theater, we seemed to be the only patrons in sight. I then turned to Murphy and said, "Gee Doc, I hope I didn't screw up on the movie times."

Just then an older gentleman walked into the front lobby. He was wearing a bright red vest and a gold tie, so he obviously worked for the theater. I then approached the man and asked him, "Excuse me sir, but is there a John Wayne double-feature playing here today at noon?"

The man replied, "Why yes, and the first movie will be starting momentarily."

As I glanced over at Lance, I saw that he had his nose pressed up against the glass of the candy counter, and he looked just like a little kid. As he stood there with his eyes wide open, he was marveling at all of the sugary treats and treasures that were inside of the display case.

Lance then impetuously asked, "Hey Uncle Jack, do you think I can get something from the candy counter before the movie starts?"

I quickly replied, "C'mon Lance, you just ate a big lunch five minutes ago. Plus I told you that we might be stopping for ice cream after the movie is over, remember."

"Yeah, I know, but I'm still a little bit hungry, please...," Lance whined.

"Alright, let me buy the movie tickets first, and then we'll go grab something from the candy counter, okay."

"Okey-dokey," Lance replied, as he flashed me his million dollar smile.

So after buying our movie tickets, we headed over to the concession stand. As Murphy and I chatted a bit, Lance was trying to decide on which tasty morsel that he wanted to get.

Lance couldn't seem to make up his mind, so he told the man behind the candy counter to give him one of everything.

Although the concessionaire was somewhat hesitant to take Lance at his word, he reached into the display case anyway, and then started to remove one candy bar from each of the racks.

When I glanced over at Lance, I couldn't believe the number of candy bars that were piled on top of the counter, which then prompted me to say, "Whoa! We can't buy all of these! Excuse me, sir. But you'll need to put all of those candy bars back into the display case, okay."

I then looked Lance straight in the eye, and firmly said, "Listen Lance, you can have one item to eat and one item to drink, that's it, okay?"

So after weighing all of his options, Lance decided to get a large tub of buttered popcorn, and a 64oz. cup of soda with no ice.

When I asked Lance if he was all set, he simply replied, "Darn tootin', fig newton."

So when we entered the theater, Lance marched right down the center aisle and made a beeline for the front row, which prompted Murphy and I to just shake our heads in disbelief.

Apparently, Lance didn't get the memo, - that you never sit in the front row of a movie theater unless you absolutely have to. Especially when there's no one else in the theater but you.

I then suggested to Lance that it might be a good idea for him to sit in the middle of the theater. That way it would provide him with a more panoramic view of the entire movie screen.

So the first movie of today's John Wayne double-feature was the classic film "True Grit," in which John Wayne plays the part of a United States Marshall named Rooster Cogburn. And this legendary role earned John Wayne an Academy Award in 1969.

Well, as soon as the movie started, Lance stopped eating his popcorn and had his eyes totally glued to the screen.

As I watched the intensity in Lance's eyes, I found myself wanting to laugh, especially since I didn't think that anything came between Lance and his total obsession for food.

Although I'm not a big John Wayne fan, I found the movie to be thoroughly entertaining. However, I'm not quite sure if I can say the same for Murphy, who kept glancing at his watch, and yawning throughout the entire film.

Lance was in seventh heaven, as his eyes were totally glued to the screen the whole time. Not only did Lance know the entire storyline by heart, but he had most of the dialogue resigned to memory as well.

In retrospect, it was probably a good thing that there were no other moviegoers in the theater today, because Lance's continuous commentary throughout the entire film would've been a definite distraction to anyone sitting around us.

At one point, there was a very funny moment in which Murphy leaned over to me and whispered, "Hey Rodney, when is John Wayne gonna say his famous line, "Well, let me tell ya something pilgrim?" It's somewhere in this movie, right?"

Lance must've overheard the question, and then quickly reprimanded Murphy by saying, "Hey Uncle Murphy, that line ain't in this movie, that line is in the movie, "The Man Who Shot Liberty Valance." Gee, I thought everybody knew that one!"

I quickly glanced at Murphy, and then playfully said, "Yeah, c'mon Doc, everybody knows that one."

Murphy just quietly nodded his head and smiled, because he knew that I didn't have the slightest idea either as to where that legendary John Wayne movie quote originated from.

Before the second movie got underway, Murphy and I decided to escort Lance to the bathroom, - seeing how he just polished off a 64oz. cup of soda.

En route to the restroom, we passed by the manager of the theater, who told us the second movie would begin momentarily, and featured the 1949 WWII classic, "The Sands of Iwo Jima."

He also said that if we wanted to purchase something from the concession stand, then he would be happy to meet us out in the front lobby before heading up to the projection room.

So when Lance heard that the second John Wayne movie was a WWII film featuring the U.S. Navy fighting against the Japanese fleet in the South Pacific, he was thrilled beyond belief.

Why?

Well, let's just say that Lance has a fascination with the Navy.

Uh, wait..., maybe I should rephrase that. Lance has an obsession with the Navy, and tells virtually everyone he meets that he proudly served in that particular branch of the U.S. military.

Just to be clear, Lance never served in the U.S. Navy. But if you didn't know any better, you'd almost think that he did. Because everything that Lance says about the Navy is spot on.

Not only does Lance know port from starboard, but he can also describe every nook and cranny of a ship that there is to know. He can show you how to swab a deck, or even tell you when it's customary to wear the dress whites.

He'll even describe what types of salty undertakings that sailors like to do while on shore leave too!

And if that still wasn't enough to convince you, Lance has a tattoo on his forearm, which supposedly represents the name of the ship that Lance was assigned to while on active duty.

Now the closest that Lance ever got to being in the Navy was listening to the escapades of his two older brothers, as they both swapped stories from their time spent on the seven seas.

In Lance's mind, the next best thing to being in the Navy was to construct his own little fantasy world, so that he could vicariously live through the experiences of his two older brothers.

Not to mention, the exhilarating sensation that he receives every time someone firmly shakes his hand, and then heartwarmingly says to him, "Thank you for your service!"

When you think about it, I guess Lance's little delusional world is a lot more interesting than telling people that he works at some fast food restaurant, or at his Uncle Charlie's carwash.

So before heading back into the theater for the second movie, Lance managed to use his boyish charm on me once again by conning me into buying him a candy bar and another 64oz. cup of soda from the concession stand.

When we returned to our seats, Murphy decided to have a little fun with Lance by asking him if he ever had the pleasure of serving under John Wayne during his time spent in the Navy.

Lance had no idea that Murphy was only pulling his leg, as he replied in complete and utter seriousness, "No, but it would have been a privilege and an honor to serve under him."

As the house lights dimmed for the second movie, Murphy thought he would take one last poke at Lance by asking him what his military rank was while serving in the U.S. Navy.

Lance proudly stated, "I was a Seaman 2nd Class!"

Murphy replied, "Really? I could've sworn that you were a Lance Corporal."

Lance glared at Murphy, and if looks could kill then Murphy would be dead. Lance then snarled, "Now why would you ever say something like that Uncle Murphy? There are no Lance Corporals in the Navy, - that rank is reserved exclusively for the Marine Corps."

Murphy replied, "Well, I guess I just assumed that you were a Lance Corporal because your name is Lance. So are you sure you weren't a Lance Corporal in the Navy?"

As I listened to Murphy and Lance go back and forth with their little give and takes, it simply fascinated me that Lance has the ability to conjure up a highly complex and sophisticated delusional world for himself. Yet, when it comes to figuring out if someone is simply playing a practical joke on him, then he doesn't seem to have the slightest idea in the world.

I actually heard through the grapevine that the living unit staff had a little wager going on amongst themselves. Apparently, everyone agreed to throw five bucks into the kitty, and the first person who gets Lance to admit that he wasn't in the Navy will wind up winning the whole pot.

In fact, Cameron even offered to buy Lance a steak dinner, if Lance would just simply admit to the fact that he never served in the U.S. Navy. But apparently, Lance wound up sticking to his guns, and he wouldn't take the bait that Cameron was dangling right there in front of him.

Throughout the movie, Murphy kept peppering Lance with all sorts of silly questions on Naval protocol, and the types of day-to-day routines that sailors would normally do on the boat.

Lance would then have to remind Murphy that he was assigned to a ship and not a boat. And even hammered the point home by using a very insightful analogy, as he carefully stated, "Just remember one thing Uncle Murphy, a ship can carry a boat, but a boat can't carry a ship."

So after guzzling down his second 64oz. cup of soda, Lance needed to use the restroom again. As Lance attempted to get up from his seat, I then informed him that he couldn't use the bathroom facilities all on his own, and that he needed to be escorted and supervised at all times.

Lance then flashed me his million dollar smile, and jokingly replied, "Ah, c'mon Uncle Jack, I'm only going to the bathroom, you know that you can trust me."

I quickly countered, "Uh-huh, just like the night of the basketball game, right?"

When I escorted Lance to the bathroom, Murphy didn't even know that we were gone, because his eyes were totally riveted to the screen the entire time. Murphy was waiting to see what trick that John Wayne had up his sleeve, so that he could save the day for the Americans.

It's funny, but up until now Murphy could care less about John Wayne, or any of his motion pictures. Yet, here he is today, sitting on the edge of his seat completely spellbound.

Upon returning from the restroom, I casually leaned over to Murphy and asked him what we missed. Murphy's eyes lit right up, as he excitedly replied, "John Wayne is single-handedly beating the Japanese, and now I understand why Lance wanted to serve under him so badly!"

A few moments later, Murphy playfully said, "Hey Lance, I think I just saw you loading some artillery shells into one of the big guns."

Lance began scouring the entire movie screen, and in a state of sheer panic he said, "Are you sure it was me, Uncle Murphy? Hey, was I wearing my peacoat, or my blue windbreaker?"

Although Murphy was tempted to keep the prank going, he decided to cut Lance a little slack, as he muttered, "Uh, it was a navy-blue windbreaker, and it said U.S. Navy on the back."

When the movie was over, we made our way toward the exits. Lance couldn't stop raving about his hero John Wayne, and how instrumental he was in defeating the entire Japanese fleet.

Lance then stopped dead in his tracks, and said with a real serious look on his face, "Listen guys, if it wasn't for John Wayne, then we'd all be speaking Japanese right now."

Once again, Lance just couldn't figure out that John Wayne was simply a Hollywood actor, and not the gutsy marine sergeant that he was portrayed to be up on the silver screen.

Now interestingly enough, but despite the dozens of military roles that John Wayne has starred in throughout his illustrious Hollywood career, it was rumored that he was actually a draft dodger during WWII.

John Wayne's decision to be a conscientious objector was highly criticized by many of his contemporaries. Especially when so many prominent sports stars and celebrities of his day decided to risk fame and fortune at the height of their careers, so that they could proudly serve their country during its darkest hour.

Well, I'm sure that John Wayne had his reasons. But good luck in telling that to all of the courageous men and women that fought so valiantly for this country, and to the families whose loved ones made the ultimate sacrifice by dying for our freedom.

As we headed for the exit, the manager of the theater thanked us for our patronage. Lance then decided to roll his shirt sleeve up over his elbow, so that he could show the theater manager the naval tattoo that he had inked on his left forearm.

Lance then shouted, "Hey mister, what do you think of my tattoo?"

As the theater manager studied the artwork on Lance's tattoo, Lance proudly said, "I got this tattoo during my last tour of duty in the Navy!"

The theater manager then looked Lance straight in the eye, and in an astonished tone of voice, the theater manager replied, "Really...! You mean, you actually served in the U.S. Navy?"

Murphy, who was standing directly behind Lance, began waving his hands in the air so that he could get the theater manager's attention. As the theater manager glanced up at Murphy, Murphy then quietly mouthed the words, "Shell shock."

Lance then asked the theater manager, "Hey mister, do you know what we use to say in the Navy?"

Although the theater manager seemed to be completely saturated at that point, he decided to humor Lance by saying, "Um, no..., what did you use to say when you were in the Navy?"

Lance proudly replied, "The Army eats the beans, and the Navy gets the gravy!"

Everyone laughed out loud, and I guess you could say that Lance's amusing little ditty was the perfect ending to a perfect day.

We left the movie theater, and as promised, we then drove directly over to the ice cream stand to get some ice cream. Lance knew exactly what he wanted, which was a gooey hot fudge sundae, with four scoops of chocolate ice cream, whipped cream, and a luscious cherry on top.

Oh yeah, and an extra-large soda with no ice.

I then leaned over to Murphy, and discretely whispered, "This is exactly why no one wants to take Lance anywhere, because he's always pushing the envelope."

Murphy and Lance sat down at one of the outdoor picnic benches, while I stepped up to the takeout window, and then ordered three extra-large vanilla cones with chocolate sprinkles.

When I handed Lance his ice cream cone, he was so excited by the enormous size of it, that he seemed to forget all about what he had originally wanted me to order for him.

So after we were all done enjoying our creamy and delectably delicious ice cream cones, we then took a nice leisurely ride back to the State School.

When Murphy pulled the van up to the front of the building, I was a little surprised to see Dick Henderson making a mad dash toward us, as if something was terribly wrong.

As Dick approached the side of the van, I rolled down the window, and then said with a satisfying smile, "Mission accomplished, Dick!"

Dick hastily replied, "Good...! Good...! Hey listen, it's getting pretty late, so why don't you and Murphy call it a day, and I'll take Lance down to his living unit now, okay?"

Murphy replied, "Sounds good, Dick. I'll just swing the van around back and park it."

Dick snapped at Murphy, and shouted, "Murphy, would you just leave the goddamn van right where it is, and I'll have the afternoon supervisor take care of it later, alright!"

Murphy glanced in my direction, and then quietly mumbled, "Okay, Dick."

As I went to open up the side door of the van to let Lance out, Dick sharply yelled, "Jack, you heard what I just told Murphy, I said that I would take care of Lance. Now I want you two guys to get the hell out of here right now, okay!"

"Alright, alright," I replied, in a somewhat agitated tone of voice.

As Murphy and I were walking toward our cars, we were both scratching our heads and wondering what the hell was wrong with Dick.

Suddenly, Mr. Hanson came charging out of the building. And with absolute fire in his voice, he screamed at the top of his lungs, "Dick, tell Jack and Murphy to stay right where they are because I wanna speak to them right now!"

In a deflated tone of voice, Dick called out to us and said, "Hey guys, wait up a minute, Mr. Hanson wants to speak to ya."

As soon as Hanson approached us, he let Murphy and I have it with both barrels, as he vehemently shouted, "So I'd like to know who in the hell authorized you two guys to go on the all-day joyride with Lance Coppenger today, huh?"

Before Murphy or I could even utter a single word, Dick replied, "Mr. Hanson, I've already been over this with you once before, I'm the one who authorized the outing for Lance."

Hanson glared at Dick and stated, "Oh, trust me, I'll be dealing with you later Dick. But right now I'm talking to Jack and Murphy, and I would appreciate it if you didn't interrupt me."

As Hanson turned his attentions back to us, I quietly said, "Actually, the outing was all my idea Mr. Hanson. I just thought that it would be nice to take Lance out on his last official day with us, that's all."

Hanson yelled, "Oh, is that right! So, uh..., what do you think we're running here Jack, summer camp? Mr. Coppenger isn't being transferred to the state forensic unit because he just won the grand prize on a TV game show, he's being transferred to the state forensic unit because he's a goddamn menace to society!"

I softly replied, "Well, I'm sorry you feel that way Mr. Hanson. It certainly wasn't my intent to undermine your authority. I just wanted Lance's last day here to be a memorable one."

Hanson snarled, "A memorable one! Uh, nicely put, Jack. Because I was just thinking the same exact thing. And almost as memorable as the night that Coppenger decided to take off from the basketball game, right?"

So after getting my ass completely chewed out by Hanson, he then shifted his attention over to Murphy, and then shouted, "And what about you Murphy, I would've expected a little more common sense out of you! Have you already forgotten about the night of the basketball game! Huh, maybe I was a little too hasty in recommending you for that promotion after all!"

Murphy didn't appreciate Hanson's cheap shot one bit, especially when Murphy has been doing everything in his power to make Hanson look good in the eyes of the Director.

To Murphy's credit, he remained as cool as a cucumber, as he calmly said, "Well, like Jack said Mr. Hanson, I didn't see the harm in taking Lance out on his last day. Frankly, I didn't think the philosophy of this agency was to hold grudges, especially toward individuals who lack the capacity to understand the gravity of their mistakes. Correct me if I'm wrong, but the last time I checked, we work for the Office of Mental Retardation and Disabilities, and not for the Department of Corrections."

Hanson was absolutely furious that Murphy would take such an insolent tone with him. Hanson is not accustomed to having his subordinates stand up to him. I'm sure Hanson thought that Murphy was going to behave like a good little soldier, and take whatever punishment he had coming to him. But apparently, Hanson doesn't know Murphy quite as well as he thought he did.

Just because Hanson gave Murphy a nice promotion, that doesn't automatically mean that Murphy is willing to roll over and play dead as a way of showing Hanson his undying gratitude.

Lest we forget, not only is Murphy a man of principle, but he is also a man of integrity as well. And come hell or high water, but he's not about to compromise on any of his convictions.

As Hanson started to inch a little closer towards Murphy, Lance suddenly jumped off of the van and knocked Hanson to the ground. Before any of us even realized what was happening, Lance had his hands wrapped around Hanson's throat, and he began choking the hell out of him.

Lance had his hands wrapped so tightly around Hanson's neck that Hanson could hardly breathe. And at that moment, Hanson looked like he was on the verge of completely passing out.

Well, just as Lance was ready to deliver the knockout punch, Murphy came up from behind and dragged Lance off of Hanson.

As Lance squirmed to get free of Murphy's hold, he was blistering Hanson with every dirty curse word in the book, like only an old salty sailor can do.

Lance was saying things to Hanson that the rest of the staff can only dream of saying.

As Hanson tried to shake out the cobwebs, he glanced down at his shirt and saw that it was badly damaged. And then he noticed that his silk tie was completely torn to smithereens.

Hanson then went totally ballistic, as he shouted, "Coppenger, you rotten son-of-a-bitch, you just ruined my brand new silk tie! This tie was a gift from my mother, you fuckin' asshole!"

Dick then decided to seize the moment by saying, "Why Mr. Hanson, how dare you speak to Lance that way. You of all people should know that we are strictly prohibited to address the clients in that manner. So based on what I just heard, I will be lodging a formal complaint with the Director, and citing you for verbal abuse and professional misconduct. And I'm also quite sure that Jack and Murphy will be lodging a formal complaint with the Director as well."

Hanson was utterly appalled that Dick would threaten him with such a heinous accusation like that, especially since Mr. Hanson prides himself on being the hammer and not the nail.

Dick then cunningly said, "Of course, I'm sure that we could overlook this entire incident altogether, if you would just simply forget all about the outing that took place today with Lance."

Needless to say, but Hanson doesn't take kindly to ultimatums. Unless of course, he's the one setting the terms.

Dick knew that he had Hanson over a barrel, and the last thing that Hanson wanted was to be accused of some type of impropriety that might blemish his illustrious record.

In a bit of a huff, Hanson headed directly toward the parking lot.

As Hanson was unlocking his car door, he then shouted, "Be advised gentlemen, but you haven't heard the last of this! Somehow I'll find a way to get you all fired! But in the meantime, I'll be placing a letter of insubordination in each of your Personnel files!"

Lance then yelled out, "Fuck you, Hanson! You fuckin' asshole…!"

So after escorting Lance down to his living unit, we chatted a few minutes with the staff, jotted a quick progress note in Lance's chart, and then finally called it a day.

As Murphy and I were walking through the front lobby, we decided to swing by Dick Henderson office, so that we could see how Dick was holding up.

When we went by Dick's office, we noticed that his door was closed. Apparently, Dick was talking to someone on the phone, and the voice on the other end of the line sounded like it was Mr. Hanson.

Hanson was yelling so loud that we could hear every word that he was saying.

Every time Dick tried to get a word in edgewise, we could hear Mr. Hanson shout at the top of his lungs, "Hey, shut up Dick, I'm talking!"

Hanson screamed, "So tell me Dick, what the hell were you thinking when you allowed O'Leary and Doherty to take Coppenger out of the building today and go on an all-day joyride? Don't you realize that I'm on record with the Director in saying that Coppenger is a total menace to society! When the Director finds out that Coppenger has been gallivanting around town with the same two idiots that got him lost in the first place, he's gonna think that I'm nothing but a total incompetent, and that I've lost complete control of my entire Unit!"

Dick countered, "Excuse me Mr. Hanson, but today's outing was nothing like the night of the basketball game. Lance was under the watchful eye of two of my most trusted staff today."

Hanson yelled, "Oh, is that right! Well, the two most trusted staff that you're referring to Dick is the reason that we're in this fuckin' predicament in the first place! And furthermore, I don't want O'Leary or Doherty anywhere near that raving lunatic Coppenger tomorrow morning when you ship his ass out to the state forensic unit! Do I make myself clear?"

"Yes sir…," Dick softly said.

Hanson continued his tirade and shouted, "And another thing, if you think you're gonna threaten me with some trumped up charge of verbal misconduct, so that you and those two Irish hooligans of yours can weasel your way out of this mess, then you're crazier than Coppenger!"

So after hanging up the phone with Mr. Hanson, Dick decided to clear his head a bit and go grab a cup of coffee out of the breakroom.

When Dick opened up his office door, he saw Murphy and I sitting out in the front lobby. As Dick approached us, he quietly said, "Hey, I thought you two guys already left for the day."

Murphy answered, "Well, Jack and I decided to swing by your office to see how you were doing. But as we were just about to knock on your door, we heard you on the telephone with Mr. Hanson. And, uh…, we kinda eavesdropped on your conversation a bit, sorry Dick."

Dick replied, "Uh-huh, so I guess you heard Mr. Hanson say that he doesn't want either of you involved in the transfer tomorrow, nor does he want you anywhere near the living unit."

"Uh, yeah…, we heard that loud and clear." I said, quietly.

Dick continued, "Well, as much as it pains me to say it, but Mr. Hanson is still my boss, and I have to respect his directives."

"Yeah, we understand Dick." Murphy replied.

I then piped up and said, "Well, for what it's worth, Lance had a great time today Dick. And I think the outing really meant a lot to him."

Dick replied, with a satisfying smile, "Well, of course he had a great time today. After all, he got to hang out with you two guys all day, right?"

I then asked, "So what time are you leaving for the forensic unit tomorrow, Dick?"

Dick replied, "Well, we're hoping to get an early start, so that we can be on the road by six o'clock. It's almost a three hour trip, so we'll probably grab some breakfast along the way."

Murphy then amusingly said, "Well, you might wanna consider going through the drive-thru window tomorrow, instead of stopping off at the diner. Because knowing Mr. Hanson, he'll probably be calling the forensic unit every five minutes to see if you've arrived there or not."

Dick let out a hearty laugh, and then replied, "You're right, and that's exactly why I told Mr. Hanson that we're leaving for the forensic unit at seven o'clock tomorrow, so that I can spend a little quality time with Lance myself."

The next day, I decided to forego my usual morning coffee with Murphy, so that I could swing by the living unit first and see how everything went this morning with Lance's transfer.

From what the living unit staff conveyed to me, Lance had absolutely no idea that he was being transferred to the state forensic unit today.

And to take it one step further, but when Lance saw all of his worldly possessions lined up outside his bedroom door, he immediately thought that he was going on a little vacation, and then he wanted to know how long he would be gone for.

Although the living unit staff wasn't exactly sure how to answer him, they told Lance that he would probably be gone for a while, which is why they decided to pack him so many bags.

Lance was thrilled with the idea of taking a little vacation, and told the staff that he was ready to leave anytime, but not until he had a chance to say "good-bye" to his Uncle Jack first.

The living unit staff told Lance that they were on a bit of a tight schedule this morning, and that they really needed to get on the road as soon as possible. And unfortunately, there just wasn't enough time for them to wait around so that Lance could say "good-bye" to me.

Upon hearing what the staff had to say, Lance dropped to his knees and began to cry, as he pleaded, "But I can't go on vacation without saying "good-bye" to my Uncle Jack first, 'cause he's my most favorite uncle in the whole wide world, and I really need to see him before I go!"

Lance was so distraught that he actually cried real tears, instead of his usual crocodile tears. And after hearing what the staff had to say, I actually shed a few tears of my own as well.

Despite all of the heartache that I was feeling right now, the one thing that was so gut-wrenching for me was knowing that I wasn't going to hear Lance call me "Uncle Jack" anymore.

According to Lance, I was his "most favorite uncle." And even though Lance has had a string of "favorite uncles" over the years, he actually considered me to be his "most favorite uncle," which is clearly a notch above the rest.

And in my book, - that's gotta count for something anyway!

CHAPTER FOURTEEN

Well, it's hard to believe, but Lance has been gone from the State School for over three months now. And other than me, no one really seems to care that he's gone.

I've been asking Dick Henderson almost every day if he's had a chance to speak with his friend who works out at the forensic unit, so that he can tell us how Lance is doing. But every time I ask Dick if he's made the call yet, he tells me that he still hasn't gotten around to doing it.

Quite honestly, but you would think that Dick Henderson could find at least five minutes out of his day to make one lousy phone call. But in Dick's defense, Hanson has been riding him pretty hard of late, and Dick can barely find time to go to the bathroom.

Lance being gone is still a very tough pill for me to swallow, and I miss him more than words can say. Since Lance has been gone, well, my days seem to be a lot longer, and my stress level has been teetering at an all-time high.

Mr. Hanson seems to be keeping a very low profile lately, and the only time that we ever see him is at meetings. Whenever Hanson runs into me he barely says "hello," which tells me that I'm still in the doghouse, and that I've probably been crossed off of his Christmas list too.

Hanson is not one to let bygones be bygones. And if it wasn't for the fact that Murphy and I are really good at what we do, then he wouldn't think twice about handing us our pink slip.

We've heard some interesting rumors circulating around the facility lately that something really big is brewing out at the State Capital, but no one seems to know exactly what it is.

Some of the rumors have mentioned Hanson as being named as the new Director at a downstate facility, and others say that he might be in line to be the State Commissioner's new right hand man.

Anyway, I've noticed a definite change in Dick Henderson since Lance's departure, and Dick's usual happy-go-lucky disposition has simply vanished into thin air. Dick rarely smiles anymore, and I can't even remember the last time that Dick came down to Murphy's office to shoot the breeze with us over coffee and donuts.

Well, I guess you could say that Hanson has finally broken Dick Henderson.

And instead of tilting at windmills, Dick has simply fallen into line to become one of Hanson's "yes" men.

Looking back, if you had asked me six months ago how I really felt about Hanson, I probably would've said that he was grossly misunderstood and generally gets a bad rap.

But sad to say my opinion of Hanson has drastically changed, and I'm now beginning to see him for what he really is, - a hypocrite and an opportunist.

On the surface, Hanson would like you to believe that he's a regular guy. But now that I've gotten the chance to know him, I've come to realize that Hanson doesn't do anything out of the goodness of his heart, because every good deed that he does comes with a hidden price tag.

Now obviously, Murphy deserved his promotion. But let's not delude ourselves into thinking that Hanson recommended Murphy for promotion because it was the right thing to do, Hanson gave Murphy the promotion because it was simply a sound investment for him to make.

 Essentially, Murphy makes Hanson look good, so why not throw a dog a bone every once in a while to make sure that the dog remains loyal and forever obedient to his master.

Yeah, I know that might sound a bit cynical to say.

But Hanson is part of the new bred, and these modern day administrators are being groomed to be a little less kind and a lot more cut-throat in their decision making.

The State School is now being operated like a business, and the days of having someone with a medical or social science degree in charge of running the place is virtually over. The administrative reins have been handed over to a bunch of young business executives, who are more concerned about the bottom line than they are with what is morally or ethically correct.

So it would seem that Mr. Wohlers was right after all, when he told me the night of his retirement party, - "Hanson is a wolf in sheep's clothing."

Although Wohlers' descriptive metaphor in describing Hanson may not have registered with me that night, it now seems to resonate with me loud and clear.

Well, it's the start of a brand new work week. And as I was driving into work this morning, I was thinking that the time has finally come for me to start making a few wholesale changes in the Work Activity Center.

The clients have been telling me for months now that they are sick and tired of working on laundry every day, and that they'd like to work on something new and a little more exciting.

It's funny, but if you had told me five years ago that I'd be in charge of operating a two-bit laundry program, then I probably would've laughed right in your face and called you crazy.

Yet, here I am today, up to my eyeballs in bed linens and bath towels.

Gee, I wonder if Dr. Stevens would get a good laugh out of this one.

Well, as much as it pains me to say it, but maybe it's time for me to pick up the phone and give Mr. Kramer a call. Perhaps Mr. Kramer and I can kick around a few ideas on how to provide the clients with some better work alternatives, so that we can make the Work Activity Center a more dynamic and enjoyable place for them to work every day.

Before calling Mr. Kramer, I decided to jot down a few ideas. I've learned from past experience that when locking horns with Mr. Kramer, then you better make sure that you have all your ducks in a row, or else he'll systematically pick you apart and make you look like a fool.

It then occurred to me that the only way to convince Kramer to buy into any of my ideas about the Work Activity Center was to make it sound like they were his ideas, and that it would be to his advantage to consider making some across-the-board changes in the work program.

So after thoroughly racking my brains, I thought I would ask Mr. Kramer if he would consider having the Work Activity Center as a satellite work program of ENCORE Industries.

ENCORE Industries is a small sheltered workshop here at the State School, and it employs roughly one hundred clients. The name ENCORE is an acronym that stands for, - Embracing New Community Opportunities and Rehabilitation Endeavors.

I actually thought the name ENCORE was a pretty catchy title for a work program. And although I'm not really sure who coined the name, I highly doubt that it was Kramer, especially since Mr. Kramer hasn't had an original thought pop into his head since the day that he was born.

Kramer considered ENCORE Industries to be the flagship program of the facility. And if you ask me, it was probably the only thing that was keeping Mr. Kramer in a job around here.

So that being said, you can only imagine how protective Kramer was of the ENCORE program, and how paranoid he was in scrutinizing every little decision that pertained to it.

Later that afternoon, I tried calling Kramer's office but his secretary told me that he was all tied up in a meeting with the Director, and that he wouldn't be back for the rest of the day.

Actually, I was kinda relieved that Mr. Kramer wasn't available to take my phone call. Especially since Kramer has a knack for putting the fear of God in you, and making you feel like you're nothing but a bumbling idiot whenever you're forced to have a conversation with him.

In the old days, Ms. Albright would always run interference for the counselors, so that she could try to protect us from Kramer and all of his unpredictable tantrums and mood swings. But now that Ms. Albright is gone, there's really no one to shield us from Mr. Kramer anymore.

So that being said, you can see why none of the counselors on staff wanted to open up their mouth and run the risk of being raked over the coals by Kramer, especially with regards to any new ideas or suggestions they might have in making the work programs around here better.

And to make matters worse, the fact that I'm currently in Hanson's doghouse right now prevents me from asking him to help grease the wheel in leveraging my position with Kramer.

So in the meantime, I guess it's back to folding bed linens and bath towels, until I can muster up enough courage to pick up the phone and call Mr. Kramer regarding any of my ideas.

Well, yesterday afternoon we finally received the new client that we were promised to get three months ago, when Lance Coppenger was transferred to the state forensic unit. The new client's name is Tony Salerno, and Tony will be residing on L.U. 513.

Apparently, the reason it took so long for Tony Salerno to get here was because of some legal complications. But now that Tony is here, I'm hoping to chat with him sometime today and see if he's interested in getting involved in the work program and maybe earning some money.

Well, since I had a few minutes to kill this morning, I decided to pay Tony Salerno a little visit on L.U. 513. As I entered the unit, I was immediately broadsided by several clients who like to camp out in the front foyer of the living unit, so that they can keep tabs on all the comings and goings, and perhaps even finagle a favor or two from someone who is entering the living unit.

Although the living unit staff frowns on this type of loitering behavior, it seems to go on all the time. And even though the living unit staff is quite vigilant in chasing the clients away, the clients still manage to scurry right back again, as soon as the living unit staff walks away.

As I ran the gauntlet of clients who were all huddled inside the front foyer of the living unit, I asked them how the new guy was doing, and if everyone was making him feel at home.

Bobby Diggs spoke right up and said, "Yeah, we're trying to be nice, but he's kind of a weird guy. He's always talking about ambulances and people dying, and it sounds really creepy."

I thought to myself, "Uh, Bobby is calling the new guy weird. So isn't that like the pot calling the kettle black?"

So in response to Bobby, I simply replied, "Well Bobby, I'm sure that Tony is feeling a little bit nervous right now, so I'm really counting on you to show him the ropes, okay buddy?"

Dan Christoff then piped up and said, "Hey Jack, I really like the new guy. I think he's pretty funny, and he likes to talk about sports and music a lot too."

I quickly thought to myself, "A funny guy that likes sports and music. Hmm…, Tony sounds like my kinda guy. And maybe I just found my new replacement for Lance Coppenger."

Jamal Buchanan then pushed his way past Dan Christoff, and brashly asked, "Hey man, is today payday? Because the staff said I gotta wait until payday before I get my new sneakers."

I then posed the question, "Well Jamal, what day is today?"

Jamal answered, in a real smart aleck tone of voice, "What kinda stupid-ass question is that cracker? It's Thursday, man! What's wrong with your dumb-ass?"

I softly replied, "Exactly, it's Thursday. So when is payday, Jamal?"

"Uh, we get paid on Friday's, aight!" Jamal said, with a real cocky grin.

I calmly replied, "Yeah, that's right, we get paid on Friday's. So if today is Thursday, then why are you asking me such a dumb-ass question like that, Jamal? Aight!"

Jamal sneered, "Chill out, man! You don't need to be flippin' an attitude about it!"

As Jamal strutted toward the dayroom, he mumbled, "Wiseass, good for nothin' honky."

Bobby Diggs mischievously whispered, "Jack, Jamal is talking bad about you again."

Tyrell Freeman then quietly said, "Mr. Jack, I've been keeping Jamal in my prayers."

I then replied. "Thank you, Tyrell. Because Jamal needs all the prayers that he can get."

So when I finally tracked down the unit charge, I asked him how Tony was adjusting to his new living situation. He told me that Tony was doing pretty well so far, and if I wanted to chat with him for a few minutes, then I could find him down in the gym with Dick and Murphy.

When I entered the gym, I saw Dick and Murphy shooting baskets with Tony. Dick then introduced me to Tony, and told him that I was the guy to see about getting a job around here.

Tony was small in stature, a bit scruffy, and he appeared to be a little rough around the edges. When I asked Tony if he was interested in having a job and earning some money here in the building, he simply shrugged his shoulders, and didn't seem all that enthused about the idea.

I then asked Tony if he had a job at the forensic unit, and he replied in a rather ominous way, "No, because they said that I was a troublemaker, and that I didn't deserve to have one."

Although I viewed this as a red flag, I really didn't want to press the issue. So I told Tony that I'd give him a tryout in the work program later this afternoon, and then we'd go from there.

Dick glanced at his watch, and then realized that he was running late for a meeting. As Dick reached for his sports jacket, he nonchalantly said, "C'mon Tony, why don't you and I head back to the living unit now, okay buddy?"

Tony replied, "No, I wanna stay here in the gym and shoot some more baskets."

Suddenly, there was a moment of uncomfortable silence, and you could feel the tension that was beginning to mount in the gym.

As I read the look of concern on Dick's face, it prompted me to say, "Hey Dick, I haven't had a chance to see Tony take a shot yet. So maybe we could stay in the gym for a little while longer, and then Murphy and I can bring him back to his living unit when we're all done, okay?"

Dick hesitated a moment, but then he nodded his head, and reluctantly left the gym.

As Murphy and I turned our attentions back to Tony, he seemed to be totally consumed in his thoughts. Tony never said a word to us, as he just kept staring down at the floor, bouncing the ball with both of his hands, as if he were trapped in some sort of deep, dark, and hypnotic trance.

Tony was definitely a strange guy. And if you ask me, I think the forensic unit got the better part of the deal when they traded him for Lance Coppenger. Tony had a real psychiatric aura about him, and I can see why some of the clients found him to be odd and a little spooky.

As Tony took shots at the basket, Murphy and I positioned ourselves on either side of the backboard, and we kept tossing him the ball, so that he could continue to take shots at the basket.

So after about ten minutes of watching Tony shoot the basketball, Murphy finally said, "Hey Tony, Jack and I have to get ready for morning programming, so this is gonna have to be your last shot. So try to make it a good one, okay buddy?"

Tony never said a word, he just kept looking down at the floor, and bouncing the ball in a trance-like manner. He then chucked the ball at the basket, but the shot he took was off the mark.

Murphy then spiritedly said, "Hey, nice try, Tony. Now, c'mon buddy, it's time to go!"

Tony looked Murphy square in the eye, and with little to no expression in his voice, he defiantly said, "No, I'm not leaving the gym until my last shot goes into the basket."

Murphy and I exchanged glances, as if to say, "Okay, let's get ready to dance!"

Apparently, Tony was drawing his line in the sand and daring us to step over it. But instead of challenging Tony, Murphy just decided to play it cool, and allow Tony to continue shooting the basketball until he successfully made his last shot.

Well, after several more attempts of shooting the basketball, Tony finally made a basket. Murphy proceeded to compliment Tony on making his last shot. And then Murphy tossed the ball into the equipment box, and we all left the gym and headed back to L.U. 513 in total silence.

The minute we stepped onto L.U. 513, it was now Murphy's turn to look Tony square in the eye, as Murphy sternly said, "Tony, if you ever try to challenge my authority like that again, then all hell will break loose. Do you understand what I'm telling you right now?"

Suddenly, the hair on the back of my neck began to stand on end. And at that moment, I honestly thought that we were on the verge of having a good old-fashioned donnybrook.

Tony then said with a deadpan expression, "Okay, but if you should happen to kill me that day, will you promise to call an ambulance, so that they can take me straight to the morgue."

Murphy replied, "Yeah, okay, it's a deal," and then Murphy and Tony shook hands.

It would seem that Tony has some sort of weird preoccupation with death. And maybe in time, I'll be able to figure out why. But in the meantime, if you wanna survive in this wild and crazy game that we call human services, then you better know your opponent's Achilles heel, and then adjust your game accordingly.

Tony's fixation on death and ambulances may not be normal. But you can bet your bottom dollar, that when push comes to shove, I'll be using it to my advantage. Tony wound up tipping his hand this morning, and Murphy and I were able to sneak a peek at his cards.

So just remember, if you wanna succeed in life, then you better learn how to sport a good poker face. And by the looks of it, - it's something that Tony still hasn't quite figured out yet.

In the afternoon, I had Tony come down to the laundry program so that I could see what kind of a worker he was. As I watched Tony fold his towels, he basically kept to himself, and he never attempted to engage in conversation with any of the clients that were working around him.

Tony had an undeniable psychiatric presence. And in some ways, Tony kinda reminded me of Henry Josephson from my days back at WEALTH Industries. Tony's quality of work was absolutely terrible, as he just kept staring out into space, folding one messy towel after the other.

Every so often, I would approach Tony and try to provide him with a few simple words of encouragement. And in a tactful and nonthreatening way, I would try to point out to him that he needed to do a better job at squaring up the corners of his towels.

But even after I demonstrated the correct way that the towels needed to be folded, Tony would simply nod his head and tell me that he understood. But the minute that I turned my back and walked away from him, he would revert back to his usual careless and sloppy ways again.

It's funny, but just when I'm ready to crown someone in the building as being the most psychiatric person we have, doesn't someone else come along who then tops the list of crazies.

As I continued to walk around the room making my clinical observations, I could hear Jamal Buchanan talking smack with some of his hommies in the far corner of the room.

I walked over to where Jamal was working, and then asked him if he would like to share his comments with the group. Jamal then boldly replied, "Listen man, I'm sick and tired of doin' punk-ass laundry all the time. So can't we work on some other kinda different shit around here?"

Before I could even respond to Jamal's heated complaint, Tony Salerno began screaming at the top of his lungs, "Shut your fuckin' mouth, or else I'll kill you! Do you hear me!"

Upon hearing Tony's blood curdling screams, I quickly turned in his direction. I couldn't figure out why Tony was yelling, especially when no one in the room was even bothering him.

As I approached Tony, I placed my hand gently on his shoulder as a way of comforting him. As I entered his personal space, he grabbed me around my neck and started choking me.

The two staff in the room then wrestled Tony to the ground, but not before he managed to tear my sweater, and destroy the St Christopher's medal that I was wearing underneath my shirt.

As the staff escorted Tony back to his living unit, I tried to shake out the cobwebs and collect my thoughts, and to also try to figure out what the hell just happened with Tony Salerno.

In the background, I could hear Jamal Buchanan laughing his head off. And then I heard Jamal say, "Damn…! That freaky white boy got the drop on your ass, Mr. O'Really. I'll tell ya man, if he tries any of that voodoo shit with me, then I'll put a good whoopin' on his sorry ass!"

Later that afternoon, I went on the living unit to check on Tony, so that I could see how he was doing, and to find out why he went totally haywire down in the work program earlier.

When I entered L.U. 513, I saw Tony sitting all by himself on one of the couches in the dayroom. Before actually speaking with Tony, I decided to chat with the living unit charge first, and get a quick update on how Tony's behavior has been since the incident occurred.

Apparently, Tony has been very subdued all afternoon. But he did ask the staff several times if he could speak with me, because he had something very important that he wanted to say.

Naturally, I just assumed that Tony wanted to speak with me so that he could apologize for attacking me earlier, and to ask for my forgiveness. So with that in mind, I decided to walk over to where Tony was sitting, and ask him what it was that he wanted to speak with me about.

Upon seeing me, Tony's eyes lit up like a spotlight, as he excitedly said, "Hey, we got 'em! And I don't think he'll be bothering us anymore!"

In a bit of a quandary, I asked, "We got 'em? Whatta mean, we got 'em? We got who?"

"Lucifer!" Tony exclaimed, without even batting an eyelash.

All of a sudden, I had a chill go right down my spine, and I'd be lying if I said that I wasn't scared. What Tony just said, coupled with the psychotic look that he had plastered on his face, threw me into such a tailspin that I nearly shit my pants.

I squeamishly asked, "Are you telling me that you actually saw the devil this afternoon?"

In an eerie, yet decisive tone of voice, Tony confidently replied, "Oh yeah, it was Lucifer all right. And he was talking to me the whole time that I was folding my towels too."

"Really…?" I said, incredulously.

Tony continued by saying, " At first, I tried telling Lucifer to get the hell away from me. But when I saw that he was beginning to choke you, then God commanded me to save you. So I grabbed Lucifer's hands, which were wrapped around your neck, and then threw him off of you. Boy, it was a good thing that you were wearing your St Christopher's medal!"

As I gazed into Tony's eyes, he seemed rather pleased with himself, as if he were some sort of superhero. Up until now, I really haven't worked with anyone this scary before. The Metro gang was certainly scary, but Tony was in a class all by himself.

Tony was a different kind of scary!

I was wondering if Hanson had any idea just how crazy Tony was, or did the forensic unit wind up pulling a fast one? Did Hanson even bother to do a background check on Tony, or did he merely take the forensic unit's word that Tony was suitable for our program?

It just doesn't make any sense to me, - why would anyone want to swap a harmless and kooky guy like Lance Coppenger, for someone as dangerous and psychotic as Tony Salerno?

As Tony continued to stare at me, I honestly think that he was expecting me to literally get down on my hands and knees and thank him for rescuing me from Lucifer's clutches.

For all I know, Tony may envision himself as being some sort of modern day crusader, who was sent by God to avenge Satan and his horde of fallen angels.

The following day, Dick came by my office to see if I was experiencing any ill-effects from my harrowing ordeal with Tony Salerno yesterday. Although Dick realizes that there is a certain amount of danger in what we do here, he still doesn't want to see any of his staff placed in harm's way.

Well…, with the exception of Hanson maybe.

As a precautionary measure, Dick has decided to assign one of the male staff to supervise Tony at all times, so that we can avoid the risk of any future injury or incident from occurring.

Also, Dick is recommending that Tony's psychotropic medications be increased, and that Cameron begin training the staff immediately on Tony's new behavior plan.

So after chatting with Dick, I headed down to Murphy's office for my morning coffee. When Murphy saw me come waltzing through the door, he amusingly said, "Morning Rodney, so I heard that you were involved in some sort of exorcism yesterday."

I quietly chuckled, and then replied, "Yeah, apparently the devil got the drop on me. But lucky for me, Tony Salerno was wearing his 3D glasses, and saved me from Lucifer's clutches."

By now it was getting close to nine-thirty, so I said "good-bye" to Murphy, and then headed down to the laundry workshop to set up for the morning session.

As I was hauling the towels out of the laundry cart, I was thinking how much the clients despise working on laundry every day. And if I don't do something about it real soon, then I'm liable to have a bloody mutiny on my hands.

Since working here at the SBU, I've totally isolated myself from Mr. Kramer. And to make matters worse, but the fact that I work for Kramer's arch enemy has placed me squarely behind the eight ball when it comes to asking Mr. Kramer for any types of favors.

So despite having the deck stacked against me, I decided to go back to my office and give Mr. Kramer a call, and see whether or not he would consider having the SBU be a satellite work program for ENCORE Industries.

Before dialing Kramer's number, I had all of my notes laid out in front of me, so that I knew exactly what I was going to say to Kramer. As I waited on the line, the pit in the bottom of my stomach was nearly the size of Gibraltar, and my sweat glands were operating on overdrive.

Suddenly, a voice come over the line and it was Karen, who is Mr. Kramer's personal secretary, as she pleasantly said, "Good afternoon, Mr. Kramer's office."

"Hi Karen, this is Jack O'Leary. I was wondering if Mr. Kramer was available."

"Oh, hi Jack. Yeah, he's here. Just hold on and I'll put you through, okay."

As I waited on the line, I was praying that this little brainstorm of mine wouldn't blow up right in my face, especially since I haven't spoken to Mr. Kramer in well over a year now.

Yet, here I am, hat in hand, asking Kramer for a pretty big favor.

The prodigal son has now returned, - but will Father Kramer welcome him back with open arms, or simply admonish him for having left the fold in the first place.

Knowing Kramer, he'll probably shoot me down the minute I ask him to consider the Work Activity Center as a satellite program for ENCORE Industries. And then once he does that, he'll want to take the conversation in a whole different direction by asking me all sorts of curious questions about Hanson, and whether or not anything unusual has been happening in his Unit.

Just then I heard Mr. Kramer's voice come over the line and say, "Jack O'Leary, so how the hell are ya? This is certainly an unexpected surprise."

I cautiously replied, "Yeah, it's been a while Mr. Kramer."

Kramer then brashly said, "C'mon Jack, how many years have you known me. What's with the Mr. Kramer, you know that you can call me Bill."

In all of the years that I've known Kramer, I've never referred to him by his first name. But if memory serves me correctly, I may have referred to him by a few other choice names.

Well, privately, of course.

As I listened to Kramer, I was wondering why he was being so chummy this morning. Kramer isn't usually this personable with his subordinates, or should I say, the bottom feeders.

Kramer then inquisitively asked, "So what do I owe the pleasure of hearing from Mr. Jack O'Leary on a Friday afternoon? Are you curious to know what my plans are for the weekend? Or, uh…, is there something else that's on your mind?"

"Well, um…,"

Kramer then rudely interrupted me, "So how are things going with you and Mr. Hanson?"

"Um, pretty good, we…"

Kramer interrupted me again and said, "Really? Because I heard about the client that you lost at the basketball game, and then the run-in you had with Hanson regarding an unauthorized outing with the same client. I even heard that Hanson placed a letter of insubordination in your personnel file. Boy, you certainly have had a pretty tough stretch with Mr. Hanson lately, Jack."

I thought to myself, "Here we go, this is exactly why I didn't wanna call Mr. Kramer."

If Kramer thinks that he's going to squeeze any relevant information out of me regarding Mr. Hanson, then he's absolutely crazy. Kramer would love to get the inside scoop on Hanson, and then use whatever information he gets as ammunition against him. This phone conversation with Mr. Kramer was beginning to go sideways, so I needed to change the subject in a hurry.

I then spoke up and said, "Well Mr. Kramer, the reason I called you today was because I'd like you to consider the SBU as a satellite work program for ENCORE Industries."

Kramer quickly snarled, "Hey Jack, I can't authorize something like that. I can't just flip a switch, and then you automatically become a satellite program for ENCORE Industries. Don't you realize that there are Department of Labor regulations that need to be followed? Oh, and not to mention, the additional workload that would be placed upon my clerical staff as well?"

I then countered, "Well, I'm not asking for a decision to be made today Mr. Kramer, only that you might consider it."

Kramer replied, "Nah, what you're asking me to do is simply out of the question, Jack."

I was actually anticipating this type of reaction from Kramer. When you draw swords with Kramer, then you better make sure that you have all of your ducks in a row. Kramer is not one to possess an open mind. Unless of course, what's being proposed is only to his advantage.

So that being said, I quickly pointed out to Mr. Kramer that it was definitely in his best interest to have the SBU be a satellite work program for ENCORE Industries because it would enable him to wield more power here at the facility, plus it would put him in the cat bird seat in keeping a closer eye on Mr. Hanson's operation.

Furthermore, I conveyed to Mr. Kramer that he would be sending a clear-cut message to the Director, as well as to all of the Unit Chief's that he was trying to bridge the gap between institutional and community based work programs.

And not only that, but this extremely innovative idea of his would undoubtedly catch the eye of the State Commissioner, who may even reward him with a handsome promotion.

As I continued to lay it on thick, I could hear the wheels in the back of Kramer's head grinding on the other end of the line, and he seemed rather pleased with what I was telling him.

Kramer said that he would give the matter some thought. But then was quick to say that I shouldn't get my hopes up, because what I was asking him to do was highly irregular, and it could possibly cost him his operating certificate with the Department of Labor.

In closing, I thanked Mr. Kramer for taking the time to listen to my proposal. And if I could be of any further assistance to him down the line, then please don't hesitate to call on me.

Well, several months went by, and I still hadn't heard back from Mr. Kramer. I couldn't understand why it was taking him so long to make a decision. Although I wanted to pick up the phone and call him, I decided not to because I didn't want him to think that I was too desperate.

It's always a cat and mouse game when you deal with Mr. Kramer. And although I pitched a pretty convincing argument to him on the telephone, he's really not one to make any hasty decisions until he's weighed all of his options very carefully.

The following Sunday, I was chatting with my friend Marty after Mass. Marty owns a small print shop here in town, and he was telling me that one of his office machines was on the fritz and in dire need of repair, specifically, the component that does all of his collating jobs.

Apparently, the parts that were needed to fix the machine were still on back order, and unavailable from the manufacturer for at least another six to eight weeks. And as a result of this, Marty has been forced to do all of his collating contracts by hand.

Obviously, collating by hand can be a very tedious and time consuming job, and Marty was very concerned that he wouldn't be able to meet all of his print shop deadlines on time.

In fact, despite it being a Sunday, Marty was heading over to his print shop right after Mass, so that he could start working on a big collating contract that was due next week.

Later that afternoon, as I was relaxing at home watching the ballgame, I couldn't stop thinking about Marty and his collating dilemma. So I decided to take a drive over to Marty's print shop and pay him a little visit, and to see if he needed any help on the collating job.

When Marty saw me enter the print shop, he was quite surprised to say the least. I told Marty that I felt bad he had to work on his day off, so I decided to come by and lend him a hand.

Marty then proceeded to tell me that even though he's been working on the collating contract for most of the day, he really hasn't made much headway in knocking through the job.

So after hearing what Marty had to say, it then prompted me to think what my dear old mother would often say to me, "Many hands makes for less work!"

I then had this wild and crazy thought pop into my head, which was, - "why don't the clients and I help Marty out on the collating job!"

So when I suggested my idea to Marty, he seemed a bit hesitant. By his own admission, Marty tends to be somewhat of a control freak, and he likes to have things done a certain way.

In addition to that, Marty said that the profit margin on the collating job wasn't sufficient enough for him to subcontract the work out, so that he could pay the clients a fair and equitable wage. I then told Marty that he wouldn't need to pay us, and that we would be more than happy to volunteer our time as a way of giving back to the community and helping out a friend in need.

However, I did suggest to Marty that if he wanted to spring for some donuts as a way of showing his appreciation for helping him out, then I certainly wouldn't object to that one bit.

Furthermore, I reassured Marty that I would oversee the entire project from start to finish, and that he had my personal guarantee that the job would be done correctly and on time.

So after giving it some thought, Marty finally said, "Sure, why not, let's give it a whirl."

The next day, I grabbed a hand truck out of the utility room and then carted Marty's collating job into the laundry workshop. I carefully arranged the stacks of paper into sequential order, and then lined them up in a row on one of the long tables along the far wall of the room.

So my game plan for today was to have half the group work on the collating job, and the other half of the group would process the laundry. That way we wouldn't fall behind in meeting any of our daily laundry quotas for any of the living units in the building.

When the clients arrived for the morning work session, they quickly spotted the stacks of paper that were all lined up on the table, and they began peppering me with all sorts of questions.

I then explained to the clients that I had a special project for them to work on this week, and that the project was for a very good friend of mine who desperately needed our help.

Jamal was the first person to pull up a chair at the table. As Jamal stared at the stacks of papers, he excitedly said, "Hey Mr. O'Really, what does this job pay, around fitty dollars?"

I quietly chuckled to myself, and then replied, "Well, to tell you the truth Jamal, we're not getting paid for this job. I told my friend Marty that you guys would do the work for free."

Jamal flew right off the handle, and then shouted, "Free! Whatcha mean, free! C'mon man, that's a bunch a bullshit! I ain't workin' on no punk-ass job for free, cracker!"

In a bit of a huff, Jamal got up from the table and then strutted over to his usual spot in the back corner of the room. As Jamal began folding his towels, I could hear him mumbling a few choice words under his breath, and comments that were just too vulgar to mention.

Although I was disappointed that Jamal wasn't willing to help us out on the collating job, I was actually proud of the fact that he didn't cause a scene, or try to turn the place upside down.

Jamal continues to be a work in progress. But I can honestly say that he has grown leaps and bounds since being here, and he's actually doing a much better job at channeling his violent outbursts than I ever would've imagined him to do.

From a very early age, Jamal has been conditioned to play the role of the tough guy. And up until now that's the only way he's learned to survive. As time goes on, I'm hoping that Jamal learns to choose his battles more wisely, so that his life won't continue to be an uphill struggle.

So after Jamal stormed away from the table, Bobby Diggs quickly took his place. Bobby couldn't wait to get started on the collating job, and he began making all sorts of suggestions on how to proceed. Although I told Bobby that I appreciated his input on the project, I made it quite clear to him that Marty gave me specific orders on how the collating job was to be done.

As the clients sat at the table and waited for further instruction, they were all wondering what the little rubber doohickey was that I had placed on top of each of the stack of papers.

To satisfy their curiosity, I told them that the little rubber doohickey was called a finger caddy. I then asked each of them to pick it up and place it on their index finger, so that it would be much easier for them to pick up one sheet of paper at a time when doing the collating project.

Russell Turner then decided to play the role of the class clown, as he blurted out, "Hey Bobby, look what I found, a condom! It's way too small for me, but I'm sure that it'll fit you!"

Suddenly, everyone sitting at the table burst out into laughter. And although Russell's comment was made in very poor taste, I must admit that what he said was pretty damn funny.

As we all laughed at Russell's wiseass remark, I happen to glance in Jamal Buchanan's direction. As Jamal looked over at us, he seemed to be wondering what all the noise and laughter was about. The look on Jamal's face indicated to me that perhaps he was a little too hasty in his decision of not wanting to help us out, and maybe he was having some second thoughts about it.

So my strategy in attacking the collating job today was quite simple. I wanted each of the clients to pick up a sheet of paper, and then pass their paper to the person sitting directly to the right of them. The person receiving the paper would then place their sheet under the stack that they just received, and then pass the papers down the line to the person sitting next to them.

The last person on the line would then hand me the stack of papers, which I would double check for mistakes, and then make sure that all of the papers were in the correct sequential order. I would then hand the papers to Francis Watson, who would staple the papers together, and then place the packet nice and neat in the cardboard box that was sitting at the end of the table.

Well, in no time at all, the clients were getting the hang of the collating job, and they had it down to a real science. Not only did they work at a steady pace, but they were as good as gold.

I kept noticing that every time I glanced in Jamal Buchanan's direction, he was watching us like a hawk. And I'm sure it was killing him that he was missing out on all of the fun today.

So for the rest of the week, as soon as the clients arrived to work each day, they would all sit at the table and get right down to business in chipping away at the collating job.

To the clients credit, they had all learned to become self-starters, and never once did they need me to coax or prod them along in any way in getting the work done.

Every day, at precisely ten o'clock, Marty would call me on the telephone and ask me how the clients were making out on the collating job. Although I was sometimes tempted to tell him that we hit a couple of snags, I would put all of my humorous thoughts aside, and simply tell him that everything was under control and that he had absolutely nothing to worry about.

Marty would always end every telephone conversation by nervously asking me, "Jack, are you sure that you're gonna be able to meet my deadline on time?"

On the last day of the collating job, there was a very funny moment that had the entire room in utter hysterics. As always, the telephone rang at precisely ten o'clock, which prompted everyone in the room to spontaneously shout in unison, "Marty's calling!"

Sure enough, it was Marty on the other end of the line. And when the clients realized that the call was actually from Marty, they all laughed hysterically.

As I listened to all of the joy and laughter in their voices, it really warmed my heart. And as far as I'm concerned, but that moment will certainly go down in the annals of my counseling career as one of the most enjoyable moments that I've ever experienced here at the State School.

By Friday, we had Marty's collating job completed. And when I told the clients that we were officially done, they all cheered…, even Jamal.

Yeah, - you heard that right!

So after sulking for two days, Jamal decided to join us at the table and give us a helping hand on finishing up the collating job. To tell you the truth, I'm not really sure why Jamal finally decided to change his mind and help us out. But intuition tells me that he probably realized that he was missing out on all of the fun and laughter, and maybe on some of the "street cred" too.

On Friday morning, I had Tyrell and Jamal ride over to Marty's print shop with me so that we could deliver the collating job to Marty.

When Marty saw us entering his shop, he couldn't believe his eyes. As Marty ran his hand across the top of the completed work, I could tell that he was very impressed.

Marty then asked me if he could use our services again sometime, which prompted Jamal to say, "Yeah, that's cool! But next time we could sure use some cold hard cash Marty, aight!"

We all laughed, and at that point Marty was quick to say, "Well, I'll certainly keep that in mind Jamal. But for helping me out this time, I think there'll be some donuts coming your way."

Tyrell softly replied, in his deep southern drawl, "Mmm, I sure like donuts, Mr. Marty."

Before heading back to the SBU, I wanted to stop somewhere and get Jamal and Tyrell a little treat for helping me out this morning on delivering the collating job over to Marty's shop.

When I asked the boys if they had a taste for something, they both shouted, "Hamburgers, french-fries, and a thick creamy milk shake!"

So after pulling into the hamburger joint, we went up to the counter and ordered our food, and then found a nice corner booth next to the window to sit down at.

As I watched the boys enjoying their food, it put a big smile on my face. Stopping to get something to eat or drink with the clients was always the best part of my job. And of course, it goes without saying, but I've been known to partake in a few tasty morsels with the guys myself.

It's always very satisfying for me to see the clients enjoying themselves out in the real world. It seems to instill a feeling of hope, and maybe even a glimmer of normalcy for them.

Well…, at least for a little while anyway.

CHAPTER FIFTEEN

Well, it's the start of a brand new work week. And as I headed down the hallway, I heard a telephone ringing in the distance, and it sounded like it was coming directly from my office.

As I fumbled for my keys, I was wondering who could be calling me this early on a Monday morning, especially since it wasn't even 7:00am yet.

So after unlocking my office door, I frantically lunged across my desk and grabbed the phone before it stopped ringing. To my surprise, the voice on the other end of the line was that of Mr. Kramer. And from the sound of his voice, he wasn't calling to ask me how my weekend was.

Kramer didn't waste any time with formalities, he simply cut to the chase, and accused me of participating in an illegal activity last week. And what's more, he intends to bring formal charges against me with the Director.

Apparently, Mr. Kramer must've found out that I helped Marty last week on the collating project, and then insinuated that my Good Samaritan act could wind up costing him his operating certificate for ENCORE Industries.

Kramer then shouted at the top of his lungs, "Listen O'Leary, if the Department of Labor finds out about this little moonlighting escapade of yours, then you can kiss your job good-bye!"

So after lecturing me for a good ten minutes on policy and procedure, Kramer threatened to have me fired if I didn't tell him every last detail of what happened last week with Marty.

In addition to reading me the riot act, Kramer also pointed out that I was guilty of breaking the cardinal rule, which was having the clients work on a contract without paying them.

And to add insult to injury, but I had the clients helping out a business that is a direct competitor of ENCORE Industries, which seemed to ruffle his feathers even more.

Although I tried several times to defend myself, Kramer wouldn't let me get a word in edgewise, as he kept blasting me with both barrels. Kramer said that my actions last week could be construed as being exploitative in the eyes of the Department of Labor, and could possibly shut down all of the work programs that were currently in operation here at the State School.

In fact, Kramer even had the audacity to say that I committed a federal offense, and that people have been sent to prison for doing far less than what I did in helping out Marty last week.

Kramer shouted, "I'd like to know who gave you the authority to be out there freelancing with my operating certificates without my knowledge! Don't you realize that the Department of Labor regulations are written in black and white, and are not subject to interpretation!"

The conversation then went completely sideways, when Kramer had the unmitigated gall to say, "Listen O'Leary, I better not find out that you received any kickbacks, or pocketed any money from this job. Because if you did, then you better find yourself a damn good lawyer!"

Well, as soon as Kramer accused me of doing something that was totally underhanded, I completely lost my temper and said, "Listen Mr. Kramer, the collating job that we did last week for Marty was done strictly on a volunteer basis. And the only reason that I agreed to do the job was because I thought it would be an ideal training opportunity for the clients, especially since the work we did for Marty was similar to the work that is being done at ENCORE Industries!"

Kramer wasn't interested in hearing any of my measly excuses or piss poor explanations, because he was only interested in twisting my words and then refreshing my memory by saying, "Just remember one thing O'Leary, even though you work for Mr. Hanson, you still have to answer to me when it comes to any of the work programs around here. Do I make myself clear?"

So instead of digging myself an even bigger hole than the one that I was already standing in, I decided to just wave the white flag, and apologize to Mr. Kramer for any improprieties that I may have been guilty of. And that going forward, I would consult with him first on all matters that dealt with vocational programming, including any volunteer work that might come our way.

It's been my experience that arguing with Mr. Kramer is nothing but a complete waste of time. And if I should happen to piss him off, then I'll only be hurting myself in the long run.

Well, getting my ass chewed out by Mr. Kramer first thing on a Monday morning wasn't exactly the way I intended to start my week off. It's funny how Kramer knew every last detail of what happened last week. I'm sure that one of Mr. Kramer's stoolies must've tipped him off, and I'm guessing that stoolie was Dave Philcox, because that guy has had it in for me since day one.

Dave Philcox is Kramer's number one henchman, and Kramer has been promising him a promotion for years, as payback for all of the dirty tricks that he has done on Kramer's behalf.

As a matter of fact, Mr. Kramer had originally promised to give Dave Philcox my job five years ago. And by all accounts, Philcox thought that he was a shoe-in for the position.

But at the last minute, Mr. Kramer decided to welch on the deal, because Ms. Albright told Kramer that Philcox was thoroughly incompetent. And she even threatened to go straight to the Director, if Kramer didn't hire someone who she felt was suitably qualified for the position.

Ms. Albright was even quoted as saying, "Why should we scrap the bottom of the barrel here at the State School, when we can skim the cream of the crop with an outside candidate."

When Kramer realized that Ms. Albright meant business, he pulled the plug on Philcox's promotion, and then the job was formally put up for bid and was eventually offered to me.

Anyway, this is why Philcox seems to harbor so much resentment and acrimony towards me. And why he would love to see me get tarred and feathered for even the slightest little thing.

When the clients walked into the workshop for the morning session, the first thing out of Bobby Diggs' mouth was, "Hey Jack, when are we gonna get another collating job to do?"

Before I could even respond to Bobby, Jamal piped up and said, "Yeah, whatta 'bout it man? That work was kinda fun, and it sure beats doin' punk-ass laundry every day, dawg."

Later that afternoon, I received an unexpected phone call from Mr. Hanson. As I've said before, Mr. Hanson has been giving me the cold shoulder for months now, so you can only imagine how surprised I was when I heard his voice on the other end of the line.

Hanson didn't waste any time with formality, as he straightforwardly said, "So Jack, I heard you had a little run-in with Mr. Kramer this morning, huh."

I then decided to lay all of my cards on the table, as I calmly stated, "Yeah, well, I wound up helping out a good friend of mine last week who owns a small print shop in town, and, uh…, Mr. Kramer felt that I may have slightly overstepped my bounds."

Hanson replied, "I see. So, uh…, did any money change hands between you and your friend?"

"Absolutely not! I think there might be some donuts coming our way, but that's about the extent of it." I answered, in a bit of a huff.

Hanson quietly chuckled, and then light-heartedly asked, "So is your friend interested in utilizing our services again?"

I replied, "Well, we didn't discuss it. But I know he was quite pleased with what we did, and I'm sure that he would welcome any assistance that we could provide him in the future."

Hanson then commented, "Okay, well, I'm sure that Mr. Kramer must've felt somewhat threatened by your actions, but I on the other hand applaud your efforts. I think the whole idea of giving back to one's community is quite admirable. Nice work, Jack!"

To which I replied, "Thanks, Mr. Hanson. I must admit that it was a nice change of pace from doing laundry every day, and the clients seemed to enjoy doing that type of work as well."

Hanson then humorously quipped, "Well, you know what they say Jack, variety is the spice of life. Okay, well, thank you for explaining things to me. And if you should have any more problems with Mr. Kramer regarding this matter, then be sure to give me a call, okay."

A few days later, I received another phone call from Mr. Hanson, who called to say that he had a rather productive meeting yesterday with Mr. Kramer and the Director. The purpose of the meeting was to figure out a way that the clients can still volunteer their services, but do it in a way so that it doesn't jeopardize Mr. Kramer's operating certificate for ENCORE Industries.

Needless to say, but Kramer made it quite clear to the Director that he wasn't sold on the idea of having the clients do volunteer work for area businesses, because Mr. Kramer felt that we were straddling the line between the Department of Labor and his precious operating certificates.

Although the Director understood Kramer's position, he felt that it was in the facility's best interest to lend a helping hand to area businesses whenever possible, especially since the Director has been trying to establish better public relations with our community leaders for years.

In wrapping up our telephone conversation, Hanson informed me that Mr. Kramer will be giving me a call later in the week, so that he can outline all of the parameters between volunteer work and paid work. And if any problems should arise, then please don't hesitate to call him.

When Kramer finally got around to calling me, I could tell by the tone of his voice that he was in a real pissy mood. Kramer doesn't like to play second fiddle to anyone, especially to Mr. Hanson, and I'm sure he must've felt like he was some sort of errand boy for Mr. Hanson today.

Lest we forget, but Mr. Kramer prefers to give the orders and not take them.

So as we concluded our little fireside chat, Kramer actually threatened to have me fired if I did anything that might jeopardize his precious operating certificates for ENCORE Industries.

And from the sound of his voice, I think he really meant it.

On Friday, Marty stopped by with three dozen donuts as his way of saying thank you for helping him out with the collating job last week. Marty and I got a big kick out of watching the guys decide on which donut to select from the vast assortment that they had to choose from.

Jamal had no problem holding back, as he helped himself to three donuts. And in the process, he wound up getting strawberry jelly smeared all over his face.

And then there was Tyrell Freeman, who had so much powdered sugar caked around his mouth that Marty suggested that we use an industrial strength power washer to clean him off.

So now that the Director has given us the green light to solicit volunteer work from area businesses, my phone has been ringing off the hook. And with this sudden infusion of new work, the Work Activity Center has come alive again, and even Marty senses the excitement.

In fact, Marty told me the other day that he likes to drop by the building from time to time and visit with us. Especially on the days when he's feeling a bit overwhelmed, and he needs to hear a funny story or two from the guys, so that it can provide him with a little pick-me-up.

Last Tuesday, Marty gave me a call and wanted to know if he could drop off a project for us to work on next week, which is the annual fundraiser for our local hospital. And this particular project just so happens to be Marty's biggest and most lucrative contract for the year.

Quite honestly, but I was a little surprised that Marty would want to entrust us with a contract of this magnitude, especially since this particular contract generates enough capital for Marty to cover all of his overhead expenditures for the year.

The day that Marty dropped off the hospital fundraiser, he appeared to be a bit more anxious than usual.

Then again, if I were in Marty's shoes, I'm sure that I would be a little bit more on edge myself.

After all, Marty is a small business owner, and reputation is everything. So if Marty should happen to foul up a particular contract, even slightly, then the chances of having that same company continue to retain his services are probably somewhere between slim and none.

Before we actually got started on the hospital fundraiser project, Marty sat down with me and painstakingly went over every little detail of the collating project step-by-step.

In fact, Marty demonstrated the collating project to me so many times that it prompted me to sarcastically say, "Geez Marty, why don't you save a few for us to do, okay?"

As Marty was heading for the door, he kept glancing back over his shoulder, as if he had forgotten to say something to me. Although Marty knew that the hospital fundraiser project was in very capable hands, I could tell that he was a bit apprehensive in leaving it behind. Especially a contract of such importance, and one that he relied on so heavily in sustaining his business.

Bobby Diggs was chomping at the bit, so that he could throw his two-cents worth in on how the job should be done. As Bobby opened his mouth, Jamal cut him right off at the knees and said, "Hush up, Bobby! We gotta get goin' on this, 'cause Marty is counting on us, aight!"

As I listened to Jamal, it brought an immediate smile to my face. Jamal has made a one hundred and eighty degree turn since coming here to the State School. And although it's been a pretty bumpy ride with him at times, it's certainly been a road worth travelling.

So for the next three weeks, we put our nose to the grindstone and worked every day on the hospital fundraiser. We had over twenty thousand invitations that needed to be done, which may sound daunting, but I had the utmost confidence that we could meet our deadline on time.

It goes without saying, but Marty was calling us every day to see how we were making out. When Marty called, he was usually on pins and needles. And it would take me at least ten minutes to talk him down off of the ledge, so that I could reassure him that everything was okay.

In fact, the clients have become so conditioned to listen for Marty's phone call every day that when the phone rings at precisely ten o'clock, they all shout in unison, "Marty's calling!"

When the clients finally realize that it's Marty on the other end of the line, they all burst out into laughter. And in a strange sort of way, the ten o'clock phone call has really galvanized us to become a more unified and cohesive group, and it's truly become the highlight of our day.

The following Thursday, I gave Marty a call. Before I could even utter a single word, he frantically cried out, "Jack, what's wrong! Is everything okay with the hospital fundraiser job?"

I lightly chuckled, and then quietly said, "Everything's fine, Marty. I'm just calling to let you know that the hospital fundraiser job is all done. So what's a good time for me to come by?"

Marty breathed a huge sigh of relief, and then nervously replied, "Well, now is as good a time as any, I guess."

"Okay Marty, we'll be right over." I calmly said.

When we pulled up, Marty was waiting for us outside his shop. Marty was a bit jumpy, and he couldn't wait for me to open up the tailgate so that he could take a peek at the invitations.

As Marty attempted to open up one of the boxes, his hand was shaking like a leaf. He then randomly selected one of the invitations from inside the box, and as he examined it with a fine tooth comb, I could tell that he was quite pleased with what he saw.

Marty then looked me straight in the eye, and said with a satisfyingly smile, "Well, if they all look as good as this one, then you guys did one helluva job!"

When Jamal heard Marty give us his seal of approval, he excitedly said, "Hey Marty, since we did such a good job for ya on those invitations, how 'bout you get us some pizza and chicken wings this time instead of donuts. And, uh…, make those wings extra crispy, aight!"

Marty laughed out loud, and then said with a big smile, "Jamal, consider it done!"

The next day, Marty called and wanted to know if he could come by with the pizza and chicken wings that he promised the guys for helping him out on the hospital fundraiser job. I told Marty that would be a great idea, because we're usually a little bit more laid back on Friday's, and his coming by with pizza and chicken wings would be the perfect way to finish out the week.

Around noontime, Marty arrived with enough pizza and chicken wings to feed an entire army. I grabbed a couple of clean tablecloths out of one of the laundry carts, and in no time at all, I was able to transform the Work Activity Center into a makeshift banquet room.

Before tearing into the food, Marty took a moment to say a few words to the guys, and to also express his gratitude for the outstanding job that they did on the hospital fundraiser project.

And if it wasn't for their help, then he never would've been able to meet his deadline on time.

As the boys listened to what Marty had to say to them, I could see how proud they were, especially since the guys don't usually find themselves in this type of position very often.

When Marty was done thanking the boys, he then excitedly shouted, "Okay, now who's ready for pizza and chicken wings!"

A resounding cheer came over the entire room. I then instructed everyone to lineup and take a plate, so that they could proceed down the buffet line and help themselves to some food.

As Tyrell Freeman was loading up his plate, he quietly said to me in his deep southern drawl, "Mr. Jack, this is the best day of my life!"

I then amusingly interjected, "Gee Tyrell, if memory serves me correctly, I believe you said the same exact thing the day that Marty brought in the donuts."

Tyrell thought a moment, and then softly replied, "Well, maybe so, I do love to eat Mr. Jack."

Bobby Diggs was beyond excited, as he kept chattering, "Oh boy, oh boy, oh boy!"

Needless to say, but when Jamal Buchanan strutted down the buffet line he had a big smile plastered on his face. And in typical Jamal style, he was quick to say, "Hey Marty, if you keep feedin' us like this, then we'll work on any job you got, aight!"

Well, the boys ate lunch faster than Grant took Richmond!

And the only thing left for us to clean up was a healthy pile of chicken bones, and a few smatterings of pizza crust.

I must say that it was certainly great having Marty with us today. And if you didn't know any better, you'd almost think that Marty and the guys have all known each other for years.

And to think that only a few short months ago, Marty had absolutely no idea what went on inside the four walls of the State School.

Yet, here he is today, sharing a meal and having a few good laughs with some of the most highly profiled and behaviorally challenged individuals in the whole state.

Once again, it reinforces to me that God works in mysterious ways. And what we might think are chance encounters, such as the one that Marty and I shared with each other after Mass one quiet Sunday morning, can be instantly transformed into something that is truly amazing.

As I've said before, things happen for a reason. And I truly believe that God, in all of his infinite wisdom, has orchestrated a divine plan for each and every one of us on Earth to follow.

Not to speak for Marty, but I'm sure it never occurred to him that a simple conversation after Mass one morning would lead to such a life altering experience for him. And put him on a direct course that would guide him onto the rocky shores of the mysterious Island of Misfit Toys.

It was probably six weeks later when I received back-to-back-to-back phone calls from Mr. Kramer, Mr. Hanson, and the Director. They all called within seconds of each other, so that they could congratulate me on the outstanding job that we did on the hospital fundraiser mailer.

Apparently, Kramer, Hanson, and the Director all attended the annual fundraiser event that was held over the weekend. Which was a black tie affair, at a cost of a thousand dollars a plate, and all of the proceeds that night went to the hospital's new cancer research wing.

From what I understand, the CEO of the hospital publicly thanked our facility for its role in putting the hospital fundraiser mailer together. Which not only raised a few eyebrows that night, but prompted many of the guests to say how surprised they were that mentally challenged individuals living in a state-operated institution actually possessed such remarkable abilities.

Well, today I'll be taking a little break from "counseling," so that I can head down to the State Capital and attend an all-day professional conference.

Although I make it a point to take advantage of all of my allotted professional days, I sometimes wonder why I even attend these conferences in the first place. Especially when much of the subject matter that is covered in these professional symposiums are completely unrelated to what I actually do here at the State School.

So that being said, if I had to characterize what the conference will be like for me today, the best way for me to describe it would be to simply say…, - it's like sitting down to a game of checkers, when everyone else in the room is playing chess!

Anyway, I may not learn much at the conference today, but I'm hoping to get the chance to see Bob Watson and Lenore Richards today, which would certainly make the day worthwhile.

Originally, Murphy was slated to go to the conference with me today too. But at the last minute he decided to back out, because he promised the clients that he would help them plant a vegetable garden today.

Although I tried to convince Murphy that one more day wouldn't matter, he said that if he didn't use the rototiller today, then it wouldn't be available for at least another two weeks.

As I cruised down the highway, I kept asking myself over and over again, if I measured up to any of my contemporaries in the field. As much as I enjoy seeing some old friends and familiar faces at these professional conferences, it sometimes makes me feel a little bit uneasy.

Especially when I mingle through the crowd, and I hear all of my colleagues boasting about some of the new and innovative counseling techniques that they are all utilizing in their respective jobs. Which then causes me to panic, and completely doubt myself. And then I start to wonder if I'm even doing any professional counseling here at the State School in the first place.

Quite frankly, but the only counseling skills that seem to be in my arsenal at the moment are telling the clients to either shape up or ship out.

Which, by the way, isn't exactly the most clinically endorsed counseling approach to take.

Anyway, it just seems like every time I attend these professional conferences, I wind up developing some sort of inferiority complex. Which makes me feel like a second-rate counselor, and that my job here at the State School is nothing but a complete and utter joke.

If only I could get some sort of validation that what I do here at the State School is really meaningful, then maybe I'd feel differently. But every time that I try to explain what it is that I do here, all of my colleagues just seem to roll their eyes and give me a strange and funny look.

Well, I guess I can't blame them. Because if I were in their shoes, then I would probably react the same way too.

Needless to say, but when I continue to get the same funny looks over and over again, it tends to play with my head. And it makes me think that I'm nothing but a rinky-dink counselor.

Ironically, I've never felt better about my job here at the State School then I do right now.

But when I get in amongst my peers, I seem to become a little insecure. And then I start to think that I'm nothing but a ham-and-egger, and not worthy of being called a true professional.

Now even though the State School may not be considered the gold standard, I still believe that our clients deserve just as much right to live a rich and rewarding life as anyone else. And at the end of the day, isn't that what really matters the most to every human service professional.

So after checking in at the registration desk, I slapped on my little name tag and then mingled through the crowd to see if I could recognize anyone that I knew.

As I watched the steady flow of people coming down the escalator, I spotted Bob Watson in amongst the fray. As usual, Bob was dressed to the nine's. And I was absolutely thrilled to be spending the day with him today, so that he could catch me up on all the news from back home.

The minute that Bob stepped off the escalator, he warmly smiled, and then said with his usual sarcastic flair, "Hi Jack, it's great to see ya! Hey, have you lost some weight?"

I sheepishly replied, "Actually Bob, I'm slightly heavier than the last time you saw me."

"Only slightly...," Bob playfully said.

I quietly chuckled, and then inquisitively asked, "So where's Lenore, didn't she come with you today?"

Bob replied, "No, I needed Lenore to stay back and keep an eye on things for me. If she had come along, then I would've been forced to have C.D. in charge of the place, and God forbid that should happen."

We both quietly chuckled, and then Bob continued by saying, "Listen Irish, I won't be able to attend the conference today, because I have a rather important meeting to get to over at the State Capital this morning."

"Really...," I said, rather disappointingly.

"Yeah, but, uh..., I had a pretty good hunch that you'd be here today, so I took a chance on stopping by. Actually, I have a little business proposition for ya that I'd like you to consider."

I curiously asked, "A business proposition? And what pray tell might that be, Bob?"

Bob hesitated for a moment, and then replied, "Well, I'm seriously thinking about retiring in a few months, and, uh..., I was just wondering if you might want to consider coming back to WEALTH Industries and take over the administrative reins. I can't think of a better person to be in charge of the place than you. So, uh..., whatta ya say O'Leary?"

Suddenly, I was at a complete loss for words. Although Bob is approaching the ripe old age of sixty-five, it never entered my mind that he may eventually step down and retire someday.

Bob has been the Executive Director of WEALTH Industries for almost forty years, and despite the hundreds of people that have worked for him, he wants to pass the baton off to me.

I quickly replied, "Well, what about Lenore? I think she'd be an excellent replacement for you, Bob. And to tell you the truth, I think Lenore is a helluva lot smarter than I am too."

Bob smiled, and then quietly said, "Boy, you haven't changed one bit O'Leary, you're still putting others ahead of yourself. Hey, Lenore is top notch, and I'm damn lucky to have her. But she's not Jack O'Leary, and I need someone like you to be in charge of running the agency."

Just then an announcement came over the public address system, saying that the morning session was about to begin in five minutes, and would everyone please report to their classrooms.

Bob then hurriedly said, "Listen Irish, I know this is a lot to digest right now. Personally, I think this is a great opportunity for you. But at the end of the day, you need to do what's in the best interest for you and your family. I'll call you in a couple days after you've had a chance to think it over. Well, I gotta go. Hey, wish me luck with those goddamn politicians today, okay."

I quietly replied, "Yeah, good luck, Bob. Not that you'll need it, because you and I both know that you could sell ice to an Eskimo," which prompted Bob to burst out into laughter.

Bob and I shook hands, and then he hopped onto the escalator.

As the escalator made its way towards the mezzanine level, Bob looked back at me and amusingly quipped, "Enjoy the conference today, Irish. And, uh…, try to learn something today, will ya, O'Leary!"

All day long, I couldn't seem to focus on any of the lectures or presentations. I guess the bombshell that Bob laid on me this morning about coming back to WEALTH Industries was just a little too much for my brain to handle.

In fact, at one point during the morning session, I was so deep in thought that the class instructor had to walk over to where I was sitting and give me a gentle nudge, so that he could tell me that the lecture was over.

When I arrived home that evening, Christine had supper already waiting for me on the table. As we sat down to eat, Christine casually asked how the conference was today, and if it was worth attending. I told her that I couldn't even remember a single topic that was covered.

Christine laughed out loud, and then amusingly said, "So it was that good, huh."

As we sat at the table, I kept pushing my food around the plate with my fork. Christine asked me if I was feeling okay, especially since I barely touched any of my dinner.

I then told Christine that I saw Bob Watson at the conference today, and Bob mentioned to me that he was considering retirement. And not only that, but he also wanted to know if I was interested in coming back to WEALTH Industries again, and be in charge of running the agency.

Upon hearing the news, Christine let out a tremendous shriek, as she jubilantly shouted, "Oh, my God! Really…! Well, you said yes, right? So when can I call my mother and tell her that we're all moving back home again!"

Christine could barely control herself, as she just kept staring at me with that starry-eyed look in her eye, and waiting for me to tell her the words that she so desperately wanted to hear.

In Christine's mind, moving back home again was simply a no-brainer. But for me I had some definite reservations, specifically, life without Murphy, if I should decide to leave the State School and take the Executive Director position at WEALTH Industries.

Trust me, the last thing in the world that I wanted to do was to disappoint my wife. But I wasn't sure if pulling up stakes and then heading back home was really the right answer either.

At that moment, Christine began badgering me with all sorts of questions, and trying to pin me down with regards to a timetable, or when a final decision had to be made about the job.

I kept telling Christine that she knew just as much about the situation as I did, and that I needed to gather more information from Bob Watson before I could make an informed decision.

The next day, I strolled into Murphy's office with two large containers of coffee and a box of jelly donuts tucked under my arm. When Murphy saw me, he lit up like a Christmas tree.

I then amusingly asked him, "So Doc, are you smiling because you're glad to see me, or because I remembered to stop off at the bakery this morning and pick up some goodies?"

Murphy smiled, and then replied with his usual Irish wit, "Why the goodies, of course!"

As Murphy took a sip of his coffee, he nonchalantly asked me how the conference was yesterday, and if it was worth attending.

Suddenly, I could feel my heart skip a beat. And my subconscious mind began to dredge up vivid thoughts of Bob Watson, and the enticing job offer that he posed to me yesterday.

As much as I wanted to discuss the WEALTH Industries job offer with Murphy, I just wasn't ready to cross that bridge yet. So I decided to take the easy way out by telling Murphy that the conference was uneventful, and that the subject matter was completely unrelated to anything that we do here at the State School.

Which, technically, wasn't a lie. Right...?

So in an effort to change the subject, I asked Murphy how he made out with rototilling the garden yesterday. Murphy leaned back in his chair and replied, "mission accomplished," but then said that he had a bit of a ticklish moment yesterday that he still hasn't recovered from yet.

Murphy then proceeded to tell me that Dan Christoff almost had his left hand completely severed yesterday, because Dan tried to stick his hand underneath the rototiller while it was still running, and it was a miracle that he didn't wind up needing emergency hand surgery yesterday.

Apparently, while Murphy was manning the rototiller, a large rock happened to wedge itself in-between the tines of the machine, which caused the axle on the rototiller to stop turning.

So at that point, Dan Christoff thought that it might be a good idea for him to reach down underneath the rototiller and try to dislodge the rock that was wedged in-between the tines, so that he could free up the axle, and thus allow the machine to continue cutting through the soil.

When Murphy saw Dan Christoff reaching for the rock, Murphy shut off the rototiller as fast as he possibly could, and then savagely tackled Dan Christoff immediately to the ground.

Dan Christoff was so angry at Murphy that he began yelling at the top of his lungs, "Hey, what the hell did ya do that for Murphy! If you just could've waited another lousy minute, then I would've been able to grab the rock that was stuck in-between the blades of the machine!"

So after hearing Murphy's harrowing ordeal, I just shook my head in disbelief, and then quietly said, "Doc, sometimes we forget just how psychiatrically impaired these guys really are."

Murphy then went on to say that Hanson held an emergency staff meeting late yesterday afternoon, and announced that the State is planning on overhauling some of its interdepartmental agencies around the state. And that many of these impending changes are due in large part to the tremendous success that the SBU has enjoyed over the past year and a half.

As a matter of fact, Hanson said that the Governor even mentioned our facility by name at a televised news conference out at the State Capital last week, and that the Governor couldn't stop singing our praises.

Furthermore, the Governor has formally announced that he will be petitioning the State Legislature to allocate emergency funds for additional SBU's to be built around the State, and he intends to use our program as the blueprint for all future statewide SBU programs to emulate.

So after making his star-studded announcement, Murphy said that Hanson began to blow his own horn by saying that he has been contacted by several Mental Health Commissioners all over the country, who are very interested in starting up SBU's in their respective States, and they would like Hanson to act as a consultant to help guide them through the application process.

Murphy said that Hanson's remarks were so nauseating that he actually wanted to vomit, and he couldn't wait for the meeting to be over.

Well, there's certainly no doubt in my mind that Hanson is hoping to get a big promotion out of all of this, so that he can continue to leapfrog his way up the career ladder, while the rest of us poor dumb schmucks are all squished together like a bunch of sardines on the bottom rung.

In wrapping up yesterday's meeting, Hanson dropped an unexpected bombshell by saying that some major changes will be coming down the pike in the next couple of months. And as a result of these changes, many of our clients may be packing their bags and heading back home.

Apparently, the reason for all of this upheaval right now is due to the new buzzword that is sweeping through the State Capital called repatriation.

The Governor is proposing that clients who are currently living in developmental centers across the state be transferred back to their original county of origin, so that these counties will now be responsible for providing them with their overall level of care.

Hanson's stunning announcement took everyone in the room by complete surprise, especially since this new line of thinking by the Governor is a dramatic departure from the way that the State currently does business now.

In the old days, the State would place clients wherever there was an available opening, and their decision had nothing to do with client rights, or any concern for the client's family.

But times have changed!

And the days of Director's making a gentleman's agreement in the back room with the shades drawn are now a thing of the past. What was once a wink of an eye, or the promise of a future favor, has now transformed itself into a world of accountability and total transparency.

Well, it didn't take long for the clients to catch wind of the repatriation rumors. And when Bobby Diggs and Jamal Buchanan heard the news, they were like two kids in a candy store.

Bobby is already dreaming about going on vacation with his family. And Jamal can't wait to get back to his old neighborhood again, so that he can spend all day playing basketball on the playground, and spend all night hanging on the street corner with all of his deadbeat friends.

So when the clients arrived to work on Monday morning, they were so excited about the prospects of moving back home that they couldn't seem to focus on a single aspect of their job.

Bobby Diggs and Jamal Buchanan were actually giving each other high fives and patting each other on the back. And what's more, they even promised to swap mailing addresses too, so that they could correspond with each other and try to stay in touch.

Uh, are you kidding me?

On a much quieter note, Tyrell Freeman is taking the news of leaving the State School pretty hard. Tyrell confided in me the other day that he doesn't want to leave the State School. And for the first time in his life, he feels safe and secure, and that he's really found a home here.

Well, it's been several months now, and there's still no word about the repatriation plan. I'm sure there's a lot of logistics that still needs to be hammered out. So that being said, I wonder why the Governor decided to let the cat out of the bag until there was a definitive plan in place?

Bobby Diggs continues to be near out of his mind with worry. And not only has Bobby been hounding me every day for information, but he's also been caught red-handed a number of times eavesdropping on conversations outside the staff lounge.

Late yesterday afternoon, we heard that there might be a fly in the ointment that could potentially dash the hopes and dreams for some of the clients being reunited with their families.

Apparently, there seems to be some sort of loophole in the repatriation plan. Or as the living unit staff likes to refer to it as, "an escape clause."

I guess this loophole would give families the option of having their "loved ones" remain at the State School, instead of having them transferred back to their original county of origin.

Of course, with it being an election year, the Governor is trying to appease as many of his constituents as possible. So there seems to be a number of families across the State who are now beginning to have some second thoughts about having their "loved ones" living directly in their backyard. And if given the choice, some of these families would much rather mail out a birthday card, then sit at the kitchen table with "Johnny" or "Mary" and enjoy a big slice of birthday cake.

Let's face it, we all know that the squeaky wheel gets the grease, - and since many of the clients that live here at the State School rarely exercise their right to vote, then that essentially means that their voice is not being heard in the Governor's office.

Personally, I think the whole idea of providing families with some sort of loophole is nothing but a bunch of malarkey. I mean, whose life is it anyway? Shouldn't the clients have some say in what goes on in their life?

Isn't it ironic, - that even though we live in an age where civil liberties reign supreme, the truth of the matter is that the game is still rigged. And unless you're lucky enough to have an ace or two hidden up your sleeve, then the chances of you remaining at the table are pretty slim.

Well, it was probably three weeks later when Mr. Hanson summoned all of us into the conference room, so that he could bring us up to speed on the proposed client transfers.

Up until now, there have been no official updates or notifications as to who might be leaving the State School.

And what's more, - even the grapevine hasn't bared any fruit either.

So you can only imagine how surprised we all were when Mr. Hanson presented us with a list of clients that are projected to be transferred back to their original county of origin, and some of these transfers could actually begin as early as next week.

As we scanned down the list of alphabetized names, the first name that jumped off of the page was Jamal Buchanan. I then spotted Tyrell Freeman and Terrence Morehouse's name listed, along with every other client that came up from Metro Psychiatric Center as well.

Now on the flip side, some of the more notable names that were excluded from the transfer list were Russell Turner, Francis Watson, and poor old Bobby Diggs.

So after scouring the list of names, I then leaned over to Dick Henderson and whispered, "Hey Dick, what about Bobby Diggs?"

Dick shook his head "no," and then said with a great deal of disappointment, "Bobby's family said that they're happy to be rid of him, and they would appreciate it if we didn't contact them anymore with regards to Bobby."

As I slowly leaned back in my chair, I felt a tremendous amount of sorrow for Bobby Diggs. And in a deflated tone of voice, I sadly mumbled to myself, "Oh boy, oh boy, oh boy…."

CHAPTER SIXTEEN

Well, get ready to strap yourself in, - because the next few months around here should prove to be a pretty bumpy ride.

Why?

Well, the minute that Bobby Diggs heard that he wasn't on the transfer list, then all hell broke loose!

For the past three weeks, Bobby has been on a rip-roaring rampage. And Bobby has logged more hours in the time-out room than a cop in a donut shop.

Bobby has been raising holy hell, - from the minute he gets up, until the minute he finally goes to sleep. And from the looks of things, there doesn't seem to be any relief in sight.

In all the years that I've known Bobby, I have never seen him act like this before. Sure, I've seen Bobby get into trouble a million times. But all of his past misdemeanors have been the result of either poor decision making, or some feeble attempt on his part at beating the system.

But this time the situation is different.

And instead of that precocious look in his eye that we've all come to know, Bobby now possesses a look of pure evil. And I'm afraid that all of the idle threats that he has been making lately may result in him doing something really drastic.

As the old adage says, "desperate times call for desperate measures," and Bobby Diggs seems to be living proof of that. Bobby has been using every trick in the book, as a way of manipulating the Director to put him on the transfer list, including playing the suicide card.

Now ordinarily, Bobby is only bluffing when he utters the magic words, "I'm going to kill myself," but Dick is soundly convinced that Bobby might actually follow through on it this time. So as a precautionary measure, Dick has instructed the staff to keep a close eye on Bobby at all times, so that he doesn't try to do something foolish and wind up seriously hurting himself.

When Bobby usually gets upset, Dick will simply pull him aside and have a little heart-to-heart talk with him, and then smooth things over with a big cup of coffee and a candy bar.

But unfortunately, - that little strategy just isn't going to work on Bobby this time.

Now even though Bobby has gotten his hopes up before about leaving the State School, I think that Bobby really thought that it was going to happen this time, especially with all of the wholesale changes that were rumored to occur.

Bobby thought that he'd finally get a taste of freedom, so that he could say "good-bye" to the albatross that's been hanging around his neck for his entire life, and preventing him from living the life that he has always dreamed about.

Now as far as the living unit staff goes, they don't seem to have much sympathy for Bobby whatsoever. Because the living unit staff feels that Bobby is nothing but a chronic complainer, and someone who just doesn't appreciate a damn thing that he has in his life at all.

The staff is sick and tired of listening to Bobby bellyache on how bad he has it here at the State School. And what's more, they seem to resent the fact that Bobby doesn't pay a penny toward room and board, health care, or any of the other amenities that he has in his life either.

Meanwhile, the staff is trying to rob Peter to pay Paul, as they struggle to meet all of their financial obligations, so that they can keep a roof over their head and put food on the table.

When Dick found out that Bobby wasn't going to be transferred, he decided to meet with Bobby on the living unit, so that he could break the disappointing news to him in person.

On the day that Dick pulled Bobby aside, Bobby thought Dick was going to congratulate him on finally getting out of the State School, so that he could be reunited with his family again.

As Bobby waited to hear the words that he so desperately longed to hear, he didn't seem to recognize the look of forlorn on Dick's face. As Dick stared deeply into Bobby's eyes, he just didn't have the heart to tell Bobby what the real reason was that his family declined the transfer.

To ease Bobby's pain, Dick wound up sugarcoating a white lie, and told Bobby that even though his family loved him very much, they just couldn't afford to feed another hungry mouth.

Despite Dick's best efforts in trying to soften the blow, Bobby took the news real hard, and dropped straight to his knees and began sobbing inconsolably.

In an effort to soothe Bobby, Dick bent down and placed his hand gently on Bobby's shoulder. But Bobby was so angry that he lunged at Dick, and knocked Dick down to the floor.

Bobby then pounced on top of Dick, and started choking the daylights out of him. And at the same time, Bobby was pounding Dick's head into submission against the hard concrete floor.

Quite honestly, but I shudder to think what would've happened to Dick if he had broken the news to Bobby down in the privacy of his office, instead of in plain sight on the living unit.

By the time the living unit staff reacted to what was happening, Dick was knocked out cold. The living unit staff then gang tackled Bobby, and dragged him down to the time-out room.

As Dick tried to regain consciousness, he could hear Bobby Diggs screaming like a wild animal down in the time-out room, "I hate you, Dick! You're nothin' but a fuckin' asshole!"

When I heard about the incident, I was absolutely appalled. Especially since Dick has done more for Bobby over the past five years than anyone has ever done for him in his entire life.

Yet, Bobby was within a whisker of killing the best thing that has ever happened to him.

This whole incident with Bobby Diggs has been a real eye-opener for me. And in a way, it kinda reminded me of what happened the night of the basketball game, when Lance Coppenger decided to take off from the Mitchell Psychiatric Center gym. It's made me finally realize that maybe the relationships that we have with these clients isn't as strong as we might think it is. And no matter how good we are to these clients, they can still turn on us at a moment's notice.

In Bobby's mind, he had Dick safely tucked away in his back pocket. And if life should happen to deal Bobby a bad card, then all he had to do was to persuade Dick to use his influence.

As time goes by, I'm sure that Dick will find it in his heart to forgive Bobby. But that being said, I wonder if Dick will ever look at Bobby in the same shimmering light ever again.

And as far as Bobby goes, I'm sure that when the dust finally settles, he'll probably be extremely sorry for what he did. And you can bet your bottom dollar, but the first chance that Bobby Diggs gets, he'll be down on his knees begging Dick Henderson for his forgiveness.

But the question that still remains, - will Bobby be sorry for what he did, or sorry because he may have just lost the best "get-out-of-jail-card" that he's ever had here at the State School.

So after raising hell for two straight days, Bobby finally ran out of gas and was permitted to leave the time-out room. The minute that the time-out room door opened up, Bobby pleaded with the staff to take him down to Dick Henderson's office, so that he could apologize to Dick, and try to smooth things over with him.

At that point, the staff quickly reminded Bobby that he was still on suicide watch. And according to his behavior plan, he wasn't allowed to have any personal contact with anyone.

Bobby then tried telling the staff that he was only joking about killing himself, and that his words were taken completely out of context. And if he could just talk to Dick Henderson for a couple of minutes, then this whole misunderstanding could get straightened out right away.

Unfortunately for Bobby, but the living unit staff wasn't buying his usual line of bullshit this time. So now Bobby was forced to improvise, and try to think of another way to get back into Dick Henderson's good graces again.

Once again, Bobby seems to think that he is above the law. And that he can play the suicide card whenever he wants without suffering any of the fallout or the consequences.

Well, that line of thinking may have worked when Mr. Wohlers was in charge. But times have changed, and the new regime that is currently in charge here at the State School doesn't take kindly to threats, especially threats related to suicide.

Just imagine what would happen if Bobby Diggs seriously hurt himself while on suicide watch, or God forbid, if Bobby even died. Well, not only would heads roll, but the State would also be forced to cough up a pretty hefty settlement check to Bobby Diggs' family as well.

Isn't it ironic, - that even though Bobby's family could give a rat's ass about him, they would all come crawling out of the woodwork if something terrible were to happen to Bobby.

And in all likelihood, they would be dragging their shyster lawyer behind them, so that they could file a wrongful death law suit against the State, as recompence for poor 'ole Bobby.

Well, it's been several weeks now since Bobby has been off of suicide watch, yet Dick Henderson continues to avoid Bobby like the plague. Although Bobby has found himself in the doghouse before, this time he realizes that the situation is different. And if Bobby doesn't do something about it real soon, then life for him here at the State School could get a little sticky.

So that being said, Bobby has been hounding the staff day and night for someone to bring him down to Dick Henderson's office, so that he can try to mend some fences with Dick. But to Bobby's chagrin, he can't seem to convince anyone to help him out at the moment.

As a matter of fact, Bobby has even resorted to bribing some of the other clients, so that they will speak to Dick on his behalf, and try to convince Dick just how sorry Bobby really is.

It goes without saying, but the other clients know that Bobby is currently sitting behind the eight ball. So in order for them to help Bobby out, they usually demand payment up front. But once the clients slide Bobby's cold hard cash safely into their pocket, then they all proceed to rat Bobby out, as payback for all the times that Bobby has double-crossed them over the years.

Now even though Bobby is a schemer and a conniver, he continues to hold a very special place in my heart. And somehow, we'll find a way to get past this latest dark chapter in his life.

So I haven't officially accepted Bob Watson's generous job offer yet. For the past month, Bob has been calling me at least once a week to see if I'm any closer to making a decision.

Bob even sweetened the pot by throwing in a few extra fringe benefits. And even though the deal sounds too good to be true, it's still not enough to convince me to sign on the dotted line.

Then of course there's Christine, who asks me every night at the dinner table if I'm any closer to making a decision on the WEALTH job.

Oh, and did I happen to mention that my parents and my in-laws have been mailing us real estate brochures and bank loan applications on a weekly basis as well.

And then there's Murphy, who still has no idea that there's even a job offer on the table.

Well, maybe it's time for me to say something to him, so that I can get his perspective on things. And when Murphy hears what I have to say, he'll probably think that I'm pulling his leg.

As I was driving into work, I was trying to figure out the best way to tell Murphy about Bob Watson's job offer. I've been regretting this day for months, especially since Murphy is the reason why I love working here at the State School so much. It's not very often that you get to work with your best friend every day, so I better weigh all of my options very carefully.

When I tapped on Murphy's door, he was talking on the telephone. So I placed a large container of coffee next to him, and then sat down in the chair that was adjacent to his desk.

As I waited for Murphy to finish up on the phone, I was thinking how much I was going to miss our little coffee klatch every morning if I decide to take the WEALTH Industries job.

Seeing Murphy first thing in the morning every day seems to set the tone for the rest of my day. And on the days that Murphy isn't here, well, my day just isn't the same.

Although I've taken these moments for granted, it seems like precious metal to me now. This incredible working relationship that I've been able to cultivate with him here at the State School won't be easily replicated anywhere else, and it's something that really concerns me.

Murphy hung up the phone, and then pleasantly said, "Morning, Rodney."

As Murphy took a sip of his coffee, he could sense that I had something on my mind. Murphy knows me like a book, and he can read me better than anyone that I've ever known.

Murphy then asked with concern, "Is everything okay Rodney, you seem a little off?"

Although I tried to act like everything was okay, I knew there was no fooling Murphy. So as I sat there with my stomach in knots, I just decided to bite the bullet and say, "Well, actually, I was offered a job a couple of months ago, and I'm not really sure if I should take it or not."

Murphy seemed rather stunned by what I just said. And as he sat there with a blank stare, he shockingly said, "Really...? I wasn't even aware that you were looking. So what's the job?"

"WEALTH Industries," I quietly uttered.

Murphy replied, "WEALTH Industries, you mean the place you worked at back home?"

I answered, "Yeah, that's right, they offered me the Executive Director position there."

Murphy responded, "Wow! You mean, you'd actually be in charge of the place?"

"Yeah, pretty scary, huh?" I replied, with a slight chuckle in my voice.

Murphy laughed heartily, and then confidently said, "Hey, I think you'd make one helluva administrator Rodney, and they'd be damn lucky to have ya!"

There was a moment of uncomfortable silence, and then Murphy asked, "So what does Christine think?"

I slightly chuckled, and then humorously replied, "Well, let's just say that her bags are already packed, and lined up at the front door."

Murphy quietly snickered, and then amusingly quipped, "Happy wife, happy life!"

I then took a moment to be serious by saying, "Listen Doc, I realize that this job offer is a great opportunity for me. But to be perfectly honest with you, I think what's really preventing me from pulling the trigger is that I won't be working with you anymore."

Murphy smiled, and then quietly replied, "Thanks Rodney, that really means a lot to me. But at the end of the day, you gotta do what's in the best interest for you and your family. And I think taking the WEALTH Industries job is an opportunity that you can't pass up. A job like that will look damn good on your resume, and certainly open up a few doors for you down the road."

I just stared at Murphy for a brief moment, and then amusingly said, "Doc, why must you always be right?"

Murphy cracked a sly grin, and then quickly replied, "Well, thanks Rodney, but I think my wife Colleen might disagree with ya on that one."

It was getting close to nine-thirty now. So I said "good-bye" to Murphy, and then beat it down the hallway towards the workshop, so that I could set up for the morning work session.

As I hustled down the hallway, I was thinking what a class act Murphy was. I'm sure he must be hurting right now, especially after hearing about the WEALTH Industries job offer. But Murphy decided to put his feelings aside, so that he could help me focus on the big picture.

Murphy's shrewd and insightful words seemed to put it all into perspective for me, and it made me realize that the WEALTH Industries job was an opportunity that I just couldn't pass up.

When I got home that evening, I was quite pleased to see that Christine had prepared my all-time favorite meal, and it was already served and waiting for me on the dining room table.

So as we sat down to eat, I was waiting for Christine to bring up the subject of WEALTH Industries, and whether I've made a decision yet regarding Bob Watson's enticing job offer.

As I've mentioned before, the WEALTH Industries job has been the main topic of conversation at the dinner table for the past two months now. But for some reason, Christine wasn't broaching the subject with me at all this evening, which I thought was a little peculiar.

We finished our meal. But before clearing the table, I told Christine that I had something urgent to tell her, and that it had to do with my decision regarding the WEALTH Industries job.

I reached for Christine's hand, and as I was about to tell her that I was going to accept Bob Watson's job offer, she jumped right out of her chair and screamed, "Jack, I already know! Colleen called me this afternoon and said that you and Murphy had a little heart-to-heart talk this morning, and that he convinced you to take the job! Oh, my God! I gotta give my mom a call and tell her the good news! Oh yeah, and we gotta get Murphy something really nice for Christmas!"

Christine then grabbed the phone and scurried into the bedroom, so that she could call her mother and tell her that we've decided to move back home again.

As I quietly sat at the dining room table, I lightly chuckled to myself and thought, "Well, so much for my big announcement. And I guess that would explain why Christine went to all the trouble of preparing me my all-time favorite dinner and dessert tonight too."

While I tidied up the kitchen, I could hear Christine laughing away on the telephone in the bedroom. And as I listened to the joy in her voice, it really seemed to warm my heart.

So after straightening up the kitchen, I spent some time playing on the living room floor with my son Rory. I then gave Rory his nightly bath, dressed him in his jammies, and then I topped off the evening by reading him his favorite bedtime story.

As I tucked Rory into bed, it didn't take long for him to fall asleep.

But then, uh…, I seem to have that effect on people.

When Christine finished talking with her mother on the telephone, she then joined me out in the living room. As she snuggled up to me on the couch, she thanked me for tidying up the kitchen, and getting Rory settled in for the night.

Christine and I chatted for about an hour, and then she decided to draw herself a hot bath. As Christine got up from the couch, she handed me the phone so that I could give Bob Watson a call, and tell him that I've finally made a decision regarding the WEALTH Industries job.

So after dialing the number, Bob and I exchanged a few light pleasantries, and then I asked him if his job offer was still on the table. And if so, I would like to accept the position.

At that moment, Bob let out a resounding cheer, as he excitedly said, "Jack, the job is all yours, congratulations!"

Well, for the next two hours, I could barely get a word in edgewise, as Bob brought me up to speed on all of the wonderful things that have been happening at WEALTH Industries for the past five years.

Bob said that the program has never been more financially solvent then it is right now. And that just the other day, he signed a lucrative three year deal for a big government contract.

As a matter of fact, Bob surprised me by saying that if it wasn't for C.D., then this multi-million dollar contract with the federal government would've never materialized.

Apparently, while C.D. was standing in line at Migliori's bakery, he struck up a friendly conversation with a guy who works as a procurement specialist for the federal government.

Anyway, one thing led to another, and then C.D. must've told the guy a little bit about WEALTH Industries, and the types of contract work that we routinely do at our agency.

Quite honestly, but the fact that C.D. even knew what types of work we did at WEALTH Industries was a complete shock in itself, especially since C.D. spends practically all of his time down in the break room drinking coffee and leisurely reading the newspaper every day.

So the government contractor then decided to give C.D. his business card, which C.D. promptly gave to Bob. And after months of negotiations, Bob was finally able to close the deal.

In addition to that, Bob said that WEALTH's profit margins and projected earnings for the next fiscal year have never been better. And that he's already consulted with an architect in hopes of upgrading and modernizing the entire building with some major capital improvements.

After listening to all of the new and exciting things that Bob had to say about WEALTH Industries, I then started to second guess myself a bit with respect to the business side of the job.

I then wound up letting my guard down, as I anxiously said, "Gee Bob, maybe I'm not the right guy for the job after all. Maybe you should really consider hiring someone with a strong business background. I mean, to tell you the truth, but I can barely balance my own checkbook."

Bob burst out into laughter, but then reassured me by saying, "Listen Irish, all you gotta do is make sure that you bring in more money than you spend. And as time goes by, you'll get the hang of it, trust me."

There was a brief pause, and then Bob continued by saying, "Hey Jack, you're gonna be great. Listen, I'm gonna teach you all of the tricks of the trade, and if you should happen to have any questions or concerns along the way, then just give me a call."

I took a moment to think, and then quietly replied, "Okay Bob, you got a deal."

In wrapping up my conversation with Bob, I told him that it was only fitting that I should be heading back to the same place where my professional career first started.

Bob then surprised me by saying, "Jack, I always knew that you'd be back at WEALTH Industries someday, because I sensed something in you that I've never experienced in any of my other subordinates before."

I was quite humbled by what Bob said, and I thanked him for having enough confidence in me to hand over the reins to a job that he has truly loved and cherished for over forty years.

So now that I'm fully committed in taking the WEALTH Industries job, I guess it's time for me to say something to Dick Henderson. I'm sure that Dick will be absolutely stunned when he hears that I'm leaving the State School, especially since he knows how much I love it here.

As I was driving into work that day, I was searching for the right words to say to Dick Henderson, so that I could break the news to him that I was leaving the State School.

Dick has been more of a friend to me than a supervisor. And he has consistently taken me under his wing and helped guide me through some pretty choppy waters, especially during the whole Lance Coppenger ordeal.

So before heading down to Murphy's office for our morning coffee, I decided to swing by Dick's office first, and inform him that I was vacating my position here at the State School.

When I tapped on Dick's door, he was chatting with someone on the telephone. Dick waved me into his office, and then pointed for me to sit down in the chair adjacent to his desk.

As I waited for Dick to finish up on the telephone, my eye seem to gravitate towards an old photograph of Dick and I from a couple of years ago. Although the photo was a bit yellowed, Dick absolutely cherished it, and displayed it proudly on the far corner of his desk.

When Dick hung up the phone, he could sense that I had something on my mind, and that my coming by his office first thing on a Monday morning wasn't exactly a social call.

As I reached to close Dick's office door, it prompted him to amusingly utter, "Uh-oh, now you're really starting to scare me, Jack?"

So not knowing how to phrase it, I just decided to bite the bullet and simply say, "Well Dick, I came by this morning to let you know that I'll be putting my notice in to leave the State School effective immediately, because I've decided to accept a position back in my hometown."

Dick looked rather stunned by what I said. And I think it would be safe to say that it was the last thing in the world that he was expecting me to say, as he simply responded, "Really…?"

I quietly replied, "Yeah, that's right, Dick. To tell you the truth, the job kinda fell into my lap, and the salary and benefits that they're offering me are just too good to pass up."

Dick nodded his head, and quietly said, "Well, I'm sure that you've given the matter a lot of thought, and there's probably nothing that I can say to make you change your mind, right?"

I amusingly replied, "Well, let me put it to you this way Dick, if I don't take this job then my wife will probably kill me. But all kidding aside, it's a great opportunity for me. Of course, the biggest downside in all of this is that I won't be working with you and Murphy anymore. But sometimes, I guess that's the price we have to pay in order to further our careers, right?"

Dick said, "Hey, sooner or later we're all forced to make some pretty tough decisions when it comes to furthering our careers. But don't worry, it'll all work out, you'll see."

There was a brief moment of silence, and then Dick continued by saying, "Well, you'll probably need to give Rita Spinelli a call over in the Human Resources Office, so that you can tell her what's going on. Also, there's some paperwork that needs to be filled out before the State can officially release you from your position. But don't worry, Rita will sort it all out for ya."

I quietly replied, "Yeah, okay, thanks Dick. I'll give Rita a call today. Um, I probably should give Mr. Hanson a call today too, right?"

Dick smiled, and then softly said, "Hey, don't worry about Hanson, just leave him to me. I just want you to focus on having a good day today, okay."

"Yeah, okay, thanks again, Dick. I'll catch ya later."

Later that morning, I gave Rita Spinelli a call over in the Human Resources Office, and told her that I was leaving the State School. Upon hearing the news, Rita was not only stunned, but I detected a hint of sadness in her voice as well.

Rita then mentioned to me that I was the first person she hired when she came on board in the Human Resources Office. And every time that she strolls down memory lane, it prompts her to think of me.

So after sharing that little piece of nostalgia with me, Rita got right down to business by telling me that it's usually customary for all employees to provide the facility with at least four weeks' notice, so that the Human Resources Office has sufficient time to backfill the position.

As a favor to me, Rita said that if I needed to vacate my position before the four week period was over, then she could probably pull a few strings and release me from my obligations.

Later that afternoon, I received a phone call from Mr. Hanson, who called to congratulate me on my new job, and to personally thank me for all of my efforts over the past five years.

Although Mr. Hanson and I have certainly bumped heads on more than one occasion, it was still very thoughtful of him to give me a call and wish me well in all of my new endeavors.

Hanson then wrapped up the conversation by saying that even though he and I have had our differences over the years, he has nothing but the utmost respect for me, and that it will be very difficult for the facility to replace someone of my caliber.

The following Monday, I received a phone call from Mr. Kramer, who apparently heard through the grapevine that I'm leaving the State School in search for greener pastures.

At first, I thought that Mr. Kramer was calling to congratulate me on my new position at WEALTH Industries, and to tell me that I will be sorely missed here at the developmental center.

But silly me, that's not why Kramer was calling at all. Kramer wanted to know when my last official day was at the State School, so that I could be available to train my new replacement.

I guess I should've realized that giving me the courtesy of a congratulatory phone call was simply out of the realm of possibility for Mr. Kramer. Because like all narcissists, Kramer lacks the capacity to be genuinely happy for others.

When you think about it, Kramer's narcissistic personality disorder is really no different than that of Bobby Diggs, except Kramer enjoys a more lavished and extravagant lifestyle than poor 'ole Bobby does.

So after taking stock of my rather contemptuous thoughts regarding Mr. Kramer, I told him that I didn't know when my last official day was. But if the interview process is completed in a timely fashion, then there should be enough time for me to train whomever comes on board.

Kramer then flippantly remarked, "Actually, there won't be any interviews to conduct, because I already have someone in mind for your position, that being…, Dave Philcox."

I quickly replied, "Well Mr. Kramer, I'm sure that Mr. Hanson may have something to say about that, because he might want to explore the possibility of canvassing applicants from outside the facility."

Kramer then got real testy with me on the phone, as he viciously snarled, "Listen here O'Leary, I'm the person in charge of Rehabilitation Services at this facility, and I'll be the one that decides on who gets hired in this department, not Mr. Hanson."

There was just no talking to Kramer. And the last thing that I needed right now was to get in the middle of a turf war between two power hungry tyrants who totally despised each other.

Anyway, I'm sure that when Hanson finds out that Kramer is maneuvering a few chess pieces behind his back, then Hanson will be picking up the phone and scheduling a meeting with the Director, so that he can put an end to whatever scheming ideas that Kramer has up his sleeve.

In the meantime, I'll just let these two Titans battle it out. So that I can wrap things up in a timely fashion, and then try to enjoy the rest of the time that I have left here at the State School.

As I was waiting for the clients to file in for the morning work session, I kept thinking about the possibility of Dave Philcox as being my new replacement for the SBU.

From an early age, I was always taught to believe that crime doesn't pay. But in Dave Philcox's case, it seems to have rewarded him quite handsomely.

In the twenty years that Dave Philcox has worked here at the State School, he's gone from being a bottom feeder, to someone who will soon command some power and influence.

As far as I'm concerned, the only reason that Dave Philcox is getting my job is because Kramer wants someone to spy on Hanson's operation. Kramer would love nothing more than to dig up some juicy gossip on Hanson. And then use it as ammunition against him, so that he can have a front row seat in watching Hanson's squeaky-clean reputation go right down the drain.

Sad to say, but I don't see much difference between Kramer's behavior and the deviant behavior of some of the hooligans that we have living here at the State School, especially when it comes to using whatever sleezy and underhanded tactics they can in settling up some old scores.

Kramer would much rather wield his power and influence to satisfy his own self-interests and petty jealousies, than he would at making the work programs here at the State School better. And devoting more of his time on personal vendettas, than on program growth and development.

When the guys arrived for the morning work session, Jamal came up to me and brusquely said, "Yo' Mr. O'Really, word on the street is that you're leavin' this punk-ass place, dawg!"

Bobby Diggs jumped right into the conversation, and then said with some considerable panic in his voice, "Hey Jamal, you're crazy! Jack would never leave us, would ya, Jack?"

I hesitated for a moment, and then quietly replied, "Well, Jamal's right, Bobby. I'm leaving the State School, and taking a job back in my hometown."

With tears streaming down his face, Bobby woefully asked, "But if you're leave the State School, then who's gonna take care of me?"

As I gazed into Bobby's eyes, I tried to reassure him by saying, "Don't worry, Bobby. Dave Henderson and Murphy are still gonna be here, they'll be watching out for ya, right?"

Bobby's shoulders went completely limp. And as he dropped his head, he mournfully replied, "Uh, Dave Henderson hates me, 'cause I choked him. But it was only that one time!"

In the afternoon work session, Russell Turner came up to me and snidely said, "Hey Jack, I heard you're leaving. So did they fire ya, or are you just sick and tired of this fuckin' dump?"

The following week, I received a phone call from Mr. Kramer's secretary, who wanted to know if she could schedule an appointment with me, so that I could meet with Mr. Kramer.

Apparently, it's incumbent upon all employees that leave state service to participate in an exit interview, so that the Human Resources Office can utilize this information for future use in their hiring practices.

Naturally, I just assumed that Dick Henderson would be conducting my exit interview, especially since Dick has been my immediate supervisor for the past three years. And to tell you the truth, but I'd much rather spend time chatting with Dick than I would with Kramer any day.

Well, maybe Rita Spinelli stuck me with Kramer because she knows that Dick has a lot on his plate, whereas Kramer is constantly scrounging around looking for ways to fill up his day.

So this morning I'm scheduled to meet with Mr. Kramer for my exit interview.

Knowing Kramer, I'm sure he'll be expecting me to stroke his incredibly large ego, and ramble on and on about how great of a supervisor he is and how much I've grown professionally while under his guidance and tutelage.

Well, if Kramer thinks that I'm going down that road then he's sadly mistaken, because I've decided to speak my mind today. Not in a cruel or vindictive way, but more in a way that is constructive and honest, especially since I may never lay eyes on Kramer again.

When I arrived for my exit interview, Mr. Kramer's secretary appeared rather surprised to see me, as she said with utter confusion, "Oh, hi Jack. Uh, didn't you get the message that Mr. Kramer won't be conducting your exit interview today?"

"Uh, no..., nobody notified me about that." I replied, with some hesitancy.

She then said, "Gee, I'm sorry that you had to come all the way over here for nothing. I specifically remember Mr. Kramer telling me that he would give you a call. Apparently, Dick Henderson will be handling your exit interview instead of Mr. Kramer."

I then decided to take the high road by simply saying, "Hey, no worries, Karen. Mr. Kramer is a very busy man, and I'm sure that it must've slipped his mind."

Well, so much for my fireside chat with Mr. Kramer.

But then it's probably a good thing that it all worked out this way anyway, because I might've said something to Mr. Kramer that I would've regretted later.

As we inch closer to the transfer date, Jamal Buchanan and Terrence Morehouse can't wait to head back to their old neighborhood again, so that they can hang out on the street corner with all of their deadbeat friends, as they hustle unsuspecting passerby's for some loose change.

Well, if that's what Jamal and Terrence both think is in store for them, then they're in for a rude awakening, because that's not exactly the way that it's going to be. These guys are all going to be living in a highly secured mental health facility, and not enjoying the freedom to just come and go as they please from their mama's one bedroom tenement apartment in the projects.

Jamal and Terrence are both under the impression that it's going to be nothing but fun and games when they head back home again. And as far as I know, but no one has even bothered to sit down with any of these guys and explain the situation to them, - probably because they're too afraid of what their reaction might be when they finally hear what their fate will actually be.

Of course, the one guy who is continuing to tug at my heartstrings right now is Tyrell Freeman. Tyrell has made it quite clear that he doesn't want to be transferred, but he's totally resigned to the fact that he doesn't have a choice, so he's placing all of his faith in God's hands.

Tyrell almost brought me to tears the other day, when he softly said in his deep and distinctive southern drawl, "Mama says that I gotta come home, so I bess' listen."

Well, it looks like Bobby Diggs is up to his old tricks again, and round two is shaping up to be just as bad as round one was. Bobby still can't accept the fact that his family doesn't want him. And when Bobby hears the other clients talking about going home and being reunited with their loved ones again, it seems to totally infuriate him to no end.

In fact, Bobby has been wreaking so much havoc that Hanson is toying with the idea of asking the Director to place Bobby into another building until all of the transfers are completed.

I'm sure that when the other Chiefs catch wind of what Hanson is proposing, then they'll be bitching up a storm, and scheduling their own private little powwow with the Director as well.

After all, who in their right mind would want to put up with Bobby Diggs every day, and all of his crazy schemes and hair-brain ideas.

Well, uh…, come to think of it, but I guess you could say that I've been down that road once or twice before with Bobby Diggs myself.

It's funny, but as much as Bobby hates hearing Jamal gloat about going home, what seems to irk Bobby even more is hearing Tyrell say that he doesn't want to leave. Especially when Bobby has been trying to figure out a way to leave the State School for over forty years.

Bobby is thoroughly convinced that the grass is greener beyond the shadow of the State School. But as a wise person once told me, - "the grass may be greener somewhere else, but you still gotta mow it."

Well, it's official, we just got word late yesterday afternoon that Tommy Gerard won't need to pack his bags and take his little dog and pony show out on the road with him after all, because Tommy Gerard will be staying right here at the State School.

Despite the fact that Tommy Gerard was born just outside the county line, the Director has decided to make an exception in Tommy's case, so that Tommy can continue to live right here at the State School.

Initially, when Tommy Gerard's parents received notification that Tommy may be forced to relocate to another facility, they were gravely concerned. So not knowing what to do, Tommy's parents pleaded with the Director to have Tommy remain right here at the State School. Especially since Tommy has lived at the State School for most of his life, and it's the only real home that Tommy Gerard has ever known.

At Tommy's last case review, his parents both remarked that they have seen a dramatic improvement in Tommy, and that they actually look forward to seeing Tommy every weekend now. Whereas in the past, they viewed their weekly visits with Tommy as a family obligation.

So I guess that means that Tommy will continue to be the featured headliner here at the State School. And if you happen to miss Tommy's live performance for the matinee show, then don't worry, because Tommy performs a live show every night of the week right here as well.

Well, after weeks of anticipation the big moment has finally arrived, and the first wave of transfers is slated to happen this week. Jamal, Terrence, Tyrell, and the rest of the Metro gang are all heading back home again.

Boy, it just seems like yesterday when they first got here.

The time that I've spent working with the Metro gang has certainly been a memorable one, and I will cherish the experience for the rest of my life.

So now that we know when the Metro gang is leaving, we decided to throw them a little going away party. When Dick asked the guys what they would like to have for their bon voyage lunch, they all shouted, "Pizza and chicken wings!"

Murphy also thought that it might be a nice idea to present the Metro gang with a little keepsake as well, so that they would all have a little something to remember us by.

So after tossing around a few ideas, we decided to tie-dye some tee shirts, and then silk screen them with the inscription, "Thanks for the memories, the SBU will never forget you!"

As a matter of fact, when the coach bus arrives tomorrow afternoon to take the guys back to Metro Psychiatric Center, everyone is planning on wearing the same tie-dyed tee shirt as well.

And yes, - even Hanson promised to show up tomorrow afternoon wearing the same tie-dyed tee shirt too!

The following day when Murphy and I arrived to work, we were surprised to see the Metro gang all camped out up in the front lobby.

Apparently, Metro Psychiatric Center called late yesterday afternoon, and informed Dick Henderson that they would be arriving earlier than planned, so they asked Dick if he could have the guys all packed up and ready to go by 8:00am.

As I mingled through the crowd, some of the guys were very excited about the prospects of going back home, and others appeared to be a bit apprehensive.

For the past two years, the Metro gang has had a taste of the good life, and almost treated like royalty. So going back home might not be the Shangri-La that some of them think it will be, and maybe some of the guys are starting to have some second thoughts about leaving.

Despite some of the tough times that we may have had along the way, we have certainly enjoyed a lot of good times with the Metro gang as well.

It's funny, but when I think back on meeting the Metro gang for the first time, I was absolutely petrified. Yet today, I can honestly say that I'm not the least bit scared. And whatever fears and apprehensions that I may have once had have now seemingly evaporated into thin air.

Now that being said, I still wouldn't feel all that comfortable walking into a dark alley all by myself with the likes of Jamal Buchanan or Terrence Morehouse, especially since both of those two guys could probably kick my ass from here to Timbuktu.

But I'm proud to say that I've learned to rely more on my wits and not my dukes, so that I can finagle my way out of some pretty tight spots without resorting to any underhanded tactics.

These skills that I've acquired along the way will serve me quite well in the future, and help level the playing field, so that I have a fighting chance at being a human services survivor.

As Murphy and I continued to make our way around the room, my eyes kept drifting over to Tyrell Freeman, who was sitting all by himself in the far corner of the room.

Tyrell had his head completely buried in his hands, as he clutched his rosary beads, and solemnly prayed to God to give him the strength and spiritual guidance he needed to get through this heart-wrenching ordeal of his in leaving the State School behind.

Despite all of the joy and laughter that was resonating throughout the room, my mind kept reverting back to Tyrell, and the agonizing heartache that he was experiencing right now.

We then stopped and chatted with Jamal Buchanan, who quickly shared some memorable moments about the basketball team. And although Jamal's comments were absolutely hilarious, I kept having ruminating thoughts about Tyrell, and all of the pain and anguish that he was feeling.

Jamal then poignantly remarked, "Yo' Murphy, you still the only white boy that has ever beaten me in a one-on-one basketball game. And if you ever get up into my neighborhood, I'll take you on my team any day, especially when we play against the bigger, bigger boys, aight!"

As I listened to the unbridled enthusiasm in Jamal's voice, it made me realize just how much he's grown as a person since being here at the State School.

Two years ago, when Jamal first walked through the door, he had a chip on his shoulder that was the size of Gibraltar, and he truly believed that white people were out to get him.

Yet today, Jamal is leaving with a totally different perspective on life, and he now has a clearer understanding that not all white people are as bad as he had originally thought them to be.

These preconceived notions of Jamal's were probably taught to him at a very early age, and continued to be drilled into him as he got older. I can't even begin to imagine some of the horrifying and tragic stories that have happened in the black community over the years.

But while Jamal was under our watch, we were able to teach him that right is right and wrong is wrong, and it makes absolutely no difference what the color of one's skin is.

As Jamal was gazing out the window, he spotted the coach bus coming up the road, and then alerted the crowd by enthusiastically shouting, "Yo', here comes the bus to Metro, y'all!"

At that point, an eerie hush seem to fall over the entire room. Dick then instructed the guys to gather up their belongings, and proceed out the front door in a quiet and orderly fashion.

As the retractable door on the coach bus swung open, I was expecting to see Mr. Jefferson hop off of the bus. But to my surprise, it wasn't Mr. Jefferson at all, but someone else.

Jamal instantly recognized the man stepping off the bus as being Mr. Washington, and then excitedly shouted, "Whadup, Mr. Washington!"

Mr. Washington nodded his head slightly, and then replied in a rather deep and deliberate tone of voice, "Jamal."

Dick walked over to Mr. Washington and cordially introduced himself, and then both of them shook hands.

As I studied Mr. Washington for a moment, he struck me as a pretty nice guy. And in a weird sort of way, he kinda reminded me of a black version of Murphy.

Washington stood about 6'11, and although he appeared to be an intimidating presence, he struck me as someone who had a certain gentleness about him as well. Washington seemed to get a big kick out of the fact that everyone was wearing the same tie-dyed tee shirt, and then made it a point to say that it kinda reminded him of his boyhood days back in summer camp.

Dick then casually asked Mr. Washington if he and his staff would like to stretch their legs a bit, or perhaps grab a quick cup of coffee in the break room before initiating the transfer.

Mr. Washington graciously declined Dick's offer, and simply said that he would just as soon get the ball rolling on the transfer, so that he and his staff could hit the road as soon as possible and try to make it back to their facility at a reasonable hour.

Suddenly, we saw Hanson pull up in his sporty red convertible. And as promised, he was wearing his tie-dyed tee shirt, which he wore over his dress shirt and fancy Italian-made silk tie.

Mr. Hanson hopped out of his car and then sprinted straight over to where Dick and Mr. Washington were standing, so that he could be brought up to speed and apprised of the situation.

As we all stood around waiting for further instruction, Murphy leaned over to me and whispered, "Hey Rodney, do you know who that big dude is over there from Metro?"

I casually replied, "Um, I think I heard Jamal refer to him as Mr. Washington."

Murphy flashed an appreciative smile, and then quietly said, "Well, his name is Marcus Washington, and I played basketball against him in college. He was the best basketball player that I ever saw. But unfortunately, he blew out his knee in his senior year, and the injury was so bad that it dashed any hopes he had of playing professional basketball. In fact, he was so highly touted by the NBA scouts, that they actually projected him to be a first-round draft pick."

"Wow! Really…? Then you should go over there and say "hi" to him, Doc."

Murphy just shrugged his shoulders, and sheepishly replied, "Nah, that's okay Rodney, I'm sure he wouldn't remember me anyway."

So after signing off on a few documents, the transfer became official. Hanson appeared to be rather pleased with himself, as if he had just solved world hunger.

Hanson began tapping the crystal on his Rolex watch, and then brusquely said, "Time's-a-wastin', Dick. So let's get these clients all loaded up on the bus, and moved out right away."

Mr. Washington then shouted, "Okay gentleman, gather up your gear and let's get goin'!"

So as the clients lined up to board the bus, Hanson made an about face and then headed directly toward the parking lot. Hanson never bothered to say "good-bye" to anyone, nor did he have the common courtesy of wishing the clients a safe trip back to Metro Psychiatric Center.

As I watched Mr. Hanson turn and walk away, it was actually quite staggering to me that he couldn't wait around a measly five more minutes, so that he could say a few parting words, or maybe even wave "good-bye" to the clients as the coach bus pulled away from the curb.

Is Hanson really that important, or is he just too socially inept not to know any better?

If you ask me, Hanson probably wanted to beat it straight over to the Director's Office, so that he could get his pat on the back, and a hearty "that-a-boy, Al" from the Director.

And to make matters worse, but before climbing into his sporty red convertible, Hanson actually had the audacity to take off his tie-dyed tee shirt, and then throw it directly into the trashcan that was sitting a few feet away from his car.

Good Lord! The unmitigated gall of that man to disrespect us like that!

I guess it never occurred to Hanson that those tie-dyed tee shirts represented more than just some token gesture on our part, they were a symbol of solidarity that bounded us together.

Once again, Hanson was merely going through the motions today.

To tell you the truth, I can almost tolerate Hanson being a complete asshole most of the time. But for him to throw that tie-dyed tee shirt into the trashcan while still in our presence, well, it was not only cruel and heartless on his part, but it was totally reprehensible as well.

At the risk of sounding overly dramatic, but I really don't know how Hanson can find the intestinal fortitude to look at himself in the mirror every day without getting nauseous. The man is simply not wired right, and he just doesn't know how to relate to any of his subordinates at all.

Despite the fact that Hanson holds a marquee position here at the State School, and earns three times the salary that I do, he's still a loser in my book. And quite honestly, but I wouldn't want to change places with him for all the tea in China.

As Hanson sped away in his sporty red convertible, Dick Henderson turned toward Mr. Washington and said, "Well, I sure hope you don't have a boss like him down at Metro."

Washington sarcastically replied, "Bosses, they're all the same man."

So as the clients all lined up to board the bus, the first person in line was Terrence Morehouse. Terrence couldn't stop smiling as he stepped onto the bus.

As Murphy and I watched the clients parade onto the bus, I said to Murphy, "Boy, it just seems like yesterday when the Metro gang got here, and now they're all leaving us."

Murphy quietly replied, "Yeah, I guess time flies when you're having fun, eh Rodney."

When it was Tyrell Freeman's turn to board the bus, he had tears pouring down his face. And I simply can't put into words how utterly devastated I felt for Tyrell at that moment.

For months now, Tyrell has been begging us to stay here at the State School. Yet here we are today, bidding him a fond adieu, and pretending like everything is going to be okay for him.

It's been my experience that the powers to be may lead you to believe that they want the clients to have some say in their lives, and to be the masters of their own destiny. Yet, isn't funny how quickly that line of thinking changes when either politics or the bottom line comes into play.

In every sensitivity class that I've ever taken, it specifically says that the clinician should always try to listen very carefully to what the client is telling them, and then act accordingly.

Yet, in Tyrell Freeman's situation this is clearly not the case. Not only are we looking the other way with Tyrell, but we seem to be sweeping his expressed wishes directly under the rug.

And to add insult to injury, but the only reason that Tyrell's mother wants him to go back to Metro is so she can get her grubby hands on his social security disability money. And not what she's been telling Tyrell all along, which is to have her baby boy back in her loving arms again.

The way I see it, if we can make an exception to allow Tommy Gerard to stay here at the State School, then why can't we extend the same courtesy to Tyrell Freeman as well.

But then realizing that the one glaring difference in this whole twisted dichotomy is, - Tommy Gerard's family wants him to stay, whereas Tyrell Freeman's family wants him to go.

As Tyrell stepped onto the bus, Mr. Washington placed his hand gently on Tyrell's broad shoulder, and then softly said, "It'll be alright, big fella. It's good to see you again, Tyrell."

Tyrell quietly replied, "Thank you, Mr. Washington. It's good to see you too, sir."

Jamal Buchanan was the next person to board the bus. Jamal was all pimped out in some colorful new threads; he had on a brand new pair of sneakers, a couple of shiny gold chains, and a real sharp looking pair of aviator style sunglasses that he had perched on the bridge of his nose.

The headphones that were sitting on top of Jamal's head could barely stretch over his enormous afro hairstyle. And the volume on his stereo headset was cranked up so high that I could hear every nasty lyric that was playing on the gangster rap song that he was listening to.

Yeah, Jamal was in his glory. Because Jamal was heading back home again, so that he could enjoy some of his mama's homemade cooking, and hang out with all of his deadbeat friends from his old neighborhood again.

Well, let's just hope that Jamal feels the same way tomorrow morning, when he rolls out of bed at Metro Psychiatric Center, instead of in his mama's one bedroom tenement apartment.

So before stepping onto the bus, Jamal took one last glimpse at Murphy, and in typical Jamal style he said, "Yo' Mr. Washington, see this dude right here, his name is Murphy Doherty. And when it comes to playing hoops, he's one bad-ass white boy! See ya around, fellas!"

Mr. Washington began to chuckle, and he seemed to be somewhat amused by what Jamal Buchanan just said.

As Mr. Washington continued to chuckle, he quietly glanced in Murphy's direction, and then Mr. Washington did a complete double-take, as if he recognized Murphy from somewhere.

In a bit of a quandary, Mr. Washington then asked Murphy, "Hey man, do I know you? Because your face looks awfully familiar to me."

Murphy smiled, and then sheepishly said, "Well, uh…, you and I played basketball against each other in college, Marcus."

Washington paused a moment, and then he slowly nodded his head while saying, "Yeah, right, Murphy Doherty. You played power forward for State College, aight!"

With a slight chuckle in his voice, Murphy replied, "Gee Marcus, that was a pretty long time ago, I'm surprised that you even remembered me."

Suddenly, Washington became quite animated, as he boisterously said, "Oh, I remember you, man! You're the guy who ended my consecutive scoring streak of thirty points a game. In fact, you elbowed me so hard under the backboard that night that you wound up cracking one of my ribs. Lordy, my ribs hurt so bad that I had to sit out the game for the entire fourth quarter."

Murphy replied, "Gee, I'm sorry Marcus, I had no idea that I injured you that night. I always wondered why you didn't finish the game. I hope there are no hard feelings."

Washington smiled, and then good-naturedly said, "Hey man, there's no hard feelings. Anyway, college seems like a lifetime ago. I'll tell ya man, I think about you from time to time, especially when my hommies start trash talking me about my consecutive scoring streak being broken by a white boy. Hey, it's good to see you again, Murphy. Listen man, if you're ever down in my neck of the woods, then look me up sometime, aight."

Murphy replied, "Yeah, okay, I'll keep that in mind. Thanks, Marcus!"

So after making sure that everyone was present and accounted for, Dick and Marcus Washington shook hands, and then exchanged a few pleasant "good-byes."

As we waited for the coach bus to pull away from the curb, my eye seemed to be drawn to Jamal Buchanan, who was still groovin' and bee-boppin' to the sounds of his hip-hop music.

Watching Jamal brought an instant smile to my face. But as soon as I caught a glimpse of Tyrell Freeman, who was sitting in the seat directly behind Jamal, my smile quickly vanished.

I guess the old adage, "One man's ceiling is another man's floor," may aptly apply here.

As the bus slowly pulled away from the curb, all of a sudden Dick Henderson started waving his arms in the air, so that he could get the attention of the bus driver to stop the bus.

Dick then shouted, "Wait a minute, you forgot the coolers!"

At that point, Dick turned to Murphy and I and asked us to grab the two ice chests that were sitting on the floor next to the front door inside the lobby.

Apparently, Dick made arrangements with the kitchen staff last night to prepare two large coolers filled with sandwiches, snacks, and assorted drinks, so that the coach bus didn't have to make a stop along the way to feed the guys on their long trip back to Metro Psychiatric Center.

Murphy and I grabbed the two coolers from inside the front lobby, and then carted them out to the bus. We then handed the two coolers up to Marcus Washington, who stowed them securely on the front seat, directly behind the bus driver.

As we all anxiously waited for the coach bus to shove off, Marcus Washington then stuck his head out of the window, and with a big smile on his face, he then yelled to us, "Hey, being here is like living in paradise! So why would anyone ever want to leave? Thanks again, fellas!"

I quietly leaned over to Murphy, and then amusingly quipped, "Hey Doc, maybe Marcus Washington should mention that to Bobby Diggs."

Murphy just nodded his head and smiled, as he continued to be deep in thought, and quietly recounting some of the memorable moments he shared with the ever popular Metro gang.

In terms of the rest of the clients who were transferred this month, everything seemed to go off without a hitch, and there was no real fanfare or signature moments to speak of.

I guess when it came right down to it, the Metro gang were the real headliners of the SBU, - from the moment they arrived, to the moment that they finally left.

And everyone else, well…, they were merely the supporting cast.

Chapter Seventeen

So now that the Metro gang is gone, Bobby, Russell, and Francis all seem to believe that one of them will emerge as the new kingpin of the building. And you can bet your bottom dollar that all three of these conniving mischievites are already hatching a plan and plotting their future.

It's certainly no secret that institutional life has its own unique pecking order. And the higher you are on the food chain, then the better your chances are for success.

Now to the casual observer, Bobby, Russell, and Francis may come across as being really nice guys. But as you get to know each of them a little bit better, it's certainly quite evident as to why all three of these shady characters require twenty-four hour supervision at all times.

In order to survive at the State School, then one must learn how to identify your enemies, and then systematically destroy them one-by-one.

But do it in a way without getting your hands dirty.

It's funny, but I've come to realize that despite the fact that many of our clients here at the State School may have difficulty grasping some of the more basic and rudimentary skills in life, when it comes to eliminating the competition, they seem to be in a class all by themselves.

And even though Bobby, Russell, and Francis have been institutionalized for their entire life, they could probably teach you and I a thing or two about the fine art of covering your tracks.

So when the new batch of recruits come strolling through the front door in a couple of weeks, I think it's safe to say that Bobby, Russell, and Francis won't be losing any sleep over it.

And what's more, Bobby, Russell, and Francis can't wait to spin their tangled web of deception, so that they can start taking the new batch of wannabies for everything they're worth.

Now on the flip side, it should also be noted that the new clients who will be arriving in a few weeks are certainly no choirboys themselves. And just because the Metro gang is gone that doesn't automatically mean that Bobby, Russell, or Francis are going to be running the show.

So it will be very interesting to see how it all plays out when the next batch of hopeful contenders shows up. And the only thing that I regret is that I won't be around to see all of the drama unfold, so I guess I'll just have to rely on Murphy to fill me in on all of the sordid details.

Well, speaking of the new recruits, Dick and Cameron are scheduled to take a little road trip this upcoming weekend, and they're planning on visiting two minimum security prisons that are located approximately two hours north of here.

Apparently, there seems to be a fairly large number of inmates throughout the state penal system that are either misplaced or misdiagnosed. And the Governor seems to think that some of these inmates may benefit from a facility like ours, which is more commensurate to their needs.

So it would seem that the landscape of the State School may be dramatically changing. And the days of taking care of cute little Down-syndrome clients, who were once relinquished by their families, and then placed into the custodial care of the State may finally be over.

Well, yesterday I received a phone call from Rita Spinelli, who informed me that she has completed all of required paperwork needed for my release from State service. And contingent upon supervisory approval, I can leave the State School as early as next Friday.

Rita then went on to say that the Director and Mr. Hanson have both signed off on Mr. Kramer's recommendation of having Dave Philcox as my new replacement for the SBU.

When Rita mentioned that Dave Philcox would be taking my job, I was a bit surprised to say the least. I really thought that Hanson would only want to consider applicants from outside the facility, especially since Hanson enjoys making life as miserable as he can for Mr. Kramer.

But at the end of the day, I guess that Mr. Hanson opted to settle for mediocrity. And he will soon discover that Dave Philcox is more of a liability than he is an asset.

As I hung up the phone with Rita, there was a part of me that was happy to hear that my timetable for leaving the State School was shorter than I had originally thought. But there was also a part of me that felt rather melancholy with hearing the news as well.

It then suddenly dawned on me that this wild and crazy ride that I have been so fortunate to be part of for the past five years here at the State School was now coming to a screeching halt.

But more importantly, I won't be working with Murphy on a day-to-day basis anymore.

So now that I have a definite release date, I decided to put my nose to the grindstone and get everything done by next Friday. And barring any unforeseen circumstances, I'm quite sure that I can tie up all of the loose ends by then.

Of course, I'll probably have to spend some time with Dave Philcox next week and show him the ropes, so that he can make a smooth transition into his new job here in the SBU.

Frankly, spending time with Dave Philcox was comparable to having a root canal done without any anesthesia. But I have always considered myself to be a team player, so I guess I'll just have to weather the storm, and set up a time to meet with Philcox next week and orient him.

Over the weekend, Murphy and his family came over to our apartment for a little get together. Since it was our last weekend in town, we wanted to spend as much time with our dear friends as possible.

So while the girls were busy gabbing away in the kitchen, Murphy and I were manning the grill and dusting off some old war stories regarding the Metro gang. Such as, meeting Tyrell Freeman for the first time, Jamal Buchanan's constant trash talking, and an endless array of memorable moments that will remain in our hearts and minds forever.

In the midst of all the laughter, I then took a moment to be serious by telling Murphy just how much I've enjoyed working with him over the past two years, and that the time that I've spent with him has been the best two years of my life. Murphy was so touched by my words that it actually brought him to tears, and then he echoed the same exact sentiments to me as well.

The following Monday, I stopped by Dick Henderson's office to let him know that Friday would be my last day, and to also find out how he and Cameron made out over the weekend.

Although Dick was pleased to hear that I was granted an early release date, the look on his face told me otherwise, and I could tell that he was totting a very heavy heart with the news.

In terms of the weekend, Dick said that the experience was a real eye-opener. And that the new crop of consideries were a lot smarter than the Metro gang, and quite a bit more devious as well. Which only stands to reason, seeing how they are currently sitting behind bars.

Dick described all of the inmates as being very friendly and engaging. And from what he could tell by reading their case files, the main reason for their incarceration was because they all ran with the wrong crowd, and were the unfortunate victims of extremely poor decision making.

As I sat there listening to all of the new and exciting ideas that Dick has in store for the new arrivals, I found myself having a twinge of regret about leaving the State School. I guess deep down inside I really didn't want to leave, and I still wanted to be part of the SBU team.

Now obviously, the die is cast and my last official day is Friday. But that being said, I still seem to have this overwhelming desire to just stick around the State School for a little while longer, and help break in the new herd of mustangs with Murphy by my side.

In my heart, I knew that taking the WEALTH Industries job was definitely the right move for me to make. But leaving the State School behind was still a bitter pill for me to swallow, and I just hope that it won't be a decision that will ultimately come back to haunt me.

So after chatting with Dick, I went straight down to my office so that I could finish tying up all of the loose ends that needed to be done by Friday. But despite my best efforts, I couldn't seem to focus on any of my work.

As I sat at my desk, I kept brooding over the fact that in a week from now my days will be consumed with figuring out profit margins, balancing the books, and keeping a steady eye on seventy-five employees, most notably, C.D., who will be even more of a challenge to keep track of now that Bob Watson is gone.

Meanwhile, Murphy will be having the time of his life, as he wiles away the hours with some amazing fun-filled activities and nonstop laughter with the incomparable Bowery Boys.

As I continued to sit there feeling sorry for myself, I then realized just how childish I was acting. It then occurred to me that the time has finally come for me to set aside all of my selfish desires, and to focus on the fact that I have a family that is relying on me to provide them with the best quality of life possible.

Well, as soon as I was able to wrap my mind around that basic concept, then the torment of leaving the State School behind seemed to suddenly vanish into thin air.

By Thursday afternoon, I finished everything that needed to be done, - including spending time with Mr. Kramer's number one henchman, Dave Philcox.

When I met with Philcox, I was able to set aside whatever acrimonious feelings that I had for the guy, and I'm happy to report that I conducted myself in a highly professional manner.

Despite the fact that Philcox rubs me the wrong way, I not only showed him the ropes, but I also provided him with a few tricks of the trade that I've managed to pick up along the way.

Well, just when I thought that my morning with Philcox was going as well as it possibly could, I then handed him the list of voluntary agencies that I have been closely networking with.

As Philcox perused the list of names, he noticed that Marty's Print Shop was one of the businesses that was listed on the sheet of paper. And from that point on my orientation with Dave Philcox went completely downhill, and it wound up leaving an extremely bad taste in my mouth.

Philcox then blurted out, "Marty's Print Shop, - hey, wasn't that the guy you helped out about a year ago, and then Kramer accused you of taking some illegal kickbacks because your Good Samaritan act almost cost him his operating certificate from the Department of Labor?"

As Philcox stood there with a real cocky grin on his face, I couldn't believe what he just said to me. The audacity of him to bring up such a sore subject like that, especially when I'm taking time out of my day to orient him so that he can make a smooth transition into his new job.

Is this the thanks I get, - to be hit below the belt by some sarcastic son-of-a-bitch, who seems to enjoy taking potshots at people that are only trying to help him out?

Up until now, I was feeling pretty good about how my morning was going. And for a split second there, I even thought that I might have totally misjudged Dave Philcox altogether.

But silly me, I should've realized that it was only a matter of time until Philcox flashed me his true colors. His snotty little remark made me feel like a ham-and-egger all over again.

Boy, I really thought that I had put all of those feelings of inadequacy behind me. But apparently, it's a psychological hurdle that I still haven't cleared yet, and it continues to gnaw at me like a giant toothache.

Well, needless to say, but at that point my orientation session with Dave Philcox came to a screeching halt. Yeah, I'll admit it, my kneejerk reaction to Dave Philcox's totally insensitive remark was pretty juvenile on my part.

But I'll be damned if I'm going to stand there and allow someone to take potshots at me. Especially when the clock is ticking, and I could be spending my last few remaining moments here at the State School hanging out with Murphy and thoroughly enjoying his company, instead of wasting all of my time and energy with an ungrateful bastard like Dave Philcox.

As Dave Philcox exited the building, he thanked me for my time, but I could tell by the sarcastic tone in his voice that his comments weren't genuine.

Before heading out the door, Dave Philcox decided to throw one last jab at me by saying, "Well, this little two-bit operation of yours may have suited you Jack, but I've got some pretty exciting ideas on how to make this a top notch program, which is why Mr. Kramer decided to put me in charge of vocational services here in the SBU. See ya, around!"

Well, it's Friday, and it's my last official day here at the State School. It's hard for me to believe that's it all coming to an end today.

When I first started working at the State School, I actually thought that I would finish out my entire career here. But like anything else in life, one never knows what tomorrow will bring.

It's certainly been quite a journey.

And as I drove into work this morning, I was thinking about some of the extraordinary people that I have had the privilege to know along the way, especially Ms. Albright.

Ms. Albright made me realize that you can't always judge a book by its cover. And if you allow yourself to get to know someone, then maybe you just might find the good in them.

Well, with the exception of Kramer, Philcox, and Hanson anyway.

Throughout the morning work session, I found it a bit odd how subdued the clients were. No one brought up the fact that it was my last official day here at the State School. And if you didn't know any better, you'd almost think that today was just an ordinary day, business as usual.

Quite honestly, but I've worked here at the State School long enough to know that the clients generally wear their heart on their sleeve. And despite their craftiness at being cunning and deceptive, the one skill that the clients really haven't mastered yet is the ability to wear a good poker face.

So that being said, you can only imagine how surprised I was that none of the clients looked visibly upset about it being my last day, nor did any of them make even the slightest attempt in telling me how much they were going to miss me after today.

When the morning work session ended, the clients all said "good-bye" and wished me a nice weekend, as if they were all expecting to see me again bright and early on Monday morning.

To be honest, I didn't say anything about it being my last day today because I was trying to take the client's feelings into account, and to spare them the heartache of saying "good-bye."

Then again, I can't totally rule out the possibility that I simply chickened out either.

Of course, one could also argue the point that the clients have developed an immunity to separation anxiety, especially since there is such a high volume of staff turnover that occurs here at the State School, and people are constantly coming in and out of the client's lives all the time.

So that being said, maybe my leaving the State School isn't quite as traumatic or earth-shattering for the clients as I may have perceived it to be.

Anyway, so once the workshop emptied out, I tidied up the room a bit, shut off the lights, and then thought I'd head down to the gym to see what Murphy was doing for lunch.

As I was locking the workshop door, I heard Dave Henderson call out to me from up the hallway, "Hey Jack, can you do me a favor and give Murphy a hand down in the gym. He has a few pieces of equipment that need to be moved around, and it should only take a few minutes. I'd help him myself, but I tweaked my back yesterday, and I really don't wanna push it."

I quickly replied, "Sure Dick, no problem. I was heading down to the gym anyway to see what Murphy was doing for lunch."

As I headed toward the gym, I was thinking that I haven't seen too much of Murphy this week, nor have I spent any measurable amount of time with him whatsoever, which is unusual.

Quite honestly, but I've been so busy trying to tie up all of the loose ends this week that I really haven't had a chance to hang out with Murphy at all. But now that I'm all squared away with everything that needs to be done, I was hoping that Murphy and I could enjoy a nice quiet meal together over at the commissary, and try to catch up on some lost time this week.

When I reached the gym, I pushed through the two double-doors, and then amusingly shouted, "Alright Murphy, you big wuss! Whatta ya need help with now?"

Well, the words no sooner came out of my mouth, when all of a sudden I noticed that the gym was absolutely packed to the gills with people. And not only that, but the inside of the gym had been completely transformed into a makeshift banquet hall as well.

As I stood there in total disbelief, everyone in the room shouted, "S U R P R I S E!"

Bobby Diggs ran straight over to me, and then excitedly said, "Hey Jack, we really had ya fooled, didn't we! You know we wouldn't forgot about ya, oh boy, oh boy, oh boy...!"

Up until now, I had no idea that a going away party was even in the works. And I simply can't believe what an incredible job that everyone did in keeping this little shindig under wraps.

If I were a betting man, then I would've bet the farm that one of the clients would've spilt the beans long before this. But knowing Murphy, he made damn sure that none of the clients said a word, because he didn't want to miss the look on my face when the big reveal got sprung.

As I slowly made my way through the crowd, people were coming up to me left and right, patting me on the back, and wishing me well in my new position at WEALTH Industries.

I was quite humbled by their kind words and thoughtful sentiments, and I must confess that it was a bit of a struggle for me to keep all of my emotions completely in check.

Just then Dick Henderson walked into the gym. When Dick spotted me, he had a big smile on his face. Before Dick could even utter a single word, I jokingly said, "Bad back, huh?"

Dick burst out into laughter. And as we shook hands, he sheepishly replied, "Well, I had to come up with something to lure you down to the gym, didn't I?"

As I gazed around the room, I couldn't believe the amount of thought and preparation that went into today. This certainly wasn't something that was thrown together at the last minute.

The room was all decked out with colorful streamers and balloons, along with decorative centerpieces on all of the tables. I never expected anything like this. I thought the gang might spring for a store bought cake and a few gag gifts, but this, well, never in a million years!

Across the way, I could see Murphy multitasking as usual. Not only was Murphy putting the finishing touches on setting up the buffet table, but he was giving Francis Watson a crash course in hooking up the sound system too.

When Murphy glanced up and saw me, he gestured for me to come over to him. As I got closer to Murphy, I noticed that there was a long table with six chairs in place, and it was set up next to the buffet. And at the end of the long table and chairs sat a podium and a microphone.

At that point, I put two and two together and then quickly realized that today's festivities was not exactly going to be a farewell party, but more in the context of a good old-fashioned roast. And instead of me being the guest of honor for today's little soiree, yours truly would most likely be the punchline of every joke that was being told today as well.

As I shook hands with Murphy, he then excitedly asked me, "So are ya ready for a couple of good laughs this afternoon, Rodney?"

I cautiously replied, "Yeah, sure, but are all the laughs going to be at my expense?"

Upon hearing my rather anxious reply, Murphy's face ignited with a devilish glow, as he roared with laughter and said, "Well, of course! It's payback for you leavin' us, pal!"

Murphy then wrapped his massive arms around me, and gave me one of his patented bear hugs. Murphy then whispered in my ear, "I'm really gonna miss not working with ya, Rodney."

As Murphy and I continued to embrace each other, I heard a voice from behind playfully say, "Uh, excuse me, but should I be jealous right now?"

When I turned around, I saw Christine standing directly in front of me. I was absolutely astonished to see her, and all I could say at that point was, "Christine, what are you doing here?"

Christine cracked a sly grin, as she precociously replied, "Well, a little bird told me that they were having a roast in your honor today, so I thought I would come by and have a few good laughs at your expense," which prompted Murphy to laugh out loud.

Murphy then excused himself so that he could check on a few of the arrangements, so I took the opportunity to introduce Christine to a few clients and some of my fellow coworkers.

A few moments later, Murphy grabbed the microphone and then addressed the crowd by saying, "Good afternoon, everybody! So before we get underway, could we please give our good friend Jack O'Leary a big round of applause, and wish him good luck in his new job!"

So after all of the fanfare died down, Murphy continued by saying, "Well, we certainly have a fun-filled afternoon in store for everyone today. We thought we'd start the festivities off with some great food over on the buffet table. And then after we eat, I thought I would go around the room and ask people to share a few memorable stories about Jack over the years. So without any further ado, I'd like the head table to go up to the buffet first, and then we'll go around the room, one table at a time, in a clockwise fashion. Enjoy your lunch, everybody!"

At that point, everyone in the room gave Murphy a nice round of applause.

Christine and I then made our way up to the buffet table. As we grabbed our plates, we both marveled at the heaping amounts of delectable delicacies that were sitting in front of us.

As I began to load up my plate, I suddenly felt a sharp elbow poke me in the ribcage. Christine whispered on the Q.T., "Uh, try to save some food for our other guests, okay honey."

The head table was positioned right next to the buffet. So as people finished making themselves a hearty plate of food, they would pass right by where Christine and I were sitting, and then briefly stop and say a few kind and parting words to us.

It shouldn't come as any big surprise to hear, but neither Hanson nor Kramer showed up for the party today. And although it might sound crazy to say, but I felt a bit slighted that neither one of them felt the urge to come by today, and shake my hand and wish me well in my new job.

Every so often, I found myself glancing at the door, and hoping that either Hanson or Kramer might come strolling into the gym to honor me with a brief cameo appearance, but no.

It then prompted me to think of Ms. Albright, and how she must've felt the night of her retirement party when Kramer decided to snub her as well and not attend her gathering either.

So after everyone finished having a second crack at the buffet table, Murphy grabbed the microphone and said, "Well, I don't know about the rest of you, but I'm pretty stuffed. So now that we've all eaten, it's time for us to move on to the entertainment portion of our program."

After a brief pause, Murphy continued by saying, "I thought it might be fun to go around the room and share a few memorable moments about Jack. So, uh…, who'd like to go first?"

Bobby Diggs jumped right out of his chair and made a mad dash for the microphone, as he cried out, "Hey Murphy, I got something that I wanna say about Jack, please…, please…!"

Murphy handed Bobby the microphone. And just as Bobby was about to speak, Murphy leaned over to him and quietly said, "Hey Bobby, try to keep it short and sweet, okay buddy."

Bobby snatched the microphone out of Murphy's hand, and then proudly stated, "Well, I just wanna say that I think Jack O'Leary is the best employee that we have ever had here at the State School. And I wanna thank him for getting me a lot of good jobs, oh boy, oh boy, oh boy!"

As Murphy reached for the microphone, Bobby decided that he had something else to say, so he blurted out, "Oh yeah, and I also wanna thank Jack O'Leary for not getting too mad at me the day that I crashed the laundry truck into the side of the building. Oh, and one more thing, for not calling the cops on me when he found out that I was stealing newspapers out of the vending machine when I was living back in Building 12, oh boy, oh boy, oh boy!"

Bobby then took a slight bow, and handed the microphone back to Murphy. And as Bobby beat it back to his seat, he was smiling as proud as proud could be.

Murphy thought he'd have a little fun with Bobby, so he raised the microphone and said, "Hey Dick, did you know anything about Bobby stealing newspapers out of the vending machine a couple of years ago? Because I think we need to contact the authorities about that, don't you?"

Dick decided to play along with the gag by saying, "Well, you bring up a very good point there Murphy. Stealing newspapers is a very serious offense. But since this was a work related issue, then I think that Jack O'Leary needs to weigh in on the matter and decide Bobby's fate."

Murphy walked over to where I was sitting, but before handing me the microphone, he asked in very dramatic style, "So Jack, what kinda jail time do you think Bobby is looking at?"

Suddenly, all eyes were now riveted on Bobby Diggs, who had absolutely no idea that we were all playing a practical joke on him. Bobby was sitting on pins and needles, as he waited to hear what his fate might be.

Just as I was about to stand up, Christine gave me a slight tug on the arm, and then gently whispered in my ear, "Jack, please try not to upset him, okay."

Before addressing the group, I casually glanced over at Murphy and Dick, who were both busting at the seams, and doing everything in their power to contain their laughter.

I raised the microphone, and then said with utter conviction, "Well, uh…, this is certainly a very serious matter, and something that I should've handled a long time ago. But seeing how the crime occurred two years ago, then I guess my hands are completely tied, because the statutes of limitations are up. And by law, I cannot invoke any punitive measures on Bobby at this time."

So after hearing what I had to say, Bobby still wasn't sure if he was out of the woods or not, as he timidly asked, "So am I still in trouble with the police, Jack?"

Russell Turner then blurted out, with his usual sarcastic charm, "It means that the cops can't touch ya dummy, and that you're totally in the clear!"

When Bobby realized that he wasn't in hot water anymore, he breathed a huge sigh of relief, and then thanked his lucky stars that his so called "crisis" was averted.

So after having some fun with Bobby, Murphy continued to go around the room and ask this one and that one if they had any fond memories that they would like to share with the group.

As I sat there listening to people dust off one unforgettable story after the other, it seemed to validate even more to me just how much I've enjoyed working here at the State School.

Sure, I've had a few bad days, who hasn't. But overall, I would have to say that working here at the State School has been the happiest time of my life.

I then chuckled to myself in knowing that no one outside the four walls of the State School would ever believe some of the wild and crazy stories that were being bantered around the room this afternoon. Nor would they ever believe that their hard earned tax dollars were being used to pay the salaries of the people who were involved in any of these stories as well.

After all, this is the Island of Misfit Toys, where reality often gets checked at the gate.

But if you're lucky enough to charter a course that steers you safely onto its majestic shoreline, then you'll soon discover what a magical place that you've been able to find here.

When I think back to my early days of working here at the State School, I can remember tossing and turning at night, and wondering how I was going to help these poor unfortunate souls. But as time went by, I managed to figure out a way to incorporate all of the madness that surrounded me, and transform it into something that made some sort of reasonable sense to me.

As much as I have enjoyed working here at the State School, it hasn't always been a bed of roses either. There were times when I felt as if I were fighting an uphill battle, especially with regards to Kramer and Hanson, and some of the idiotic regulations that the State is famous for.

Now I realize that regulations are needed, or else anarchy would exist in every nook and cranny of the State system. However, many of the state and federal regulations that are on the books seem to go a little overboard in what they deem as being in the best interest of the client.

And if you don't believe me, then just go ask Bobby Diggs!

Often times, I would come home at night and wind up taking my frustrations out on Christine by telling her that the State system was completely flawed, and that the types of jobs that I was offering the clients in the Work Activity Center was nothing more than busy work.

As a matter of fact, I wish I had a nickel for every time I heard Jamal Buchanan say to me, "Hey Mr. O'Really, this work is nothin' but a bunch of bullshit! So when are we ever gonna get some real work to do, dawg!"

What Jamal failed to realize was that if I procured work from outside of the State School, then I could get into a lot of trouble, and maybe even find myself on the unemployment line too.

And according to Kramer, I might even wind up behind bars for not following the proper chain of command, or for not complying with the Department of Labor's laws and regulations.

Essentially, I was trapped between a rock and a hard place. Do I make the clients happy by finding them work that they can really sink their teeth into? Or do I want to stare down the barrel of a gun, when Mr. Kramer tells me that I'm fired because I'm not playing by the rules?

So as Murphy continued to make his way around the room, I was suddenly jarred back into reality, when I saw Murphy reach over and hand Mary Beth the microphone.

Mary Beth had a rather precocious look in her eye, as she playfully said, "Hey Murphy, before I share my fondest memory about Jack, would you like me to tell everyone in the room about the time that I single-handedly wrestled you down to the floor in our training class?"

At that point, the entire room erupted into uncontrollable laughter. And I was actually laughing so hard that my eyes began to water.

Christine then quietly leaned over to me and whispered, "Jack, I remember you telling me that story. Boy, what I wouldn't give to have Colleen here right now."

So despite taking a blow to his ego, Murphy just laughed at Mary Beth's comment, and then simply said, "Ah, c'mon Mary Beth, no one is interested in a dull story like that. Anyway, weren't you just about to tell us your fondest memory about our good friend Jack O'Leary?"

Mary Beth then affably replied, "Yes, yes, I was. But before I do that, can we all give our good friend Murphy a big round of applause for being such a great sport!"

So once the room finally settled down, Mary Beth then light-heartedly said, "Well, we have certainly heard some terrific stories about Jack O'Leary this afternoon, and that's exactly why we're all going to miss him so much. For me, I think my fondest memory of Jack was the day that he and I took a group of clients on a little tour of the farmers' museum. And then after the tour was over, we all went over to the State park to enjoy a nice bag lunch by the lake."

Bobby Diggs shouted, "Hey Mary Beth, I remember that day, oh boy, oh boy, oh boy!"

Mary Beth chuckled, and then continued by saying, "So last summer, after enjoying a very educational morning at the farmers' museum, Jack and I took some clients over to the State park to eat a bag lunch. As we all sat around gazing at the water, I noticed that there was a lot of boat traffic out on the lake, so I thought it would be fun to play a little game of I Spy.

Bobby Diggs kept squirming in his seat, as he feverishly rubbed the back of his head with both of his hands, while excitedly mumbling, "This is gonna be good, oh boy, oh boy, oh boy!"

Mary Beth continued by saying, "So for those of you who are not familiar with the game I Spy, the object of the game is to identify something, and then have someone in the group find whatever it is that you are looking for. So in starting off the game, I told everyone that I saw a yellow sailboat out on the water, and could anyone identify it for me."

Bobby Diggs chimed in and excitedly said, "Hey Mary Beth, I was the one who found the yellow sailboat out on the water that day remember, oh boy, oh boy, oh boy!"

Mary Beth smiled, and with a slight chuckle in her voice she replied, "Yes, that's right, Bobby. So since Bobby was the one who spotted the yellow sailboat out on the water, then that meant that it was his turn to I Spy a boat. And if memory serves me correctly, I think Bobby may have I Spied a blue sailboat out on the lake."

Bobby excitedly shouted, "Yes, that's right, a blue sailboat, oh boy, oh boy, oh boy!"

Mary Beth chuckled, and then continued by saying, "So with Bobby in control of the game, he I Spied a blue sailboat, which Francis Watson then spotted off in the distance. So now it was Francis' turn to I Spy a boat."

Russell Turner then shouted at the top of his lungs, "Hey, wait until Mary Beth gets to the end of the story, because I guarantee that we'll all be laughing our asses off! Right, Jack!"

Murphy walked over to where Russell Turner was sitting, and then firmly but politely said, "Hey Russell, try to keep it down so that Mary Beth can finish telling her story, okay."

Mary Beth continued by saying, "So after about eight or nine rounds of I Spy, it suddenly occurred to me that Jack hadn't made any attempts to I Spy a single boat out on the water yet, so I amusingly said to him, "Hey Jack, you can jump into the game at any time now, okay."

Bobby Diggs quietly mumbled, "Get ready, 'cause she's coming up to the good part, oh boy, oh boy, oh boy!"

Mary Beth continued, "By now, we've been playing the game for about fifteen minutes, and everyone has had at least one or two turns to I Spy a boat out on the water except for Jack. So since Jack hadn't had a turn yet, I asked everyone in the group if they wouldn't mind if Jack could have a chance to I Spy a boat out on the lake."

Bobby Diggs could barely control himself, as he kept scratching the back of his head with both of his hands, while excitedly mumbling over and over again, "This is gonna be good, this is gonna be good, this is gonna be good….!"

Mary Beth continued, "So with Jack in control of the game, he looked out onto the water, and although there were a number of boats to choose from, Jack was still having a lot of trouble finding one. And by rule, he could only I Spy a boat that hasn't already been identified yet."

Suddenly, the room resonated with a murmur of excitement and anticipation.

Mary Beth continued, "As I glanced at the clients, I saw that they were all shaking their heads and wondering why Jack was having so much trouble locating a boat. And I could hear all of them quietly whispering amongst themselves that there were plenty of boats out on the water to choose from, so why hasn't Jack identified one of these boats yet."

At that point, Mary Beth then quietly glanced in my direction and warmly smiled.

Mary Beth then continued by saying, "Poor Jack, he kept squinting his eyes and trying as hard as he possibly could to find a boat out on the water. And at one point, Jack even mistook a seagull for being a sailboat, and then Bobby Diggs actually had to correct him on his mistake."

Which, at that point, prompted everyone in the room to quietly snicker.

Mary Beth continued, "So in a fit of frustration, Jack threw both of his hands up in the air and then said, "Well, I'll be darned if I can find even one lousy boat out on the water to identify, which may sound crazy, especially since I'm the one who drove the van today."

All of a sudden, the entire room broke out into utter hysterics, and it was by far the funniest and most entertaining story of the day.

Russell Turner's voice then rose above the clamor of the crowd, as he brashly shouted, "Hey everybody, I told ya that we'd all be laughing our asses off!"

As Mary Beth handed the microphone back to Murphy, everyone in the room gave her a big round of applause. And what's more, they all said that her I Spy story was the funniest story that they've ever heard in all their years of working here at the State School.

Murphy noticed that Dick Henderson had something that he wanted to say, so Murphy walked over to where Dick was sitting, and then handed Dick the microphone.

Dick then affably said, "Well, that was one helluva story Mary Beth. And to tell you the truth, but I don't think that I've ever laughed that hard in my entire life."

As the crowd settled down, Dick addressed the group by saying, "Well, I guess it's no secret that Jack's eyesight isn't exactly 20/20, and that was certainly highlighted in some of the terrific stories that we heard today. But if you ask me, I think the clients would probably tell you that Jack's vision isn't as bad as you might think it is, especially since Jack doesn't miss a trick."

Russell Turner then mumbled, "Huh, yeah, you got that right."

Dick continued, "Well, I think it would be safe to say that Jack has certainly made a positive impact on all of our lives, and that he has a real knack for making people feel good. Although, uh…, I think that Mr. Hanson might beg to differ," which prompted the entire room to burst into laughter, coupled with a few spirited and uncensored remarks regarding Mr. Hanson.

So after the room settled down, Dick continued by saying, "When I first took over as Team Leader for the SBU, the Director instructed me to assemble a team of professionals, and the first person I chose to be on the team was Jack O'Leary. I needed someone who would lead by example, and someone who didn't mind rolling up his sleeves and getting his hands dirty."

Bobby Diggs then shouted, "Let's hear it for Jack! Hip, hip, hooray…! Hip, hip, hooray…! Hip, hip, hooray…!"

Dick then concluded his remarks by saying, "Well Jack, I just want you to know that we're all going to miss you very much. But we also know that you're going to make one helluva administrator at WEALTH Industries too, and they're damn lucky to have ya!"

At that point the crowd cheered, and then everyone in the room stood up and gave me a standing ovation.

Dick waited for the room to quiet down, and then added one more thing by saying, "Jack, I'd just like to say that it has been an absolute pleasure working with you for the past five years, and we would all like to thank you from the bottom of our hearts. Not only have you helped us to become a top notch program, but a program that other facilities would like to emulate as well!"

Russell Turner then shouted, "Way to go, Jack!"

As the crowd continued to cheer, Dick handed the microphone back to Murphy. As Dick Henderson took his seat, I noticed that he quietly slipped his handkerchief out of his pocket and then wiped the corners of his eyes, which told me just how much Dick was going to miss me.

It was now time for Murphy to say a few words. As Murphy raised the microphone, he paused momentarily. As we all sat on the edge of our seat waiting for Murphy to say something witty or profound, he seemed to be having a great deal of difficulty in organizing his thoughts.

Everyone in the room, including myself, was a bit taken aback by Murphy's inability to seize the moment. After all, Murphy is our superhero, who's always in control of the situation, and someone that never seems to crack under pressure. So for him to just awkwardly stand there without having the ability to utter a single word, well, it was certainly a rare sight indeed.

Bobby Diggs then turned to Russell Turner, and in a bit of a quandary he asked, "Hey Russell, what the heck is wrong with Murphy?"

Russell Turner then replied, in classic Russell style, "He's too choked up to talk, dummy!"

What Russell may lack in social grace, he seems to make up for in sizing up an awkward situation.

At that point, Murphy was so overcome with emotion that he simply couldn't get the words out.

In all the years that I've known Murphy, I've never seen him this upset before. Murphy has always managed to keep his emotions in check. Especially during pressure packed situations, when the game was on the line, and everyone was relying on him to lead us to victory.

So that being said, is it even conceivable to think that this moment in time may actually trump every other pressure packed situation that Murphy has ever known. Could our friendship possibly mean more to him than any game winning basket, or touchdown that he's ever scored?

Murphy Doherty, this mountain of a man, who single-handedly tamed the Metro gang, was now standing in front of us weeping and utterly speechless.

As Murphy continued to stand there in suspended animation, the only sounds you could hear in the room were the long deep breaths that Murphy was breathing into the microphone.

Suddenly, Murphy ended the silence, as he quietly said, "Well, uh…, if I had known that Jack O'Leary's eyesight was as bad as what's being reported today, then I never would've asked him to keep an eye on Lance Coppenger, the night that he ran away from the basketball game."

Upon hearing Murphy's deadpan remark, the crowd erupted into uncontrollable laughter, and the energy that the crowd generated was enough to give Murphy the strength to say, "Well, I didn't think that I'd have to face this day for a very long time, because I thought that Jack and I would be working together for many more years to come, but I guess I was wrong about that."

At that point, Murphy glanced over at me and warmly smiled.

Murphy continued, "I'm sure that many of you know that Jack and I have known each other since we were kids. Now although Jack never had the chance to play sports in high school, he never missed any of my games, and I always considered him to be my biggest fan. Every time that I glanced up into the bleachers, Jack would be right there cheering me on. And he was always the first one to pat me on the back when we won the game, and the first one to console me when we lost. Jack is someone that you can always count on through thick and thin."

Once again, Murphy glanced in my direction and warmly smiled.

Murphy continued by saying, "Well Jack, today the shoe is on the other foot, and I'm the one who is your biggest fan. Up until now, I've never had the opportunity to work with disabled individuals before, so I guess you could say that I was the one sitting up in the bleachers, while you were the one who was down on the field playing in the game."

Upon hearing Murphy's insightful and thought provoking analogy, a murmur of reflective laughter resonated throughout the entire room.

Murphy continued by saying, "When I first came on board, Jack took me under his wing and taught me all the tricks of the trade, so that I would be successful in my new career. It's gonna be tough not working with him anymore. I'm gonna miss all of his corny jokes, and all of his long-winded stories. But most of all, not sharing my morning coffee with him every day, and those gooey glaze donuts that he loves to bring in. So Rodney, we wanna wish you all the very best at WEALTH Industries, and thanks again for all the great memories that you've given us!"

As the crowd stood up and applauded, Murphy walked over to where I was sitting and gave me a giant bear hug. And he hugged me so tight that he almost squeezed the life out of me.

Murphy then turned to Christine, and with a sly grin on his face, he amusingly said, "So Christine, I'm sure you have one or two interesting stories that you'd like to share with us about Jack, right?"

I then pleaded, "No Doc, please, don't hand her the microphone. Isn't there some kinda law on the books that prohibits wives from speaking at their husband's farewell party?"

Murphy laughed, and then he began to laugh even harder, when he heard Christine say, "Jack, honey, c'mon, you've always said that our life is nothing but an open book, right?"

I humorously replied, "Well, yeah, but that doesn't mean that I want everyone in the room to know what a complete numbskull that you're married to!"

Murphy quietly chuckled, and then he handed me the microphone, so that I could say a few closing remarks to the group.

As I stood there trying to think of what to say, I had a sea of thoughts and emotions going through my head, and memories that were just too precious for me to share with the group.

Such as, the on-grounds apartment, locking horns with Ms. Albright, and all of the wild and crazy moments that I experienced back in Buildings 12 and 13 in Mr. Wohler's Unit.

My thoughts then shifted over to the Metro gang, and thinking how scared I was when they first walked through the door. But then as time went by, I was able to overcome my fears, so that I could handle any situation that the big bad Metro gang was willing to throw at me.

And then finally I had thoughts of Murphy, and realizing that the time that I've spent with him here at the State School has been the best time of my life. This magical and wonderous ride that I have been so privileged to share with Murphy was now coming to a screeching halt.

Well, despite the fact that the Irish are blessed with the gift of gab, I just couldn't find the right words to say at that moment. Which is pretty ironic, especially since I've been known to have some rather spirited conversations with myself on more than one occasion.

So at the point, I decided to keep my comments short and sweet, and simply say that I'm very grateful for all the support that I've received over the years, and that I'll miss everyone here at the State School very much. But intuition tells me that our lives will continue to cross paths.

And on that note, - the luncheon was over.

Murphy asked a few of the clients to stay back and help him clean up the gym, and then everyone else just headed straight for the door and went back to their respective locations.

As Christine and I were leaving the gym, I turned to her and whimsically asked, "So just out of curiosity, but when Murphy handed you the microphone so that you could say a few words to the group, what exactly were you thinking of telling them?"

A devilish smile then swept across Christine's face, as she replied, "Oh, well, I was just going to say what a gifted counselor you are, which was certainly quite evident the day that you and I were both in the elevator together heading up to the maternity unit when Rory was born."

I then quietly said, "Uh-uh, well, as I recall, I was having a bit of a meltdown that day. And, uh…, I think that story is a story that is better left untold, wouldn't you agree?"

Christine began to laugh, and as she threw her arms around me, she amusingly said, "Don't worry Jack, you're secret is safe with me. Well, for a price, of course."

As Christine and I exited the gym, I happen to glance over my shoulder, and I saw Bobby Diggs whimpering in the hallway. I quickly approached Bobby, and asked him what was wrong.

In an angry and resentful tone of voice, Bobby replied, "What do you care, I'm not your fuckin' problem anymore! Because you're leaving me, just like my family did! I hate you, Jack!"

Bobby then took off running down the hallway towards his living unit.

I quickly glanced at Christine, who nervously said, "Jack, you better go talk to him right away, so that you can try to straighten things out. I'm afraid he might do something foolish."

To which I replied, "You're right, Bobby has a history of hurting himself. Why don't you head down to my office, and I'll catch up with you later after I finish talking to Bobby, okay?"

As I rounded the corner that led to L.U. 513, I saw Bobby slumped on the floor outside his living unit door. Bobby had his face buried in his hands, and he was crying uncontrollably. As I approached Bobby, I wasn't quite sure what to say to him.

I then placed my hand softly on Bobby's shoulder, and calmly said, "C'mon Bobby, you know that I'll be coming back to visit with ya. Plus, I'll be talking with Murphy on the telephone almost every day, so that he can tell me how good you're doing here at the State School, right?"

Bobby blubbered, "Yeah, I know, but it's still not the same Jack."

At that point, I felt like I needed to say something to Bobby that would not only pick up his spirits, but help take away some of the pain and heartache that he was feeling right now too.

So that being said, I decided to take a giant leap of faith by saying, "Listen Bobby, I'll make a deal with ya. If you can ever find a way to get out of the State School someday, then I'll see if I can get you a job working for me at WEALTH Industries. So whatta ya think of that idea Bobby, do we have a deal?"

Bobby's face lit up like a Roman candle, as he emphatically exclaimed, "Yeah, okay, we have a deal! Hey Jack, you're the best counselor that I ever had, oh boy, oh boy, oh boy!"

So thinking that all of his troubles were over, Bobby flung open the door to L.U. 513, and as he ran onto the living unit, he jubilantly shouted, "Hey everybody, Jack O'Leary just promised to give me a job at WEALTH Industries, as soon as I get the hell out of the State School, oh boy, oh boy, oh boy!"

I then quietly thought to myself, "Geez Bobby, if only it were that easy!"

Hey, who knows, maybe I'll wind up being Bobby Diggs's rabbi someday, so that he can start living the life that he's always dreamed about.

Well, as much as I'd like that to be true, my gut tells me that Bobby Diggs will continue to find ways to sabotage his life. And in all likelihood, he'll probably be stranded on the Island of Misfit Toys for the rest of his days, staring at the horizon, and hoping that a ship will come along someday and rescue him from all of his heartache and misery.

So after squaring things with Bobby, I went back to my office. Christine had already gathered up all of my personal effects, and packed them neatly into a small cardboard box.

Christine then asked me how I made out with Bobby, and I quietly told her, "Crisis averted, well, until the next disaster hits anyway. Which could be five minutes from now."

As I took one last look around my office, Christine then innocently asked, "So do you have everything that you need, Jack?"

I then turned directly towards Christine, and as I lovingly gazed into her eyes, I quietly replied, "Yeah, I've got everything that I need, as long as I have you and Rory by my side!"

POST SCRIPT

Well, I certainly hope that you enjoyed the story, and I would welcome any feedback you may have regarding the book. Please feel free to make any comments on social media, or if you feel so inclined, you can forward me your comments to stemmer947@gmail.com - thank you!

ABOUT THE AUTHOR

Jack Dempsey was born in New York City in 1954 and lived his formative years on Long Island, New York. In 1976 he graduated from SUNY Brockport with a BA in Psychology. He earned his Master's degree in Rehabilitation Counseling in 1979 from Hofstra University on Long Island. After graduate school he worked thirty years as a Vocational Rehabilitation Counselor for NYS OMRDD and retired from that position in 2010.

Dempsey's main intent for writing this book was to provide the reader with a light-hearted fictional story of a profession that he has enjoyed being associated with for all of his adult professional life. Mr. Dempsey is married to his wife Kristin for over thirty-eight years and has four children and currently resides in Upstate NY.